Also by C.E. Standley

Pawprints All Over Me

FATE-Seven Days in January

The Shaman's Legacy

C.E. "Stan" Standley

*JAY (DR. SCHEFFER) -
THANKS FOR ALL OF YOUR
HELP. OVER THE YEARS.
BEST WISHES!*

Stan
1/6/11

All rights reserved. No part of this book shall be reproduced or transmitted in any form or by any means, electronic, mechanical, magnetic, photographic including photocopying, recording or by any information storage and retrieval system, without prior written permission of the publisher. No patent liability is assumed with respect to the use of the information contained herein. Although every precaution has been taken in the preparation of this book, the publisher and author assume no responsibility for errors or omissions. Neither is any liability assumed for damages resulting from the use of the information contained herein.

Copyright © 2010 by C.E. Standley

ISBN 0-7414-6343-1

Printed in the United States of America

This is a work of fiction. Names, characters, places, and incidents either are the product of the author's imagination or are used fictitiously. Any resemblance to actual events or locales or persons, living or dead, is entirely coincidental.

Published December 2010

INFINITY PUBLISHING
1094 New DeHaven Street, Suite 100
West Conshohocken, PA 19428-2713
Toll-free (877) BUY BOOK
Local Phone (610) 941-9999
Fax (610) 941-9959
Info@buybooksontheweb.com
www.buybooksontheweb.com

Foreword

There are things in this world that we simply do not understand. These are often explained as a coincidence or a rare occurrence whereupon they are relegated to an abnormal status and usually discarded. What then are we to do with a persistent series of coincidences?

Mental telepathy is usually explained as another form of coincidence and those of us who have either experienced it or been next to one who experienced it know that something extraordinary has happened. I am not referring to an incident which occurred in a room where both parties were in attendance and visual signs or conversation could have been the actual cause of the 'mental telepathy.' I refer to an occurrence where twins, a sister and brother, separated by approximately 4,000 miles were involved. The brother was severely injured while felling a tree in Ohio; his sister was in Hawaii and suddenly stated, "Paul's been hurt!" I scoffed at the idea, but watched her make the frantic phone call to Ohio. She told her sister-in-law who rushed to check on her husband. Two hours later she called to say that she had found him and he was now in the hospital undergoing surgery. He would not have survived the combination of the cold and his internal injuries. As a skeptic, I searched for answers and came up empty. There were no physical means for the two to communicate. Mental telepathy?

Likewise, the writing of this book has been a collection of strange coincidences. The site of the Lewis' farm was based on the need to be located north of the 'dust bowl' area of the 1930s near a river and a major north-south highway. Having never been in that part of the country, I wrote in vague terms. Several months later I was selected to assist with a security assessment at a nuclear power plant; at the end of the first day of the assessment I realized that I was at the Lewis' farm location.

Research sometimes did not provide certain items that I required. The golden eagle appeared on a poster of endangered North American species that was in front of me while I huffed and puffed through a stress test. Other bits and pieces appeared in casual magazines and newspaper articles that were given to me and just happened to be next to an article that the provider wanted me to read. Then there was the nice lady seated next to me on an airplane who noticed the words as I worked on this book; she is an expert on Native Americans and especially the Lakota.

I used a casual co-worker as a model for one of the characters. I chose names for three lesser characters to be her relatives; I picked the real first names of her mother and nephew. We both were astounded.

Our subconscious minds often help us locate things that we seek. However, sometimes things just happen and we briefly wonder 'why' or 'how' and then forget all about them.

CHAPTER ONE

HOWLING WOLF – The Beginning

Howling Wolf had descended from a long line of powerful Lakota medicine men. His abilities and potential had amazed his father, *Eagle Feather*, beginning when the boy was only in his fourth year. He took instruction willingly and somehow seemed to instinctively know the medicinal value of many plants. It was readily apparent that he was destined to follow in the traditions of his lineage. Howling Wolf continued to grow in the knowledge of the tribe and in answers to the many mysteries which were relegated only to medicine men. Eagle Feather had tried to encourage him to play and enjoy his time as a child, but the boy would not relent. He possessed an insatiable hunger for knowledge and learned quickly.

By his seventeenth year, Howling Wolf had established himself as an exceptional young man both within the tribe and external to his people. He was already held in high esteem throughout the Sioux nation and was beginning to spend more and more time in a solitary lifestyle as he sought more wisdom. He searched for additional visions with the most spectacular of all occurring when he was in his twenty-first year.

He had sat alone atop a small rise on the rolling plains awaiting an approaching afternoon storm. He sat patiently within a circle comprised of numerous artifacts, stones and symbols with his eyes closed. The sky darkened and the air became unnaturally still; there was a vague rumble of thunder in the distance. There was no other sound and he basked in the silence, waiting for what was to come.

Howling Wolf suddenly opened his eyes and noticed the darkened sky. He was amazed at how rapidly the clouds had replaced the sun and how the air was somehow different. There was that unusual smell and then he felt his hair stand on end. In a split second he realized what was about to occur.

The bolt of lightning struck the earth just outside his circle! He *felt* rather than *heard* the instantaneous clap of thunder. Howling Wolf was briefly aware of a blinding flash and searing pain before slipping into total blackness. He was suddenly lying on his back, unmoving; a tendril of smoke rose from his hair.

After several moments, Howling Wolf revived somewhat. He tried to breathe, but could not. His head hurt and his lungs screamed for air. He was unable to move any part of his body and was slowly losing consciousness. He was vaguely aware of the first few raindrops that fell and suddenly felt a cold wind. Then, somehow, he was able to draw in a ragged breath. He became acutely aware of his pounding heart and willed his lungs to refill once more. It was terribly painful and yet so wonderful. And then he saw an eagle...a large, majestic eagle. It spoke to him yet he would never be able to recall the spoken words. As suddenly as the eagle had appeared, it disappeared. Howling Wolf's pain remained and he fought to remain conscious.

It was almost dark before Howling Wolf was able to sit up. He was unable to stand and thus crawled painfully over to his meager supplies. He drank some water and realized that some of his hair had been burned away. Then he noticed that his right ear was severely charred. He was also deaf, but his hearing would return. Howling Wolf wondered how long he had left his body and then fell asleep without warning.

The next morning he had awakened in great pain. Every muscle ached and his right ear throbbed. It had taken almost an hour for him to stand and he had experienced great difficulty just maintaining his balance. He had regained his hearing somewhat, but it would be several days before it returned completely. He was extremely unstable as he began his journey; when he stumbled and fell it took considerable time to regain his feet. He was a pathetic sight as he lurched along.

Hours later, Howling Wolf staggered into his village and collapsed. He was quickly moved to his own tepee and made comfortable under the watchful eyes of his father. He slept fitfully, constantly tossing and turning with long periods of unintelligible murmuring. He had awakened the next day and was immediately questioned by his father. He related his experience as best he could. Eagle Feather listened carefully and then convinced Howling Wolf that he had died and returned to life. His father was elated and Howling Wolf knew that it was far more than just relief that he had survived the ordeal.

His father told him how the death and re-birth symbolized that Howling Wolf would now be able to communicate with the spirit world; he was now or was to be a *shaman*. He was clearly destined for greatness and would be able to harness his new powers for the good of *The People*. Howling Wolf knew that he had changed, but the extent was unknown to the young man.

After that a large eagle often came to him, sometimes in dreams and sometimes in the flesh. He would receive knowledge and guidance which were not always clear. The eagle would look at Howling Wolf and communicate yet the young man could not respond or ask questions. The eagle would then disappear for days or sometimes weeks at a time. The arrival of the eagle always foretold of some event in which Howling Wolf was to play a major role.

Word spread rapidly of Howling Wolf's experience. People came from numerous camps and villages, hoping to witness his new powers. His injured right ear was quickly noticed and added immensely to his new image. His singed hair was being replaced by solid white hair and one area of his scalp had no hair at all. The overall effect was to make it clear that this man was very special. Children looked at him with a mixture for fear and awe; adults looked at him and saw hope. He became a part of many decisions which were made throughout the Lakota lands and even beyond. He sat with the great leaders from all tribes and advised them of things which were to come. He was not considered an enemy by those tribes that were either at war with the Lakota or had been in the past. These leaders knew that he was special and granted him safe passage through their lands. Howling Wolf traveled alone and carried no weapons...he did not need them.

He was soon courted by the Whites for his access to those powerful leaders of several tribes in the hope that he could persuade them to accept various treaties and occasionally to assist in returning some of the 'renegades' to their reservations. He did not trust most Whites; they did not respect the earth and were filled with greed. They failed to honor their own treaties and showed no real concern for his people who now included far more than just the Lakota. There were exceptions among the Whites, but they were rare. In later years they would speak of *the great depression* and how difficult life had become yet would remain completely blind to the fate of his people. Sweeping changes had already come to the many nations as the white man relentlessly moved westward.

Shortly after the turn of the century Howling Wolf had sought another vision; there was so much that *The People* could not understand. He had hoped to return with knowledge of what was in store and how to break free of the overbearing restrictions placed on *The People* by the white man. He had finished his sacred potion just as the rising sun struck his eyes. He was never truly aware of any changes occurring within his body even though it seemed that time had slowed considerably. He seemed to be drifting and then suddenly he was lifted into the air by his friend, the eagle.

They climbed high into the air and Howling Wolf marveled at the fertile land below. He saw none of the prairie animals which normally roamed the land and there were no buffalo. He saw herds of cattle and the fences with the sharp points and he was saddened. They were flying toward the northeast and Howling Wolf felt neither fear nor pain as he was held by the powerful talons. He was uncertain how far they had traveled until he spotted the large city of the white man. He could see the huge lake on the east side. The white man called the city *Chicago* and he remembered that he had been there before. Actually, he had been to several of these cities as the white man sought his help in convincing *The People* to accept those conditions thrust upon them by the greed of the Whites.

As they approached the outskirts of the city, the eagle flew lower and suddenly Howling Wolf possessed the visual acuity of the eagle. The eagle dipped one wing and Howling Wolf's attention was captured by a young man with a slingshot. He watched the youth pick up a rock and place it into the pouch. He then saw the young man draw the pouch to arm's length and then release it. He watched in awe as he followed the path of the stone and saw it strike a small bird, killing it instantly. He observed the youth as he rushed over and picked up the bird by one leg to observe it. Howling Wolf noticed that the young man was smiling in triumph and he felt a distinct chill throughout his entire body. The youth suddenly looked up and spotted Howling Wolf; he smiled and it caused Howling Wolf to jerk as if he had been physically struck. The young man drew the empty slingshot to arm's length and pointed it toward Howling Wolf; the look on his face was that of pure evil. Then he winked and Howling Wolf somehow knew that he would see him again.

The eagle abruptly turned toward the southwest and climbed skyward. Howling Wolf looked back in an attempt to glimpse the *Evil One* once more, but the young man was gone. He was suddenly aware of a feeling of tremendous fatigue and felt himself slowly losing consciousness; he was helpless to ward it off.

Then he was on the ground and somewhat dizzy. The eagle was gone, if it had even been there at all. He took a drink from his water bag and stood shakily. Although he was completely disoriented, it was imperative that he return to his camp. He briefly closed his eyes and then began turning to his left. When he stopped and opened his eyes, he knew that this was the route back to his camp. The spirits would guide him as they had done many times before. His vision had left him puzzled and with nothing to share with *The People*.

That was more than thirty long years ago.

CHAPTER TWO

The Later Years – Summer, 1937

Howling Wolf staggered and fell face-down on the parched earth. He was breathing heavily and tried to rise, but was unable; he felt the relentless afternoon sun burning into his exposed skin. He knew that he must return to his camp if there was any hope of survival. His water bag had slipped from his grip long ago and he knew that there was little chance of finding water due to the drought.

Now his life was in jeopardy as he tried to re-create those events which had produced the vision of the eagle, but this time the eagle did not come. He wondered why the Great Spirit had not sent the eagle and wondered if his own powers had lessened. The heat and dehydration were now rapidly taking the last of Howling Wolf's strength. Perhaps the eagle would come to him now.

Gerald and Martha Lewis were headed south on U.S. 75 after a visit with their oldest daughter and her family. It was far too hot to be making the afternoon trip home, but Gerald did not like the thought of driving at night if he could avoid it. The couple had the window vents turned to maximize the amount of air coming in and the cowl vent was wide open for the same reason. That lessened the effects of the hot summer air somewhat and made the interior of the car almost bearable. Both occupants were sweating and the iced tea provided by their daughter was refreshing for only a few brief seconds.

There was not much scenery to enjoy. There was very little green vegetation along their route except for the trees lining the occasional dry creek. The drought had continued longer than expected and was exacting an incredible toll on both crops and pastures. Rain was not forecast for anytime in the near future and that fact had allowed the couple to make this visit. There was a chance that they could visit their other daughter later on if the drought continued. Gerald was aggravated and a little hurt that both daughters had moved away after they married; they should have married farmers and remained in the local area. At least their son would be remaining even though he wanted no part of the farm and selling insurance was a respectable vocation. Times were difficult, but they would manage. After all, they had survived the depression.

The couple had spoken very little during the last hour mostly due to the heat. Once they turned off the highway and onto the unpaved shortcut, they resumed their conversation. Another twenty grueling minutes and they would be home.

"How hungry are you?" Martha asked suddenly.

"Oh, I don't know. I hadn't really thought about it and this heat seems to kill my appetite. Maybe after we get home we could go over and get something at Jill's," referring to the small diner which was perpetually in danger of closing for good. "Lord knows they could use the business."

Gerald wiped his brow automatically.

"That's fine with me. I don't really feel much like cookin' in this heat."

Martha smiled knowing that her husband was anxious to find out if anything interesting had happened during their absence. There were always several people at Jill's either drinking coffee or iced tea. Nobody spent much money there, especially with the uncertainty that the endless drought had brought.

At that moment, Martha turned her head and looked through her open window.

"Stop the car! There's somebody out there!"

Gerald hit the brakes while turning his head to see where Martha was looking. As the car slid to a stop on the gravel road, he saw a man stumble and fall face-down about a hundred yards away. Exiting the vehicle he noted that the man had not risen.

"Stay here," he commanded as he crossed the road ditch, carefully parted the barbed wire fence and swung his body through with the ease of one who had done this hundreds of times.

He trotted directly toward the fallen man while Martha grabbed the last of the iced tea and the towel used for insulation. She crossed the fence, ripping her dress in the process. She was not worried about the stranger being dangerous...he appeared to be in trouble. She spotted a buzzard, no, an eagle circling overhead, but thought nothing of it as she rushed to help.

Gerald approached the fallen man with a certain amount of caution. As he came closer, though, he could see that the man was in bad shape and mumbling incoherently. He turned to motion for Martha to come and was surprised to see her already on her way.

"Mister, are you okay?"

He did not want to startle him and at the same time hoped for a response. Receiving none, he knelt so that his shadow would shield the man's face from the sun. He carefully rolled the man over and was astonished at what he saw. This was no local resident nor was it a person of means. The man was probably past middle age and was dressed strangely, but the most striking thing about him was the scarred ear and the white hair with the bare skin next to it. He was breathing with great difficulty and was not sweating. His skin appeared quite red and Gerald knew that it was the heat.

"Hurry up," he yelled over his shoulder to Martha.

Then he realized that he could hear her approaching. He wished that he had told her to bring the jar of tea.

And then she was kneeling next to him holding the opened jar.

She looked at the man and gasped, "He's an Indian."

She quickly poured some of the iced tea onto the towel and gently wiped his forehead.

"Let's raise his head a little and get some of this tea into him, he's terribly dehydrated."

Gerald eased the man's shoulders up and shifted so that his own right thigh would support the man. He stabilized the stranger's head while Martha placed the jar to his lips. A small amount of tea spilled before the stranger's mouth opened and she was able to pour perhaps half a cup which disappeared with a series of swallows.

"Pour the rest of the tea over him while I run back and get the water."

Gerald eased the man back down and headed for the car. He was glad that his daughter had insisted that they take the big jar of water, "just in case."

Martha poured the remainder of the tea over the man and began trying to cool his head with the dampened towel. Periodically, she would shake the towel so that evaporation would cool it. She thought she noticed his eyelids flicker and leaned over to stare closely at him.

"Are you okay?" She did not really expect a response.

Howling Wolf slowly regained his consciousness, but did not move. He opened his eyes just enough to see the face of the one who had spoken to him in the language of the Whites. As he gathered his wits, he realized that he was weak and his heart was pounding. This was not a vision and this was not a dream. He felt the cool towel and realized that this woman was not to be feared and lapsed back into unconsciousness.

Gerald returned with the water and thoroughly doused the stranger. He saved half of the water and poured some of it into the jar that had held the tea.

"We need to get him up and wet down his back; he's still burning up. I think he tried to open his eyes once, but he didn't respond to my voice. We've got to get him out of here. If you can roll him over, I'll wet him down."

Martha spoke with the authority and confidence from years of caring for others. She helped Gerald roll the man onto his stomach.

Once the couple had poured the remainder of the water from the big jar over the stranger, they tried valiantly to carry him to the car. After realizing how difficult that was, Gerald finally lifted him as best he could and dragged him down the gentle slope toward the car. He was forced to rest several times before reaching the fence. Once there, he carefully moved the man as close to the fence as possible and then helped Martha to ease between the strands of barbed wire. Once through the fence himself, he had Martha hold the bottom strand as high as possible while he pulled the man clear. They tried once again to force some water into the man's mouth, but only succeeded in causing him to cough and gag.

"Let's just get him home right now. We must bring his temperature down and we're getting low on water."

Gerald somehow managed to get the stranger into the backseat and Martha sat with him to keep him more or less upright. Gerald drove as fast as he felt he safely could on the gravel road. The warm, dry air entering the car was cooling the old man while drying his clothing, but each minute brought them closer to home.

Fifteen minutes later Gerald parked the car as close to the front porch as possible and carefully eased the stranger out of the car and onto the porch. Martha had already opened the house and pumped water into a large bowl and a pitcher. She brought out the pitcher first and poured the cool water over the stranger.

"Gerald, we've got to get him into the tub. Let's move him next to the tub and get him undressed."

She looked at her startled husband before speaking.

"Oh, for God's sake, you know I used to be a nurse. Now let's get moving!"

Once they had the old man in the tub, it was a simple matter of bringing water and pouring it over him. It took another twenty minutes before his temperate dropped significantly. After that they were able to remove him from the bathtub and dressed him in a robe before putting him on the bed in their son's old room. They tried again to give him water, but very little made it down his throat.

They took turns watching him through the night and Gerald was awakened by the stranger as he stirred just before dawn.

"Martha, come here quick! I think he's waking up."

Martha arrived almost immediately and went to the stranger.

"How are you feeling?"

She saw the stranger turn his head and look at her, his face showing total bewilderment before gradually softening.

Howling Wolf remembered the gentle voice and looked around at the strange surroundings. He then looked directly at Martha and spoke.

"Thirsty."

Gerald held out a glass of water which Martha took and moved closer to the stranger. The stranger stared warily at Gerald and then turned his gaze first to Martha and then to the glass of water. He reached for the glass, but Martha shook her head and gently eased the glass to his lips. He drank sparingly as if he knew that it would not be wise to drink too much. There was complete silence in the room.

Suddenly the stranger's eyes widened and he reached below the sheets. He had a quizzical expression for a few moments and then smiled. He then gestured for another sip of water. After that he nodded and looked around the unfamiliar room for his clothes. He was clearly confused, but asked no questions. Then, without warning, he fell asleep.

Howling Wolf slowly recuperated from his ordeal. While he did not trust his benefactors, he had not yet acquired the strength necessary to venture off on his own. He appreciated the warmth and gentleness of the nice lady and the man seemed to be equally kind. They began to talk to him.

They recounted how they had discovered him, delirious and terribly dehydrated. They both were certain that he belonged on one of the reservations farther north, but made it clear that they would not be transporting him anywhere. He listened, but said very little. These were complete strangers and they were Whites.

The old man's suspicious nature began to soften as he recognized their genuine concern for his well being. In the past he had met some Whites who seemed to understand the ways of his people and even considered a small number of them to be his friends. Still, he would wait cautiously to see what developed; he had very little choice, at least right now.

On the third day of his recovery Howling Wolf sat with the white man while the latter talked about his past and how he had come to be in this place. Gerald explained how his family had settled here as farmers which had created problems with the growing number of ranchers who considered these vast grasslands essential to their success. And, yes, there had been occasional raids by small bands of Indians, but no one had ever been injured...at least none of his family. The Indians seemed to recognize that these farmers were not a threat to them, but had settled in areas where they were not welcome. The evolving tolerance had resulted in some strange partnerships which benefited both groups. The settlers often traded grains and vegetables for meat and hides to augment the small amount of beef they raised. This strange alliance angered the ranchers even more; there was some retaliation, but it soon stopped.

After the Civil War, as more settlers moved westward, the Army was brought in to protect them. As their traditional hunting grounds were ravaged, the Indians fought back and were ultimately decimated or forced onto reservations. One of Gerald's relatives had fought Indians as a soldier until one event had changed his life forever. He had heard of occasions where old men, women and children had been slaughtered in their camps by troops as they searched for the warriors, the braves. He had initially dismissed these stories as fiction until he listened to the stories told by a trusted eye witness. He left the Army a few months later at the end of his enlistment. He had repeated these stories much to the horror of his audience that just happened to include a very young Gerald. That startling revelation had made a terrible and lasting impression on the small boy.

Howling Wolf had listened quietly and politely to the story. His face looked even more haggard than it had three days earlier.

"I am called Howling Wolf by my people," he said quietly. "I did not enter the world quietly."

He smiled widely before beginning his own tale. Gerald was soon joined by Martha. They listened in awe as he told them about his brief, unique childhood and the process of growing up in such changing times. It was obvious that he was proud of being asked to sit with the elders as a young man. Much to their surprise, he explained that he had been schooled by the Whites for one year. He made numerous references to the inequities and injustices brought on by the Whites.

Howling Wolf watched his small audience and noted their sympathetic understanding. He told of the starvation and illness which had swept through the reservations and the lack of assistance from the Whites in spite of all the promises.

"These are good people," he thought as he watched tears run down Martha's face. He then concentrated on educating the couple from the perspective of one who had witnessed massive change in a relatively short period of time. He verified many of the horror stories, having witnessed some of the results in person. He did not blame the two Whites for the hostilities any more than they blamed him.

Howling Wolf explained how he had traveled to various locations throughout the nation. He was presently in this area in an attempt to summon a great eagle that was his guide. He had tried to re-create all of the details leading up to an earlier vision, but there was no vision this time and there was no eagle. Perhaps it was due to the many changes in the lives of his people. He was discouraged.

Martha did not mention the eagle that she had seen on the day they found him; surely he was not speaking literally.

Howling Wolf took his meals with his new friends even though he was anxious to return to his normal routine. There was a growing bond as he learned more about them and as they, likewise, learned more about him. He was fascinated by Martha's use of spices and asked a multitude of questions about their origin and purpose. He seemed intrigued that they were for cooking and none were used for medicinal or ritual purposes.

The Shaman's Legacy

After several days, Gerald was able to help him return to his camp to collect his things and was surprised that nothing, not even food, had been touched by animals or insects. He saw the circle and the numerous artifacts and symbols; the grass was green within the circle in contrast to the dead grass outside. He watched in silence as Howling Wolf carefully gathered each item and spoke softly in a language that Gerald did not understand. He noticed that none of the artifacts had left an impression or discoloration in the grass. Once each item had been retrieved and carefully placed into a blanket, the two men returned to the farm in relative silence. Gerald was now convinced that this was no ordinary man. He had many questions but chose not to ask them.

Howling Wolf became more restless and longed to return to his old ways. Since his bout with severe dehydration, he had realized that his stamina was not as it had been. He was an old man who was approaching his 90th year, but appeared to be much younger than that. His hands and face were as smooth as those of a man in his early twenties. His movements and range of motion were akin to someone in his late forties or early fifties and his vision was perfect. Even so, his restlessness was evident to both Martha and Gerald. They were reluctant to let him leave in his weakened condition.

The couple discussed allowing Howling Wolf the use of an old cabin located down near the river if it were acceptable to him. Gerald knew that it would certainly require some repairs and would definitely require cleaning. There were also a few outbuildings and the soil would grow just about anything. That area was approximately 15 acres and was no longer under cultivation. There was even access from the road. The well was questionable since it had been unused for some time.

Martha suggested that perhaps they could give the land to Howling Wolf; they would not even miss that small chunk of land. Guilt? Perhaps that was the impetus or maybe it was the hope that he would remain and continue sharing his incredible experiences. The couple decided to take him down to look at the site and see his reaction. After a half-hearted protest, Howling Wolf agreed to accompany them.

Howling Wolf saw the river and the willow trees and smiled. He was clearly pleased with the location, but did not understand the implications of the proposed gift. When they tried to explain that he would own the land, he was quick to point out that people could not *own* the earth. He had no objections to living on that piece of land but considered his benefactors foolish for thinking that a piece of paper was even relevant. Besides, all of the treaties had been written on paper and most were not followed so why would this paper called a *deed* be any different. Reluctantly, he accepted the offer if only to please his benefactors.

Gerald subsequently assembled a small group of handymen who quickly made necessary repairs to the old cabin and fenced the acreage.

They soon had the well functioning and replaced the hand pump in the cabin. They even installed a new cast iron stove. Howling Wolf protested the improvements, but was pleased at the availability of fresh water. Martha provided an assortment of bowls, glasses and tableware; these went virtually unused.

Howling Wolf moved his belongings to the cabin and timidly asked Gerald if he would drive him to a location three days distant by horse so that he could retrieve some necessary items. Gerald agreed and dropped Howling Wolf at the specified location: there was no one there to greet him. Howling Wolf said that he would return to the farm in two weeks. He thanked Gerald and walked away. Puzzled, Gerald watched him for a minute or so before commencing the return journey.

In two weeks Howling Wolf returned in a battered pickup truck pulling a trailer. Gerald and Martha drove down to the cabin and noticed the horse immediately. Two men had helped unload the other items from the truck and drove away while Howling Wolf explained that "Every Indian needs a good horse." His laughter convinced the couple that all was well. He showed them some of the items that he had brought and even explained the significance of some. He told them that he would also have some sheep delivered in the near future. He hoped that the animals were allowed since he might need them for trading. Gerald assured him that the sheep would be welcome since it was *his* land.

Howling Wolf's main concern was preparation for the coming winter and setting aside all of the things that he would need. He was reassured that they would help with anything he might require. Howling Wolf was truly humbled by this generosity. His trust in the couple along with a special fondness was continuing to grow.

Within a few days, six sheep were delivered and shortly thereafter a tepee was erected next to the cabin. The couple saw less and less of Howling Wolf as he resumed his mysterious routine. They were sometimes able to hear the sounds of some rituals, but were careful not to ask about them. They were uncertain how he would react to their questions.

Usually Howling Wolf would advise them of any planned absence. On some occasions he was picked up and driven to his destination; other times he simply rode away on his horse. Gerald noticed the regular appearance of an eagle near the cabin and considered it odd, yet somehow not really surprising. He also noticed that the grass and other vegetation now thrived within the fenced area in spite of the drought.

Howling Wolf mentioned a strange growth on Gerald's forehead. "Too much sun," he said and treated the growth with a mixture derived from various plants. He also mumbled a few words and the growth disappeared during the next few days. He also told Gerald that his "blood was too much" and told him not to worry about those things that he could not control. Those were not words that consoled a farmer in the midst of a long, continuous drought.

The following spring Howling Wolf asked permission for a young man to live at the cabin to help with planting and caring for the animals. Once again Gerald reiterated that Howling Wolf could do as he pleased with *his* land. One week later Howling Wolf introduced them to *Wounded Hand*, a young man perhaps eighteen years old with a partially amputated little finger on his left hand. He would assist Howling Wolf as necessary.

In a few weeks there was an abundance of thriving vegetables and other plants that seemed to appear overnight. Shrubs which were clearly not native to the area were flowering and several fruit trees were in bloom. Neither Martha nor Gerald asked about them even though their curiosity was causing them to lose sleep.

On one occasion Howling Wolf knocked on the door and surprised the couple with a gift. He asked them to sit while he explained the gift and its relevance to them. He spoke to them as a storyteller addressing an assemblage of children.

"Long ago, an old spiritual leader sat on a tall mountain and experienced a vision. In this vision, *Iktomi*, a great prankster and wise man, appeared in the form of a spider. *Iktomi* spoke in a sacred language known only to our spiritual elders."

"*Iktomi* took the elder's willow hoop with beads, feathers, horse hair and special symbols on it and built a web inside the hoop. He spoke of the cycle of life; how we begin as helpless infants and we move on to childhood and then become adults. Finally, we reach old age and must be taken care of as infants, thus completing the cycle of life."

"*Iktomi* said, 'In each part of the cycle of life there are a great number of forces and actions that can affect our harmony with nature and the Great Spirit.' *Iktomi* gave the hoop to the elder and said, 'The web is part of a perfect circle with a hole in the center. If you believe in the Great Spirit, the web will catch your good dreams while the bad ones will go through the hole.'

"The elder later passed his vision along to our people who now use the dreamcatcher as the web of their life. It is placed in our homes to cleanse our dreams and our visions. The good of our dreams is captured in the web and remains with us while the evil passes through the hole and is gone forever."

"Now take this gift, this dreamcatcher, and let it help you in your own lives."

With those words Howling Wolf unwrapped the gift. Martha and Gerald gasped at the sight of the dreamcatcher. The simple beauty of it was readily apparent, but its exquisite detail was only revealed upon closer inspection. The hoop was a perfect circle almost the size of

Martha's treasured cast iron skillet. It was made from a willow sapling and seemed to have neither a beginning nor an end. The web was woven from horsehair, a departure from the deer sinew normally used. There were ten eagle feathers attached to the hoop; there were four pairs, one high and one low on each side with single feathers centered top and bottom. A set of four short beaded strings dangled from the outer portion of each lower side of the hoop. There were various symbols on the beads.

Howling Wolf explained that the feathers were there to carry their dreams along and that the eagle was the most majestic of all birds. Thus this dreamcatcher was the best that he could fashion for his friends. When asked the meaning or purpose of the beaded strings, Howling Wolf said simply, "So that you will always remember me."

Gerald suffered a massive stroke ten months later and never recovered; he passed away shortly thereafter. Martha then began a downward spiral as her health deteriorated. She seemed not to care about living anymore and died quietly six months after Gerald's death. Howling Wolf attended both funerals and lingered afterward on both occasions. Some thought it odd that this strange man was there wearing full Indian regalia; others were somewhat angered by his presence. Still others knew of the close bond between the Lewis family and Howling Wolf and were pleased to see that he had attended the funerals.

During the ensuing weeks, the Lewis family survivors debated the fate of the farm. The long drought years had devastated the farming business and none of them had any desire to even attempt to continue farming. They agreed to dispose of the farm equipment by auction. They would divide their parents' personal effects among themselves and proceeds from the auction would be divided equally. The acreage and buildings would be sold as best they could. The extended drought had decimated the market for land although not to the extent of the 'dust bowl' area farther to the south. Their hope was to get what they could from the sale of the farm and perhaps move even farther away from this stricken area.

As was to be expected, there were those visionaries who foresaw the future of these lands and sought to purchase them at these current rock-bottom prices. They were buying up these farms at every opportunity knowing that some day the value would increase astronomically. The favorite tactic was to purchase adjacent properties and create huge blocks of land that could later be divided or sub-divided as needed.

It was one of these opportunists who learned about the Lewis farm and its 465 acres. The same individual had already purchased three neighboring farms which bordered the river. He toured the Lewis farm and quickly concluded that this was the best of the farms and was surprised to learn of the small block of 15 acres which was owned by someone else. He needed to have the entire parcel. He would contact the legal owner and persuade him to sell. He could offer a hefty sum if necessary since it was only fifteen acres. The following day he approached Howling Wolf to make an offer. He considered it strange that an Indian owned the land. Regardless, he would sell...just like everyone else. After all, money was always a great persuader.

Howling Wolf did not like the arrogance of the stranger who wanted to purchase the land where he was living.

Before abruptly walking away, he stated simply, "You cannot own this land."

This was in reference to his belief that men could live on the earth, but could not *own the earth*.

The stranger was furious.

"We'll see about that," he shouted at the old man.

He strode angrily to his car and headed back to Chicago. He would have that property one way or another.

Lawrence Alexander was a professional. He was completely unremarkable in appearance and nothing about him would draw the slightest amount of attention. It was almost as if he did not actually exist. He could make a purchase in a store and minutes later the clerk would not be able to describe him at all. He never wore flashy clothing and even the automobile he drove was inconspicuous although he could afford to purchase any vehicle he chose. He spoke very little in public and on those rare occasions when he did speak, his voice was very soft and his words were soon forgotten. He seemed to have no friends, but there were those who always knew how to find him and employ him to eliminate their problems. He had no criminal record and not even a medical record. He had no bank accounts and always paid with cash. He went by the name of *Charles Alexander*. And *Charles* had no permanent address.

Lawrence (Charles) stopped on the main road next to the sign that read "For Sale – 465 Acres." He checked the crude map before continuing a little farther and making the right turn onto the rough road leading down toward the river. He spotted the old cabin almost immediately. "My god," he thought, "there really *is* a tepee next to the house." He left the Ford sedan in first gear as he bounced along the rutted path. He gratefully stopped near the cabin and noticed a young man working next to one of the outbuildings. He shut off the engine, eased out of the sedan and walked toward the young man. This was clearly not the man he was here to see.

Wounded Hand had heard the approaching automobile and had stopped chopping on the last of the support posts for the extended roof of the old barn. He had realized that the structure was now almost ready to collapse and he would soon be able to take a break. After that he would move the debris. It was his good fortune that this stranger had appeared and could help stabilize the post while he made the last few swings with the axe.

"Hey mister! Could you steady this old roof while I finish chopping the post?"

Wounded Hand had no qualms about asking for help, not even from a stranger. "Just hold this rope for a minute."

"Glad to help, but I'm actually here to see an old man that supposedly lives here," said a very cautious Lawrence as he accepted the end of the rope.

"Oh, he's inside. I take care of him and help him with all of the hard work. Just hold the rope and as soon as this thing falls down, I'll take you to him."

Wounded Hand turned away and picked up the axe. He took a couple of deep breaths before taking careful aim.

As soon as Wounded Hand turned away, Lawrence dropped the rope and picked up a piece of discarded two by four. He silently moved toward the young Indian and swung it with all of his strength. It was a solid blow to the base of the skull and Wounded Hand collapsed without uttering a sound. Lawrence checked for a pulse; finding none, he quickly and carefully repositioned the body.

He removed the rope from the end post and after retrieving the axe, very carefully made a few swings on the opposite side of the post where Wounded Hand had been working. At the sound of the first crack, he placed the axe next to the body where he thought it should go. Then he located a small branch and obliterated his own tracks that were under the roof area. He then moved to the end post and pushed. The roof extension moved slowly and then suddenly came crashing down onto the lifeless body of Wounded Hand.

Lawrence surveyed his handiwork and was pleased. He returned to his automobile and grabbed the small wooden case. He removed a syringe and a vial of clear liquid. He took the needle, twisted it onto the syringe and pulled back the plunger. He then injected air into the vial and once again withdrew the plunger. He carefully held the full syringe with the needle pointed up. He closed the door of the sedan and headed for the cabin. He immediately felt a touch of uneasiness or perhaps it was fear. Yet somehow, armed only with the syringe, he continued toward the door to the cabin.

Howling Wolf had finished the final touches to the last of five elaborate and identical dreamcatchers when he had heard the approaching of an automobile. Not expecting any visitors, he had looked through the window just in time to see a man walking over to Wounded Hand. "Perhaps he will send him away," he thought as he left the window and placed the last dreamcatcher next to the others on the table. Returning to his chair, he sensed that something was about to happen. He waited patiently.

He finally heard the automobile door close, but knew that the man was not leaving. He also knew that the man was here to see him. He remained seated in his favorite chair and waited for the knock on the door.

Lawrence felt the uncomfortable and foreign sensation intensify as he approached the door to the cabin. "He's just an old man," he thought to himself as he fought to control the fear that was slowly building. This was a new experience for him; his planning was always perfect with nothing left to chance. He was fully cognizant that he had taken on this job with very little planning simply because of the circumstances. He was beginning to regret that lapse in judgment. "It's just an old man," he reassured himself and swung the door open.

Howling Wolf made immediate eye contact with the stranger and immediately remembered the flight of the eagle and the boy with the slingshot. He knew why he was here, yet had no fear. He continued to stare at the stranger, the *Evil One*.

Lawrence looked at the old man for several seconds while his eyes adjusted to the dim light in the cabin. Something was vaguely familiar about this old man and yet he could not understand how that was possible. He knew that he had never traveled to this part of the country before and tried to shrug it off as one of those things that just seemed to happen. Still, his brain continued to search for some previous encounter. Something caused the hair on the back of his neck to stand on end.

"Do I know you; have we met before?" Lawrence quietly asked both questions as one.

"Many years ago I watched you kill a small bird and then you saw me and pretended to shoot a stone at me. You were just a boy."

Howling Wolf watched the stranger's eyes widen and his brow furrow as the memory of the incident returned.

"I saw a huge bird, an eagle, I think; I did not see you. Are you telling me that you were an eagle, old man?"

A smirk replaced his puzzled expression as Lawrence relaxed somewhat. Even so, the feeling of dread remained. He slowly looked around the cabin at the numerous articles and symbols. Something was urging him to leave immediately, but as a professional he still had work to do. He would not, *could not* leave...at least not yet. Even so, his internal warning system that had served him so well in the past, urged him to flee.

Howling Wolf watched the stranger yet had no fear; he knew what was to be, although the method had not yet been revealed. He needed to know what was about to happen.

"I know why you are here and I know that Wounded Hand is no longer among the living. How do you intend to complete your visit?"

The question seemed almost absurd to Lawrence. There were no promises or begging; there was not even a simple "Why?" There was no fear in the old man and that was unnerving. It was as if he had known that this day was coming and was prepared for it. He doubted that the old man would put up much of a fight and that was intriguing. Lawrence had never encountered a situation like this before. He suddenly brought the syringe into view and immediately felt an inexplicable need to describe the process. His expression softened and he spoke just above a whisper.

"This syringe contains potassium *something*. I will inject it into your body and it will go to your heart. It will make your heart stop beating. The needle is not too painful and shortly thereafter your heart will stop and you will go to sleep."

He could not tell the old man the truth about the body's reaction. He actually admired the old man, but this was just business.

"I have seen this thing, this *syringe*, and it was used to heal people and now I know that it can kill, too. I am ready for what is to be."

Lawrence initially expected some sort of a trick, but began to realize that it was just someone accepting his destiny. He felt the need to know so much more about this man who appeared to be so confident and serene. Then suddenly his mood changed.

Howling Wolf watched Lawrence's facial expression change from one of sadness or perhaps sympathy to a cold, emotionless stare. He watched as the stranger stepped over to the table and placed the syringe there before picking up the closest dreamcatcher. He examined it very carefully before turning toward Howling Wolf.

"What is this?" He was obviously impressed.

"It is called a dreamcatcher. My people use it to catch their good dreams and remove their bad ones," he said knowing there was no point in further elaboration.

"I always take a souvenir from each of my jobs and I really like this one. Besides, you won't be needing it." His voice was now cold and hard.

"These are special gifts for some of my people. They know that they are here and will come to claim them. You must take something else."

There was a hint of rising anger in his voice.

"No, I will take this thing and there is nothing you can do about it, old man," he growled as he returned the dreamcatcher to the table and picked up the syringe.

He stepped over to Howling Wolf and roughly grabbed his right arm.

Howling Wolf closed his eyes and began mumbling softly. A wave of anger unlike anything he had ever experienced washed over him as Lawrence began a series of failed attempts to locate the vein on the inside of the elbow.

"Go ahead; let the happy hunting ground know you're coming."

The Shaman's Legacy

His frustration was evident as he continued seeking the elusive vein.

Howling Wolf's eyes suddenly flicked open and he glared momentarily at Lawrence and then closed his eyes while murmuring more words. This time his brow was furrowed and his jaw was clinched as he spoke. If the *Evil One* wanted to take a dreamcatcher then he would receive far more than he expected. An angry Howling Wolf had summoned powers that he had never used before...powers for use against extreme evil. His rage was uncharacteristic for such a gentle man.

On the table, all five dreamcatchers suddenly quivered briefly rather than just the one chosen by Lawrence and then the webs rearranged, *eliminating the hole in the middle*. Neither man was witness to the transformations. At that same instant, Lawrence was finally able to penetrate the vein and then quickly inject the contents of the syringe into Howling Wolf's bloodstream. He withdrew the syringe and stepped back.

After a few seconds Howling Wolf suddenly took a deep breath and looked directly into the eyes of his executioner. Almost immediately he was completely paralyzed by a crushing force deep within his chest. He welcomed the relief as his vision became only black and white followed by reduced vision which slowly faded along with the crushing force. His last vision was that of his tormentor's face. Then he joined his ancestors.

Lawrence was unable to turn away from the old man's gaze. He was now sweating profusely and that strange feeling had returned. He felt no remorse...he was a professional. Still, there was something eerie about the last few seconds. He was certain that the old man was dead, but was still unable to break eye contact. It was as if Howling Wolf was still watching him, condemning him. His pulse was racing. Suddenly the vision of an eagle replaced the old man's face and then disappeared. He heard a flapping sound, and seeing movement in his peripheral vision, glanced toward the table. He noticed the feathers on the five dreamcatchers as they moved briefly as if disturbed by a rush of air. Lawrence blinked and shook his head. "My mind is playing tricks on me," he thought aloud. He was suddenly very anxious to leave.

There were three golden eagles that suddenly appeared in the lands of the Lakota. They were larger than those that populated the earth and they could be seen only by those who were pure in heart and soul and believed in the Great Spirit. They had been summoned to that place by a fourth eagle, one that been around as long as *The People* had existed. Their task was to seek out the location of a sudden disturbance in the natural balance of things; they were to locate the dreamcatchers that had gone awry. The eagles commenced a systematic search and soon pinpointed Howling Wolf's cabin as the location. Five mortal eagles would soon keep watch over the small cabin and would serve as locating sentinels should the dreamcatchers begin to move. These five golden eagles could be seen by children and those close to the one in possession of the dreamcatchers; others would never notice them.

Lawrence moved to the table and picked up the dreamcatcher which he had selected earlier. It was now imperative that this unusual item should be his; it would be a lasting reminder to fully prepare for each job. He located a towel and then very carefully placed the dreamcatcher onto it. Lawrence did not notice the subtle change in the dreamcatcher. He folded the towel over his prize and carried it out to his automobile where he placed it on the back seat before returning to the cabin.

He checked Howling Wolf for a carotid pulse; finding none, he struggled before finally getting the old man over his shoulder. He staggered out to the old barn amazed at how heavy the old man was. He placed him on the ground near Wounded Hand and arranged the body to look as if the old man had experienced heart failure while trying to help the younger man. The cause of death would be obvious. He noticed that there was neither blood nor anything else that indicated that there had even been an injection. That was odd. Once again he shook his head in confusion and then dismissed the thought; it was time to leave.

He erased his tracks with the same branch that he had used earlier. Then he returned to the cabin and washed his hands and face. After that he retrieved the syringe, closed the cabin door behind him and climbed into his car. He carefully removed the needle from the syringe and re-packed everything in the wooden case. He glanced around the area for anything he might have disturbed and mentally reviewed everything he had done. Satisfied, he started the engine and slowly crept up the rutted path to the main road. He eased onto the gravel road and headed back to Chicago. He knew that he would need to stop for the night rather than attempt to drive straight through.

Overhead, a golden eagle followed the path of the black Ford sedan.

At the same time, something seemingly unimportant and unrelated was occurring in San Diego, California. Carlos Martinez Montoya was one of many illegal aliens who had crossed into southern California in search of a better life. He spoke no English and lived with several others who shared the same fate. He was extremely lucky to be picked for a construction job at the San Diego Zoo. As a laborer, he was assigned mostly difficult tasks such as digging and preparing sites for the pouring of concrete foundations. He took his directions from a bi-lingual laborer who would provide any necessary clarification.

Once the preparation work was complete, he transported concrete by wheelbarrow to those locations where the concrete trucks could not reach. Periodically, he would do the concrete spreading and tamping plus removal of air pockets along the edges of the forms. This was a welcome relief from the monotonous and sometimes dangerous job of maneuvering the heavy wheelbarrow along the narrow planks to the dump location. During one of these tamping assignments, Carlos accepted the shovel from a co-worker and noted that the handle had fresh concrete in the area where he would place his left hand. He intended to remove the concrete, but was distracted while avoiding one of the loaded wheelbarrows; he forgot about removing the wet concrete. A few seconds later he placed his left hand on the wet concrete. It was only a matter of time until Carlos wiped the sweat from his brow with his left hand and deposited a small amount of concrete on his forehead. A few minutes later he became acutely aware of his mistake as his left eye was subjected to intense pain from the caustic cement that entered his eye with a bead of sweat.

Carlos forgot about tamping the corner of the form as he sought relief from the pain. After flushing his eyes he returned to his task and unintentionally failed to remove a substantial air pocket from the corner. The next day when the forms were removed, the crew was directed to immediately bank the fresh concrete with moist sand which would remain in place after the curing was complete. In the rush to complete that task, the weakened corner foundation was overlooked; it would remain undetected for years.

CHAPTER THREE

The Legacy Begins

Lawrence drove northbound on U.S. 75 to Omaha where he stopped for gas and a sandwich before crossing the Missouri River into Iowa. He would try to make Davenport if possible. He was fatigued from the trip out to Nebraska and could not take the chance of falling asleep at the wheel. He had remained irked by the late notification of this job and the urgency expressed by his client. He thought about the events of the last few hours. That old man was certainly not a risk or threat to anyone; he was, though, really quits strange. Actually, he was creepy. Lawrence had already forgotten about the haunting image of the eagle and the sound of the flapping wings.

He stopped briefly and tossed the glass vial with the remaining potassium stuff into a small river...just in case. He thought for a few more seconds and then also tossed the remaining contents of the box. He also remembered that he had a meeting with his sister, Charlotte, and that was something he could not miss.

Lawrence continued eastbound to Des Moines and stopped for gas next to a small diner. He decided to have dinner rather than to wait until he stopped for the night. After the filling station attendant completed his task, Lawrence paid for the gas and drove over to the diner. He visited the restroom before sitting down at a table near a front window. A waitress appeared almost immediately and automatically filled a coffee cup without bothering to ask. He scanned the menu briefly and ordered the pork chop dinner. After sipping the coffee, he told the waitress to "Keep the coffee coming." He then took a few seconds to carefully observe the other four patrons in the diner and continued working on his cup of coffee. Seeing nothing amiss, he relaxed somewhat.

Something suddenly caused him to glance out the window and he noticed a huge bird perched atop an electrical pole on the far side of the highway. He was certain that the damn bird was staring at him. A slight chill enveloped him as he suddenly remembered the vision of the eagle at the old man's cabin. "It's just a coincidence," he said softly to himself. He remained seated for another minute or so before moving to a table on the far side of the diner. He held up his coffee cup so the waitress could

The Shaman's Legacy

see it and he noticed that his hand was trembling. This was something new and it made him extremely uneasy.

The waitress returned and replenished his coffee, seeming a little perturbed that he had re-located. Lawrence broke from his self-imposed avoidance of conversation.

"Is that an eagle that nests somewhere around here?"

The waitress stared blankly at him for a few seconds before speaking.

"What are you talking about?"

"Come over to the window," he said as he rose from his chair, "Please."

She followed cautiously; there were lots of strange people who passed through this area.

"Look up on that pole right there," he said as he pointed at the eagle that was still looking at him.

The waitress looked at the pole and then looked back at him with a quizzical expression.

"I don't see any eagle. Where is it?"

"It's right there on the pole, staring at us."

There was a touch of aggravation in his voice.

"I'm sorry, mister, I don't see an eagle. You've probably just been driving a little too long."

She rolled her eyes and quickly walked away thinking, "He's probably not really dangerous."

Visibly shaken, Lawrence returned to his table. He must not create a disturbance that might cause him to be remembered. He sat quietly until his dinner arrived. He picked at his meal for a few minutes as he tried to come up with some sort of an explanation. He was suddenly no longer hungry and was anxious to leave. He put five dollars on the table and left the diner. He glanced up at the eagle; it was still there, it was *real* and it appeared to be almost completely black. That was unsettling, but perhaps it was only because he was looking into the late afternoon sun. His only concern right now was to put some miles between himself and this place before it got dark. A minute later he caused a great deal of gravel to spew from the rear wheels of his car as he pulled onto the highway.

Lawrence did not observe the eagle as it launched itself from the pole to follow him.

He drove for more than two hours before fatigue began to dull his senses. It was now dark and he found himself dozing off. He would stop at the next place where he could get a room. Six miles later he was passing though a small populated area and spotted a sign with the word 'Rooms' on it. He turned onto the side road and followed the signs. There was a building with a sign designating it as the office. There were ten very small cabins, five on either side of the office.

He parked in front of the office and asked if the cabin on the far end was available. The clerk, Jerry Powell, assured him that for one dollar it was definitely available. He also mentioned that the cabin was closest to the train tracks, but that only one train was coming through that night. Lawrence was handed a key and advised that the men's room was in the back half of the office and was accessible from the outside. Lawrence tipped the clerk with a five-dollar bill before visiting the facility and then drove down to cabin number 10. He was now wide awake.

He unlocked the cabin and then took his souvenir from the back seat so that he could look at it more carefully. He was amazed at the workmanship; surely the old man had not actually made these things. He looked over at the cheap painting that was hanging above the headboard and smiled. He removed it and hung the souvenir in its place. It really added class to the small room. This was certainly the finest souvenir in his extensive collection.

Without warning, Lawrence suddenly felt thoroughly fatigued. Two minutes later he was sound asleep on the saggy bed, fully clothed with the lights on. He snored softly at first. After a while, he began dreaming and it was that same one from his childhood.

Twelve minutes after midnight, the southbound freight train came through the small town moving at approximately 30 miles per hour. Without any warning or indication of a malfunction, the caboose uncoupled from the boxcar in front of it. A split second later it de-railed and, remarkably, remained upright as it continued rolling.

Lawrence awoke to the vision of an eagle, a very angry eagle. He immediately thought of the old Indian just as the caboose came through the back wall of cabin number 10. The sound of snapping and splintering lumber filled the room and then the lights abruptly went out. The caboose and a portion of the wall collided with the bed before continuing through the front wall amid the sound of more splintering wood. The movement through the darkened shambles terrified the man who rarely felt fear. The caboose slowed just as both of Lawrence's legs snapped causing him to scream in anguish. The large coupling on the caboose then slammed into his chest and remained there as it propelled his body first through the grille, then the radiator and finally into the engine block of Lawrence's car. Death followed after a few seconds of excruciating pain.

The night clerk heard the commotion and arrived at the scene before anyone else. Jerry spotted the crushed bed and the lifeless body. He noticed that the caboose from the *Southern Eagle* appeared to be undamaged. He did not panic, but surveyed the area and noticed that the end wall of the cabin had fallen outward. Unconsciously, he walked over to a strange object that had caught his attention. He picked up the dreamcatcher, examined it briefly and returned with it to the office to report the situation. People were just beginning to leave their cabins to investigate the noise. The clerk hesitated as he opened the door to the office; he thought he heard the sound of flapping wings. Spotting nothing, he entered the office. Jerry was anxious to examine his prize since he knew it did not belong in the cabin and he knew it would not be missed. And it must have belonged to the nice but strange man who had given him the five-dollar tip. He realized that he could not even remember what the man had looked like.

CHAPTER FOUR

The Trading Post

Two days after the unfortunate deaths of the two Indians out at the Lewis farm, two men came to clean out the cabin and either take away or burn any personal items which might have remained behind. One man concentrated his efforts on the items that had belonged to the old Indian while the other man collected everything else. There were numerous items which could be sold. They would each be paid fifty dollars cash to make the property presentable. That also entailed the burning of the outbuildings which were in poor condition.

Both men had marveled at the taller grass on the property which had turned brown recently; it was a sharp contrast to the thin grass on the adjacent property. It seemed to them that somehow the property had died along with the two Indians, but then that was ridiculous. The two men were glad to complete the job and stopped by the bank to collect their money. Then they went their separate ways.

Walter Hawkins stopped at Jill's Diner for two reasons. First, he had fifty dollars and was hungry for a good meal. His second item of business was to find out if anyone knew where he might sell his truckload of 'Indian stuff.' As a carpenter and handyman, he had suffered from the lack of construction work in the area and had taken on numerous side jobs just to feed his family. This windfall would allow the family to move farther north and perhaps allow him to find steady work.

He spoke with Jill who told him about a place on the west side of Omaha that sold a little bit of everything and would probably do right by him. And, of course, Chicago would be even better. Unfortunately she had no contacts there. Walter decided to try the Omaha location, but had some work to do first. He wanted to build wooden cases for the four circle things with the feathers and beads on them. That would protect them and would probably raise their value significantly.

He stopped at the small local grocery store on the way home and picked up the basics along with some candy for the kids. He drove home full of hope for a better future. After taking the groceries inside his house, he took the four dreamcatchers to his so-called shop and commenced the construction of four identical wooden boxes, each 18 by

30 by 3.5 inches. After five hours he was able to step back and admire his handiwork. Each dreamcatcher was now nestled inside a wooden case with a small latch which held the case securely closed. Walter was amazed that the four objects were *exactly* the same size which was a factor in how quickly the boxes could be assembled. As a final touch, he rubbed lemon oil on the pine cases and smiled at the simple beauty of the pine wood. These would fetch a handsome price just for the boxes alone; the real value was the object inside resting on the liner made from a woolen blanket which had been sacrificed. He would head for Omaha tomorrow morning and hopefully be home before dark…unless he had to go to Chicago. Walter was unaware of the four golden eagles that would now escort his cargo.

After a good night's sleep, Walter arrived at Bailey's Trading Post just before 10:00 A.M. and eagerly went inside. There were several cars parked outside and at least 20 customers wandering around the many aisles. He waited in line patiently until he could talk to the man at the counter.

"I've got some stuff out on my truck that you might be interested in," he said as calmly as he could.

It would be nice if he could sell everything right here.

"What kind of stuff, mister?"

"It's mostly Indian things including a tepee," grinning as he spoke.

Immediately a small crowd formed and looked at Walter.

"Is it a real tepee?" asked a man wearing a suit. "I'm asking if it is an *authentic* Indian tepee."

"It was owned by an Indian so I guess that would make it a real tepee."

Walter wondered if there was some way of knowing if it was authentic. It certainly looked real to him. He remembered that the tepee had a buffalo and a large bird on it plus numerous symbols.

"What else do you have?" asked a woman.

The small crowd inched closer to hear.

"I don't have an inventory, but there are all kinds of things and I don't know what most of them are."

"Let me get Mr. Bailey," said the man at the counter as he rushed over to the small office.

He knocked and entered quickly, closing the door behind him.

Moments later an older man with thick glasses approached the counter area followed by the other man. He looked around and then addressed Walter.

"Okay, let's see what you have," and headed toward the front door with the crowd in hot pursuit.

Walter's Chevy truck with the poles for the tepee was easily identified as the place to go. Mr. Bailey was not happy that this merchandise, if genuine, would be seen by these customers before he purchased it. He knew that they would rather buy from the man with the truck.

"I tell you what Mister...I'll give you a hundred dollars for the whole truckload so you can be on your way," Mr. Bailey whispered to Walter.

"Mister, I'll give you a hundred dollars just for the tepee if it's real," said the man wearing the suit.

He stared at Walter and then at Mr. Bailey.

Mr. Bailey turned beet red, but tried to conceal his anger with the way things were progressing. There was a good chance that the tepee would be sold to the man in the suit. He needed to get control of the process.

"Look folks, deliveries normally come in through that gate over there and I do an inventory of all the items that I buy. Then I move them into the store and assign a fair price for them. Then you folks can look around and decide what you want to buy. This man has not had a chance to show me what he has for sale. I'll open the gate so he can drive the truck around back and we can work something out. Okay, Mister?"

"Sure."

Walter was pleased; he had hoped for perhaps fifty or maybe as much as sixty dollars for the whole load.

"Wait a minute; what about the tepee? I am serious about the hundred dollars."

The man in the suit wanted to deal with Walter. He knew that Mr. Bailey would raise the price.

Walter realized that he was now in command; perhaps he could get more.

"This man has offered me the same amount for the tepee as you offered for the entire truckload. I would be a fool to turn that down."

"Then I will give you one-ten." The response was instantaneous and Mr. Bailey was sweating.

Walter looked at the man in the suit.

"One-twenty, cash!" hesitating before adding, "I'll give you ten more than whatever Mr. Bailey offers."

Walter turned toward Mr. Bailey hardly believing what he had just heard; he smiled.

Knowing that he was beaten, Mr. Bailey upped the ante just for spite.

"One-thirty."

"One-fifty."

"Take it!" Mr. Bailey threw up his hands. He had considered playing a few more rounds, but feared that he might end up with the final bid.

"Now let's get your truck inside the fence."

Smiling, Walter climbed into the cab and started the engine. Once the gate was open he drove into the compound and stopped near the back of the trading post. The man in the suit had walked alongside the truck and was waiting when Walter stepped down from the cab.

The Shaman's Legacy

"Do we have a deal? For one-fifty, I mean?" he asked anxiously.

"Yes we do. If you wanted it delivered, I'll be happy to do that. Are you from around here?" Walter hoped he was a local resident.

"I own a restaurant about 3 miles from here. It's called the Broken Arrow and I think an authentic tepee would really bring in the customers. I'm sure that you have other items that I might be interested in as well."

Walter observed Mr. Bailey approaching.

"Well, Mr. Bailey gets first crack at the rest of the load, so you'll be dealing with him."

Mr. Bailey smiled smugly at the restaurant owner; he just might be able to get back some of the potential money he had lost on the tepee.

The three men began unloading the boxes and crates from the truck. Mr. Bailey wrote down each item or a description of it and showed it to the man in the suit. He tried to see how much interest the man had in each object so that he could price it accordingly. Once each item had been inspected, he assigned a price and totaled it for Walter. He was careful to keep the actual figures away from the man in the suit.

The total was just shy of $100 and Mr. Bailey whispered to Walter, "Let's just call it an even hundred."

Walter was elated and soberly agreed with a nod. He turned to the restaurant owner.

"Why don't you ride with me and we can drop off the tepee. I'll bring you back here and maybe by then Mr. Bailey will be ready to do more business with you. I need to head for home pretty soon."

Mr. Bailey nodded his approval and started toward the gate. He was anxious to get rid of those two for awhile. He had a lot of treasure to sort through.

The restaurant owner immediately spoke, "I'll take care of the gate. Don't sell everything before I return!"

He walked swiftly toward the gate.

Mr. Bailey had no intention of letting this man get away! He had a score to settle; every item would have two prices.

Walter drove the truck out of the compound and waited for the restaurant owner to close and latch the gate. It was then that he spotted the four wooden cases on the floor of the cab. In the excitement of the monetary windfall he had forgotten about them.

When the restaurant owner opened the door, Walter told him to hand the four cases to him. He stacked the four cases next to him on the seat and waited for the man to climb in.

"What are these?"

The restaurant owner carefully touched the top case.

"I don't really know, but see what you think of them...they're all the same. I forgot that I had them here in the cab."

The other man placed one of the cases on his lap and opened it. Walter heard the man take a deep breath. It was several seconds before he spoke.

"This is beautiful, simply beautiful. What is it and is it for sale?"

He sat there staring at the dreamcatcher.

"I'm not sure what it is, but I think that they're a set."

He knew what the next question would be.

"Sorry, you'll have to deal with Mr. Bailey."

"Why don't you just sell them to me...if they all look like this, I'll take all four and pay you more than Bailey will. He doesn't even know about them."

"I'm sorry; I just can't do that. It wouldn't be right."

Walter sighed and looked at the restaurant owner before adding, "He has to make a living, too. By the way, my name is Walter Hawkins," he said as he extended his hand.

"Aaron Polk."

The firm handshake showed the character of the two men.

They chatted amicably as they drove to the restaurant. After unloading the tepee, Walter wrote down some assembly instructions based on what he had learned from taking it down. Aaron was ecstatic. He gave the one hundred fifty dollars to a very grateful Walter.

Twenty-five minutes later Walter parked his truck in front of the trading post. He carried the four wooden cases and walked in with Aaron close behind. Mr. Bailey spotted the two men and rushed over. He noticed the four wooden cases immediately and knew that something wonderful was inside even though it probably was not of Indian origin.

"What have we here?"

He could not stop staring at the boxes. He produced an envelope with Walter's hundred dollars from his pocket.

Walter carried the cases over to the counter and selected the uppermost from the stack. He opened the case and stepped back. Mr. Bailey looked at the dreamcatcher without speaking. Aaron crowded closer for another look and was once again startled by the magnificence of what he saw.

"I'm sorry; I forgot that I had these in the truck. Mr. Polk here seems to be interested in them. I will let you make an offer and if it is reasonable I will sell them to you; if it is not, then I will sell them to Mr. Polk."

Walter knew that Mr. Bailey was going to have very special prices for Aaron if he sold anything to him at all.

Mr. Bailey picked up the opened case and tilted it so that the light struck the dreamcatcher from different angles.

"I have seen similar objects, but none as striking as this."

The Shaman's Legacy

Still clutching the money envelope, he placed the case on the counter and selected the next case. He fumbled with the latch and then opened it. Once again he just stared. Then he placed the case next to the other.

"They're identical," he whispered after a few seconds.

"And the other two are the same," said Walter as Aaron moved closer so that he could see.

Walter opened the other two cases so that the two men could draw their own conclusions. Aaron whistled softly as he looked at the four objects. Mr. Bailey said nothing as he compared each to the others.

"I would like to meet the person who made these. You brought in a war bonnet that has the same high-quality craftsmanship. These feathers come from golden eagles; these are genuine Sioux articles," stated Mr. Bailey speaking just above a whisper.

"The man who fashioned these things died a few days ago. He was supposedly a special medicine man with great powers," Walter spoke in a whisper, unconsciously mimicking Mr. Bailey. "There are no other items like these."

"I'll give you five dollars for each of these," ventured Mr. Bailey.

"I need seven."

"Okay, seven dollars each. Agreed?" Mr. Bailey held his breath as did Aaron Polk.

"Agreed."

"I'll be right back," said a relieved Mr. Bailey as he left for the office.

"I would have given you ten," grumbled Aaron as he shook his head.

"Sorry, I couldn't go back on my word. Besides, I think the tepee might have been the best bargain of the whole lot."

Mr. Bailey returned moments later and counted out the twenty-eight dollars. He then counted out the contents of the crumpled envelope. Walter collected the money and placed all of it into the envelope, shook the hands of both men and headed for the door.

"Thank you both and perhaps I'll see you again," he said as he departed. He was eager to return home with the good news.

The two men waved and then turned to face each other. Mr. Bailey spoke first.

"These boxes are not for sale; everything else is. All of the new items are located on those tables near the front of the store except for the war bonnet. I will keep it in the office because I don't want people touching it. Look around and see if there's anything you like."

Mr. Bailey was smiling triumphantly. Aaron shrugged and moved toward the front of the store.

Mr. Bailey took one of the wooden cases into his office before returning to place the other three out of sight on top of a tall cabinet. He would get more for these items if it appeared that there was only one. He was shrewd when it came to promoting his merchandise. He admired the beautiful object for a few more minutes before taking it out to the main counter.

The following week a nice lady by the name of Eleanor Taylor would stop in on her way home from a trip and would purchase the dreamcatcher as a housewarming gift for a dear friend. She would pay ten dollars for it and, unknown to her, she would have an eagle for an escort when she departed.

That sale would be Mr. Bailey's last due to a fatal automobile accident as he pulled out of the parking lot onto the highway while congratulating himself on a very profitable day; he never saw the truck that killed him. His wife reluctantly took over the task of running the trading post.

CHAPTER FIVE

The Original Dreamcatcher

Jerry Powell spoke to the police and representatives from the railroad about the caboose and poor Mr. Charles Alexander. There was very little information that he could provide other than the name of the occupant of cabin number 10. His car was there, so that should provide more information. He certainly did not mention that the round thing with feathers had probably belonged to the deceased; it was now his and he had no intention of parting with it.

A reporter from Cedar Rapids had come down, taking notes and photographs. Jerry spoke with him and was pleased to learn that he would be mentioned in the news article. Jerry was also hearing comments about the unexplained derailment of just one railroad car and the fact that it had remained upright throughout its deadly path. These men were referring to the deceased as "just plain unlucky."

Jerry was sent home two hours before his scheduled shift ended. The owner had arrived and thought that Jerry was just a little too cozy with the strangers investigating this terrible mishap. Jerry carried home his special prize knowing that his wife would love it. He would tell her that he got it just for her. She would be waking up just about the time he reached home. He thought about the strange occurrence throughout the fifteen minute drive home. Stepping out of his car, he spotted a large, dark bird overhead. He watched it for a few seconds before picking up the feathered object and walking to the front door.

Jerry awkwardly unlocked his front door and stepped inside; the feathered thing had made it difficult to open the screen door and unlock the front door while simultaneously protecting the prize from damage.

"Jerry, is that you?"

He was surprised to hear his wife's voice.

"Yeah, it's me...I got out early and, boy do I have a story to tell! I also have a present for you. I'll be right there," he said as he walked toward the bedroom.

Nancy Powell met her husband before he reached the bedroom. She had been motivated by the mention of a present; Jerry was not one to surprise *anyone* with a present. She kissed him lightly and looked around for the present.

"Take a look at this," he said as he thrust the dreamcatcher toward her.

"I'm not sure what it's called, but it sure is beautiful."

"Oh, Jerry, that's gorgeous! Where did you find it?"

He hesitated, surprised by her choice of words.

"A guy came in last night with it and I just had to get it for you, so here it is," he said while avoiding the details.

Nancy examined the present and was impressed by the high quality and craftsmanship. She carried it to the kitchen and placed it on the dinette before starting a pot of coffee.

"Now what happened last night that was so exciting?"

She sat down at the dinette and admired the dreamcatcher.

Jerry told her about the stranger and the train wreck being very careful not to mention the dreamcatcher. He told her that he had been interviewed by several people and that he would be mentioned in the newspaper. He was excited about it even though it was not a happy occasion. Once the coffee was brewed they pondered their breakfast options and were surprised when their oldest daughter arrived.

Sarah (Powell) Simpson knocked and opened the door as she had done so many times before.

"We're in the kitchen, sweetheart," her mother said as she rose to get another coffee cup.

"Dad, are you okay? I heard about the train wreck on the radio and came over to ask Mom if she had heard from you. I didn't expect to see you here."

She removed her sweater and sat at the dinette.

"It's all right, Hon; they sent me home early due to all of the excitement and investigations."

Nancy brought the coffee over and placed it in front of her daughter.

"Look what your father brought me," gesturing toward the dreamcatcher.

"Oh, Mom, it's beautiful. Do you know what it is?"

"I know that it's some sort of decoration and I'm pretty sure it's Indian."

"Yes it is; it's called a *dreamcatcher* and it's supposed to bring you good luck or something. It has something to do with your dreams and making them come true."

Sarah had exhausted her knowledge of dreamcatchers.

"Well, I don't believe in that sort of thing and Lord knows I'm not an Indian, but it sounds like it belongs in the bedroom and it's much too beautiful to be sitting in a cardboard box somewhere."

Nancy knew exactly where to hang it.

"C'mon, let's see how it looks."

The two women left the kitchen with Nancy carrying her very special gift. Jerry smiled before rising to refill his cup. He used a match to light the burner under the coffee pot and turned the burner all the way down. A few seconds later he filled his cup. He was starting to feel really hungry. He had enough money to take the three of them to breakfast and he was lucky to be alive; that caboose could have come right through the office.

"Dad, come here!"

There was obvious excitement in Sarah's voice.

"Coming," he sighed as he headed for the bedroom.

He saw the dreamcatcher hanging above the bed before he even entered the room. It had replaced an old (and in his opinion) ugly painting of poor quality that had been there for years. It was a welcome change; in fact, it looked magnificent. It needed to be about six inches higher, though.

"What do you think, Dad?"

Sarah was actually beaming.

Nancy was smiling with what seemed to be a hopeful expression and Jerry carefully crafted his reply.

"Wow! That looks really nice. I like it better than the painting."

"To tell the truth, I've always hated that painting, but knew that you liked it so I never said anything," said a still smiling Nancy.

"I stopped liking it the time it fell and hit me on the back of the head about ten or twelve years ago. Sarah, would you like to have the painting?"

He knew what the answer would be, but was interested in how she would gracefully decline the offer.

"No, Dad; no offense, but I also *hate* that painting."

"Well ladies, I think the *dream thing* needs to be about six inches higher and that I should take care of that *after* we return from breakfast. Grab your things and let's go."

The two women shrieked with delight and complied while Jerry preceded them to the car. Sarah dutifully took the back seat and Nancy climbed in next to her husband. Just as Jerry started backing out of the driveway, Nancy spoke.

"Jerry, did you make sure the fire under the coffee pot was off?"

"Uh, I think so. Don't worry, it'll be okay."

"Sure, burn the house down. Then what would we do? I'll be right back," she said good-naturedly as she opened the car door.

She was surprised to see a huge bird circling overhead. A minute later she returned wearing an exaggerated smug expression.

"Lucky I checked. At least we'll have a roof over our heads for another night."

"Yeah, Dad...you know Mom and her nightmares about the house burning down. I'm surprised that you forgot to turn off the stove."

"Okay, I'm sorry. I think I might still be a little addled by the train wreck after all. Let's go get something to eat."

"Honey, I just remembered; I think the bathroom light switch is broken. Could you take a look at it when we get back?"

Nancy knew the answer, but Jerry handled all of the finances so she would let him make the decision.

"I'm not touching that switch. I'll get someone to come check it 'cause it might not be the switch. I'll swing by Joe Rogers' shop after we eat; he won't over-charge us. And remind me to get a newspaper."

Breakfast was a pleasant affair and afterward, Jerry stopped to pick up a newspaper to verify that he was mentioned as promised. To his chagrin there was no article since the information had arrived after that edition had been printed. Disappointed, he would check for it tomorrow. On the way home he stopped in at Joe Rogers' little shop and arranged for him to drop by the following day to check on the bathroom lighting problem. Then he drove his two favorite women home and promptly chose to get some sleep before the night shift. Prior to lying down, he moved the nail above the bed up approximately six inches and placed the dreamcatcher in its new location. Ten minutes later he was sound asleep.

Nancy and Sarah visited for almost an hour before the latter left to run some errands. Nancy chose that time to do some grocery shopping and to swing by the post office to check the mail. Upon returning home, she spotted what probably was a large eagle circling overhead and wondered briefly if it was the same one she had seen earlier. That seemed a little odd, but she was more concerned about getting the groceries into the house. After that, she checked on Jerry who was sleeping fitfully as he often did. She smiled as she looked up at the dreamcatcher; it was just so beautiful. She stroked Jerry's forehead and he immediately began to breathe easier and then to snore softly. She left the room and resumed working on the special quilt that she was making for one of her friends. The quilt would fetch five dollars which she could stretch into their meals for almost two weeks. Her other sewing jobs would take care of the remaining bills for that month. It was important to leave their meager savings alone. The depression had taught them a lesson.

Six hours later, Jerry awoke. He went to the bathroom and was immediately reminded that the bathroom light was not working. He knew that checking the bulb would be a prudent course of action and quickly located a replacement bulb in the living room closet. He could change a light bulb; that did not bother him at all. He grabbed the small stepstool from the kitchen and placed it under the light fixture in the bathroom. He removed the glass globe and placed it on the floor next to the tub. As he prepared to unscrew the bulb, he realized that he had to lean awkwardly and needed to relocate the stepstool. However, for expediency purposes, he simply placed his bare left foot on the lavatory for balance and commenced to remove the bulb. The light switch was in the 'on' position so he would immediately know if the new bulb solved the problem.

As the old bulb came out of the socket, it began to slip from his grasp and he moved to try and catch it. His left foot slipped until it hit the hot water faucet and as his weight shifted, he instinctively tried to grab something with his right hand. His right index finger entered the bulb socket and made contact with the 'hot' side of the circuit. Electricity immediately entered his body through the index finger and exited through his left foot where it contacted the faucet. Electricity continued to flow until Jerry's body collapsed and gravity pulled him clear of the electrical current. It was too late; Jerry was dead. The last thing that had registered in his brain was the image of a very angry eagle.

The new widow was devastated; her two children were in a state of shock. Sarah replaced the light bulb in the bathroom and spent that night at her mother's house. After family and friends left, the two women sat at the dinette alternately laughing and crying as they shared their best memories of their husband and father. Nancy mentioned how Jerry had gotten her that dreamcatcher thing from some guy who was staying at one of the cottages and how surprising it was that Jerry would spend money on something like that. Sarah agreed. The evening contained another surprise when Jerry's boss arrived to find out why he had not shown up for his shift. His anger had quickly changed to sorrow when he heard the news. He had expressed his condolences in an embarrassed and awkward manner and rushed to take over the position as night clerk.

It was almost 2:00 A.M. before Nancy fell asleep on the sofa while Sarah slept in her dad's favorite over-stuffed chair. After awakening several hours later, the two women once again relived the sad realization of what had occurred the day before. Funeral arrangements were made in a dazed state and the service would take place in three days. Friends and neighbors arrived throughout the day; most brought food of some sort and the largest percentage was some type of dessert. Joe Rogers came by to fix the light switch, but Sarah met him at the door and sent him away.

About an hour after sunset when all of the visitors had departed, Nancy told Sarah to go home. She wanted to be alone with her thoughts; she would be okay. A good long sleep in her own bed would be best for her. Sarah knew better than to argue with her mother and left reluctantly. Nancy grabbed a piece of chocolate cake and some milk, amazed at the amount of food in her house. After polishing off her snack, she washed and dried the dishes. Finally, she went to the bathroom and finally was able to get the light to illuminate; she gazed at the stranger in the mirror. Nancy was appalled at the unkempt image staring back at her.

"I just don't care," she sighed wearily and went to bed.

She cried for a short time and then, mercifully, fell asleep.

Unknown to Nancy, the broken light switch was now becoming warm to the touch. The temperature continued to increase as time progressed. There was charring which was followed by a pronounced glowing and finally the wall burst into flames.

The bathroom was located next to the bedroom. It did not take long for an escape through the door to be eliminated. The fire spread rapidly throughout the wooden structure. Nancy was awakened from her deep sleep by a dream of a ferocious looking and very dark eagle. Confused, she sat up and noticed the smoke and heat from the roaring fire. Just as she realized the danger, the entire room flashed.

By the time the fire truck arrived, there was little that could be done. One of the firemen stood helplessly near the structure and was startled as the roof collapsed. He watched embers shooting skyward and then thought he saw movement in the flames and rubble. He continued to stare and right before his eyes, a huge bird briefly appeared and looked directly at him with eyes that reflected the glowing embers. Moments later, it spread its massive wings and disappeared into the night. He stood there not believing what he had seen...and yet he knew it was real. He decided that he would not discuss this with anyone.

A second fireman also witnessed the rise and ascent of the big bird, but decided to keep his mouth shut since he had been drinking before being called out for this fire; right now he needed a drink to calm his shaking hands. He looked at the other fireman that had been standing right in front of the spectacle and made eye contact. Both men shook their heads slightly and then went about their duties. Their thoughts were no longer focused solely on the task at hand.

CHAPTER SIX

The Second Dreamcatcher

Thelma Wells walked through the dining area of her small home and smiled as she once again congratulated herself on purchasing the house for such a good price. She was not normally one to haggle excessively over money, but this had been a major purchase and certainly the largest one since her husband passed away. She almost felt guilty for talking the sellers into reducing the price so low; they fell for her 'poor widow' routine, complete with crocodile tears. Oh well, it was their decision, not hers. If her useless husband had carried more insurance or earned more money then she would not have been placed in such a predicament.

She had looked for her sweater and finally remembered that she had taken it off while moving some of the junk in the storage building in the backyard. She wanted to wear it when her friend Eleanor picked her up. It was just a little too cool in the late afternoons and she hated to be uncomfortable. It seemed that each year she was a little less tolerant of the cold. Maybe a move to Florida was not such a bad idea after all. She needed to think about that some more.

Thelma stepped out onto the back porch and let the screen door slam behind her. She made a mental note to find a way to stretch the spring so that the door would close a little less violently. Carefully easing herself down the steps, she remembered that she needed to find someone to mow the yard. Surely there was a boy in the area who would mow the yard for a low price and maybe she could use the 'poor widow' routine on him. Fall would soon be here and the grass was just about ready to go dormant. She noticed an eagle or perhaps a buzzard circling overhead, but thought nothing of it. She plodded on toward the shed and unlatched the door.

The contents of the shed were a surprising array of old worn tools, battered furniture and assorted odds and ends. They came with the house simply because it was not worth the effort to move them. It was doubtful that anyone would even remove the contents just for their value. Regardless, Thelma had spent considerable time earlier digging through the boxes and crates just hoping to find some *treasure*. At some point in time she had realized that it was warm and her exertions were causing her to sweat. She had removed her dark blue sweater and draped it over an old rocking chair which was completely beyond repair.

Finally spotting the sweater, Thelma cautiously navigated to a point where she could retrieve it. She grasped the heavy sweater carefully and slowly eased her way back toward the door. Once outside, she placed the sweater around her shoulders and headed for the house. She wanted to be ready to go when Eleanor drove up. Timeliness was a virtue which was not cherished as it should be. Younger folks just did not seem to be concerned with promptness. This was just another example of how the country was going to hell in a hand basket.

She opened the screen door and checked the clock; Eleanor would be there in less than ten minutes. She ambled through the kitchen and paused to catch her breath in front of her old oval mirror in the short hallway. She checked her hair and noticed some fuzz or lint on her sweater and tried to pick it off with her right hand. Just as she was about to grab it, she saw it move and immediately recognized the unique shape of a rather large black widow spider. She could feel her heart pounding.

Thelma screamed in terror as she tried to remove the sweater and was immediately immobilized by a tremendous crushing sensation in her chest. She was now staring into the mirror and could see the spider moving slowly toward her neck. Unable to move, she watched as the colors in her immediate field of view were replaced by black, white and shades of gray. As tunnel vision closed in, she saw the spider as it touched the skin of her neck and then a brief vision of an eagle. She was dead before she hit the floor.

Eleanor arrived four minutes later and knocked on the door.

"That's odd, Thelma always meets me at the door," she said aloud. "She must be getting dressed. I'll just let myself in."

She swung the door open and immediately spotted her friend.

"Thelma!"

She rushed to her side and knelt. She spotted a huge spider on Thelma's lifeless cheek and brushed it away. Only then did she realize what type of spider·it was. She rose to her feet and crushed the slow-moving arachnid with her shoe. Kneeling at her friend's side, she noticed that Thelma's eyes were wide open. Eleanor knew that she was dead.

She rushed next door and knocked frantically at the front door. The startled neighbor who answered the knock was given terse instructions.

"Get the doctor! Thelma's been bitten by a spider and I think she's dead. Hurry!"

Eleanor returned to Thelma's house. She knelt over her friend once again and tried to listen for sounds of breathing, but could only hear the sound of her own heart pounding. She struggled to her feet and moved to the nearby rocking chair to await the arrival of the doctor. She was deeply saddened, but did not shed a tear.

The Shaman's Legacy

Forty-five minutes later, Thelma's body was taken out to an ambulance which drove away quietly. Sheriff Owens dropped by just as the ambulance was leaving. He spoke briefly with the doctor and then knocked on Thelma's door. Eleanor opened the door and was surprised to see the Sheriff standing there with his hat in his hand. Her pulse quickened immediately.

"Ma'am, I'm Sheriff Owens and I need to ask you a few questions if you don't mind."

He slowly shifted his weight from foot to foot.

Eleanor stepped back, "Come in, Sheriff. I'm Eleanor Taylor."

"I understand that you discovered the body; I just need to ask you a few routine questions and I'll be on my way," he said as he hung his hat on the rack next to the door.

He had an immediate calming effect on Eleanor and he was quite handsome. She also remembered that he was single.

"I made some coffee a few minutes ago, Sheriff; would you care for some?"

"As a matter of fact I would. I take it black, please. First, though, where did you find the deceased? Show me where. Oh, and call me Tom."

"Okay, Tom. She was right in front of that mirror with her head toward the kitchen. I saw the spider that killed her and knocked it away. Then I squashed it with my shoe. You can still see where I killed it."

Eleanor pointed to the wet spot on the floor.

"I think the doctor took the dead spider."

"The doctor examined her briefly, but didn't find any evidence of a bite during his quick examination. He doesn't believe that it would have killed her, anyway. He thinks her heart just gave out. I am puzzled about one thing, though; this house is immaculate and not the kind of place where this type of spider prefers to live. They normally want a dark, secluded location. The doctor showed me a web and egg case that was on her sweater and there was quite a bit of dust on it, too. I think she brought the spider in with her from somewhere else."

"Well, there's an old shed outside and an old garage. Come to think of it, she did mention that she wanted to clean out both of them. Maybe the spider came from one of them. You can check if you like. Anyway, let me get you that coffee," said Eleanor as she headed for the kitchen.

The sheriff glanced around the room and then followed her to the kitchen. He stood patiently while Eleanor located a coffee cup and filled it from the ancient coffee pot. She handed the cup to him and watched him take a careful sip; he nodded his approval.

"Thank you, ma'am," said the sheriff as he walked to the back door. "I'll just make a quick check of the garage and the shed."

He took another sip of coffee, hesitated briefly and then carried the cup with him as he left the house.

Eleanor watched the sheriff enter the garage through the side door and was surprised to see him exit almost immediately. He walked across the yard to the shed and went inside. He came out after a minute or so and returned to the back door. She heard the screen door swing and opened the door just as he reached for the doorknob which startled him somewhat.

"I wasn't expecting that," he laughed; "I almost spilled my coffee."

He downed the last of the coffee and carried the empty cup to the sink.

"I'm sorry. That door sometimes sticks. Did you find anything?"

"Well, the garage was almost empty and very clean. The shed was a disaster, though. I would guess that the spider came from there. I'll be leaving now. This was just routine checking, nothing sinister or suspicious. Can you lock the house up when you leave?"

He paused for a few seconds.

"I'm sorry. I just assumed that you lived nearby or were a relative."

"Actually, I'm a friend and just came over to pick her up for a trip to the store. I can go see her granddaughter. She'll tell me what she wants to do. She lives about five miles from here."

"Well, ma'am, I don't know…maybe it would be better if I made the notification. I mean, it's not easy to do and she might handle it a little better coming from me. She will know that something's up as soon as she sees my car. I don't mind doing it unless you feel really strong about doing it yourself."

He leaned against the refrigerator waiting for a response.

"No, I'll do it. I'll lock the house and give her the keys. She may need me to help her a little and I have no immediate plans."

Eleanor moved toward the front door and opened it.

"Thanks for the offer, Tom."

Sheriff Owens followed her lead and retrieved his hat from the rack near the door.

"Thanks for the coffee and I hope everything goes smoothly. I'm sorry about the loss of your friend."

He stepped through the door, nodded and placed his hat on his head. He smiled weakly and walked away.

Eleanor waited until he entered the car and then closed the front door. She walked straight to Thelma's bedroom and stood at the foot of the bed. She looked at the magnificent Indian thing hanging over the bed for a long moment and then went to the closet and retrieved the wooden case. She carefully removed the dreamcatcher from the wall and gently placed it into the case.

"Thelma doesn't need it anymore and since I gave it to her as a house warming gift, I guess I can keep it," she said aloud as she left the room with her prize. "It would be such a waste to allow something this beautiful to go to someone who might not appreciate it."

That Bailey man at the trading post in Omaha had overcharged her, but she just had to have that beautiful thing. She locked the house and carried her new possession to her car. It was time to notify the granddaughter.

Fifteen minutes later Eleanor parked her car next to the small house where Thelma's granddaughter lived. She walked across the yard to the front steps and knocked on the screen door. She immediately heard movement within and soon saw the granddaughter rushing toward her, frantically drying her hands on a dish towel.

"Hi Eleanor, what brings you out here? What's wrong?" she asked pushing the door open and stepping back.

"Mary, it's bad news. Your grandmother was bitten by a spider and it killed her. I am so sorry."

She stepped inside uncertain if she should hug the young woman since they were mere acquaintances. She kept her distance.

"The doctor said her heart quit, but I found a black widow spider on her...they're poisonous, you know."

Tears streamed down Mary's face and she sat quietly on the sofa. Eleanor sat down next to her, unsure of her next move.

"When did it happen?"

"I don't know, maybe an hour and a half ago. I found her; she had already passed."

There was the sound of an approaching vehicle.

"That's Clyde. He was able to leave work early today."

"Would you like me to stay for awhile?"

Eleanor was dreading the possibility that Mary might soon become hysterical. It would be better if she left now and allowed the husband to console his wife.

"No, I'm okay. It just doesn't seem fair; she had *nightmares* about spiders. She was terrified by them and one of them killed her. I'll get in touch with Momma and let her know. She can be here in a few hours. Thank you, Eleanor. You've always been such a good friend to Grandma."

Eleanor squeezed Mary's hand and rose. After clearing her throat she removed the house keys from her pocket and gave them to the young woman.

"I locked the house when I left. I'm so sorry."

She turned and left, encountering Clyde as he approached the front steps. She looked at him briefly, raised her right hand and shook her head, unable to speak. She continued to her car and drove home. She considered returning to Mary's house and giving her that beautiful Indian thing, but chose to keep it. Besides, she knew exactly what to do with it.

Eleanor drove to the local grocery store and purchased those few items she needed for the rest of the week. Once she reached home and put away her meager supply of groceries, she had time to reflect on the loss of Thelma. They had not been the best of friends, but Thelma did offer a certain amount of companionship and that helped ward off some of the loneliness that Eleanor often felt. She missed her daughter and this was a good time to drive to Florida and visit. She would write her and let her know that she planned to drive down there in two weeks. Actually, she now had a gift to deliver!

She remembered that the wooden case and its special contents were still in her car. On her way to the car she noticed a large bird circling above; Eleanor watched it briefly and then remembered why she was outside. She retrieved the case, placed it on the dining room table and opened it. She was struck by the simple elegance of what she saw; it seemed to become even more beautiful each time she saw it. She closed the case and placed it on the top of her china cabinet where it was to remain until she took it to Florida.

Her excitement about the trip continued to grow as her departure date approached. The day prior, she removed the wooden case from its resting place atop the china cabinet. Placing it on the nearby table, she was surprised to see that no dust had accumulated on the top of the case. That seemed odd since dusting was a necessary and constant battle. "Perhaps," she thought, "dust doesn't settle that close to the ceiling." The more she thought about it, though, the more she knew that a lot of dust collected on top of that cabinet; she just hated to get up on that flimsy stepstool to remove it. She dismissed it from her thoughts as she packed her things for the long drive. She planned on a week to make the trip down. Upon her departure she failed to notice that she was being escorted by a rather large bird.

She arrived at her daughter's home on the seventh day after a surprisingly uneventful trip. Well, she did experience one flat tire which was changed by a nice man who stopped to assist. There was also a problem with her room on the second night of her journey; otherwise, it really was uneventful. She tried to drive for six hours each day and some days she covered over 200 miles and other days she managed a mere 100 miles.

She was exhausted when she pulled into her daughter's driveway just before noon. She honked the horn, shut off the engine and breathed a huge sigh of relief. She was already dreading the return trip.

She smiled as she saw her daughter, Frances, peek through the living room window. Seconds later she came through the front door, drying her hands on a dish towel. It seemed that she always arrived at someone's house when they were washing the dishes.

"I wasn't expecting you until tonight or tomorrow! How was the drive?"

Eleanor eased out of the car very much aware of her new aches and pains. She hugged her daughter and stifled a tear without saying a word. Frances broke the hug, eager to get her mother into the house.

"Are you hungry? I have plenty of food ready. I'll come back out and get your things, but I'm sure you're ready to stay out of the car for awhile."

"I'm a little tired and you're right about the car. Let's just go inside and visit for a little bit. I think I could eat a sandwich or something like that...nothing heavy, though. I could really go for some ice tea if you have some made."

The two women slowly walked to the house, both thinking how much the other had aged in the last seven years. Frances was saddened that it took the death of her mother's friend to convince her to come visit her only daughter and her two grandchildren. She and John had offered to send her train fare so that she could visit; they were not able to go visit her since John could not leave his hardware store. Frances knew how hard it must have been for her mother to make such a trip alone, but she *did* have the time.

Eleanor's thoughts concerned the guilt she felt for missing out on the growing years of the grandchildren. The trip had been difficult, but certainly not as bad as she had thought. Her fear had been simply that of traveling *alone* and all of the bad things that could happen along the way. Carrying a considerable amount of money had been frightening along with all of the 'what ifs' of driving a car for more than a thousand miles. Yet here she was and in pretty good shape. Oh, there was the return trip, but then she would worry about that later.

Frances opened the screen door for her mother and stepped back for her to enter. Eleanor walked inside and looked around at the unfamiliar room. She placed her purse on a nearby chair before turning to face her daughter. She cleared her throat before speaking.

"It's so good to see you; I've missed you so much!" Eleanor said as she stepped forward and hugged her daughter a second time.

"I know, Mom, I've missed you, too. The kids will be home from school soon and they are so excited. C'mon in the kitchen and I'll get you some tea."

She broke the embrace and walked to the kitchen.

Eleanor followed, searching the walls for a location for the special gift she had brought. It would not be her choice, but it would be nice if she could point out a special place where it could be prominently displayed. Of course visitors would surely comment on it and Frances would tell them that her mother had given it to her after driving all the way down here to see them.

Frances selected a large glass from a cabinet and filled it with iced tea. She placed it on the table and indicated that her mother was to sit.

"I have some meatloaf that I can warm up for you along with some mashed potatoes and gravy. That would be quick and I don't have much in the way of fixin's for a sandwich."

"The meatloaf sounds good, but don't bother with warming it up. Of course if you heat up the gravy I can pour it over the potatoes. That would be fine."

She was now seated and busily adding sugar to her tea.

"I'm tired of eating food along my route. It's not the same as eating at home."

Frances poured the gravy into a small pot and let it heat up while she sliced the meatloaf and placed a rather large helping of potatoes on a plate. She quickly transferred the meatloaf to the plate and grabbed a knife and fork which she placed on the table before her mother. She checked the gravy and stirred it.

"Where's your bathroom? I need to freshen up a little."

Eleanor struggled to her feet; her entire body had stiffened up.

"Right through there, second door on the right."

Frances mistook her mother's obvious distress for the aging process rather than the results of driving for seven days.

Several minutes later they were catching up on all that had happened in the last seven years while Eleanor polished off her lunch. After an hour or so, they remembered Eleanor's things and set out to bring them in. It took them three trips and Eleanor mentioned that she had left one item in the trunk of the car. Frances volunteered to retrieve it and Eleanor was more than happy to let her.

"It's a wooden case, you can't miss it. Be very careful with it."

She could hardly wait to see her daughter's reaction.

Frances returned a minute later and handed the case to her mother without saying a word. Eleanor carried the case over to the kitchen table followed by her very curious daughter.

"It's for you; I hope you like it," Eleanor said stepping back slightly.

Frances flipped the latch and opened the case. Eleanor heard her daughter draw in a deep breath as she saw the dreamcatcher. Even Eleanor was once again captivated by the beauty of this unusual object before them. Frances reached out to touch it, but suddenly drew back her hand.

"Can I pick it up?"

She could not take her eyes off this fascinating thing.

"Of course you can. It's yours."

Eleanor was beaming. This had been a good decision.

Frances carefully lifted the dreamcatcher from its resting place. She shook her head gently from side to side as she examined it from top to bottom. Eleanor watched in eager anticipation, hoping that her daughter would like this unusual gift. She was more excited than Frances. She sat down.

"Where in the world did you get this? I've never seen anything like it."

"I found it in Nebraska a few weeks ago. It is supposedly genuine Sioux Indian. It holds some kind of a special meaning for them, but I can't remember what it is."

Try as she might, Eleanor just could not remember what that Bailey man at that trading post had told her; she should have listened more carefully instead of admiring the thing.

"John will probably come home about 5:30; he normally stays open until six, but wanted to close early to spend more time with you. He has adjusted to the hardware business, but I think he still misses the alligator farm. The danger and excitement of wrestling alligators for the tourists just made him seem so much more alive. Of course, the money from the tourists was awfully good, too."

Frances lowered her eyes as if embarrassed or possibly something else.

"Well, you did the right thing." It was time to change the subject.

"And when are my grandkids supposed to be home?"

"Oh, they should be here in the next twenty minutes or so."

"Let's go sit on the porch so we can see them get off the bus," Eleanor said as she pushed back her chair.

She rose unsteadily as her muscles revolted once again.

"I'll bring the tea and some sugar; in fact, I think I'll have some, too. Go ahead, I'll be right out."

Eleanor walked out to the porch and felt the slight rise in temperature. She was glad that the house faced east; the sun would not be a problem. She sat in the rocking chair closest to the steps. Getting out of the chair might be difficult if her muscles stiffened up again.

Frances joined her shortly thereafter and placed a tray with the pitcher of tea, two glasses, spoons and sugar on the small table next to Eleanor. She then moved a second rocking chair next to the table. She refilled her mother's glass and placed it next to her. Finally, she poured a glass for herself and sat.

The two women chatted about the last few years and the changes they had undergone. It was only a few minutes before they heard the sound of the approaching school bus. Eleanor struggled to her feet and stood in eager anticipation.

"Do you think they'll remember me? I mean Molly...Jeff was much too young. It's hard for me to believe that it's been seven years."

She realized that her heart was pounding.

"I know that Molly remembers you, but you're right about Jeff."

And then came the sound of squealing brakes as the bus rolled into view. It came to a stop and the door opened almost immediately. Jeff was out the door and running toward the front porch as soon as the door opened; Molly was right behind him, but walking. Both children were smiling and staring at Eleanor.

"Hi, Grandma!"

Jeff was certainly not shy. He rushed into the arms of his grandmother and allowed her to do those grandmotherly things that he would find embarrassing in a few short years.

Eleanor pushed him back slightly.

"Now let me get a good look at my handsome little man."

Molly arrived just in time to steal the spotlight from Jeff.

"Grandma, you're not as tall as you used to be!"

The two adults laughed as Eleanor hugged her granddaughter.

"That's because you've grown so much and you're *so pretty*!"

She realized that Molly was destined to be a very attractive woman; her blue eyes and facial features were simply perfect. Yes, she would be a beauty.

"Grandma, did you bring us presents?" Jeff was *definitely* not shy.

"Jeff, mind your manners!" Frances was horrified.

"It's okay. I don't know, Jeff. I *might* have something for you and come to think of it, I *might* have something for Molly, too. Go in the living room and bring me the box tied with a red ribbon."

Both children raced into the house and Jeff returned carrying the box with the ribbon and Molly had the wooden case.

Molly spoke immediately as she looked at the wooden box, "Is this for me, Grandma?"

"No, Molly, that's for your mother. You and Jeff have something in the other box."

She took the wooden case and placed it on her lap. She suddenly realized that the gift for Molly had been a poor choice.

Jeff tore the ribbon from the package and opened the box. He removed a small box that had his name printed on it; he passed the larger box to Molly who looked inside. Eleanor watched Molly's expression go from excitement to disappointment as she removed the doll. Meanwhile, Jeff had opened the small box and discovered a yo-yo and a wooden top.

"Look! A yo-yo and something else!"

He stared at the top and the string that had been wrapped around it. He placed it on the table and concentrated on the yo-yo.

"Thank you, Grandma," Molly smiled as she said it. "I can put it with my others."

"Oh, honey, I still think of you as just a little girl. I think you and I will need to go look for something else. Maybe we could do that tomorrow."

"Grandma, what's in the wooden box?" Molly still had hopes.

"It's something special for your mother. Let's take a look."

She opened the case and watched Frances move so that she could see Molly's face.

"It's so pretty! What is it?"

Molly was completely captivated by the dreamcatcher.

"It's just so pretty!"

She looked at Eleanor, full of hope.

Frances looked at Eleanor and nodded slightly.

"Well, Molly, if you really like it and if your mother says it's all right with her, then I guess you should have it."

Eleanor was rewarded with a huge smile and a hug.

Molly looked up at her mother and was overjoyed when she saw the big smile and the nod of her head. She hugged her mother fiercely and took the wooden case with its special contents into the house.

"I'm sorry, the doll just seemed like the right thing; I just forgot that she was growing up. I'll find you another gift."

"No gift is necessary; the look on Molly's face was the best gift I could ever have. I think Jeff will need some help with the top, though. The yo-yo is easy...I was pretty good at it years ago."

Hearing his name, Jeff looked up. The yo-yo was now dangling by the string and the boy was wondering what he was supposed to do with it. He was sitting on the porch steps and suddenly pointed into the sky.

"Momma, Grandma, look at the big bird!"

The two women looked, but only Eleanor saw the eagle, a very large eagle as it slowly circled nearby.

"I've seen several of those things on the trip down here. Before that, I think I've only seen two of them in my entire life. One was near my friend's house...you know, the one that died a few weeks ago."

"I guess I need to have my eyes checked; I don't see it."

Frances was not really interested in seeing a big bird, anyway.

At that moment, Molly shoved the screen door open and exclaimed, "I know where I want to hang it...wow, look at that eagle! I want to hang it over my bed."

"Why would you want to hang an eagle over your bed?" Frances teased her daughter.

"Oh, Mom, I was talking about the circle thing with the feathers. And you knew what I meant! Can you get Daddy to hang it up for me?"

"Maybe I can get him to do it, but I could do it right now if someone would ask me."

"Mom, please?"

Frances left her chair and several minutes later, with help from Molly, placed the dreamcatcher in the perfect position over her daughter's bed.

She returned to the front porch while Molly sprawled on the bed staring at her new addition.

After a few minutes, Molly saw a spider move across the wall from the window area toward the dreamcatcher. Approaching the dreamcatcher, the spider stopped abruptly. It remained motionless for several seconds before quickly fleeing in the direction it had come. Molly wondered why it had run away like it was frightened. She did not like spiders anyway and continued her admiration of *her* dreamcatcher.

Frances shortened the string on Jeff's yo-yo and showed him how to use it. The two women continued their visit amid a series of calls by Jeff to watch him. Then Frances announced that it was time to start supper. They adjourned to the kitchen and Eleanor soon excused herself to take a quick nap.

Molly walked in and sat at the table.

"Where's Grandma?"

"She's taking a nap; it was a long trip and she's really tired so you kids need to be real quiet."

"Mom, can I let Rascal come in?"

She loved that dog and had forgotten to play with him when she arrived home from school. She felt guilty.

"Okay, but just for a few minutes and then he goes back outside."

Molly hurried to the back door and was met there by a happy and excited young dog that waited for her to open the screen door.

"C'mon, Rascal! Come look at my present."

Frances smiled at her daughter and was glad that she had allowed her daughter to have the Indian thing. She watched the twosome disappear.

Molly opened her bedroom door and stepped aside knowing that Rascal would immediately rush past her and jump onto her bed. Instead, the young dog took a few steps into the room and stopped. He looked around very slowly and Molly noticed that the hair on his back was standing up. He growled very softly and then gazed at the dreamcatcher. His tail stopped wagging and he lowered it. He then backed out of the room and headed for the back door. Confused, Molly followed him and watched him as he looked back repeatedly. When he reached the door, he tried to push the screen door open with his nose while whining softly. Molly pushed the door open and Rascal ran to the middle of the backyard before turning and looking at Molly.

"Come here, Rascal."

She was surprised that he remained where he was.

"Come here boy!"

There was still no movement.

Molly walked out to the dog and noticed that he was shaking. She petted him and then walked back toward the house. He followed, but stopped short of the small porch.

"Okay, you can come in later," she said as she walked back into the kitchen.

"What's wrong with Rascal...you usually have to push him outside."

"I don't know. He didn't want to stay in my room. Remember when that panther came around? Well, he's acting just like he did then. Maybe the panther came back."

"I don't think so...he wouldn't have gone back outside. He sure didn't want to stay in the house. Maybe he knows that Grandma is here, but hasn't seen her. Dogs sometimes act funny when they smell something unfamiliar."

"I think he was afraid of the thing with feathers. He was looking at it and growling."

"There's your answer. He sees the feathers and probably thinks it's some kind of bird and he knows that it should not be in your room. Don't worry, by tomorrow he'll be all right. Want to help me with supper?"

Molly shrugged. "Okay."

It was six o'clock when they heard the sound of John's pickup truck just before it pulled into the driveway. The two kids rushed to greet their dad while Frances and a much-refreshed Eleanor stood on the porch and watched. Eleanor wondered if this greeting was the norm or just something for her benefit; perhaps it was a subtle reminder of how families should be. She watched her two grandchildren clinging to their father and knew that it was genuine.

"Well, there's Grandma," he said as he spotted Eleanor.

The mood immediately became a little less festive. The trio dissolved as John climbed the steps. He gave Eleanor a brief hug before speaking.

"How was your trip?"

It was a sterile question and he really did not care what the answer was. He kissed Frances and detected a certain amount of aggravation. He had promised to be civil and he thought that he was doing well under the circumstances.

"It was a long trip, John. I've had a nap and feel pretty good now although I am a little sore from driving for a week."

She was hesitant to add any other information.

"Honey, why don't you get cleaned up, we're ready to start putting everything on the table."

Frances desperately hoped that they would both relax by mealtime.

"You probably noticed the smoke; we've got a couple more grass fires going now. Maybe this approaching rainstorm will knock 'em out," John commented as he went inside.

Frances walked out in the front yard and looked toward the southwest. The smoke was now apparent, but the darkened sky had her attention. Perhaps they would finally get rain this time. She headed for the porch.

"Okay, time for supper. We've got a storm headed this way."

Five minutes later all five were seated at the table. They all turned toward John and then bowed their heads.

"Lord, thank You for this day and for this food. Help us mind our thoughts and our words. In Jesus' name, amen."

Frances kicked his right leg and gave him a brief look of disapproval before lifting a bowl of green beans and passing it to her husband. John had winced, but he had a slight smile on his face. Eleanor heard his subtle message and vowed to avoid those areas which were certain to provoke arguments. The kids were oblivious to the drama.

"Grandma brought us presents," Jeff said as his dad spooned some green beans onto his plate. "I got a yo-yo and a top. I can do the yo-yo, but I can't make the top spin."

John passed the beans over to Eleanor.

"I'll show you how to spin the top after supper."

"Grandma got me a thing for my wall; it's got feathers and beads and stuff and it's really pretty. Oh, and she got me a doll, too. And, Daddy, we saw an eagle today!"

"Are you sure it was an eagle...they're pretty rare around here. Maybe it was a hawk."

"Daddy, it was too big to be a hawk. Grandma and Jeff saw it, too."

"It was probably a bald eagle."

"No Daddy; its head was not white."

The meal continued with small talk and courteous questions about Eleanor's trip. Only those safe topics were chosen and after a few minutes things settled into dialogue that allowed Frances to breathe a sigh of relief.

After everyone finished, John took the kids out on the front porch and began showing Jeff how to wind the string around the top. Eleanor and Frances remained inside cleaning the kitchen. They all heard the first rumblings of thunder and quickly noticed the wind increasing. John soon had the top spinning while Molly and Jeff watched in amazement. Everyone saw the first flash of lightning which was followed several seconds later by some impressive thunder. A nervous Jeff received some additional help with the top and then tried once again to make it spin. He succeeded in making the top land on its side rather than the metal point and watched as it rolled off the porch. He raced after it, hoping to spot it in the dim light.

Kaboom! The flash of lightning was just a split second ahead of the crash of thunder. A wide-eyed Jeff returned to the porch visibly frightened. Molly screamed and ran inside. John laughed.

"Did that scare you, Jeff?"

"Uh, a little. Maybe we should go inside."

They joined the rest of the family just as another flash occurred accompanied by yet another extremely loud roll of thunder. Frances had already lit one of several lamps. There was another flash and the lights flickered twice before going out.

"Time to light the rest of the lamps," Frances said very calmly.

Both kids thought that the lamps were special while the three adults thought of past days where they were used constantly. The adults carried out a civil conversation although interrupted regularly by the two youngsters who were becoming bored. After roughly two hours, the entire household called it quits and went to bed. They left one dimmed lamp burning.

John awoke just after 4:00 A.M. and smelled smoke. It was the smell of burning vegetation. He quietly left the bed, took the dimmed lamp and walked to the back door. He could see the glow of the fire and even occasional flames; the fire was moving toward them!

"Everybody up! Wake up; we've got to get out of here!"

The smell of smoke coupled with the urgency in John's voice caused everyone to respond without questioning. He lit several of the lamps and placed them where they would do the most good. Then he responded to some heavy scratching at the back door and let Rascal into the house. The dog headed straight for Molly's room, yelped and raced to the front door. Cowering there, he whined pathetically.

Frances dressed quickly and grabbed some bare essentials while Eleanor concentrated on just a few things. The children took a few small items and were soon waiting next to the frantic dog.

"Let's go! We have to leave now! We're going in the truck. You kids hop in the back. Now go!"

John opened the front door and followed the kids; the two women were right behind him. Ash was raining down and the smoke was rapidly intensifying. They could now hear the approaching fire.

After putting Rascal in the back with the two kids, John entered the cab and started the engine while Frances and then Eleanor climbed in from the passenger's side.

"Hang on, kids," John yelled as he backed into the side yard. "We'll be forced to go south...it looks like the fire's jumped the road north of us."

He turned right from the driveway and sped down the road. Molly and Jeff stood and held on to the wooden cab protector that their father had constructed; it was their preferred way to ride since they could see where they were going.

They could all see the fire on their right and it was close! Rascal was lying next to Molly instead of riding with his head out in the wind stream. John noticed that the fire was more distant ahead and after the left curve in the road he should be able to easily outrun the fire. Right now, though, it was still a race for their lives.

The pickup truck raced through the smoky darkness. The two kids did not understand the seriousness of the fire and certainly had given no thought to the possibility that their house might not be there when they returned. The adults knew all too well that everything would probably be gone.

Up ahead they could see that the fire was extremely close to the road. John accelerated and they flew past the threat but were exposed to both the heat and the acrid smoke. And then they were at the curve.

John took his foot off the gas but did not brake. As he steered into the curve, he felt the rear wheels lose traction. He tried to correct, but only succeeded in moving onto the shoulder. He then eased the steering wheel back to the left and the truck slammed into first one and then a second concrete post which were placed there to prevent vehicles from crashing into the water next to the road. The road was banked slightly as it followed the up-sloped soil which was meant to serve as a flood barrier.

A combination of the upslope, the skid and the sudden lateral stoppage launched Molly from the truck; she had taken that exact second to attempt to reposition her hands for a better grip. She screamed as she flew through the air. There was a muffled 'thud' and an abrupt end to the scream. She had observed a mean looking eagle as she flew through the blackness.

Jeff had squatted down and had a better grip at the moment of impact, but still slammed into Rascal who voiced his pain. Eleanor heard Molly scream; obviously the girl was frightened. John and Frances had been concentrating on the path of the truck and had not heard the scream. Jeff began pounding on the back window.

"Stop! Stop! Molly fell out! Stop!" He was panic-stricken.

Meanwhile, John had gained control of the truck and was driving slower. He was now aware that the fire was no longer an immediate threat. And then the rain began! He turned on the wipers, braked hard and hopped out of the truck.

"C'mon, both of you get into the cab with us!"

"Daddy, Molly fell out when we had the wreck! Why didn't you stop?"

John grabbed his son and pulled him into the cab.

"Molly fell out when we hit the post!"

He slammed the transmission into first gear, cut the steering wheel hard to the left and pulled forward to the shoulder. He stopped and shifted into reverse and turned the steering wheel in the opposite direction. Seconds later they were headed the opposite direction. The windshield wipers would not work during acceleration due to the lowered vacuum levels so he eased off the gas pedal momentarily and the wipers resumed their task. And then he was accelerating again. This time he eased off the gas and strained to see through the heavy rain.

"Be careful, she might be standing in the road." Frances' voice showed extreme concern but not fear.

John stopped just prior to the dirt and gravel that marked the location where he re-gained control of the truck. He left the truck, oblivious to the rain.

"Molly, where are you?" He trotted along the road trying to stay clear of the light from the headlights while listening for a reply. "Molly! Molly, can you hear me?"

He reached the two concrete posts where the impact had occurred. He mentally calculated where he thought she might have landed. It was obvious that she had gone over the slight embankment. He moved as far as he could, trying to peer through the darkness and the rain. They had no flashlight and there was no way to maneuver the truck to light up the area where she must have landed.

"Molly, where are you? Can you hear me?"

And then he heard the sound of approaching footsteps.

"Molly, it's Mommie. Can you hear me?" She was sobbing.

They both heard the sound of the truck as it slowly approached; Eleanor was trying to help. She stopped the truck so that the headlights illuminated most of the shoulder.

"I'm going in the water."

John eased down the embankment to the waterline and commenced a frantic search for his daughter. He knew that there was a gentle slope, but was surprised by the amount of vegetation. He moved as quickly as possible, calling Molly's name as he stumbled through the shallow water.

"John, there might be gators...oh my God! Molly! Molly, can you hear me?"

Her voice now carried the terror that she suddenly felt.

The impact of his wife's words hit him hard; he had not even thought of alligators. This new fear only motivated him to search faster. He traveled perhaps 50 feet before moving into deeper water and reversing direction. The headlights from the truck gave him enough illumination to navigate and he was beginning to realize that Molly's chances were not good if she had landed in the water. She could swim, though, and surely she could see the shore backlit by the glow from the fire. He would continue past his approximate entry point for about the same distance and then move back up to the waterline. After that he would search the slope. She might be unconscious on dry land...he had possibly walked right past her. He was vaguely aware of the two women as they called to her. His brain was becoming numb. He moved on through the water and slammed into something solid. Then he realized exactly where he was...the big sign for the alligator farm. John moved around the pole and continued.

He thought he felt something brush his right shoulder, but dismissed it. He proceeded for what he estimated to be about 50 feet and then moved to the edge of the water. His calls to his daughter had slowed.

"Mom, go back to the house and get a flashlight. Take Jeff with you...he knows where we keep them. Hurry!"

Frances had no other ideas and this seemed like the only solution. Eleanor climbed back into the truck with Jeff close behind.

"Grandma, why not use Rascal to look for Molly?"

"Frances, see if your dog can find her; we don't need him with us!"

Frances called Rascal to her and waited for the truck to leave. Then she told him to go find Molly. The dog simply whined and stayed at her side.

Eleanor sped down the unfamiliar road. She tried not to think of what had happened to Molly; she knew that silence was not good. She prayed that Molly had just been knocked unconscious.

"Help me find the house, Jeff. I can't remember how far it is."

"Don't worry, Grandma...it's not far."

She realized that Jeff did not understand the seriousness of the situation. Then she realized that the rain had stopped. Up ahead she could see the glow of the fire and suddenly she knew what was burning.

"Oh, no. Please don't let it be."

She turned onto the driveway and stopped. They both got out and walked cautiously toward the remains of the house. They stood there, fascinated by the speed at which the house had been transformed into ash and embers. They could make out the icebox, stove and a few other items but it was clear that nothing was salvageable.

They stood there mesmerized by the sight before them. Suddenly, there was movement and a large bird suddenly arose from the hot coals. With ember-reddened eyes, it stared at the two witnesses before spreading its wings and launching itself into the darkened sky, headed northwest.

"Grandma! Did you see it? Did you see the big bird?"

Eleanor simply nodded her head. What she had just seen was impossible and yet Jeff had also seen it.

"Yes, honey...I saw it too. Now let's go back."

Neither saw the sentinel eagle cock its head to one side momentarily before returning to its normal predatory state.

Eleanor drove slowly back down the road, doubting her sanity but comforted by the knowledge that Jeff had also witnessed whatever that thing was. She tried not to think about it; her focus should remain on Molly.

Another vehicle arrived just seconds before Eleanor and Jeff. The driver jumped from his car waving a flashlight and Eleanor breathed a sigh of relief. She could see Frances rushing toward the other vehicle and stopped the truck so that the headlights illuminated the road shoulder where she thought the search had commenced.

John climbed up from the swamp having completed his search as best he could without lights. He quickly walked up to the Good Samaritan where Frances was frantically trying to gain his assistance. They were illuminated by the light from both vehicles. Frances was hysterically explaining how Molly had been thrown out of the truck and they could not locate her in the darkness.

"Oh my God, John you're hurt! What happened?" asked Frances, jolted by the sight of her husband.

"Aw, I walked smack dab into one of the poles for the alligator farm sign. I'm not hurt, though."

He was anxious to borrow the flashlight and resume the search.

"You're bleeding pretty bad, mister."

John looked at his left arm and saw no blood.

"No, your right shoulder."

John looked at his shoulder and saw the blood which had now spread all the way to his waist. His fear intensified.

"Oh, no!"

He remembered brushing something lightly with his right shoulder. A sense of panic enveloped him.

John grabbed the flashlight and rushed to the concrete posts, shining the flashlight out over the water. He finally lit up the sign and stared in numbing disbelief; Molly, his pride and joy, was hanging by her neck from the open mouth of the huge gator that reached out from the sign. He was vaguely aware of the scream from Frances before he collapsed.

The stranger rushed over, grabbed the flashlight and managed to place the beam on the young girl; there was no movement. There was no sound except for the loud sobbing from Frances and Eleanor's tearful attempts to comfort her. Clearly the girl was dead; he could see the blood dripping from her shoes. The fact that she had landed with her neck on the sharp metal teeth was amazing...a few inches in any direction could have spared her life. It was almost as if she had been delivered to that one small area during those brief moments after being thrown from the pickup truck.

The stranger then noticed that John was beginning to move and walked over to assist him. He knelt, gently placing a hand on John's shoulder and allowing him to slowly return to full consciousness.

Rascal chose that instant to express his own grief as he sensed that something terribly wrong had happened. He sat, pointed his head skyward and commenced a long mournful howl that carried across the quiet, smokey Florida landscape. Numerous animals ceased their movements as they evaluated the sound. The stranger shivered and wiped the tears from his own eyes.

As the wail from the dog ceased, Frances struggled to her feet and staggered over to her husband. Respectfully, the stranger stepped aside.

"You bastard; this is all your fault! You killed Molly...you killed my daughter! You...killed...my...daughter!"

She began pummeling her husband while sobbing hysterically. John felt the most pain he had ever experienced and it was not from the physical assault by his spouse.

"You thought it was so funny, holding a three year old child over that damn alligator pen while the alligators snapped at her! It's your fault that she's dead now. You gave her nightmares that have never gone away. God has punished you for what you did to her and the results of your sin have been bestowed on the rest of us. I hate you!"

Frances ceased her ineffective physical attack and collapsed into her husband's arms and cried as John just held her, rocking back and forth.

Eleanor walked over to Jeff and took his hand. Jeff did not understand that he had lost his sister, but was acutely aware that his mother was awfully mad at his dad. Rascal, Molly's dog, came over to Jeff and licked his hand as he trembled. Jeff was pleased that Rascal actually sought him out. Boy, Molly was really going to be mad at him now. And then he remembered that their house was gone.

"Grandma, where are we going to live now?"

"I don't know, Jeff."

She wondered when Jeff would grasp the reality of his sister's death.

The stranger walked over to Eleanor.

"Ma'am, I'm gonna get the sheriff out here. We need to get the little girl down from there. Keep the flashlight. I'm so sorry for all of you."

He walked to his car and drove away.

John thought back to that day, years ago, when he had held Molly over the alligators. He knew the gators well and she was not in any real danger. They were well-fed. The tourists were shocked and then angered when Molly began screaming. He had immediately returned her to safety and into the arms of her hysterical mother. It was a stupid thing to do, but he had felt that Molly would know that he would never allow anything to harm her. Molly had watched her father feed the alligators several times and now she was being handled just like the fish or chickens that were usually offered to the big reptiles. It was suddenly clear to him how Molly had felt...and now she was gone. His tears began anew as his body shook in his unbearable grief. He had resented Frances' ultimatum 'to leave the alligator farm or else.' Perhaps if he had remained at the farm...but then, Frances was right.

Two weeks later, Eleanor sadly headed north. The funeral had been very nice with hundreds of people in attendance. There was even newspaper coverage and the story went out over the wire services. In a bizarre twist of fate, Rascal died on the day the funeral was held, adding to the sorrow. A new house was already being constructed on the same spot as the old. They had a lot of friends and a lot of help, but their lives could never be rebuilt.

Frances cried every morning and every night; in her opinion, her relationship with her husband had been damaged beyond repair. Surprisingly, Eleanor and John were able to overcome the old hostility between them which had been brought about by Eleanor's support of her daughter's ultimatum. Jeff gradually realized over the next few months that Molly was never coming back. And John would carry his guilt feelings for the rest of his life.

They would never associate the dreamcatcher with Molly's death. It was considered just a freak accident by everyone except Frances.

CHAPTER SEVEN

The Reporter

Thomas Stevens, age 25, had been a reporter for the Chicago *Daily Illustrated Times* for almost a year. As a 'cub' reporter, he was only allowed to cover local stories of general interest and to perform research and background acquisition for the more notable and experienced reporters. He had demonstrated a flair for writing coupled with exceptional spelling and grammatical skills. Thomas actually loved the investigative side of news leads, but sometimes had a tendency to continue digging for information longer than necessary. This resulted in the newspaper being 'scooped' by competitors on several occasions; that fact was not appreciated by the publisher and Thomas' editor had threatened him with dismissal on two occasions. In his defense, Thomas had pointed out that he "had *never* provided anything but accurate information and wasn't that extremely important?" Regardless, he always managed to discover more information which should have appeared in the original or follow-up story.

Thomas religiously checked the wire service teletype for stories and read through the competition's papers for items which were, in his opinion, incomplete or erroneous. He would point out inconsistencies or errors to the editor hoping that he might be allowed to do further research and write his own article. The typical reply was "Not worth the effort" or a simple, emphatic "No!" The editor had recognized the potential of this young reporter, but wanted to keep him 'hungry.' It was almost time to give him some leeway. That would certainly not go over well with some of the other reporters who astutely recognized his potential and knew that if he moved up then someone would most certainly lose his job or place in the reporting 'food chain.'

During one of his checks of the wire service information, he noticed a death caused by the derailment of a train caboose in Iowa. The story contained too many unknowns regarding a mysterious derailment plus an acute shortage of information on the victim who was from Chicago. Perhaps it was just a rush job to get the information out, but maybe it was yet another example of the lack of in-depth reporting that he found so fascinating and yet so frustrating.

Once again, Thomas paraded into the editor's office with a request to see what he could uncover. He was informed that the story would be carried just as it came from the wire service; if he wanted to research it further, it was to be done on his own time. This was certainly not his preference, but it would be a chance for him to show the editor what he could do by just following his instincts and using his abilities.

"By the way, you look terrible; have a rough night?"

The editor smiled as he awaited a brief tale of the young bachelor's steamy evening.

"Yes, sir. I had a strange dream about an old Indian with an injured ear. He was talking to me, but I can't remember what he said. I've had the same dream several times."

Thomas just wanted to leave the office; he had work to do.

The disappointed editor dismissed the young man with a wave of his hand. He had really hoped for some great spicy details of a wild evening. Apparently this younger generation just did not take advantage of their youth and resilience.

Thomas utilized the sparse information from the article to eventually track down the victim's sister. The late Mr. Charles Alexander appeared to be the victim of poor or incomplete record keeping on the part of the city of Chicago. While that was not an unusual occurrence, it did hamper his efforts to complete his research. It appeared that he might have picked the wrong subject and the wrong time to impress his editor.

His first surprise was to learn that Mr. Alexander apparently had not maintained close contact with his family even though his mother and siblings resided in or near Chicago. He had never married, had owned no property and apparently had not worked anywhere. He had owned a car (which now had serious damage from the train accident), but had never lived at his listed address. Thomas was puzzled; it was as if Mr. Alexander had been hiding. If that were the case, from who or what and why? The reporter, was suddenly energized; he was on to something.

Thomas discovered that the local law enforcement agency that had performed the preliminary investigation had determined that Mr. Alexander's car had been registered in Chicago. They had also found no personal identification in the car or on his body. His sister, Charlotte, came forth to identify him when the story appeared in the paper and after he failed to appear for one of their rare visits. She identified the body and that was about all of the information which she could provide. The lack of information from a family member bothered Thomas and he wondered why no one else seemed concerned about this blatant absence of essential information.

On the morning of the Alexander funeral, Thomas was hailed by a colleague concerning an interesting item from the AP wire service. The night clerk from the place where Mr. Alexander died had been electrocuted in his own home; that was quite a coincidence. Thomas just shrugged it off; he had another appointment...an important one.

Thomas attended the small funeral and was able to pick out the sister of the deceased from the small assemblage of close family members who were seated; he also noticed the presence of a few individuals who he knew were the subject of scrutiny by the Chicago police. He wondered why they would be in attendance at the funeral of what appeared to be an insignificant individual...and then he remembered his gut feeling that the man was hiding. He knew that Mr. Alexander had something to do with them and he would find out what it was. He would be especially discreet because he had heard several rumors of mysterious disappearances which were attributed to some of these same men.

At the conclusion of the ceremony, Thomas wandered over to the family to express his condolences. He purposely allowed everyone else to go ahead so that he could be the last to speak to the family. He expressed his sorrow to the mother and two brothers and waited until the daughter was alone.

"Pardon me, ma'am. I just wanted to pay my respects. I barely made it here in time."

He shook her offered hand while she looked at him, obviously puzzled.

"So you knew Charles. Did you work with him or something?"

She now seemed suspicious and stepped back slightly.

"Well, you know how private he was. I knew he had two brothers, but I just recently found out that he had a sister. He probably thought I was just too nosey. By the way, my name is Tom, Tom Stevens."

He thought she seemed to relax somewhat. He must be careful not to scare her away.

"I'm Charlotte. Were you a close friend?"

She was still being cautious. She was also looking at him very intensely.

"Not really close, but we did bump into each other on a regular basis. In fact, we were going to get together for a beer or two when he got back to Chicago from his last trip. He never dropped by so I assumed that he was delayed until I read in the paper about the... well, you know."

It appeared that she was beginning to relax again.

"Tom, can we go somewhere to talk? I mean somewhere, perhaps a restaurant. I could sure use some coffee or something stronger right about now."

She glanced around the cemetery as she spoke. She was definitely becoming comfortable now. The tough scrutiny seemed to be over. Now he could get some answers, but he had to go slowly.

"Sure, do you know where Al's Diner is? We could meet there if that's okay with you."

He was trying not to sound too eager.

"I've eaten there before. I'll be there in about ten minutes."

She offered her hand again and then walked toward the remainder of her family.

Thomas returned to his car and drove to the diner. He was able to park right in front and quickly entered the nearly empty diner. He ordered a cup of coffee and placed a dollar on the table. He was halfway through his cup of coffee when Charlotte arrived. She walked over to him and slipped into the booth across from him. Thomas waved the waitress over and pointed at his cup and then at Charlotte. The waitress acknowledged the silent order and turned away.

"You're not a cop and you're not one of those other guys. Who are you and what do you want?"

She was blunt. Her expression was that of anger.

Thomas took a deep breath. He would be completely honest and hope for the best.

"Please do not get upset with me. Let me finish before you make any decisions. I gave you my real name and I am a reporter for the *Daily Illustrated Times*. I read the story about your brother and there is a lot of information missing. I just wanted to talk to you and figured that the funeral would be a starting place and I apologize for being so crude. I noticed some, well, unsavory characters in attendance and some of the lack of information suddenly seems to make sense. I now feel that Charles might have been associated with them in some way. Your husband did not attend the funeral and that strikes me as strange. Please understand that I am seeking information, but I promise not to mention anything we might discuss without your permission. Please feel free to say whatever is on your mind."

He watched her squirm and held his breath awaiting her reaction. It was a gamble, but she obviously was very direct in this matter.

"Your early comments about Charles gave you away. Nobody knows anything about what he has done. We, my family, are convinced that it was not good. Charles was always a loner and really had no friends. There were some guys that he associated with, but they were misfits and were usually in some sort of trouble. Charles was smart enough to not get caught doing the same things those guys did. When he turned eighteen he more or less left the family and occasionally would visit briefly just to let us know he was alive. He never talked about what he was doing and we were afraid to ask. We had no way of contacting him which worried Mom to death. Around Christmas he would show up and usually give us money or gifts and then just disappear again. He has never met my husband or my two sons, but he has seen all of them. My husband chose not to attend the funeral and forbid me to bring the boys. He knows that something bad is associated with my brother's lifestyle. After seeing those guys and hearing them tell me what a good man he was, I know my husband was right. I honestly do not know what he has done."

"My husband says that the train wreck was not an accident; train wrecks don't happen like that. That leaves only one possibility: those men had him killed. Do you think I want my name in your story? I am asking you, no, *begging* you not to write anything about our family. By the way, his real name is...was *Lawrence*. He told us that he was known as *Charles* to his associates."

She was no longer angry, but she was now trembling.

"You know, there is one other thing. Lawrence was terrified by trains. He was almost run over by a freight train as a young child and he refused to even ride on one after that. He actually had nightmares about trains coming at him. Ironic isn't it? I mean, he was killed by the thing he feared the most."

Thomas sympathetically shook his head.

"I promise not to print anything about you or your family. I might look into the train wreck since there seems to be a lot of unanswered questions. I have no intention of ever contacting you again and this goes against everything I know about the newspaper business, but I will not take the chance of possibly causing harm to come your way. Good bye, Charlotte."

Thomas rose and left the diner without looking back. He would keep that promise. She seemed to be very nice and she had been open and honest as far as he could tell. Then it dawned on him: *Charles* no longer existed and the family should be safe. Even so, he would keep his word.

Once back at the newspaper, Thomas remembered the mention of the night clerk that had been electrocuted. He considered that to be unusual, but not anything that warranted spending any time on it. He read the article before the paper went to print and went on with his other assignments. He was unable to proceed with his inquiry the next day, but he was able to clear up almost all of his pending research. He would approach his editor tomorrow.

The following morning he reported to work amid a frenzied discussion among several co-workers. The wife of that same night clerk had died in a house fire. Thomas was now certain that it was no longer coincidence. That clerk must have witnessed something or discovered something and had been killed. Apparently his wife was also killed just in case the clerk had shared some information with her. Perhaps Charlotte's husband was correct; perhaps Charles had been murdered.

It took almost five minutes for Thomas to convince the editor to grant him a few minutes in private. The editor saw this as just a bizarre series of events that happened in close proximity and nothing more. Thomas hinted that he was in possession of knowledge that appeared to tie these three deaths to some people in Chicago, but could not elaborate without possibly endangering some innocent people. The editor demanded specifics, but Thomas refused. The editor thought it over for a minute and then told him go with his instincts. He also wanted a major update in three days. This was finally Thomas' big chance; he would either sink or swim. The editor smiled as Thomas left his office.

Thomas phoned the reporter in Cedar Rapids who had covered the three deaths. Armed with some names and directions, he quickly packed and headed for the site of the train wreck. He arrived several hours later.

Nothing useful remained at the crash location. Everything had been cleaned up except for the path of a bulldozer that had obliterated the route of the errant caboose and the site where the cabin had been. Thomas was fortunate to encounter one of the workers who had assisted in the cleanup. There was not much information of any real significance until the man mentioned one item which was quite puzzling: "The caboose wheels had made shallow impressions in the ground all the way to the building. When the caboose was moved away, the impressions were much deeper. One of the investigators said it was as if the caboose *had been lifted slightly or was much lighter before the crash than after.*" The worker had seen the tracks and had overheard the conversation. That was all he had to offer. Oh, and it had not rained since the crash so the ground was not any softer when the caboose was moved.

Thomas thanked him and scribbled down all he had just heard. He followed the path of the caboose to the point where it left the tracks. The path had been perfectly straight and there was no apparent disturbance of the railroad bed, the ties or the rails. Nothing had been replaced. He scoured the area looking for any indication of anything which might have caused the caboose to somehow roll up over the rails. Surely the heavy gravel would have been disturbed and the caboose could have overturned. Instead, it had somehow tracked straight to the doomed cabin, the wheels barely leaving an imprint. He was completely baffled. Every photograph of a derailment that he had ever seen showed the railroad cars had never traveled very far and had never gone perfectly straight.

He went to the office hoping for more information. Had it not been for a talkative desk clerk, Thomas would not have located the automobile belonging to the late Mr. Charles Alexander. The police had finished their investigation and the vehicle now rested in a nearby salvage yard; he arrived there 15 minutes later. Thomas had no idea what he was looking for as he inspected the crushed automobile, but managed to find a crudely drawn map wedged in a crevice in the back seat. He placed it in his shirt pocket with the intention to drive to the night clerk's house, or what was left of it.

He checked with the local fire department and was told that the probable cause of the fire was a problem with electrical wiring in the bathroom. It might possibly have been aggravated by the electrocution the day before. They might know more in a day or so. Perhaps he would like to talk to one of the firemen who had been summoned to the Simpson fire. Thomas declined.

Thomas had one more stop for the day. He wanted to meet with the daughter of the two victims, a Sarah Simpson. He was reluctant to do so since the funerals had not yet been held. Perhaps the Powell house could provide some clues. And maybe he could come up with a tactful way to meet with the daughter. He somehow felt the *need* to go to the house.

Small towns are always a reporter's delight. Although they typically produce only a small amount of news, tracking down leads is easy since everyone usually knows everyone else. Thomas drove to the blackened rubble which had been the Powell house and walked around trying to get a sense of the two victims or maybe find some item that would point him in the right direction. Finding nothing, he stood in the front yard pondering what he should do next. He was in no hurry to leave.

He heard the sound of an approaching vehicle and was surprised when it stopped right behind his old car. A woman carrying two red roses exited and walked past him to what had been the front porch. She knelt and gently placed the flowers on the ground. After a moment she arose and walked directly toward Thomas. She was fairly tall and quite attractive.

"Did you know my parents?"

Her eyes were filled with tears, but her voice was strong. She extended her right hand.

"I'm Sarah."

"Tom Stevens."

He shook her hand gently, noticing how frail it seemed. He was not certain how to deal with this woman who was in such obvious distress. He would go slowly.

"No, I didn't know your folks. I'm a reporter and I want to know more about what happened; something just doesn't seem quite right to me. I apologize...I was not trying to meet up with you and I am truly sorry about your loss. This may not be a good time for us to talk and maybe there never will be such a time, but I cannot believe that this was just an accident or a series of accidents."

She was *really* attractive.

"What are you saying? Are you implying that my parents were killed, murdered? That is absurd; they had no enemies."

Sarah's voice was losing its strength. Suddenly she was anxious to talk to this man even though he was a reporter.

"Okay," she sniffed, "what do you want to know?"

"Tell me everything you know about what happened in the days before the train wreck. I am only concerned with your conversations with your parents or anything that you may have observed them doing or talking about which was out of the ordinary. Did they have any visits from strangers? Were there any changes in their normal routines? This is what I need. I don't really know what I am actually looking for so just try to remember *anything* that was different."

"There is not much to tell...not really. Dad was always tight with money, especially after the stock market crash. He lost his job and finally was able to get this last one. He came home early the night of the train crash because they sent him home. He took Mom and me to a restaurant to eat breakfast which was very unusual. He was in good spirits considering what he had been through. Actually, there *was* something unusual: he brought a gift home to Mom. It was an Indian thing called a *dreamcatcher*. He got it from some guy who was staying in one of the cabins. Dad did not buy gifts except for birthdays and Christmas, so this was quite a surprise and then to buy breakfast for us...."

Her voice broke; she was becoming upset.

"So he bought a gift and treated the family to breakfast, but you said he was very tight with money. Was it payday?"

This did not seem worth pursuing.

"No," she sniffed, "it was not payday; he paid for breakfast with a five-dollar bill and he also bought a newspaper because his name was supposed to be in it."

"Why did he think his name would be in the paper?"

"Dad was excited about being interviewed by a reporter and never considered that it was too soon for the story to appear."

"Did he mention how many people spoke with him about the accident?"

"Not really. He spoke to a reporter and some of the people who were staying in the cabins. There were some railroad people and I'm almost certain that he said there was someone from the government who was especially interested in the caboose. Beyond that, I don't remember anything. Oh, and of course the owner of the motor court, Mr. Griffin, sent him home early."

"Did Mr. Griffin give him a reason for being sent home?"

This could be the key to the mysterious deaths. It was now time to start checking on the owner.

"Dad said that he was sent home because he had been through enough, but Dad sensed that it was for some other reason. Are you thinking that he, Mr. Griffin, was involved in this? My dad was just a night clerk."

"Sarah, I have just begun my own investigation. I am trying to answer a lot of questions and track down facts. You have just given me another part of what seems to be a huge puzzle. I promise that I will not release any information until I have spoken to you. There is definitely something strange going on here and I must be very careful. I need you to keep a record of anything unusual that you remember. There may be strangers who ask you questions about your parents. Letters to your folks...anything and I mean *anything* that is unusual. I know that this is a very difficult time for you, but I know that there is an explanation for all of this and it is *not* just a coincidence. Take this card; it has my address and there is a telephone number. Speak only to me. I need to leave now. I am truly sorry for the loss of your parents."

Thomas handed her the card and was surprised when she hugged him. "Okay. Thank you, Tom."

She felt better now, but there was some anger building; she needed to know who was responsible for the untimely death of her parents. This man was nice and she knew, somehow, that she could trust him. He seemed rather...*special.*

Thomas walked to his car and drove away without looking back at Sarah. He would check his notes for anything on Mr. Griffin; he was anxious to find out what role he had played in this. Thomas was certain that he was now headed in the right direction. Encountering Sarah had been pure luck and had saved a considerable amount of time. What a lucky break! It was almost as if they had been brought together for a reason. And what a nice lady.

Thomas abruptly changed his mind and decided to check with the Fire Department about interviewing one of the firemen who had responded to the Simpson fire. He could possibly obtain some information about Mr. Griffin under the guise of investigating the fire. He was certain to be known by virtually everyone in this small town. Twenty minutes later he on his way to Taylor's Filling Station to talk to a Samuel Jones, a volunteer fireman who had been there that night.

Thomas parked his car out of the way and walked past the gasoline pumps to the open door where cars were serviced and repaired. A young man, probably in his mid-twenties, leaned around the front of a black sedan and spotted Thomas. He grabbed a cloth rag and began wiping his hands as he walked toward Thomas.

"Can I help you?" He had a pleasant voice and a friendly manner.

"I'm looking for Sam Jones."

"You're looking at him. And you are...?"

"My name is Tom Stevens. I'm a reporter and would like to talk to you about the fire a few nights ago. I understand that you were there and I would like just a few minutes of your time."

"Sure, what would you like to know?"

"Was there anything unusual or suspicious about this particular fire?"

"Why, did someone mention something unusual that happened?"

Thomas was surprised by Sam's choice of words; also, something in his voice changed and he suddenly appeared to be nervous. He definitely knew something and Thomas hoped that he would be able to coax it from him.

"Well, let's just say that there has been some talk about something unusual concerning the fire," Thomas ventured.

He wanted to sound like he knew something.

"Are you talking about the bird we saw in the fire?" Sam sounded almost relieved.

Thomas tried to hide his bewilderment. He was not sure what to say next. He looked down at his shoes momentarily and then looked up at Sam. He inhaled deeply and exhaled loudly before speaking.

"Yeah, what can you tell me?"

Sam looked around and then eased closer to Thomas.

"I know it sounds crazy, but the roof had just collapsed," he whispered. "It surprised me since it happened so quickly. Anyway, lots of sparks and embers flew up and then I saw something move in the rubble. I thought it was someone who had been trapped in the house and I just froze. I mean, I just couldn't even move. I didn't know what to do. And then I saw this huge bird stand up. He looked right at me for a few seconds and then leaped into the air and flew away. I know for certain that one of the other guys saw it too, but neither one of us mentioned it to anyone, at least not that night. It's been driving me nuts. I'm glad someone else finally brought it up. With that much heat, nothing could have lived. I am not crazy...I *saw* it! I just thought it would be better to keep my mouth shut, for obvious reasons."

He waited for a response from Thomas.

The reporter just looked at Sam, uncertain what he should do next. It was apparent to Thomas that the man was telling the truth or at least what he *believed* was the truth. He had been hoping for information, but this was certainly unexpected.

"I think I would just continue to not mention this and let it just go away; it will, you know."

"But you don't understand; that bird could not have survived that inferno, *but it did*! The feathers would have burned, but they *didn't*. So what happened? What kind of creature was it? It was *not of this world*!"

Sam was now shaking and his voice had ceased to be a whisper.

"There's got to be a logical explanation, but I don't think we should do any more with it. Let me see if I can find something in our files at the newspaper."

Thomas was now reluctant to inquire about Mr. Griffin. He thanked Sam and left.

As puzzling as the bird story had been, Thomas felt that he had lost any chance of gleaning any useful information from Sam. Perhaps it would be possible at a later date. He thought about the map which he had found in the late Mr. Alexander's car; he removed it from his pocket.

He unfolded the map and studied it for several minutes. He realized that the map showed the route from Chicago to Omaha and then south on what appeared to be U.S. 75. The last town on the crude map was *Brownville* or perhaps *Brownsville*. It was north of the Kansas border. There was an unmarked road heading east, toward the Missouri river and the words 'For Sale sign.' He needed to report his findings to his editor in three days, but did not have any strong leads. If he left now and drove hard, he should be able to reach Omaha and spend the night there. Then he could head south, and if his good luck continued, find out how the Alexander guy was involved.

Fifteen minutes later he was westbound and wondering if he were wasting his time. He reached Omaha after four and one-half hours and found a cheap place to spend the night. Once settled in his room, he reviewed the map and checked his notes. He had a small note about the large bird arising from the fire. He thought back to his recent stop in Des Moines at that diner. He had told the waitress to "Keep the coffee coming."

He had been surprised at her comment as she filled his cup: "The last guy who said those words to me was sitting right where you are and then tried to show me an eagle that didn't exist."

He had shrugged it off. He thought back; he had felt *compelled* to stop at that particular diner. He had not been really hungry and had plenty of gas, but stopped for dinner and filled his gas tank at the filling station next door, anyway. Thomas had dismissed the eagle reference as just some strange coincidence.

Thomas slept fitfully and awoke anxious to hit the road. He ate a quick breakfast at a small restaurant and headed south on U.S. 75. He reached Brownville after three hours and one flat tire. He waited at the filling station while the inner tube was patched. During that time he struck up a conversation with the mechanic who was doing the work. He explained that he was searching for someone who could help him track down some information about a man who had recently died.

"You mean the two Indians out at the Lewis place? Now that was really a shame."

"No, this man died when a train derailed and crushed him. Let me show you this map; it's not very good, but it's a start. I think he was here somewhere and then headed back to Chicago but never made it."

The mechanic studied the map for a few moments.

"Mister, I think this map tells you how to get to the Lewis farm. That was a sad case. Old man Lewis had a stroke several months ago and ended up dying. Then his wife just gave up and *she* died. Their kids put the farm up for sale and this map looks like a map of how to get there. There are a lot of *out-of-towners* who are buying up local farms that are failing due to the drought and the Lewis farm is one of them. That's where those two Indians died."

"Do you know of anyone who could give me some additional information?"

"Sure, just keep going about a mile farther and stop at Jill's place; she knows everything that goes on around here. The food is pretty good, too."

The mechanic finished the inner tube repair and checked for leaks before putting the tube back into the tire. After inflating it properly, he placed the tire into the trunk. Thomas paid him fifty cents and thanked him profusely for the repair and especially for the information. He drove away, hoping for a major revelation at Jill's place.

Thomas had no trouble finding the little restaurant, diner or whatever it was. There were several vehicles parked outside. All conversation ceased as he opened the screen door and stepped inside. After the locals finished sizing up the stranger, they resumed talking. A tall, pleasant-looking woman walked over to him and spoke.

"Welcome to Jill's. Have a seat and what can I get for you?"

"I'd like some coffee and I need some information."

"I'm Jill and I can probably help you out or someone else here can. Let me get that coffee...you drink it black?"

"Yes, ma'am, that's fine," he replied as he took a seat at the nearest table.

Jill returned with a large cup of coffee and sat across from Thomas.

"My name is Tom Stevens and I am a reporter from the Chicago *Daily Illustrated Times*. I am here trying to finish a story on a man who died in a strange train crash a few days ago. He had been here in the area and then was on his way back to Chicago. He was spending the night at a place near Davenport, Iowa when the caboose from a train jumped the tracks and crushed him in his sleep. There is not much information on the man and something just isn't right. My editor is letting me investigate the original story and I have traced that man back here. I am trying to find out what he was doing here and maybe even talk to someone who might know more about him or who he worked for."

"I read about the train wreck, but I don't recall any strangers stopping in here on that particular day except for some families."

"Here is a map that I found in his car. Could you look at it and tell me what you think?"

He removed the map from his pocket and handed it to Jill.

She unfolded it and stared at it for a few seconds.

"This is a map to the Lewis farm. It's supposedly being bought by some big shot from Chicago. The guy was out here about a week or maybe ten days ago asking how to get there. He was also asking about the Indian that owned a small part of the original land next to the river.

He said that he wanted to buy the whole property including the part owned by the Indian. I gave him directions, but I never saw the man again. He supposedly made an offer on all but the small part, but I've heard that it's going up for sale, too. The Indian and the Lewis family were friends. They deeded over that small portion of the farm so that the Indian, he was called Howling Wolf, could live in peace. He was supposedly a big medicine man and there really was something special about him; he *knew things*. He was in here a few times and really seemed like a nice guy, for an Indian. Anyway, a few days ago one of his friends came by and said there had been an accident and that the old Indian and his young helper were both dead. Apparently the young Indian was killed while trying to tear down an old barn. They think that the old man tried to rescue the young guy and suffered heart failure. The bank had a crew out there yesterday cleaning up the place probably so that it will sell faster. One of the guys stopped in late yesterday with a lot of Indian stuff and was taking it up to Omaha to see if a trading post up there might want to buy it. In fact, I think he was hauling it up there today. If you just came down 75, you probably passed each other."

Thomas considered her comments briefly and looked at the map.

"I see the road that goes toward the river; how far is that from here? I want to go by the old farm."

"It's about two and a half miles...just past a farm with two big silos on the right hand side of the road. Follow that road and turn left when it dead ends. The farm will be down about a mile on your right. You will drive right past the old Indian's place. If you keep going down that road you can take the next left turn and it will bring you right back out to 75."

"I certainly do thank you for your help," Thomas said as he rose from his chair.

He fished in his pocket and placed a quarter on the table.

"Thanks again, I'm on a tight schedule."

"Maybe it's none of my business, Tom, but what are you lookin' for?"

"I honestly don't know; perhaps I'll figure it out when the time comes."

"We're open for lunch and you'll pass right by us on your way back to Omaha."

"I'll keep that in mind," he said as he smiled and left the diner.

Fifteen minutes later he drove up to the farmhouse at the old Lewis place. The house was locked so he walked around looking for something that might give a hint why the map was needed. He spotted what appeared to be a small house close to the river. He had driven past it, but did not recall seeing it from the road. Thomas went back to his car and backtracked, looking for the house he had just noticed. He finally located the dirt road leading toward the river and slowly crept down the rough, but recently traveled path. He arrived at the small house and noticed that several outbuildings had burnt to the ground. He left his car and walked around the general area. He noticed that the grass was brown, but was much longer than on the other side of the barbed wire fence. He also noticed that the various trees and shrubs were dying, but were not completely barren like other similar vegetation in the area. It was strange, but not worthy of any real scrutiny. He returned to his car and started up the lane toward the road.

He spotted an old pickup truck as it slowed and turned onto the same lane. Realizing that the path would not accommodate both vehicles, he stopped and slowly rolled back down the hill to level ground. The pickup truck continued down the lane and stopped nearby. An older man, apparently an Indian, exited and walked toward him. Thomas shut off the engine and stepped out of his car.

"Can I help you?"

He was not certain what to do.

"I am here to take back five gifts to some of my people. Howling Wolf, the man who lived here, made them and I need to find them. They are very important to me and my people."

"Maybe they are in the house," Thomas replied, hoping that his presence on the property was not a problem; the Indian did not seem angry.

"I looked before and nothing is in the house. I was told you were here and asking questions so I came to talk with you. We did not learn about Howling Wolf and Wounded Hand for two days. Much has happened since then and many sacred things are gone. We need to find these things so that they are not lost. Can you help me?" It was a simple request.

"I am sorry; I am searching for people who can help me answer questions, too. I do not know what I am looking for."

The Indian nodded and stared at Thomas for a long moment before speaking.

"Howling Wolf had great powers. He knew many things and was favored by the Great Spirit. He was watched over by a great eagle that guided him and helped him to see things that we could not see. We are seeking answers and want to know why Howling Wolf and the eagle were taken from us. We do not believe the story told by the Whites."

He immediately regretted his last words and lowered his eyes in embarrassment.

"I, too, have many questions about another man who came here, but no one has seen him. I am looking for someone who spoke to him and I am now trying to follow his trail. I am sorry that I am unable to help you. I hope you find the missing things."

Thomas returned to his car and drove away, turning right onto the old gravel road.

The Indian had not spoken again, but nodded and later waved at the reporter's car as it disappeared to the north. He knew that this man, this white man, had a good heart. Others must be made aware of his quest. The Indian would seek advice from his elders.

Thomas turned left onto the westbound road and made his way over to U.S. 75. He turned north and a few minutes later pulled in at Jill's. He walked in and noticed that several of the same people were still there.

"Glad to see you back. Care for some lunch?" Jill asked, obviously pleased to see him.

"Sure. How about bacon and eggs? Eggs over easy and soft bacon."

"You can have lunch, you know."

She smiled broadly, wondering if he was being cheap or just doubted that she served good food.

"Bacon and eggs are fast and I'm headed for Omaha. I need some directions to that trading post you mentioned earlier."

"It's called Bailey's Trading Post and it's on the west side of Omaha. I'll draw you a map...it's real easy to find. Are you looking for something to buy?"

"No, just looking for answers."

He sat at a table and looked around the room. None of the occupants paid any attention to him.

Jill brought his bacon and eggs and some toast. He thanked her and watched as she sketched a rough map. He wolfed down the food and drank a glass of water that had mysteriously appeared. Finally, Jill spun the map around and explained it although it was very clear and simple. He thanked her, paid for his food and headed north up U.S. 75.

Two hours later he parked in front of Bailey's Trading Post. He climbed out of his car, grateful for the opportunity to stretch his legs. He then entered the trading post and looked around. There were tremendous numbers of very ordinary items on display and most customers were wearing clothing which showed the effects of the poor economy. He immediately spotted a man wearing a suit; he stood out in sharp contrast to the other customers. The man was intently examining several objects and was oblivious to anything else.

Curiosity got the best of Thomas and he wandered over to the man. He watched him for several moments before speaking.

"Are those Indian artifacts? I'm sorry; I didn't mean to be rude, but you seem so interested in them. Tom Stevens," he said as he extended his hand.

"Aaron Polk. Apparently these are genuine Sioux articles."

He shook Thomas' hand.

"They just came in today."

"Were they hauled in on a truck? I was told that a truckload of things came up from down near Brownville. I was hoping to talk to the driver."

"He left about thirty minutes ago. He's a really nice guy, Walter something. I bought a tepee from him; it belonged to an old Indian. The Bailey guy, the owner of this place, bought a real war bonnet from him and you've gotta see this thing in a wooden case. He brought in four of them, all identical. Come up to the counter with me...you gotta see them!"

Aaron realized that this sense of urgency was unusual; this stranger probably had no real interest in those things.

The two men walked over to the counter and waited for the clerk to acknowledge their presence.

"Pardon me, could you show us that thing in the case," Aaron asked as he pointed to the wooden case at the end of the counter.

Without speaking, the clerk stepped over to the case and opened it and then carefully watched the two men for their reactions; extreme interest would raise the selling price by one dollar.

Thomas whistled softly as he gazed at the dreamcatcher. He did not know what it was, but he knew that it was special. He wanted to touch it just to convince himself that it was real. It was, well...perfect. It also seemed as if it were calling out to him to take it, to possess it. He suddenly noticed that he was breathing rapidly.

"You said there were four of them."

He remembered the old Indian at the farm.

"Don't you mean *five* of them?"

It was somehow important, but he did not know why.

"He only had four and he never said anything about five. Maybe he kept one. The bank down there paid him and some other guy to clean up the Indian's place after he died. Actually, *two* Indians died. He brought the stuff up here to sell. He's on his way back to Brownville."

Thomas felt an overwhelming need to talk to that Walter guy; he might have the information that he was looking for. He could probably catch up with him. Something was urging him to dig further.

"Thanks, I'll try to catch him. You've been a great help!"

Thomas was soon southbound knowing that the truck was at least forty minutes ahead of him. He realized that he had no description of the truck, but surely there would not be too many trucks on that stretch of road. He racked his brain trying to focus on what his subconscious was trying to tell him, but nothing was forthcoming.

He spotted the truck at the same filling station where he had stopped that morning to have his flat tire fixed; he *knew* it was the right truck. He slid to a stop on the gravel and rushed from his car. He spotted the driver...it *had* to be the driver.

"Is your name Walter?"

Startled, the man next to the truck nodded his head.

"Yeah, I'm Walter," he said as he assumed a defensive stance while Thomas continued walking toward him.

"My name's Tom Stevens. I'm a reporter and I'm hoping you have some information for me. Did you deliver some Indian things to Bailey's Trading Post near Omaha?"

"Maybe. Something wrong?" He was obviously being cautious.

"Those things in the wooden boxes…did you keep one?"

"No, there were only four at the old cabin. They were on a table in the little house and I built the boxes to protect them from damage. I sold all four to Bailey. I swear there were only four."

"I'm just curious. This morning I ran into an old Indian who was down there to collect five special gifts for some of his friends, I guess. Anyway, he was upset because there were no gifts and all of the other old Indian's possessions were gone, too. He seemed extremely angry about the missing gifts; apparently they were really special."

"Well, did he say what the gifts looked like?"

Walter chose not to mention the other items.

"I never thought to ask. I saw one of the things in the box and it sure looked special to me, but I'm no expert on Indian things. If those were the gifts, then someone took one and I think maybe I know who might have taken it."

"Come to think of it, the four feathered things were perfectly lined up on the table; there was room for one more on the end closest to the door. And you made me think of something else. Those two Indians died out there and this other guy and I were hired to clean up the property just a couple of days later. Things don't normally happen that fast around here. I've also heard that the Indian's place is already for sale. How could that be? There is supposed to be a deed for that property and I don't see how the land could possibly be ready to change hands that fast. At this point I'm just thinking out loud."

"Are you implying that perhaps the deaths of the two Indians might be tied in with the quick sale of the land? What makes that piece of land so important?" Thomas was merely curious.

"The Lewis farm was bought by a man who already owned the farms on either side of it. The Indian owned that little chunk right in the middle…that made it very valuable. Isn't it a little too much of a coincidence that the Indian dies and his property suddenly becomes immediately available? And who do you think would be first in line to buy the property? And of course the Indian didn't know that he was supposed to register the deed and so it turns out that the property had never changed hands at all…the Lewis family had never actually relinquished ownership of that piece of land. So, technically the little piece of land was never for sale at all. There's just one little thing wrong with that idea: *Gerald Lewis personally registered the deed for the*

Indian when he updated his own deed."

"So what happened to the deed or the record of the deed?"

"Well someone obviously made the record disappear and you can be sure that the person is working for the man who bought the three parcels of land. You're a reporter; it looks like you have a story and maybe even a murder to cover."

Thomas paused to consider what he had just heard. Suddenly he remembered that he needed to call his editor in two more days and give him an update as he had promised. This was now a big story and it had been handed to him by this Walter character. Still, there were the unusual deaths of the Powells; how did they figure in? And what about that Mr. Griffin...what role did he play? He tried to fashion a scenario.

Either the man who wanted to purchase the land or one of the unsavory types who attended the Alexander guy's funeral had probably sent him to kill the old Indian so that the land could be purchased. Someone else had disposed of the record of the land sale to the old Indian...someone with access to the records. The killer was probably murdered so that he would not reveal who his employer was. The clerk at that motor court was murdered because he might have known something or talked to the killer before he died. The wife was killed because her husband might have mentioned what he had been told. The only person left alive was the one who had removed the record of the land sale. Was he or she aware of the other murders? And one more thought suddenly chilled him to the bone.

"Walter, how do you know that the Lewis guy registered the deed for the Indian?"

"He told me so...he was afraid the old Indian wouldn't do it because he thinks, or thought, that men cannot own the earth. So he personally made sure that the deed was registered."

"Who knows that he told you what he did?"

"Nobody. You're the only one I've told. Why, what's the matter?"

His voice now showed a certain amount of stress.

"There may be some very nasty people involved in this. Almost everyone involved in this scheme has died under very mysterious circumstances. The one who manipulated the deed records probably lives here and he is still alive only because he is looking for anyone who might know something about what really happened or someone who is asking too many questions. He would probably let the appropriate people know and then another murder would probably occur. It would not be wise for you to mention any of this to anyone and I'm certain that this helper will have a fatal accident in the very near future."

Walter was silent as he considered Thomas' statement. He understood the idea, but found it hard to believe that it could happen in a small town like this. Even so, he would not be seeking any answers or talking to anyone about this whole mess. Besides, he would soon be moving his family up to the Omaha area.

"Tom, since you're a reporter, you'll be asking a lot of questions. You are also a stranger and I guarantee that everyone around here will be at least a little suspicious of you. You will be putting yourself in danger if you pursue this. I'm moving my family to Omaha and starting over up there. That area is starting to grow and I'm sure that I can do better for my family there. It seems to me that this is a story to leave alone. Someone here will either kill you or make sure that someone else does. Since you don't know who you're looking for, word will spread fast and something bad will happen to you."

Walter was being very candid and his concerns sounded valid.

"Thanks, Walter. I'm not sure how to pull this off, but I just can't let someone be killed because he or she knows too much. I'm supposed to talk to my editor and maybe he can tell me what to do."

"Look, you're a reporter. You never did say where you were from and how you ended up out here."

"I work for the Chicago *Daily Illustrated Times* and I persuaded my editor to let me chase down a story that seems incomplete. Anyway, he gave me three days to come up with a good story. I've been looking for a link between some shady characters from Chicago and the untimely death of a man that was here a few days ago. He was killed by the caboose from a train. Each time I speak to someone I get another perspective and a new set of leads. And here I am."

"Yeah, I'm familiar with the *Southern Eagle* caboose story."

"Wait a minute; did you say *Southern Eagle*? I never thought of that before."

Thomas thought back to some of his earlier conversations.

"There was a fireman that witnessed what he said was a big bird that arose from a burning house where two people died; one of them had dealt with the guy who was killed by the caboose. Then there was a waitress who mentioned that a guy saw an invisible eagle...he could see it but she couldn't. There was also an old Indian that stopped at the Lewis farm while I was there and he mentioned that one of the Indians who died out there was supposedly guided by an eagle. That seems odd to me."

"Well listen to this: those Indian things in the box have feathers that come from golden eagles. Golden eagles are not native to this area. This sounds like voodoo magic or something, not that I believe in that sort of thing. But there's something else...several people had mentioned seeing an eagle out near the Lewis farm, but I haven't heard anyone mention it in the last few days. Most people around here have never seen an eagle, so it was a big deal. Oh, and the tepee that I removed from the old Indian's place had a buffalo and a large bird on it and I'm willing to bet that it was an eagle."

Thomas considered the mention of the eagle. Surely it was a coincidence. And then he remembered that the daughter of the couple that was killed, Sarah, had mentioned that her dad had obtained a gift for his wife from someone at the motor courtyard. It was an Indian thing, a *dream* something.

"I just thought of something else: there was a feathered gift that the night man at the motor court where the train wreck occurred had taken home to his wife. Both died within two days."

"So you think that feathered thing carried some sort of disease like the *plague* or something?"

Walter held his breath since he had handled the others.

"No, it happened too quickly. That type of thing takes days or maybe weeks to show up. This is going to sound crazy, but suppose that this thing somehow caused the deaths of those three people."

Thomas waited for a response, feeling a little foolish.

"Uh, do you realize how preposterous that sounds? Do you honestly think these things are alive? I think it's just a coincidence. Let me think for just a minute. All right. Now, for example, show me the change in your pocket."

Puzzled, Thomas reached into his pocket and held out an assortment of coins. He silently stared at Walter waiting to see what was next.

"There is a nickel which is 5 cents. Your hand holding the coins has five fingers. You are standing here talking to me along Highway 75. This truck of mine was built in 1925. And if we keep trying, we can come up with even more. Of course, there might have been 5 of the feathered things. So I think you're concentrating too much on the eagle thing."

Walter was obviously pleased with himself, perhaps even a little smug.

"You're right. I've been trying to relate the deaths of three people to some people in Chicago and just got carried away. I do that sometimes. My editor actually hates to see me coming for that very reason. I shudder to think what he would have said if I had mentioned the eagle idea. Walter, thank you for your help. I have a lot to do. Remember that there is someone here who has connections to those Chicago people and you cannot give him or her any reason to mention your name."

Thomas stepped back slightly and extended his hand.

"Good luck, my friend."

"You be careful, too. You are trying to find out who is ultimately responsible for those deaths or at least one of them and I don't want to hear that you had some sort of an accident."

Walter clasped the offered hand.

"One more thing: have you always lived around here?"

"No, I was a teacher up in Minneapolis and I accidentally killed a guy in a fight. I spent five years in prison. When I got out, I came here to start over; it's hard to resume your old vocation when there has been as much publicity as I received. Are you surprised?"

"Yes, but then I know that there were circumstances that caused you to end up in prison and I somehow think that you got the short end of the stick. Good bye, Walter."

"So long, Tom."

Thomas walked to his car, glanced back at Walter and smiled. Walter waved and each man went back to his own life after briefly wondering what was in store for the other.

Thomas drove back to Omaha to spend the night. He mentally reviewed everything that he could remember and even pulled off the road more than once to check his notes. Tomorrow would be the second day of his investigation and he needed to check in with his editor on the following day. He wanted to talk to that waitress that had served the man who saw the eagle. He was now certain that it was Mr. Charles Alexander. He was also certain that Mr. Alexander had been in possession of one of the feathered things...the *fifth* one.

He stayed at a motor courtyard just outside of Omaha and dreamed of eagles. There were actually several dreams about eagles and each one seemed to foster a recurring sense of vague importance. It was as if the dreams were trying to tell him something or perhaps *warn* him about something; he was helpless and unable to find the meaning. Upon awakening, Thomas considered trying to explore his new compelling need to resolve the issue of the eagle yet did not know where to begin. He knew that his editor would not even consider granting him any leeway. Still, he would try to speak with the waitress and speak once more with the daughter of the two people killed near Davenport. *Then* he would contact his editor. He was extremely tired, having not slept well due to the dreams.

Thomas skipped breakfast, but did get a container of coffee since he was eager to get to Des Moines. He felt no *compulsion* to stop at that diner this time. He arrived feeling fatigued and suddenly realized that the waitress might not even be there. If not, he would eat and continue on to try and find Sarah Simpson.

He walked in with his fingers mentally crossed. He spotted the waitress immediately and breathed a sigh of relief. She noticed him shortly thereafter and motioned him toward a booth near the far end of the counter.

"I knew you'd be back, but this is really strange. The girl who always works the morning shift needed to swap with me due to a doctor's visit; otherwise I would not be here. I'll keep the coffee coming and take your order. Then you can ask your questions."

She smiled and walked away.

Dumbfounded, Thomas sat and watched the waitress as she grabbed a cup and a coffee pot and returned. She *knew why he was here* or was just quite perceptive, but the change in her schedule was exceptional good luck...or was it luck? Thoughts raced through his mind.

"Okay, what will it be this morning?" She was poised and ready to take the order. Obviously it was business first.

"Two eggs, over easy, bacon and toast. Oh, and a glass of milk."

He ordered quickly to speed her return. He was anxious to hear what she had to say.

"Coming right up."

She disappeared.

A minute or so later, she returned and sat opposite Thomas.

"Sherry, the other waitress, came by late yesterday and told me about needing to go to the doctor today. I was supposed to spend some time with my cousin this morning and she came by to cancel while Sherry was here. Okay, things like that happen and I agreed to switch. Then last night I went to bed early because of the earlier work hours. This is the scary part: *I dreamed of an eagle and he told me to 'keep the coffee coming.'* I *knew* you were coming here today. I don't know why or how, but I *knew* it. This is crazy and nothing like this has ever happened to me before. Surprisingly, I am not frightened, but I am confused and am hopeful that you can help me make some sense of this." She abruptly rose and returned to the counter.

Thomas sat there thinking about his own dreams and realized that his fatigue had left him; he was now wide awake. This eagle thing was now beginning to take over his thought process, but now it was affecting others if he were to believe this waitress. She had his attention; she had his *full* attention. He would not mention his own dreams.

The waitress returned with his breakfast and left to fetch his glass of milk. Returning, she once again sat across from him.

"What is it that I apparently *know* that you seem to *need*?" She was wasting no time.

"The man that saw the eagle, what did he look like?"

"I can't remember. I have tried, but I can't tell you anything about him. He was driving a black Ford sedan with an Illinois license plate; I remember that because he parked directly in front of the door. He was really aggravated that I couldn't see that eagle. He also moved from that table over there at that window to this booth. He became nervous and didn't finish his meal and then left in a big hurry."

"What about a name?" Thomas ate quickly as he listened.

"Nope. He was very quiet and I think he was tired. He ordered his food and then asked me to go with him to the window to look at that eagle. I just thought that he might have some problems and tried to avoid him. Oh, and he had told me to *keep the coffee coming* and then just drank two cups."

"What time of day was it?"

"It was still light outside when he left. Maybe six-thirty or seven."

"Can you think of anything else? The man I'm looking for was also driving a black Ford sedan with Illinois plates, but I'm sure that there are lots of them driving by on this highway. I desperately need a description."

"I'm sorry. I've told you everything I can remember." She seemed to be sincere.

"Here is a telephone number and an address where you can reach me. If you think of anything else, please contact me." He handed her a small card.

"Wow, you're a reporter. Okay, Mr. Stevens, I will get in touch with you if I remember anything else. Are you married?"

"No," Tom laughed, "I'm not married. Thank you for your help. I just wish that I could understand or explain what has happened regarding your dream."

"Well, come back any time. Remember, I normally work nights," she said as she displayed her best smile and resumed her waitress duties.

Thomas wolfed down the remainder of his breakfast and left. He filled his gas tank at the filling station next door and headed east. He realized that he had not gotten the name of the waitress. "Oh well," he thought, "I don't think I'll get any more information from her."

As he drove he considered her account of her dream and how their chance meeting seemed to be much more than just chance or luck. How could the eagle appear in her dream and an eagle appear in his dreams on the same night? He shivered suddenly as he remembered the fireman's comment that the eagle he saw was *not of this world*. He had also said that the feathers would have burned due to the intense heat. What if the fireman had actually *seen* that eagle? Thomas dismissed that thought immediately. What if the eagle sightings just carried over as an illusion or just the result of an over-active imagination? Yet neither he nor that waitress had seen an eagle. Perhaps just the *mention* of an eagle triggered the dreams. No, the waitress said that the eagle spoke to her and used the phrase 'keep the coffee coming' and she had mentioned that phrase to him when he stopped there the first time. That did not mean anything special to Thomas; she just had a good memory and her brain was working too hard. She also appeared to be interested in him and maybe that was all there was to it...but that did not explain her dreams.

He continued to struggle as he searched for something to tie all of this together. He needed facts and they were not forthcoming. He decided that if he contacted Sarah and *she* mentioned dreaming about an eagle, then he would start to worry. He tried to dismiss all of this and concentrate on the Chicago people who were involved in the murders, but he kept thinking back to the eagle and the repeated references to it.

CHAPTER EIGHT

Revelations

Thomas wearily parked in front of the burnt structure that had been the Powell house. He realized that he had not asked Sarah when the funeral for her parents would be held. He had her address but was reluctant to go there. He would sit here and go over his notes which were rapidly becoming divergent rather than convergent. In less than five minutes he heard the sound of an approaching car. Looking through his rear view mirror, he recognized Sarah Simpson's car. She parked in the driveway. He was both pleased and somewhat confused that she had appeared.

Thomas stepped from his car, walked over and opened the car door for her.

"Hello, Tom. I didn't see you at the funeral, but I *somehow* knew that you would be here. I didn't really come here to see you; I was checking to see if the funeral home had delivered some of the extra flowers. Have you learned anything about what happened?"

She appeared weary, but otherwise seemed to be holding up well. She seemed genuinely pleased that he was there.

"I just arrived about ten minutes ago and I'm sorry I missed the service. I wish I could tell you that I had some great news, but I have nothing new to tell you. I have, however, discovered some confusing things that do not make any sense at all. I must ask this question, though: does the word 'eagle' have any special meaning for you or have you seen an eagle recently or have you *dreamed* about an eagle?"

She stared at him with a frown that made him wish that he had not brought that up. The frown gave way to a soft smile and she shook her head and rolled her eyes before speaking.

"A what? An eagle? What could that *possibly* have to do with the death of my parents?" She looked like she was almost ready to flee.

"Sarah, just trust me right now. Has an eagle, in any form, entered your thoughts?" He wasn't sure what he wanted to hear.

"No. Now would you please tell me what's going on?" She was becoming slightly agitated and that was very clear.

"As you know, I've been trying to track down those responsible for the death of your parents. I've been to a little town in Nebraska and a series of very strange coincidences just keep showing up. I didn't pay any attention to them at first, but now I think that they're very important; I just can't figure out how they fit in. The worst part is that the whole idea is preposterous." He paused and considered his next few words. "An eagle is somehow involved in this." He waited for her to speak.

Sarah rolled her eyes again and then took a long look at Thomas. She could tell that he was serious and was waiting for her reaction with an expression that just melted her heart. Abruptly, she stepped forward and kissed him. He resisted momentarily and then returned the kiss. He felt her arms encircle him and pulled her closer to him. When their lips parted, the embrace continued for several seconds and then Sarah quickly pulled away.

"I'm sorry; I didn't mean to do that. Well, I really did, but the way you were looking at me and I didn't know if I would ever see you again and then it just happened. I'm sorry. I hope I didn't offend you. I knew you would be here and I wanted to see you. I was just so afraid I might miss you if you came by."

"I wasn't offended, but I was a little surprised. And it was a very *pleasant* surprise." Thomas was actually blushing.

He stepped closer and took her face in both hands and gently kissed her. This time she returned the kiss and this one lasted much longer than the first. They smiled awkwardly at each other, both wondering what to do next. Thomas spoke first to break the awkward silence.

"I need some coffee. Is there any place nearby?"

Sarah carefully crafted her answer to avoid scaring him away; she briefly considered inviting him over to her house. "We can go to the place where the three of us had breakfast for the last time." Tears ran down her face as she briefly thought about that day.

Thomas produced a handkerchief and gently dried her tears. He took her hand and walked her to his car. She squeezed his hand causing him to wonder what it meant. He opened the passenger door, moved his notes to the back seat and then allowed her to enter. He closed the door very carefully and walked around to the driver's door. Getting in, he wondered if he should talk business or talk about what had happened in the last few minutes. This was new and certainly unexpected. She was grieving and maybe he just happened to be nearby. That was probably all there was to it. Still, she did imply that she had missed him. He started the engine without saying a word. Sarah was first to speak.

"You can turn around or just follow the road and come out at the same place. It's about a mile from here. Years ago it was a home and then the owner decided that it would make a good restaurant and it has survived through some hard times. It's not on a main road so the customers are almost exclusively the local residents. And the food is always good."

Thomas had hoped that she might speak of something else. Oh well, he was, in fact, a reporter. He took a deep breath.

"Sarah, I know so little about you and I want to know more. I see no wedding ring, but your last name is Simpson and not Powell. After what just happened, I have a few questions before I get shot by a jealous husband."

She hesitated briefly. "I married when I was eighteen. The guy was going to take me away from here and we would have a great life. My folks were against it and that just made it that much more attractive to me. We never even left town. He said he was waiting for the right job to come along; he was killed in a construction accident six months after we married. He slapped me around a lot, but would not let me leave. So I guess you could say that things just worked themselves out for the best. That was almost six years ago. Now it's your turn."

"You know that I'm a reporter. I'm very good at it, but don't have the experience. The older guys get the best stories to pursue. Right now I am onto what seems to be two separate stories that are related. One story could launch my career in a way I never imagined or get me killed; the other could get me classified as a crackpot and end my brief career. Now you have thrown another aspect into an already complicated life that has changed considerably in the last few days."

"And now I suppose that you're going to tell me about your wife and eight kids." She smiled as she spoke, but was fearful of his next words.

"There is no...," he said as he looked at her. "I'm sorry; I was taking this very seriously."

He chuckled before continuing.

"There is no wife and there is no girlfriend...I've just never taken the time and the pay is not so good for fledgling reporters. Most women I've met are expecting lavish meals and entertainment and, well, here I am. I would just need to meet the right woman and so far I haven't."

"Does that include present company?"

This was certain to provoke a response, although it might not be what she was hoping for. Regardless, Sarah wanted to know where she stood.

"Well, I, uh...I don't know. I thought initially that you were just a little too forward for me, but I considered it part of your grieving and it was okay. Now I'm just numb and hopeful I guess. I'm not frightened, though."

Sarah reached over and patted his hand. "Now turn right and then take the next left."

Silence prevailed for the next minute or so with each hoping the other would reveal something that would give some sort of encouragement.

"That's it ahead on the right, where that car just turned in."

Thomas pulled to a stop near the front door and quickly walked around to Sarah's door. He opened it with a flourish which made her laugh and then her face saddened as she remembered the significance of this place. Thomas detected the change and took her arm.

"Would you rather go somewhere else?"

"No, Tom, this is where I want to be right now and I'll be okay. It got awfully quiet for the last couple of minutes and I'm anxious to hear about this mysterious theory of yours."

They entered the restaurant and found it to be essentially empty. Sarah led Thomas to a booth and they sat just as their waitress arrived.

"And what can I get for you two lovebirds?"

Sarah shrieked with delight while Thomas cringed.

"Coffee for me," laughed Sarah. "If he could speak, I think he'd say that he would like a cup, too."

"I'll be right back with your coffee," she said softly as she wondered what she had said that caused this reaction. Still puzzled, she frowned and walked away.

Thomas reached across the table and took Sarah's hands; he gently squeezed them and swallowed.

"I asked you about an eagle because it keeps coming up over and over again. I don't know what it means, but it is somehow related to my investigation. I deal in facts and I do my research. What I am about to tell you might make you question my sanity. I am only going to relate what I have been told and what I know and I want you to let me tell you everything without interruption."

He told about the waitress and the invisible eagle and how he was certain that Charles Alexander was the man who tried to show it to her. He mentioned the eagle sightings near the old Indian's place. He spoke of the eagle on the tepee and realized that he had meant to stop and see it. He watched her reaction when he told her about the fireman and the eagle that rose from her parents' home. The last thing Thomas mentioned was a description of the feathered ring thing that had the eagle feathers on it.

Upon hearing those words, Sarah abruptly pulled free of his hands and covered her mouth as in disbelief.

"The dreamcatcher! Oh my God! Tom, I forgot...my dad brought a dreamcatcher home to my mom on the night or actually the morning of the train wreck!"

Thomas sat back in the booth as a chill engulfed him. He saw the two cups of coffee at the end of their table and briefly wondered when they had arrived. His thoughts immediately returned to Sarah's last words. He was now certain that the Indian thing, the *dreamcatcher*, had come from Charles Alexander.

"Sarah, what did this dreamcatcher look like?"

She described it in great detail and Thomas was certain that it had to be proof that Charles Alexander had taken it from the old Indian. Still, there were other questions.

"Sarah, this will sound a little strange, but do you know which train jumped the track?"

"Of course, everyone knows that it was the caboose from the *Southern Eagle*...." Her voice trailed off and her eyes widened as she stared at Thomas. "Tom, this is becoming a little too scary for me."

"Our coffee is here. I drink mine black. It looks like the waitress brought cream and we have sugar if you need it. Let's drink a little coffee and then resume our conversation. At least now you know why I tried to warn you about how this sounds."

"I was a little concerned when you began preparing me for this and now I know why." She re-located her cup, adding cream and sugar.

Thomas sipped his coffee and mentally pronounced it as 'very good.' Now he had more questions and they would concern Sarah's parents. He was uncertain how she would handle this, particularly since she had just come from their funeral. He watched her as she tasted her coffee and noted no reaction at all. Now he would need to ask some tough questions.

"There are more questions now. Did your father mention how he got the dreamcatcher...did he buy it?"

"Mom said he got it from a man that was at the place where Dad worked; I assume that he bought it."

"Could your dad have taken it?"

"You mean did my dad *steal* it? Tom, my dad was not a thief." There was a touch of anger in her voice.

"It's just that there was no mention of the dreamcatcher in Mr. Alexander's personal things and I'm certain that he took one from the old Indian. You must admit that the dreamcatcher was too nice to be thrown away. Perhaps he just *rescued* it; I know that I would not have let it be destroyed or be lost at the crash scene. And it *obviously* had nothing to do with the train wreck."

Sarah had calmed down realizing that if this Alexander man had bothered to take it initially, he probably would not have sold it or given it away. She listened as Thomas resumed.

"Now I need you to tell me everything that happened with this dreamcatcher thing."

"Okay. I dropped by the house when I heard about the train wreck on the radio. Dad was home and they were having coffee. Mom showed me the dreamcatcher and couldn't stop talking about how beautiful it was. She wanted it hung over their bed to replace an old ugly painting that we all hated. Before doing that, we came here for breakfast and I left their house just before Dad went to sleep. After Dad, you know...died, she said that he had slept for several hours and then decided to change the light bulb in the bathroom and that's when it happened." Sarah was very close to tears.

"Where was the dreamcatcher; was it hanging up?"

"Yes, Mom said he hung it up just before going to sleep."

"Sarah, why is it called a *dreamcatcher*?"

"Tom, it's supposed to bring you good luck when you sleep. No, it catches your dreams...maybe that's why it's called a *dreamcatcher*. And you know something, Dad was scared of electricity. He was shocked by electricity years ago and actually had nightmares about it. Mom said that while he was sleeping the last time, he was having a bad dream and she was wondering if it was about being shocked. Isn't it strange that a few hours later he died from electrocution?"

Thomas inhaled deeply as his mind raced. "So what if this dreamcatcher caught his bad dream, his nightmare?" He immediately regretted making that statement aloud.

"You mean this thing somehow made his bad dreams come true?"

"I don't know. I'm just trying to sort out things. Did your mom have bad dreams, too?"

"Oh, yes. She just knew that Dad was going to burn the house down. She made him quit smoking and even made sure that were no candles in the house. She used to have nightmares where the house was burning and she could not escape." Sarah's eyes widened and then she frowned slightly as she considered the words she had just uttered. Then she began to shake.

"But Sarah, she didn't die that same night, so I guess that I was wrong about the dreamcatcher." He searched for other possibilities.

Sarah took a deep breath and thought for a few seconds.

"Wait a minute; Mom didn't sleep in the bed that night. I stayed with her and we both ended up sleeping in the living room. They found her in the bedroom the *next* night, the night of the fire. You don't seriously believe that this thing killed my parents. I was in the house, too and it didn't kill me."

Thomas' memory had another critical piece of the puzzle. It took a few seconds before he remembered. "I spoke with Charles Alexander's sister and she said that he had nightmares about being hit by a train. She said it was ironic that he was killed by the thing he feared the most. This is going to sound crazy, but...."

"All three were killed by their nightmares! My God, this is too much to be a coincidence. But Tom, I have nightmares, too."

"Then there must be some other common thread. Maybe you must sleep in the room with the dreamcatcher or touch it. Did you touch it?"

"Yes, I held it several times, but I never slept in the room with it. Do you realize how ridiculous this sounds? What about the Alexander guy...maybe he gave it to my dad and that would void your theory."

"Why would he take it, carry it this far and then just give it to a complete stranger? I think that your dad might have found it *after* the crash and took it home. Okay, there is something else: there were *two* firemen that saw an eagle arise from the ashes but I only spoke to one of them. He really believed that he saw it. He said that it stood in the hot embers and looked right at him. Then it spread its wings and flew away. He pointed out that the feathers should have burned and that nothing could have survived that heat. He also said that it *could not have been from this world* and he was obviously frightened."

"Tom, maybe he was mistaken. Maybe it was one of those eagle dreams that you asked me about; maybe he just *thinks* he saw it. I can't think of any other explanation."

"But what if we *are* dealing with something from beyond our normal world? The dreamcatcher is supposedly a *good* thing and yet this one seems to selectively kill certain people. It's obviously not alive, but it seems to have power. I examined one of the ones at the trading post and I felt a strong, overpowering urge to pick it up and I did. Since I started this bizarre investigation, I have had a series of things happen that have caused me to stop somewhere or talk to someone for no apparent reason. I have good reporter savvy, but these were things that I *just did* and they all provided answers or more questions. It's as if I am being directed. I originally went to your parents' house looking for clues and trying to think of a way to approach you and you appeared. I showed up today and you arrived minutes later. I stopped at the diner in Des Moines and the waitress was there after changing her shift and she said that she *knew* I was coming. And these are just a few examples of some things that are not my doing. Each time, though, I find something that I need. I cannot consider that to be simple coincidence. I don't know *what* or *how* or even *why*, but I think that I am being guided to each one of these meetings and it's becoming very unsettling."

"I had the same feeling on both occasions when we met, but those were the only times. The first time, I knew that something was going to happen. I was just taking flowers to our old house, but as I got closer I had this feeling that something was going to happen. When I saw your car, I immediately felt that everything was going to be okay and that strange feeling went away. Today, I just *knew* that I had to go there and that you would be there also. I didn't even question or consider that you *would not* be there. I don't understand it either, but I'm not actually afraid. I am really confused, though."

"There is one other thing: the old Indian was supposedly a very powerful medicine man. Apparently he constructed the dreamcatchers and they were special gifts for some people. What if he gave them special powers of some sort; maybe they were guardians or something like that."

"Guardians that kill people for no reason? Tom, I think you're way off on that one. Besides, how would my parents fit in? I mean, they had no enemies; they were not evil."

Thomas looked deep into her eyes; it was as if he were seeing her for the first time. He forgot all about eagles and reporting and investigations. She was very attractive and such a joy to be around. He just wanted to be in this place right now...with her.

"Are you okay?"

"I'm falling in love with you as silly as that might sound."

Sarah's concerned expression was replaced with a slight frown as she leaned back.

"Silly? Why would that sound silly?"

"I've known you for a grand total of only a few minutes. You have suffered terrible losses and are grieving. You are very vulnerable right now and I want to help you, protect you from something or someone. To me, that already sounds a little crazy and then I throw in a declaration of love."

"Tom, I'm an adult. Maybe I'm not really experienced in matters of the heart, but I am an excellent judge of character. You are destined for great things and I want to be part of your life. These are not the words of a small town girl that just desperately wants to get away and see the world. I can see a future with you and it just seems right. And Tom, I've known you for the same length of time. I could not be any more certain that this is right."

Sarah blushed as she realized that she had just bared her soul. How could she have been so stupid! She had just placed the poor man in a very bad situation, but she had been completely honest. If only she could withdraw those last few words. Sarah closed her eyes. "Please, don't leave," she thought to herself.

Thomas swallowed; this was not what he had expected. He was thrilled and yet he was puzzled by her complete honesty. He had listened to other men discuss women and the games that seemed inevitable. Everything was happening much too fast. He did not regret his own words, but hers had come too soon. It was almost desperation and that bothered him. He was supposed to pursue her and win her, but that was not the case.

The silence was unbearable. They sipped their coffee and each glanced briefly at the other. Thomas was first to speak.

"Well, I guess we need to talk about this."

"Tom, I'm sorry I said what I did. I'm just afraid that you will go back to Chicago and I'll never see you again. I know that you are supposed to court me and I'm supposed to make you chase me, but we are separated by a long distance and your job controls you. It is not my decision...you know my true feelings and right now I feel foolish that I spoke so quickly."

"You realize that you would have to come to Chicago." He was giving her a way to back out gracefully. He hoped that she would not change her mind.

"There's nothing here for me anymore. Mom was a seamstress and had a few friends in the fashion industry. I occasionally supply designs for Sears, Roebuck and Company and you know where their headquarters is located. I don't see a problem; in fact, this would be a good move."

Now it was all out in the open; she felt foolish, throwing herself at this man that she hardly knew. Perhaps desperate was a more apt description, but she could not let him get away.

Thomas had feelings just short of terror but was flattered that a woman, particularly this woman, would be so open and so honest about her feelings for him. She was not concerned about how difficult their life might be as long as it was *their* life. There was so much to think about and discuss and yet he was no longer fearful; he was rapidly becoming comfortable with this new possibility.

In the ensuing days, Thomas put together a story involving a wealthy Chicago business man, Charles Alexander and the deaths of the two Indians. Armed with his research and some information already in their possession, the Chicago police were able to bring charges against three individuals and also implicated a man in Nebraska who had made the old Indian's deed disappear. Thomas was able to launch his story as the indictments were handed out; there were no references to dreamcatchers and eagles. He received an immediate promotion and pay raise along with his new fame. He also had the attention of those who did not wish him well.

Thomas and Sarah were married two weeks later and spent a week at Niagara Falls. She was able to devote more time to designing women's clothing for Sears and was approached by the newspaper to join the fledgling fashion segment of the Society Department. She accepted the position and was able to continue submitting designs; she was happy.

On his fourth day back at work, Thomas came across a wire service teletype story concerning a twelve year old girl who had died in a freak accident down in Florida. She had been thrown from a speeding pickup truck as her family fled from a wildfire. She had come to rest in the jaws of a large alligator that was part of a sign advertising a local alligator farm. The child's grandmother had mentioned that her granddaughter had experienced nightmares about alligators. Ironically, the grandmother had also recently lost a good friend who had nightmares about spiders and had died from a spider bite. There were numerous similarities to the other recent deaths. He placed the teletype in his top drawer for further investigation. He did manage to send a brief letter to the grandmother, a lady named Eleanor Taylor.

Thomas now found himself in the midst of the big stories, no longer doing the research for other reporters. He became an expert with a camera and was usually able to add immensely to his stories with a well-crafted and well-captioned photo. He was now being sent to cover stories in other cities and was often allowed to take Sarah with him to fashion locales like New York City, Boston, Houston, Dallas, San Francisco, Atlanta, Miami and Los Angeles. His research into the eagle-dreamcatcher phenomena essentially stopped as his free time evaporated.

Thomas awakened one night after a vivid dream involving an old Indian who stared at him and said simply, "Find them; burn them." He was unable to return to sleep. He thought about the dream on a daily basis. Sarah thought it was just a coincidence, but inwardly considered the possibility that there was some special meaning...especially after Thomas had a second similar dream. The Indian had a bald spot near what appeared to be an injured right ear. Once again he repeated the simple message and then became an eagle and flew away; Thomas awakened in a sweat.

He received a reply from Eleanor Taylor the following day and was convinced that the death of her granddaughter was somehow connected to the dreamcatcher things. He was unable to find a telephone number for her and quickly fired off a second letter with very specific questions; her reply arrived two weeks later. It seemed that Eleanor had purchased a dreamcatcher from Bailey's Trading Post in Omaha, Nebraska. That revelation caused his heart to pound. The following paragraph caused his heart to skip a beat: 'I returned to my daughter's house to find a flashlight. By the time I arrived, the house had been almost completely destroyed by the wildfire, but something inexplicable happened. A big bird with red eyes stood up in the burning house, looked at me and my grandson and then flew away. I know it happened and my grandson saw it too. He said it was just like the eagle that we saw the day before.'

Thomas re-read the paragraph several times and remembered the fireman's story about the eagle that arose from the ashes of Sarah's parents' home. These were almost identical accounts of something very strange that happened hundreds of miles apart yet none of which was public knowledge. The only remaining link was Bailey's Trading Post and Thomas was now certain that both dreamcatchers had come from the same source. At that instant, the old Indian's directive flashed through his mind: 'Find them; burn them.'

Carrying the letter, Thomas rushed over to Sarah's desk amid some bawdy comments about newlyweds from the mostly male workers. He ignored the comments and dropped the letter on her desk as he sat.

"You're not going to believe this!"

"Oh, I'm doing fine and I'm glad to see you, too."

Sarah smiled warmly, but knew that the message had been received. She quickly read the letter down to the paragraph that had shocked Thomas and then read slowly. She read that paragraph a second time and then whistled softly.

"Tom, this is no coincidence. This dreamcatcher must have killed her friend and her granddaughter, and this eagle did the same thing that the other one did...*in a fire*."

"Sarah...the dreamcatchers are *destroyed by fire*! That's what the old Indian was telling me in my dreams! 'Find them; burn them.' That's what must be done with the other three to stop them from killing anyone else!"

Sarah and Thomas were suddenly aware that the huge room was now silent. They both looked around and watched as most co-workers quickly avoided their gaze; others just stared at them.

"I'm going to call Bailey's Trading Post and see if they still have the other dreamcatchers!" Thomas did not wait for Sarah to speak.

He returned to his desk and called the Omaha operator; he was soon connected to the Trading Post. Once Mrs. Bailey came on the line, he introduced himself by name only and asked about the dreamcatchers in the wooden boxes. She was unaware of anything of that description and did not recall any that had been sold. When Thomas asked to speak to Mr. Bailey, she informed him that Mr. Bailey had died in an automobile accident right in front of the Trading Post several weeks earlier. He expressed his sorrow and asked if he could speak to the man that normally ran the counter. Thomas was dismayed to learn that he had quit two days after the tragic loss of Mr. Bailey. Thomas then asked about sales receipts that might show that the dreamcatchers had been sold and was assured that there were none.

"It's possible that he sold them on his last day. It was extremely busy that day and maybe he just didn't get around to completing a sales receipt." Thomas winced before he thanked her and again extended his condolences before hanging up.

Sally Bailey hung up the phone and walked out into the large display room. She surveyed the thousands of items in front of her and sighed. Behind her and carefully hidden atop the tall cabinet were three wooden boxes, each containing a dreamcatcher. Sally wiped tears from her eyes and returned to the office for a good cry. How she hated this place!

The world was now beginning to pay serious attention to a man named Adolph Hitler. There was talk that a war in Europe was inevitable. Most Americans considered that to be a problem for other people...certainly nothing to affect the United States. After all, this country had enough problems just trying to re-build the economy. Newspaper coverage now presented almost daily updates on the increasing turmoil that surrounded Germany.

Then on September 1, 1939, Germany invaded Poland and things began to change. Thomas was summoned to the editor's office and told to close the door. He was informed that things were relatively quiet in Europe in spite of the invasion of Poland, but that things would probably become worse. He was asked how he felt about becoming a war correspondent. Having never considered that possibility, Thomas felt honored yet apprehensive. Neither man was certain what the actual role of a war correspondent would be other than to report what was actually occurring. The editor explained that military and civilian leaders were certain to carefully screen news reports that were destined for release to the public. Since the United States was to remain neutral, he would probably be sent to London. No timetable was discussed.

Thomas broke the news to Sarah whose first question was, "When do we leave for London?" Two weeks later she found out that she was pregnant and plans for her to accompany Thomas to London were scrapped. Kathleen Nancy Stevens was born seven months later.

Thomas covered the war in Europe and then part of the campaigns in North Africa and Italy. In spite of the strict censorship, he was able to bring the progress of the war to the American people through his exceptional writing skills and superb photography. He covered the plight of the American soldiers and showed them and their surprising humor in spite of the danger and the often miserable conditions.

Immediately after the attack on Pearl Harbor, Thomas had been summoned home for three weeks to relax. He met his daughter and had been swept away by her already-evident charm. Sarah had watched him as he awkwardly played with Kathleen and had seen a side of her husband that had melted her heart. Their short time together before his return to London had been mostly a family matter, but Thomas had been summoned to the newspaper several times. The return to the European theater had been difficult and Thomas had received word several weeks later that Sarah was expecting another child; Thomas Jr. was born in September.

In May, 1944 Thomas was sent to the Pacific theater. There he was sent to cover the stories of U.S. Marines. He was initially resented as just someone who had to be kept out of danger until the day he was forced to pick up a rifle and join a kill-or-be-killed battle. He was surprisingly effective and immediately gained the respect of those who witnessed his aggressiveness. He never told anyone that his motivation had been the sniper round that mortally wounded his favorite camera.

Thomas would often pick a Marine and stay with him for days and sometimes for weeks. His photos and stories were well-received back in the 'States' and even those with sad endings instilled a great sense of pride in the many readers who now looked forward to his reports.

He moved toward Japan with the Marines as they pushed forward. Then came Nagasaki and Hiroshima. Shortly thereafter, Thomas was aboard the USS Missouri in Tokyo Bay where he took his final photos of the war. Thomas soon returned to Chicago and was considered a hero of a different sort; he was now a world-renown journalist and photographer. He had been nominated for a Pulitzer Prize in two separate categories, but lost by very narrow margins on both accounts. He now commanded great respect throughout the newspaper industry and could do just about anything he pleased. His editor prided himself in his decision to let the young man venture out to show what he could do; he conveniently forgot that he had originally done so just to have some peace and quiet. Thomas had been surprised that there had been no dreams of eagles or the old Indian during his entire tenure as a war correspondent; apparently the remaining dreamcatchers had been destroyed.

Then suddenly in March of 1946, the old Indian and an eagle would appear once again in a dream. "Find them; burn them" would be the message. Thomas would suddenly be thrown back into his previous quest. He would bring out his collection of notes on everything he had learned thus far. A few days later he would check the wire service and be saddened to read about the death of a heroic Marine and friend. He would call Sarah immediately and tell her that he needed to visit the family of this man who had impressed him so much. He would then search through countless photos before departing for St Louis.

CHAPTER NINE

Post-War

Sally Bailey looked around the trading post one last time. The War had affected so much in her life. The shortages and rationing had prompted the population to clean out their stashes of wonderful treasures while they searched for scrap metal and other items vital to the war effort. She bartered and purchased and, in general, increased her inventory of all sorts of things which would not normally appear in her place of business. She made it through the war, but did not envision the growth that would soon begin. She was tired and her hatred of the trading post had remained. Truly luck was on her side when that nice man from New York, Mr. Pollard, offered to purchase the place and the entire inventory. The large eagle that had recently taken up residence nearby had certainly brought her good luck. One customer said that it was a golden eagle.

The new owner shared the same feelings about good luck and would rename the place *Eagle's Nest Trading Post*. A flat tire had forced him to pull over in the parking area and he had wandered inside the trading post for help. Sally had watched him as he walked around looking at the shelves and the variety which they contained. He was not a customer; there was something more to this man.

"Make me an offer," she had said in jest. Winter was coming and she wanted to leave this place with all of its bad memories.

"And what would you take for the entire place, land and all?" He had been serious.

The next day they had agreed on a price and started the process which had brought her to today. Sally stepped outside and looked over at the tree where the eagle spent much of its time. The eagle looked at her and then flew away as she walked to her car. Sally never bothered to look back; she would not miss this place, this albatross.

For the new owner, the priority was to get the new sign up. While he relied on the goodwill of the Bailey name, he was anxious to see the trading post as *his* enterprise. There was certain to be a period of prosperity following the war and he wanted to be prepared for it. He had plans to upgrade the display area and make the trading post more appealing on the inside. He initially let things settle down while he formulated his design. He would start at the front of the building and work back. Winter was certain to be a slow time and he could do most of the work himself. He commenced this huge project on the day of the first snowfall. He rearranged the store just enough to provide some working space and slowly worked his way through the trading post. He was able to conduct sales which varied from just a few customers each day to days where he found himself completely overwhelmed; on those days he was unable to complete any of his planned upgrades.

On March 14, 1946 he reached the rear portion of the store. He noticed the huge cabinet that looked so hideous now; he decided that the monstrosity had to go. Two days later he found three beautiful wooden boxes atop the ugly cabinet. Surprisingly, there was no dust on the three boxes although there was a large accumulation on the remainder of the upper surface of the cabinet. His bewilderment disappeared after he moved the three items over to the main counter and opened the first one. He gasped at the sight of the contents...he did not know what it was, but it was unlike anything he had ever seen. With trembling hands he opened the two remaining boxes and was overjoyed to see that all three of the things were identical. He stared at them, eager to lift one and examine it, but afraid that it might be so fragile as to disintegrate upon being touched. Even so, he felt an irresistible urge to touch these magnificent things. He resisted as long as possible.

Finally, Mr. Pollard reached down and lifted the first dreamcatcher; it remained intact. He studied it carefully and wondered how it had been constructed. Surely the precise workmanship had not been accomplished by human hands, but what type of machine or machines could produce such precise results with these materials? He shrugged, at least he had three of them and perhaps he could find more. He had no idea what he should charge for them, but he would start at twenty dollars and adjust downward if necessary. He was afraid to leave one out in its opened box and thus placed it inside one of the display cases near the counter.

Two days later he sold it to a young lady on her way to St Louis; it was a present for her brother who had just returned home from the war. She did not hesitate when she heard the price and quickly departed with her prize. Unknown to her, an eagle followed overhead.

The following month the remaining two dreamcatchers were purchased by a man named Bob Starnes, a buyer from a similar type of store in El Cajon, California; the set of two cost the eager buyer forty dollars and brought a smile to the face of Mr. Pollard. He would try to find more of those things. Surely *someone* around here would know where they came from. And that was the last day that he saw an eagle...the two that had remained in the area for the last few weeks departed the same day that Mr. Starnes left with the last two dreamcatchers.

Bob Starnes drove away from the Eagle's Nest Trading Post and headed south on U.S. 75. He was particularly pleased with his purchase of the two feathered objects in the wooden cases. He was amazed at how he had been drawn to them; it was almost as if they were calling out to him. Bob had walked away from them twice and had returned only to purchase them in a near-hypnotic state. And now, suddenly he felt so good about the purchase. In reality, Bob was overjoyed; he rarely became excited over anything. He even began humming as he drove. He was unaware of the two golden eagles following overhead.

Two days later he arrived in Houston and was able to visit with an old friend for several hours. Bob had failed to mention to his brother, Carl, that he wanted to drive down to Houston before turning west toward San Diego. Now it was necessary to make up the time and be back at the store without hampering his brother's precious vacation. Best of all, though, he would surely make a nice profit on the two feathered treasures and a few of the other prizes that he had secured. This would help him financially as he migrated into his new business.

Even if he did not realize a great profit, he could show that he had access to unique objects of incredible beauty and quality. The car was loaded with an impressive array of Indian items that would quickly sell to the endless stream of tourists that stopped at the store in El Cajon, California. Bob was weary of being sent on buying trips by his domineering older brother. He should be a *partner*, not merely an employee. He had put up a third of the money needed to buy out the previous owner and his brother had quickly paid him back without even an offer to share in the ownership. Thus Bob began to pick up additional items separate from the 'must have' list that his brother always provided.

He was slowly building up a network of suppliers that would be loyal to him; it was only a matter of time until he would be able to open his own store. Bob wanted to be situated closer to Los Angeles and had a friend watching for a good location on the preferred route down to San Diego. When he made his move, it would be a complete surprise to his brother. Then his brother would realize that he had brought this on himself. Bob knew that it would be the best day of his life.

The following day Bob was headed west on U.S. 90 completely oblivious to the two eagles overhead. After spending the night in Van Horn, Texas, he picked up U.S. 80 and continued his westward journey. That night he stayed in Casa Grande, Arizona and was confident that he would reach El Cajon the following afternoon.

Bob did not sleep well that night; he was thinking about venturing out on his own and possibly moving up his timetable. This trip had just been too taxing; he was tired and now motivated only by the knowledge that he must endure his humiliation for just a little longer.

He was on the road at 8:30 A.M. and passed through Yuma, where he refueled just after noon. Crossing into California brought a smile to the face of the weary driver; he only had about four, maybe five more hours left depending on the traffic. Of course he would start up into the mountains after passing El Centro and Plaster City and that would be the worst part.

The two eagles continued trailing the unsuspecting man.

Just over two hours later he commenced the spectacular passage through the mountains. Traffic was moderate and he was able to keep up with most of the other vehicles except for some of the steeper grades on the mountain road. Bob made a mental note to have the engine tuned up in the near future.

Twenty-five minutes later he was struggling up yet another steep incline with the accelerator pedal floored. As he reached the apex, he could see that the highway made a gentle curve to the left, hugging the side of the mountain. He yawned and blinked his eyes several times as he started into the curve. It was at that instant that Bob suddenly dozed off.

He awakened abruptly and realized that the curve had tightened. He instinctively turned the steering wheel and tried to hit the clutch and brakes, but it was too late. The car left the roadway, became airborne and somehow missed a huge rock on the left but smacked the last post of the crude guardrail on the right. There were no witnesses except for a pair of golden eagles.

Bob uttered an extended "Nooooo!" as he gripped the steering wheel; he closed his eyes and waited. The front of the car had commenced a downward movement as soon as the front wheels left the ground; the rotation continued slowly until impact. The front of the car slammed into the ground and then continued until coming to rest on the roof and leaning against a small tree. Bob died instantly. There was no fire and the wreckage was hidden from view by the surrounding vegetation. There was one odd thing; the two wooden boxes in the back seat that had been covered by a genuine buffalo robe were now resting in plain sight on top of that robe.

The two dreamcatchers began a slow process of gaining strength under the watchful eyes of the two eagles. They would reappear when the time was right. The two eagles patiently maintained their vigil, awaiting the time when they must signal the movement of the dreamcatchers. They would be replaced by younger eagles as they approached the limit of their lifespan; this would occur twice for one of the eagles and three times for the other.

Carl Starnes did not become concerned about his brother's failure to return for two more days. He was aggravated that he had received no contact, but he was aware of the building anger that Bob had displayed recently. On the third day which was the day before he was to depart on his annual two week vacation, Carl decided to lock up the store and let Bob take care of things when he finally decided to appear. He knew that his brother would put the store back into perfect order with the new items ready for sale.

Two days into his vacation Carl phoned the store, but received no answer. He was somewhat concerned although he understood that Bob might be assisting a customer. Efforts to reach his brother at his home were futile and yet Carl was aggravated with rather than concerned about his brother. Regardless of the circumstances, Carl was not going to interrupt his vacation.

After his return and seeing that the store was exactly as he had left it, Carl commenced efforts to locate his brother. Bob *always* utilized the same return route. He checked with state police along the anticipated route and received nothing helpful. Carl called Bailey's Trading Post since that was always a stop on the route. He was surprised to learn that it had a new name and new owner. The good news was that Bob had stopped there and purchased several items for the El Cajon store and even several items for himself. The personal items did not seem relevant; Carl was worried about the new items that should have already been in the store.

Armed with this information he renewed his efforts to track down his brother unaware that Bob had traveled down to Houston. After six months he concluded that Bob had just walked away; he never considered any other possibility since his car was never located.

CHAPTER TEN

The Third Dreamcatcher

John Rawlings, Jr. felt like the luckiest man alive. He had returned from the war in the Pacific virtually unscathed in spite of the heavy fighting as the Marines moved toward Japan atoll by atoll. He had lost countless friends and acquaintances; several had died in his arms as he sought to help and console them while waiting for a corpsman. By all rights he should have been wounded or killed on numerous occasions, but it was if he led a charmed life. His photos had appeared in newspapers all over the nation and he was often recognized as 'that Marine in the photos.' Six months after the Japanese surrender he had been informed that his services were no longer required by the Marine Corps and he returned to civilian life.

John now found himself in a country that regarded him as a hero. He was twenty-five years old and single. He had money in his pockets and decided to see some of the country that was suddenly filled with opportunities for those able to take advantage of them. He visited with his family for two weeks and then set out on his new adventure with an eye peeled for something substantial in the form of employment or possibly a business venture. He chose to hitchhike rather than to purchase an automobile and was amazed at the ease with which he could travel. Once his status as a returning veteran was revealed, he was treated with respect and awe that simply overwhelmed him. He grew to enjoy the attention and free meals that accompanied his revelation or recognition and the word was passed along to all of those in the vicinity. Nothing was too good for this returning veteran.

He was a genuine hero and would talk about many of his experiences, but there were some things that he would not divulge. His audience would quickly realize from his expression that these things were just too painful for him to discuss. There was often an embarrassing silence before the conversation was re-directed to some other topic. His audience would then be extremely careful to avoid similar questions that might bring further discomfort to this special guest.

It was a sunny, comfortable Wednesday morning. John had just concluded a visit with his family in St. Louis and was now riding with a

Texas family on their way from Texarkana to Houston. They had picked him up at a little town named Diboll several miles south of Lufkin and had quickly completed all of the introductions. Marvin and Janet Holmes had two children: George, age six and Mary who had just celebrated her fourth birthday. The adults had been making small talk and were in the process of discussing a stop for lunch. They had not recognized their hitchhiker, but they had learned that he was a veteran.

"There's a little restaurant not too far from here," said Marvin. "We usually stop there since it's handy and the food is good. Jesus, look at that!"

Ahead of them a north-bound car had sustained a blowout of the left front tire and suddenly crossed over into their lane. The driver had immediately turned the wheel to the right and driven onto the shoulder, headed for the trees. Suddenly, the car contacted a pine tree and spun violently to the left. It rolled over, coming to rest precariously on the passenger's side and the roof; a small tree prevented it from rolling completely onto the roof.

Marvin had begun braking immediately and they watched the scenario as they passed. He stopped the car on the shoulder and ran after John who was already halfway to the overturned vehicle. Mary stayed with the two children.

John initially tried to open the door to assist the unconscious driver, but the door was jammed by the partially crushed roof. "I'll have to crawl inside to get him. Flag down a car and have them get some help. The driver is apparently unconscious, but breathing. I'll know more once I get inside!"

While Marvin spoke to the occupants of the first car to stop, John shattered the rear window with his boot and carefully crawled into the vehicle. The driver was in the front seat area on the passenger's side. John checked his pulse, noting that it was strong and his breathing was regular. He heard Marvin approaching.

"Help is on the way. How's the driver?"

"He seems okay, but I really can't tell much from here. We'll have to wait until more help arrives to get him out."

"John, I don't think that's an option. Gasoline is leaking from somewhere!"

"Yeah, I thought I smelled it, but it seems stronger now. See if you can tell where it's coming from."

John realized that it was imperative to get the driver out now. He leaned into the front seat area and switched off the ignition. He was able to force the driver's seat toward the steering wheel, thankful that this was a two-door rather than a four-door sedan. He squeezed into the front seat area and tried to think of the best way to remove the driver. The gasoline fumes were definitely getting stronger.

The Shaman's Legacy

"The fuel tank is leaking somewhere, but I can't tell where! Wait, it's collecting under the car! We need to get him out of there right now!"

"Okay, come over to the passenger's side; we should be able to get him out though the window," John was calm but forceful. They could not wait for additional help.

Marvin rushed to the driver's window. The small tree which prevented the automobile from rolling over onto its roof was located next to the window. Marvin broke off several small branches in order to gain access and then reached inside to grasp the driver's arms.

"Go easy, Marvin, and I'll try to stabilize his head. Once we get his head out, I want you grab him under the arms and try to cradle his head with your elbows if you can. I will push him out. Let's not waste any time because gas has soaked through the seat back and the fumes are really bad in here. Just drag him well clear and I'll help you after I get out. Okay, let's get him out!"

Marvin pulled while John pushed. The driver groaned in obvious pain which caused both men to pause. They both resumed their tasks immediately and with an increased sense of urgency. The combined effort brought the driver clear and caused Marvin to move rapidly and strike the small tree which restrained the sedan. There was a cracking sound as the tree ceased to support its metal burden.

Inside the sedan, John was now face-down with his legs up into the floorboard area and his arms fully extended as the result of the surprisingly easy exit of the driver. He heard the tree crack and felt the sedan shift violently. He also heard something large shift in the engine compartment. He pulled forward with his arms and dropped his legs in order to push himself free. During the push, his left boot went through the driver's window vent assembly.

In the engine compartment, the six-volt battery had broken loose from its normal position; it was now suspended by the positive cable which was resting against a jagged piece of sheet metal.

John tried to pull his left foot clear of the window vent, but the upper part of the boot would not pass through the opening. He shifted his weight and tried to reach his boot laces, but was unable. He pushed his left foot a little farther through the opening and braced himself for a hard jerk that might allow him to pull his foot free, either with or without the boot. He jerked his leg as hard as possible and felt the sedan shift position again; his left leg did not come free. John then heard the unmistakable sound of electrical sparking and tried once more to pull his leg free. He gave his leg another violent jerk and once again was unable to pull free. He heard the electrical crackling sound again and took a deep breath while closing his eyes. He had a brief vision of an angry eagle.

Marvin had moved the driver approximately fifty feet from the wreckage and was attempting to make him as comfortable as possible.

He knew nothing of first aid and would wait for John who seemed to be fairly knowledgeable of those things. He looked back at the sedan.

Ka-whoomp! The sedan jumped slightly and then was completely engulfed in flames and thick black smoke. The screams began almost immediately, but did not last long.

Marvin comforted his family and wished that they had not witnessed the death of this pleasant hitchhiker who had seemed so much older than he appeared. They were completely unaware of his war record. Young George pointed out a large bird circling overhead and the adults searched for it but were unable to see it. Even little Mary spotted the bird, but then she often saw things and spoke about things that did not actually exist. The large bird then flew northward, toward St. Louis.

A police car appeared shortly thereafter and was soon followed by an ambulance. Marvin provided the details of the accident and the family continued on toward Houston. Two days later they returned and visited with the injured man who was being released from the hospital.

The driver, William White, had spent two days in the hospital and was anxious to return home. He asked the Holmes family for John's personal effects so that he could return them to John's parents. Two weeks later he drove to their Missouri home and returned John's luggage and other personal articles. Bill explained how John had saved his life and that he wanted to meet the parents of a young man who would ignore his own safety and ultimately lose his life for a complete stranger. The sad but proud parents took him to John's final resting place in a small local cemetery. He was amazed to see dozens, perhaps *hundreds* of flags adorning the gravesite. It was one of the most impressive sights that he had ever witnessed. Tears ran down his cheeks as he thought about the man he had never met.

Later, at the parents' home, Bill was shown John's room. There were photos of him as a boy and one taken just before he left for the Marine Corps. Two things impressed him: a display of his medals and a beautiful object hanging above his bed. John's father explained that his oldest daughter had proudly presented it to John when he had returned home two weeks earlier; it was called a 'dreamcatcher.'

Seeing his interest in the dreamcatcher, the elder Rawlings removed it from the wall, placed it into a beautiful wooden case and presented it to the man who had so thoughtfully returned John's personal articles to them. The older man explained that John had operated a flame thrower during the mop up of several islands in the Pacific campaign. Going from cave to cave he would unleash an inferno that was difficult to imagine; death was never quick unless the cave occupants rushed outside, screaming, only to be met by a hail of gunfire. Others simply fell on their own grenades to quickly end the inevitable, having been told by superiors that the Marines took no prisoners. He had told only his father about these experiences and it had been obvious to the older man that it stirred up horrible memories. John had nightmares of being burned to death and his family had been awakened almost every night that he was home. The nightmares had commenced shortly after his return from overseas.

"It is not right that he would survive the war and then perish in the very manner he feared the most," said the tearful father as he shook Bill's hand in farewell.

The stranger thanked John's father and humbly returned to his car. He would give the gift to his daughter along with the information he had learned about the man who had saved his life. An eagle silently followed his car as he headed for his Oklahoma home.

Two days later John's family was surprised by a knock at the front door. John Rawlings, Sr. unlocked and opened the front door. A young man stood on the porch with a leather satchel in his hand.

"Is this the Rawlings residence?"

"Yes it is. Can I help you?"

This man did not appear to be a salesman.

"Mr. Rawlings, my name is Thomas Stevens and I am a reporter for the Chicago *Daily Illustrated Times*. I am so sorry for your loss. I met your son during the clean-up operations on some of the Pacific islands. I have a series of photos of John that I took during his daily routine. I was impressed by everything he did when I followed him around for several weeks. We spoke at great lengths and I came to consider him a good friend. I have a number of photographs that I think you should have. You may recognize some of them, but many were perhaps too personal and showed him as a kind and caring man rather than just a very proficient Marine. He spoke of all of you and regretted that he had not written home more often. I feel like I have known you for years."

"Mr. Stevens, please come in. This is my wife, Helen. We would love to hear everything you can tell us. John mentioned you in several of his letters and we've read your stories in the newspapers. Please have a seat. This is an honor for us. Would you care for some coffee?"

"No Sir, I'm fine."

The senior Rawlings was soft-spoken, but it was obvious that he was a tough man who was proud of his son. Thomas sat on the badly worn sofa and was joined by the parents...one on either side.

Thomas produced a folder with dozens of 8 by 10 photos, each one showing a young, handsome man with a ready smile and surrounded by other young men who obviously looked up to him. There were photos of him sleeping amid the rubble of war. There were a few that showed him relaxing near the water, but with his rifle close by. Still others showed him with his flame thrower and full battle gear. There were even some that showed him comforting some of his fellow Marines who had been wounded. There was also one of him and the famous man who was now seated on their sofa.

Thomas then produced a second folder. "These are photos of your son at work. Some of them are not pleasant and you might want to discard them. Some were not released to the wire services simply because I felt that they were much too graphic. This was what John had to do and not what he *wanted* to do. It troubled him deeply. I regret that I missed his funeral, but I am comforted to know that he died saving another man's life; that was the Marine that I came to know quite well. He was certainly one of the bravest men I ever met. He was truly a hero and I am extremely proud to have known him as a friend. If there is ever anything that I can do for you, please contact me." He handed one of his cards to each of them.

Mr. Rawlings nodded and shook the reporter's hand and his wife hugged this famous man who had made a special trip to bring those wonderful photos. They would never forget this special act of kindness just as they had so deeply appreciated the return of John's personal effects by the man whose life he had saved. That was what had made John so special...he always brought out the best in people.

There had been no mention of John's nightmares and in a quirk of fate, Thomas returned to Chicago unaware that he had narrowly missed information that could have quickly led him to the third dreamcatcher. That dreamcatcher was now hanging over the bed of a young woman in northern Oklahoma. Thomas would find out about John's nightmares upon returning to Chicago and he would depart for St. Louis the following day.

Meanwhile, Navy Lieutenant (Junior Grade) James "Jimbo" Prescott Johnson had just leveled off at four thousand feet of altitude and was in the process of setting his North American SNJ trainer for maximum range cruise testing. This was also a scheduled navigation training flight with some required segments to be flown in instrument conditions. He enjoyed flying the SNJ; it was a stable and predictable airplane with no really bad characteristics. In a few weeks he would be transitioning to a real fleet airplane instead of a trainer, but this was just one of the necessary evils. He understood the value and the wisdom of honing basic skills while gaining experience; some of his peers were only anxious to fly the newest and hottest aircraft available. He was convinced that many of them would perish in the process. Thus he methodically absorbed as much knowledge about flight characteristics of different aircraft as possible. He would be ready at the proper time; there would be a need for experienced pilots to test and evaluate new aircraft and he would be one of those pilots.

He smiled. "I was fine until I tried to climb through the fence...." He spotted the car beneath his airplane. "Oh my God!" He dropped his 'chute and rushed to the wreckage, his heart pounding.

The crowd turned as one and followed his progress. The only sound was that of an approaching siren. The crowd automatically turned toward the sound and then returned its gaze to the pilot.

Jimbo reached the wreckage and spotted the lifeless body of Elsie White; his heart sank. Tears filled the eyes of the young Naval Aviator as the full realization of what had happened sunk in. He had caused this; he had killed this woman. He immediately thought of other possibilities that he could have chosen. He could have picked a different heading before bailing out. He could have waited longer. Maybe he should have stayed with the stricken plane. He would agonize for almost three weeks before returning to flight status.

Thomas Stevens drove from Chicago to the Rawlings home near St. Louis. He had dreamed of the eagle and the old Indian again; this time the Indian repeated his message only it somehow seemed to stress urgency. He drove fast but carefully, reaching the Rawlings home in record time.

His knock on the door was answered almost immediately. He was greeted by the pleasant smile of Helen Rawlings.

"Mr. Stevens, how nice to see you again! Please come in."

"Hello Mrs. Rawlings. How are you today?" He stepped into the living room and glanced around for her husband.

"He's still out working on a tractor. May I ask what brings you back here? And thank you so much for the pictures...you were right about some of them being hard to look at."

Thomas noticed how her facial expression softened as she spoke of the photos. "I'm only glad I was able to locate them and deliver them to you. Now this may seem odd, but did John have an Indian thing called a 'dreamcatcher' here or somewhere else?"

"Oh yes, our daughter bought it for him as a 'welcome home from the war' gift. It was so beautiful." Helen's face lit up just thinking about the dreamcatcher.

"Can I see it please? And did John really have nightmares? This is very important to me."

"I'm sorry, but we gave it to Bill White...the man that John rescued from the burning car. He brought John's things to us and was fascinated by the dreamcatcher thing, so we gave it to him. Were we wrong to do that? Oh, and yes, John did have terrible nightmares; he would not discuss the nightmares with us, but it had something to do with the war." There was obvious concern in her voice.

probably from the base in Olathe. I'll stay here just in case the pilot shows up."

The woman returned to her car and sped away while the man listened and watched for approaching traffic. He wandered back and forth through the intersection alternately checking the highway and the wreckage.

Neither saw the eagle that ceased circling overhead and returned to monitor the dreamcatcher.

Meanwhile, Jimbo was descending into the lower overcast layer and straining to see through the mist. The lack of visual references was unnerving and he moved his head very slowly to avoid vertigo. He hoped to spot the ground with enough time to prepare for contact with whatever was in his path; his main concern was trees or power lines. He was quite fortunate and spotted what appeared to be open land or maybe pasture. He had just enough time to prepare for landing. He hit hard and rolled with his inertia just like he had been taught. His parachute collapsed immediately and he released the three harness buckles. He stood, arched his back and rolled the harness straps from his shoulders. Then he evaluated his condition; he was terribly thirsty but otherwise fine and his worries switched to finding a way out. He knew that most roads were oriented north-south or east-west. The side roads were usually the same except where terrain features forced a deviation. He had no hints and decided to move south since he remembered that there was a small town in that general direction. He thought about continuing west and perhaps locating the plane, but with this poor visibility, the odds of finding it were poor. He gathered his parachute and made it as small as he could before locking the harness straps over it; he hefted the 'chute' and headed south.

He walked for approximately five minutes before spotting the barbed wire fence and then the gravel road. He tossed the parachute over the fence and then spent several minutes trying to slip between the strands of barbed wire. He eventually made it, but cut himself several times before completing his task. "I survive the bailout, but get hurt crossing a fence," he thought wryly to himself.

Once on the road, he headed west. Thirty-five minutes later he reached the intersection and spotted his airplane. There was now a crowd of twelve people who stared at the wreckage from a respectable distance...just in case.

One of the men spotted Jimbo and exclaimed, "There's the pilot!"

The remainder of the crowd turned and stared at the approaching pilot, but did not move and remained completely silent.

"Well, I've had better days," he stated in an attempt to let them know that he was okay.

"Mister, you're bleeding," said a woman who noticed some of his new scratches. The others nodded in agreement.

problems: loss of smooth, continuous engine power and imbalance due to the loss of the piston which was now welded in place at the top of its cylinder.

A suddenly sweating Jimbo immediately pulled the throttle back to idle and felt the vibration decrease substantially. Pulse racing, he quickly broadcast a 'mayday' as he began preparing to bailout. He slowed the aircraft and turned to a westerly heading, knowing that a town was ahead on his planned route. As far as he knew, the cloud cover extended all the way to ground level. He really did not want to bail out, but attempting a forced landing on instruments would probably be fatal. His decision was made; he opened the canopy, pulled the mixture lever to *Idle Cut-Off*, moved the fuel selector handle to *OFF* and moved the battery switch to *OFF*. He 'popped' his lap belt, threw the shoulder harness straps toward the rear of the cockpit and disconnected his radio cords. Jimbo sighed, raised the seat slightly and stepped up onto the seat cushion. He took a deep breath and dove from the stricken aircraft. He counted to three and pulled the ripcord; he was soon rewarded by the abrupt blossoming of the canopy and visually confirmed a good 'chute.' He was then able to locate his airplane just before it disappeared into the cloud cover. He hoped that he would have decent visibility and would come down near a road.

At that same instant, Elsie White slowed to a stop at the intersection of her road and the main highway. Visibility was not that bad, but she still hated turning north onto that highway since some drivers just drove much too fast and those Oklahoma roads were hilly. Therefore she would accelerate quickly once she made up her mind to go. The sudden vision of a ferocious eagle briefly entered her thought process. Confused, she hesitated for a minute or so and then decided to roll down her window and listen for approaching traffic before making her turn. With the window down, she listened and briefly heard a strange sound just before the stricken Navy trainer slammed into her car. The car and airplane continued across the intersection right in front of two cars headed opposite directions; Elsie was the only fatality and there was no fire.

Shaken, the drivers of both cars quickly stopped and cautiously approached the wreckage. It appeared that there was only one occupant in the car and she was obviously dead; the pilot of the plane had apparently bailed out. One of the drivers thanked God for sparing her and prayed for the soul of the deceased and as an afterthought, prayed that the pilot or pilots were safe. The other driver just felt lucky that he had not been killed.

The man suddenly realized that fuel was leaking from the damaged airplane. "We need to move away...this thing might explode. You're headed north; the next town is about three or four miles from here. Let someone know what happened so they can get the police out here. That's a Navy plane, so they need to let the Navy know, too. The plane is

Jimbo eased the throttle back to 16 inches of manifold pressure and brought the propeller control back to 1,800 rpm. He then reset the throttle to 18 inches of manifold pressure and slowly brought the mixture control back from 'rich' to 'normal.' He made his final trim adjustments and checked his fuel quantity. He wrote down the fuel quantity and the time; he could now evaluate this power setting for speed and rate of fuel consumption. Then he could concentrate on the navigation portion of the flight. He was presently on a southerly course with approximately fifteen minutes until his turn to the southwest. He would cross-check his bearings from at least two offset radio stations to verify his progress. His confidence was bolstered by both readings which confirmed that his groundspeed was just under his projected estimate.

He was flying above a low overcast which was predicted to reach the surface farther south and below another cloud layer that darkened the sky above yet did not contain any significant turbulence. While he was actually encountering visual flight conditions, he was unable to see any physical reference points other than the stratus type clouds. He knew that clouds were not normally a good source of reference, but they did serve as a backup for the sparse instrumentation in the aircraft. Jimbo was acutely aware of the hazards of relying on only one reference point; one of his instructors had survived a crash caused by assuming that a cloud layer was perfectly horizontal. Using the cloud layer as a reference rather than cross-checking his other instrumentation had caused him to experience vertigo and ultimately lose control of the aircraft. He regained control, but not in time to prevent the aircraft from impacting a large pine tree. The instructor was extremely effective in communicating his mistake and sported a very impressive scar on his forehead from impact with the canopy bow. His wide-eyed students would always remember his warning to "never fixate on just one attitude reference."

Jimbo motored on, making his turn to the southwest right on cue. According to his chart, he had crossed over into Oklahoma a few minutes earlier. This new leg was forty-seven miles in length and would culminate in a turn to the northwest. Unknown to the young pilot, an oil ring on the piston of the number four cylinder had broken which drastically altered the lubrication process; this started a steady deterioration of that cylinder. Initially, the only indication in the cockpit was a slight, but slow increase in cylinder head temperature and engine oil temperature. Minute metal shavings began to appear as the condition worsened. This process continued as the moving piston ground its way along the cylinder wall generating more and more friction. Finally, the number four cylinder piston seized as it reached the top dead center position and the retreating connecting rod snapped.

The effect was instantaneous. A violent vibration threatened to tear the engine from its mounts. The vibration was caused by two distinct

"No, you were not wrong to give it away. I'm just doing a story and tracing how things like this move around." He had no desire to even attempt to try to explain.

"You're not telling me everything; there is more to this story." She walked to the worn sofa, sat and then patted the cushion next to her. "I reckon I have time to listen."

"Mrs. Rawlings...."

"Helen."

"Helen, you would think that I was crazy if I told you what I'm trying to do." He walked to the sofa and sat.

"Not long ago I stumbled onto a very bizarre set of circumstances involving these dreamcatchers. I think there were originally five and two have been destroyed. I am searching for the other three."

"Why?"

"According to everything I have learned so far, bad things happen to those who possess them."

"Bad things such as...." She stared deeply into his eyes.

"It seems that they die and it has something to do with their nightmares." Thomas braced himself for her next words.

"So you think that John's dreamcatcher killed him? Do you realize how farfetched that sounds?" Helen sat back on the sofa and exhaled loudly.

"I don't have time to go into great detail, but I need to know how to find the guy who received John's dreamcatcher."

"We gave it to a Bill White. He lives near a small town in Northern Oklahoma...same name as one of the states."

Helen hesitated for a few seconds, her brow wrinkled in concentration.

"Delaware! That's it, Delaware. He was going to give it to his daughter."

Thomas stood abruptly. "I'm sorry, Helen I must leave now; I must locate that dreamcatcher. I will try to explain more later. Please say hello to your husband for me. I'm afraid that I have a long trip ahead of me."

He hurried to his car and was soon on his way, leaving a bewildered Helen Rawlings staring at him from the front door. He would reach Delaware, Oklahoma two days later after a mechanic replaced the water pump in his car.

Elsie White's family was overwhelmed by her death. Her dad had only recently recovered from an automobile accident in east Texas. After a brief hospital stay, he had delivered to a grieving family the personal effects of the man who had sacrificed his life to rescue him; the family had given him a special gift that had belonged to his rescuer. He had presented the gift to Elsie who loved surprises. She was completely overwhelmed by the beautiful gift and had him immediately hang the Indian thing over her bed.

The local paper carried the sad story. The interview with the family revealed that Elsie refused to fly because of her fear of being involved in a plane crash. She had heard and read of so many terrible stories that there was absolutely no possibility that she would ever set foot in an airplane. Unfortunately, she sometimes had nightmares about plane crashes. Her father told the local reporter that "It was unfair that she would die in a plane crash without even flying." The story soon appeared on the wire services accenting the irony.

A war-hardened photo-journalist would find out additional information when he checked back with his boss in Chicago. He was already enroute to Delaware, Oklahoma.

Bill White sadly helped remove his daughter's belongings from the house that she had shared with another young woman, Sally Benson. Elsie's roommate could not afford the entire rent and chose to return to her Little Rock hometown; she apologized for not staying for the funeral. Bill gave her the dreamcatcher since it brought back too many painful memories for him. Sally accepted the gift in its beautiful case and presented it to her brother, Terry, in Little Rock, Arkansas late that night. She had felt a compulsion to deliver the dreamcatcher as soon as possible; there was a sense of urgency that she did not understand and yet she never questioned it. She never saw the eagle that had taken up residence nearby.

Terrence Benson was a school teacher and would surely appreciate it; he did not need to know the circumstances behind the gift. To Sally's delight, he was clearly pleased with it and felt the need to immediately place it over his bed. He left town the next day in an attempt to obtain a better teaching job in Texas. Overhead, an eagle followed his path.

"What a horrible place to stop," Terry thought as he stepped from his overheated automobile. The red Oklahoma dust and his dry throat made a lousy combination. This particular day was not going well for the single school teacher as he attempted what should have been a routine trip from Little Rock, Arkansas to Amarillo, Texas. He was hoping to land a job in the Amarillo school system. He was certain that his mere presence in early May would give him the job in September. Now he was at the mercy of a local mechanic who seemed less than enthusiastic about repairing his car. That was due to the heat that was beginning to rise in the morning hours.

After a late start the previous day, Terry had spent a terrible night in eastern Oklahoma and could not even remember the name of the little town if it even had a name. Every truck that went past his place of lodging had honked at someone or something and it was far too hot to close the window; the anemic fan in the small room was of little value. He had arisen extremely aggravated and tired, just eager to leave that awful place behind. He had driven for almost an hour before realizing that he had not eaten breakfast and was really hungry. He had stopped shortly thereafter at a small place with a huge sign that bragged about its home cooking. It had been cool inside and was absolutely spotless. He had been certain that he could get a decent meal and plenty of coffee.

He had ordered his standard breakfast: two eggs sunny side up, sausage and toast. He had also ordered a cup of coffee and promptly received it along with a glass of cold water. His waitress, Millie, was pleasant and efficient even though he thought that she smiled too much. He had begun to forget about the previous night; today would be a much better day. It would be hot, but not too bad as long as he was not forced to stop for road construction or repairs.

Terry's breakfast had arrived in record time. The eggs were over easy instead of sunny side up, the toast was much too dark and the sausage was essentially tasteless. He considered telling Millie to take it back and try again, but that would just take more of his valuable time. He wondered how things so simple to fix could turn out so badly. After thinking about it as he ate, he had realized that there was no competition in the area and therefore no motivation to do a better job. The coffee had been excellent, however, and he really needed it. He drank two cups of coffee and even polished off the glass of water, noting a slightly metallic taste. He had left two dollars on the table and departed; Amarillo, Texas was still a long drive. He had driven away hoping to make up for the time he had spent at the little restaurant.

Now he was stuck in this hick town waiting for the filling station mechanic to figure out what was wrong with his car. Terry could feel the increasing heat and made a point of trying to stay in the shade as he wandered slowly through the town. There was nothing spectacular about the little town; there was a bank, a restaurant, a doctor's office and several stores. He felt the sweat trickle down his back and wished for a breeze. There was a small grocery store ahead and it seemed like a good time to stop and grab a Royal Crown Cola.

He sauntered into the store and went straight to the ice cooler. He grabbed an RC and popped off the cap using the built-in opener on the cooler. He savored the first big swallow even though it burned his throat. He spent several minutes walking around the store and listening to the floor creak under his weight. Finally, he paid for the soft drink, placed the empty bottle in the wooden crate located next to the cooler and returned to the sidewalk. He wiped his brow and then continued his exploration of the town. He considered it odd that there were very few people moving about, but then the heat was likely the cause. He looked up at the bright, cloudless sky and slowly shook his head. He just wanted to leave this place.

It was 10:17 when Terry walked past the bank. There was a car parked at the end of the block, directly in his path and he noticed that the engine was running. He thought he could see someone sitting behind the wheel. He thought of earlier days when that sometimes indicated that a robbery was in progress, but immediately dismissed the thought; the Bonnie and Clyde days were gone.

Suddenly he heard the sound of rapid footsteps behind him and turned just in time to be shoved aside by a man leaving the bank with a bag in his left hand and a pistol in his right. Frightened, Terry flattened himself against the building just as another individual armed with a rifle stepped out onto the sidewalk.

"Stop right there!" yelled the second man.

Terry watched as the robber slowed to a stop, turned and pointed the pistol at his adversary. Both men fired simultaneously and Terry saw the robber fall. He glanced back at the pursuer and saw him drop to a sitting position against the bank building, moaning and clutching his neck with the now bloody rifle across his lap. Visibly shaken, Terry turned back toward the robber and noticed that he was still breathing, but with great difficulty. There was a widening pool of blood emerging from beneath him. Terry walked cautiously over to the man who was sprawled facedown on the sidewalk, the pistol next to his hand. Afraid that the robber might arise and start shooting, Terry bent down and carefully picked up the pistol while keeping his eyes on the robber; he was ready to run if the guy even moved. In a trance-like state, he straightened up and stared at the man, wondering what to do next. He then realized that he was shaking. The car that he had noticed earlier suddenly backed around the corner and stopped beside him.

"Throw me the bag of money," commanded a deep voice from inside the car.

"Turn around, mister!" This voice came from behind him.

Startled, Terry spun around to see what was going on; he heard the car drive away.

"Drop the gun," said a very nervous bank teller who had retrieved the bloody rifle from his fellow bank employee.

Terry unconsciously raised the pistol and started to explain, but never had the chance to utter a word. The rifle fired for the second time that day just as Terry's eyes widened and he realized that he was in serious trouble. It was his last conscious thought. He died moments later after mumbling to an angry eagle, "I asked for them sunny side up."

Overhead, a lone eagle ceased its circling and headed eastward, back toward Little Rock.

The Shaman's Legacy

Terry's funeral was a sad affair. There were numerous former students who turned out still in shock that this man, a great teacher in their eyes, had been killed. The details of his shooting had included questions as to why he had picked up the robber's pistol. The family was unable to give an answer citing a terrible experience that occurred when he was five years old.

Terry had been left with his thirteen year old brother, Jerry, while their parents spent a long day making plans to have a new house built. Jerry and several of his friends were going to do some serious target shooting with rifles and a shotgun. Jerry told his brother to stay home until he returned. As soon as he left the house, though, Terry followed while remaining out of sight. He watched Jerry meet up with four friends but needed a better vantage point. He carefully worked his way around to the far end of the lot where they had met; the lot served as a repository for junk. Terry crawled over to an old metal sign and then chose a large wooden box as a superior place from which to observe.

The four boys with rifles were pretending to be deputies having a shoot-out with Bonnie and Clyde; the wooden box was Clyde's automobile. Just as Terry started to peek around the side of the box, the four rifles and the shotgun began firing.

Terry screamed as the wood chips flew! He was afraid to run and kept screaming as he tried to flatten himself against the ground. The five boys fired for almost thirty seconds before someone thought it to be prudent to investigate the screams. Once they had determined that the screams were coming from the far end of the lot, they rushed to the general area and discovered Terry with his eyes closed, hands over his ears and still screaming.

Terry was not injured by the gunfire, but suffered a different kind of injury. He developed an acute aversion to guns of any type. Loud noises would cause him to freeze and then begin trembling. He would never lose his overwhelming fear and suffered occasional nightmares involving people shooting at him.

The newspaper carried the story with an abbreviated account of the childhood experience. That, coupled with the narrative of his death, produced a statement of how bad luck had intervened and he was killed by something that had haunted him for years.

The wire services picked up the story due to the ironic content; once again, a famous photo-journalist was jolted by a familiar theme and would depart Delaware, Oklahoma immediately for Little Rock. He had just confirmed that the dreamcatcher had been owned by the late Elsie White and that her roommate had taken it with her to Little Rock. He was weary, but knew that he was closing in on the elusive dreamcatcher. He headed for Little Rock after quickly checking his maps; time was critical.

Sally Benson once again removed the dreamcatcher from the wall; this time it was her late brother's room. She placed it into its wooden case and delivered it to a long-time friend who had admired it when she had presented it to Terry. Sally had once again felt an unmistakable urgency to give the dreamcatcher to someone else. This time it seemed that it was even more important than before to quickly find a new owner for the magnificent gift. She briefly thought that the dreamcatcher itself was urging her to acquire a new owner; she dismissed the thought as silly.

Ewell Hill gladly accepted the dreamcatcher from Sally and quickly opened the case to assure himself that it was indeed his. He stared at this special gift and quickly forgot about the circumstances that had brought it to him. He thanked Sally profusely as she left and then sat on his sofa admiring his new prize. He made the perfectly logical assumption that a dreamcatcher would naturally be placed in a bedroom and decided to hang it on the wall opposite his east-facing window. That way the morning sun would properly illuminate this marvelous treasure. Ewell felt a sudden *need* to hang his new treasure immediately. He measured the width of the wall, halved it and then made a mark for future reference. Then he brought the dreamcatcher into the room and placed it so that the bottom of the hoop was at eye level. He placed a mark for the nail directly above the mark for the center of the wall. Ewell quickly placed the dreamcatcher on the bed and went in search of a hammer and nail. He soon had his magnificent prize hanging perfectly. It was clearly the focal point of the room and he felt immensely proud, no, *relieved* that it was now hanging there in his room.

Ewell awoke early the next morning. He would celebrate his twenty-fifth birthday tomorrow and knew that his friends and family had planned some sort of surprise. He was not aware of any details and was not looking forward to the necessary requirement to act surprised. It would be exactly eight years since his accident; he would rather just forget the whole thing. After all, he was not a little boy; he was much too old for birthday parties.

He had quietly turned seventeen years of age back in 1939 with just a small acknowledgement from his family. After finishing his part-time job, he had returned home and eaten supper with his family. He had then borrowed the family car and left soon thereafter to catch up with his friends. It was Friday night and he met up with three of his pals, one of whom produced a bottle of booze. Another had purchased a case of soda and the four boys along with the bottle of cheap whiskey soon migrated to the car with the soda in it. Initially, they each sipped from the whiskey bottle and each commented on how great it was even though each thought it tasted horrible. Ewell mentioned that they could pour it into their bottles of soda and lessen the risk of being spotted drinking alcohol. Everyone agreed that it was a smart thing to do while silently cheering the fact that the bad taste would be lessened.

They had sat in the parking lot at their favorite hangout which was an early version of the 'Malt 'n Burgers' or 'Dairy Queens' that would eventually become commonplace. Being teenagers, they still required excessive amounts of food and would purchase food periodically which allowed them to remain in the parking lot for extended periods without angering the owner. The four boys sat and talked about girls, their jobs and the remainder of their final year of high school. It had rained for the previous three days and they were glad that it had finally ceased. After an hour, the booze was gone yet they lingered and chose not to try to obtain more. Ewell was the first to call it quits for the night.

"I've gotta work tomorrow. I think I'll head on home." He waited for the inevitable verbal assault on his stamina.

"Yeah, me too," said his closest friend, Chuck. That stopped any comments from the other two boys.

Three of them went to their own cars and left. Ewell was following Chuck who lived on the same road, but farther out of town. Ewell thought that Chuck was driving a little too fast, but chose to travel at the same speed. All went well until the left turn just before the bridge over Rock Creek. Chuck had slowed slightly for the curve and Ewell followed suit.

Halfway through the curve, a raccoon chose that instant to dart across the road in front of Ewell. He instinctively swerved to the right to avoid the raccoon, but it was not out of concern for the life of the animal. He cut the steering wheel back to the left, over-correcting, and then back to the right in a vain attempt to regain control. Once the right hand tires touched the soft shoulder, he realized that he was leaving the roadway. He braked hard to no avail and tried to steer clear of the rapidly approaching trees. He was able to steer between two large trees that were close together, but that was better than hitting either one head-on. At the last second he realized that the car would not pass though the narrow opening and saw the blackness of the flooded creek. He braced himself as best he could.

He was moving at perhaps twenty-five miles per hour and braced against the steering wheel when he struck first the tree on the left and then the one on the right. He was aware of a 'crack' from his right wrist and a sharp pain. That was followed by the front of the car splashing into the flood waters and submerging. Water immediately rushed into the car as it came to an abrupt halt when the rear bumper snagged the two trees. Ewell's body had shifted to the right when his wrist snapped and his left foot had slipped between the clutch pedal and the brake pedal. He was now trapped as the water continued to pour into the half-submerged automobile. Ewell initially panicked and tried to yank his foot free. The driver's window had broken and was the source of most of the inrushing water. He was finally able to pull against the flow with his left hand and move enough to push the clutch pedal in with his right foot and to pull his left foot free. He was just barely able to keep his head above the cold water. The front of the car continued to submerge and Ewell tried frantically to open the driver's door. Unable, he tried the passenger door reaching around with his left hand; it was also jammed. The water was rising rapidly and the pocket of air was retreating!

Hampered by his useless right wrist, he somehow managed to crawl into the back seat as the water continued to rise. He tried to kick out the windows for the back seat, but could not brace himself adequately. Time was running out!

Chuck had seen the sudden erratic pattern of Ewell's headlights and wondered what the crazy fool was doing. Then he saw the headlights disappear. He stopped and backed up as best he could by looking out through the windshield; there was no room to turn around. He located the car approximately one minute after Ewell crashed. Using the tail lights as a guide and with some illumination from his own headlights, he rushed to find his friend.

"Ewell! Ewell! Where are you?" There was no response.

Inside the car, Ewell was holding his head in the air pocket near the rear window hoping somehow to escape. He tried breaking the rear window, but could not. He was running out of ideas. The water continued to rise and Ewell, a non-swimmer, briefly considered trying to escape through the driver's window. He was too frightened to try; he was out of options! He screamed for help and pounded on the rear window as the air pocket continued to shrink.

Chuck jumped onto the trunk of the sedan. He heard the muffled screams and pounding. Chuck spotted Ewell's head tilted back in an attempt to stay with a small pocket of air; he also saw bubbles escaping from the edge of the rear window. As the pocket of air disappeared, he raised his right foot and stomped as hard as he could. The rear window partially shattered and Ewell's head soon popped into view; he was coughing profusely! Chuck knelt and helped his friend exit the doomed car just as water rushed out where the window had been. They fell clear of Ewell's car and caught their breath.

Ewell had subsequently developed a great fear of drowning which continually plagued him. He had tried to forget the terrifying incident, but could not. He had religiously avoided all possibilities that could put his life in danger from contact with water. He had even tried to avoid bridges, but that was not always possible. He had been encouraged to learn to swim, but had adamantly dismissed that possibility as rather stupid. Thus he had never set foot in a boat or even fished from the shoreline just in case; taunts by his friends fell on deaf ears. Worst of all, the nightmares had begun.

Late in the afternoon Ewell went next door to care for the neighbor's dog. Tomorrow the neighbor would return and relieve him of this minor inconvenience to his life. It was not that he hated to be tied down while caring for the dog...the neighbor had just assumed that he would relish the opportunity and did not even consider the possibility that Ewell might have other plans. And, of course, tomorrow was his 'surprise' birthday party.

Ewell had entered the yard through the back gate and was immediately welcomed by the six-month old German shepherd mix; in his haste, he failed to check the latch on the gate. He played with the dog for a few minutes before going into the house and getting some food. It would soon be dark and he was anxious to return to his own home. He had hoped to see the eagle again, but he missed it this time; perhaps it was roosting or whatever eagles did when it got dark. He felt that the eagle was a sign of good luck; this was the first one he had ever seen.

He remembered that he needed to water his neighbor's new rose bush on the West side of the house and after feeding *Buster*, he filled his huge water dish and then filled the bucket with water for the rose bush. He carried the water out to the thirsty plant and was soon joined by 45 pounds of happy puppy. In the fading light he watched as Buster suddenly ran toward the back gate which was now standing wide open.

Ewell dropped the bucket and sprinted after the dog. He briefly saw what seemed to be a very angry eagle staring at him. So intent was his focus that he forgot about the clothesline. Running at full speed, the first steel wire caught him just below the nose. His head snapped back violently and all motor skills in both arms and both legs immediately ceased. He crashed to the ground in pain from the violent contact with the clothesline and confused by the abrupt cessation of running ability. His non-responsive body bounced once and he came to rest face down in Buster's large water dish. He instinctively held his breath and tried to use his arms to lift his head clear of the dish. Realizing that his arms did not function, he still tried to lift his head clear but was not able. On the verge of panic, he tried to turn his head, but could not move it far enough. His lungs were now screaming for fresh air! Then he realized that he was going to drown in a dog's water bowl and all alone. Ewell held his breath as his heart pounded and his lungs urged him to breath. He tried to will his body to respond, but it was to no avail. Lungs bursting, he finally inhaled as his tears mixed with the water. He never heard the flapping sound when the sentinel eagle took to the air from its perch in a tree fifty feet away.

Upon his return the next morning, the neighbor found his overgrown puppy running loose and was furious; he found Ewell's lifeless body thirty minutes later and was ashamed of his earlier anger.

The tragedy and the irony were sent over the wire service as the only news out of Little Rock, Arkansas that day. Forty-five minutes later Thomas Stevens, the famous photo-journalist, became aware of Ewell's death after speaking to his editor by telephone and quickly resumed his now frantic search knowing for certain that he was very close to the elusive dreamcatcher.

Thomas had tremendous flexibility when it came to picking his assignments. The editor knew that this famous man could do no wrong in the eyes of his adoring public. He even excused the preposterous notion that these dreamcatcher things were killing people...a spectacular story was certain to emerge. Of course, going public was certain to bring ridicule to this famous man. But as long as Thomas continued to produce, he could do mostly as he pleased much to the chagrin of his fellow reporters who had gradually ceased their hero-worship over the last few months.

The February, 1946 return of the dreams with the eagle and the old Indian along with the "Find them; burn them" message had been a surprise after their absence during the war years. Thomas took the return to mean that the dreamcatchers were suddenly active again instead of destroyed as he had hoped. He discussed what he had previously learned with his extremely skeptical editor and showed him the notes and what he perceived to be truth rather than coincidence. The editor was polite and asked questions which hinted at how crazy the whole idea was. However, Thomas did have some convincing arguments about the involvement of at least one wealthy individual from Chicago who had been involved in the 'Lewis Farm Incident' as the editor loved to refer to it. That story and a few follow-up stories had really launched Thomas' career. The editor would humor him...at least for the time being.

The editor was now in regular contact with Thomas as he worked his way across Missouri, Oklahoma and now Arkansas. He truly wanted to believe that Thomas was right, but was terrified that he might be. Even so, he could not jeopardize the reputation of the paper. He was formulating his own story of how a well-known reporter lost touch with reality probably as a result of his terrible observations during the war. It would be a great story, although heartbreaking. He was saddened that such a story would end a brilliant career, but he was a realist.

Thomas was now enroute to the residence of the newly-deceased Ewell Hill. He had been impressed with the speed with which the dreamcatcher changed hands...it was almost as if the dreamcatcher itself were attempting to do as much destruction as possible while eluding its pursuer. Did the dreamcatcher have a will of its own or was it completely inanimate and not capable of protecting itself? Was the dreamcatcher learning how to survive? What would happen if and when he confronted it? Thomas shuddered as he thought about it. Nevertheless, he pressed on with the search.

Thomas arrived at the small house that Ewell shared with another young man. Those who had chosen to extend their condolences and those who were relatives had already gathered at the Hill family residence located two miles away. Thomas walked up to the front door and knocked. Upon realizing that no one was home, he tried the door and found it to be unlocked. He entered cautiously.

"Anybody home? Hello!"

The lack of a response strengthened his resolve to locate the dreamcatcher. He started down the hallway and was startled by the sudden appearance of an image of the old Indian on the door on his right. Thomas felt a building feeling of anxiety. He cautiously opened the door and there was the dreamcatcher hanging on the wall across from the window. The wooden case was on the floor next to a small table. His anxiety continued to increase.

With shaking hands, he grabbed the case, opened it and placed it on the bed. Then he removed the dreamcatcher from the wall and quickly placed it into the case. He carefully closed the case, latched it and left the house. His anxiety decreased somewhat as he walked to his car. Thomas never noticed the eagle that had suddenly taken great interest in him.

Thomas initially toyed with the idea of taking it back to Chicago, but decided that it needed to be destroyed immediately. He drove out of town and stopped in a rural area off the main road. He carried the wooden case to an open space, placed it on the ground and collected some brush. He took some newspaper and a box of matches from the car and then built a pile almost two feet high before placing the opened case on the top. He briefly admired the deadly beauty of the dreamcatcher and then stuck a match; a sudden breeze extinguished it. Thomas made repeated attempts to bring a lighted match in contact with the newspaper and each time a gust or sudden breeze would blow out the flame. He tried shielding the flame with a cupped hand and that failed. He finally fashioned a paper shield and was able to bring the flame to the newspaper. The paper caught quickly and the fire began to crackle almost immediately. Thomas breathed a deep sigh of relief. He wondered if the dreamcatcher was somehow fighting for its own survival; he dismissed the thought as just coincidence. Then he realized that there was not even a hint of a breeze...leaves on nearby trees were motionless. This dreamcatcher had apparently become stronger!

Thomas watched as the wooden box began to burn and then the dreamcatcher suddenly erupted into flame. He watched it intently to see what it would do; he did not know what to expect. The pile of brush was now burning fiercely and suddenly he saw movement! Unconsciously, he stepped back.

Thomas watched an eagle emerge from the middle of the small inferno. He shuddered as it turned and looked, no, *glared* at him. Then it screeched! A chill like he had never experienced before enveloped his body and his pulse raced. Then suddenly the eagle launched itself in a shower of sparks and embers and flew away toward the West, toward the lands of the Lakota.

The sentinel eagle observing from a nearby tree cocked its head briefly as if listening to something and then returned to its normal lifestyle.

Thomas was shaken, but glad to know that he had destroyed the third dreamcatcher. That left two more. Then he wondered aloud, "Could the two remaining dreamcatchers also be growing in power?"

He shuddered at the thought. At that moment he realized that his camera was still in the car; an image of the eagle emerging from the fire would have been some of the proof that he would soon need. That is, if the image could have been captured on film. He did not even have a picture of the dreamcatcher...how could that have happened? He wondered briefly if the dreamcatcher had somehow blocked the thought of taking a photo from his mind; perhaps it was just his eagerness to eliminate the dreamcatcher.

Now he could head back to Chicago. Now he had an amazing story to tell; that is, if he dared. He phoned Sarah and let her know what had happened and that he would leave Little Rock tomorrow after getting some sleep. He would now be able to spend some time with his family for a change. Even so, he still had to locate and destroy the remaining dreamcatchers. Yet there would be no clues, no visions nor dreams to send him in pursuit of those last two dreamcatchers...not for a long time.

Meanwhile, Sally Benson asked Ewell's family if she could have the dreamcatcher. She wanted to keep it to remember the two friends she had lost; it was suddenly very important to her. Ewell's parents assured her that it was indeed hers. Then, without warning, her urgent need to own the dreamcatcher abruptly disappeared. Sally was subsequently unable to find it and wondered briefly where it had gone; then she forgot about it entirely. She was never even aware that Thomas Stevens, the famous war correspondent, had been in town. And, of course, that knowledge would not have mattered to her, anyway.

CHAPTER ELEVEN

Quiet Times

Thomas and Sarah now had more time on their hands. Thomas was in great demand for speaking engagements and the newspaper was pleased to have him as a nation-wide reminder of the rising importance of the news media field. He was also free to pick stories which either interested him or would capture the hearts of this post-war nation. He wrote of veterans who returned home to a world that sometimes made no sense to them. He covered the plight of those whose injuries and experiences would lead them down a path of self-destruction. His delight, however, was the celebration of those who returned and prospered through hard work and good ethics.

Thomas also commenced a campaign to educate the American public about the plight of Native Americans. They had been cheated, lied to and even murdered. He would periodically provide historical and current information which slowly began to take root throughout the nation. His revelations never failed to touch the hearts of many, some of whom would begin to take up the cause of attempting to right some of the past wrongs.

Sarah turned over the reins of the Fashion Department to an ambitious successor, but was able to continue with her designs and started her own affordable fashion line. This arrangement allowed her to work from her home and raise little Kathy and Tom Jr. in a truly nurturing environment. She was extremely happy with her life. The children were always shielded from the dreamcatcher information.

Kathleen showed a knack for clothing design at an early age and eventually became successful as a designer of children's clothing. As a small child she had demonstrated a natural ability for drawing as she 'worked' with her mother. Tom Jr. was just a happy-go-lucky kid who waited for an adventurous lifestyle to catch his fancy.

Thomas spent eighteen months covering the Korean War and once again provided the American people with his special brand of coverage that emphasized the human side of war. His photographs provided details of the conditions under which American military personnel were forced to operate and especially the brutal conditions of the Korean winters. He was able to capture the effects on the Korean people who were continuously re-locating and struggling to survive. Thomas chose not to cover the policies and decisions that shaped the way the war progressed or failed to progress...he left that to the other correspondents. Once again he picked a Marine or soldier and followed him around for several days or weeks and reported the daily routine or the occasional terrifying attacks that became a scramble to survive. He was readily accepted by the military and that opened many doors for him.

He spent one month aboard an aircraft carrier and was amazed by the ship itself; he became lost on numerous occasions. Flight deck operations were, in his words, organized chaos orchestrated by a few men who seemed to be unflappable. Flight operations were extremely noisy, but so incredibly exciting. Pilots were gregarious and always provided tales that made Thomas wonder how much was truth and how much was embellishment. The food was quite good plus warmth and a dry place to sleep gave him a pleasant respite from his land-based assignments. He was treated to one winter storm which convinced him that those pilots had to be a little crazy to fly in weather like that. He left the ship reluctantly, but so glad that he had been allowed to observe things that he would never forget. The American people were rewarded with an in-depth account of life aboard an aircraft carrier through the words and photographs of their favorite correspondent.

Thomas returned from Korea just before the conflict ended and this time he did pick up a Pulitzer Prize for journalism. Once again he was that larger-than-life reporter who had won the hearts of the American people. Once again the editor patted himself on the back for his innate ability to have chosen the right man for the job.

Thomas remained in constant demand as a guest speaker. Colleges sought him for commencement speeches and virtually every type of business wanted him if only to impress their employees. He functioned as a photo journalist to a lesser degree as he traveled the nation on the numerous speaking engagements. Whenever possible, he took all or some of his family.

Thomas had hoped that Tom Jr. would follow in his footsteps, but through the years it became apparent that the young man had no desire to embrace the field of journalism or photography; the young man chose engineering instead. He worked at General Motors for three years before taking a job selling automobiles at a Chevrolet dealership in Chicago. In five years Tom became Service Manager and bought the dealership six years later...the first of three that he would ultimately own in the Chicago area. It was certainly an advantage to have his name prominently displayed where it could easily be confused with that of his famous father. He even had many of his father's photos displayed inside among the special promotional photos and posters showing the latest models. He was extremely proud of his father, but had always been fearful of trying to emulate his father's role in journalism. He would never be compared to his father by virtue of his choice to work in the automotive industry.

Kathy married in the fall of 1963 and Deborah arrived on the last day of November in 1964. John was born two years later. Tom Jr. married his high school sweetheart in 1965 and Marilyn was born in 1968; her brother, Michael, was born after a three year wait.

The proud grandparents now had plenty of time to lavish on their four grandchildren; then things suddenly changed. The television industry had already assumed a huge role in the reporting of the Vietnam War and then the space program. Thomas became a regular guest speaker on the major networks discussing the role of television reporters covering the war. In addition to the need to avoid disclosure of information that would assist the enemy, he always explained his personal feelings of showing the 'human' side of war as opposed to the political side; this resulted in numerous lively debates on the true role of reporters.

There was now a new generation that learned about the war by watching the news and were not interested in the comments of "some old guy who was no longer in touch with the people." Nevertheless, Thomas was pressured to cover the Vietnam War using his old style. He refused, but helped edit and performed 'voice overs' and commentary for numerous television specials about that unpopular war. He authored a book, *The Human Side of War*, which was a collection of his experiences and observations in WWII and Korea. It became a best seller due to the thousands of fans who had been comforted by his reporting. It also became a favorite of a new generation of readers.

Thomas was soon chosen by NASA to cover the astronauts for the wire services, but decided not to use him for television coverage due to his controversial reputation. His newspaper articles were well received by his loyal readership which actually grew in spite of his television controversy.

He officially retired from the newspaper (which was now known as the *Chicago Sun-Times*) on December 1, 1978 and turned his attention to his children and grandchildren. The four grandchildren now ranged in age from eight to fourteen. It was a joyous time for Sarah and Thomas. They were financially able to do anything that struck their fancy. Travel had always been part of their lives but that was not a priority. They had the ability to 'open doors' for their grandchildren and guarantee that they could receive entry into the best schools and ultimately into the best jobs; they chose otherwise.

Thomas had desperately hoped that one of the boys would follow in his footsteps. He relished the thought of providing guidance that would assure a rewarding career in the field of journalism, but that was not to be. It was a very serious ten year old Marilyn who walked up to him and said simply, "I want to be a reporter like you, Grandpa."

This was quite a shock to a man who had yet to accept the thought of women as serious reporters or photo journalists. Thomas dismissed the idea as something that would eventually be replaced by other dreams and wishes as the young girl grew older, but that did not happen. Marilyn persisted and her focus remained and even intensified. Thomas began to coach her and even took her to his old place of employment where she was amazed at the huge complex; she was also very much aware of the respect that the employees had for her grandfather.

He came to fully accept her growing desire to follow in his steps and introduced her to concepts which had served him so well. He purchased a camera for her and taught her how to compose a photo without making it appear staged. "You might take fifty photos and end up with only one that tells a story all by itself." Those words left a lasting impression.

Marilyn subsequently became the photographer and editor for her junior high school yearbook and then the photographer for the yearbook throughout her high school years; she was the editor in her senior year. That first camera had long since been replaced by one of near-professional quality and her darkroom skills were remarkable.

Her neighborhood newspaper contacted her and asked if she would care to contribute a few articles on local residents and she complied. This was in response to a local businessman who had advertised in the school yearbook and had been impressed with his ad; he mentioned her name to the newspaper publisher. That started her on a career without benefit of any influence from her grandfather. Her relationship to the famous reporter with the same last name was always mentioned by the newspaper in spite of her protests. Marilyn had mixed emotions about that repetitive fact; she wanted to be judged on her own merits.

College truly revealed her skills and further enhanced her potential. Marilyn was a thorn in the side of her professors as she continually challenged them on their presentations and techniques. She was also a major contributor to the campus newspaper. She had little time for a social life as she juggled her busy schedule. She graduated with honors and had several job offers which she declined; she did not want to rush into anything. She moved into an apartment with two other young ladies and continued building her reputation as an excellent reporter. She received numerous requests for articles and was able to pick and choose. She would travel if necessary, but was beginning to search for something more permanent. It was the first week of June in 1997 and she was approaching twenty-nine years of age.

Patricia Gail Favret had arrived in San Diego on June 2, 1997. Trish had dreamed of this visit for years and even though her plans had been placed on hold for what seemed to be an eternity, she had finally made it to San Diego. She probably knew more about this city than almost everyone who lived there. She had one whole glorious month to see how much she really enjoyed San Diego and she could certainly live there if she chose. Or, if things were not to her liking, she could return to the nuclear power plant in Massachusetts where she worked. The hectic refueling process at the power plant had recently been completed and she had been more than ready for a break. June was supposedly a great time to visit San Diego and her travel plans had been finalized more than three months earlier.

Trish had been the typical tourist for the first few days and had visited the landmarks that she had seen on television. Most of her special 'must see' places came from the old *Simon and Simon* television series, augmented by travel brochures and countless forays into her newly-discovered internet. Of course, she had gone to Sea World and the Wild Animal Park...those were everyone's priorities.

She had eventually located a cousin, Lieutenant Commander Don Ahern, who had taken time to show her some of his favorite places. A pilot, he had given her a tour of most of the naval facilities in the area including a tour of the *USS Kitty Hawk* berthed at the North Island Naval Air Station. She had known that aircraft carriers were huge, but to actually walk around on one had been mind boggling.

She was particularly impressed with the two plaques on the island structure mounted 120 feet apart...the same distance flown by Orville Wright on December 17, 1903 at Kitty Hawk, North Carolina. Looking around at the massive flight deck, Trish had wondered what the two Wright brothers would have said if they could have stood on this ship at this same spot.

Trish was glad that Don had saved the ship tour for the afternoon; it was a fitting end to her first Thursday in San Diego. They made plans to meet at a small coffee shop at 9:00 A.M. the following day. Don had one more tour in mind.

Don met Trish at a small coffee shop and drove her out to Fort Rosecrans National Cemetery on Point Loma where she saw the hundreds and hundreds of white markers that contrasted with the rich green grass. She was both humbled and awed by the thought of those who had spent their lives in sacrifice for this country. She stood a little taller and was not embarrassed by the tears that had run down her cheeks. She thought she noticed a tear on her cousin's face, but did not mention it; it gave her a warm feeling to know that he, too, had been moved by this experience. Don then drove her down to the Cabrillo National Monument. Trish already knew the significance of the monument but read the information as if she knew nothing about the man who was the first European to set foot on what was to become known as the West Coast of the United States.

The incredible blue color of the Pacific Ocean was overshadowed only by its calm vastness. The North Island Naval Air Station and the city of Coronado were equally spectacular and farther to the east the mountains seemed so close. She watched a nuclear submarine depart Ballast Point and slowly make its way seaward, wondering what life must be like aboard such a vessel.

Her cousin pointed out countless landmarks including the 'bull ring by the sea' across the border in Tijuana, Mexico. Don also pointed out the ominous-looking fog bank that lurked several miles offshore and would probably work its way eastward later that day. The beauty of the area had been simply breathtaking and Trish had wondered why it had taken her so long to make this trip. Don drove Trish back to her car and she was surprised that they had spent nearly three hours out on Point Loma. It had been a very pleasant Friday.

"Why don't you come over for dinner tonight, nothing special. Joan and the girls would love to meet you and I'm sure that you're ready for a home cooked meal by now."

"Are you sure it's okay? It's really short notice." Trish had been unable to hide her excitement.

"It's not a problem. Let me draw you a quick map...it's real easy to find and only about a 20 minute drive from your hotel. How does 1800, I mean 6 o'clock, sound?"

"I'll be there."

Don had quickly sketched a map and put his phone number next to the address...just in case.

"I have a couple of errands to run. Can you find your way from here?"

"Sure. I'll see you at six."

Back at her hotel, Trish had checked her San Diego map and traced her route to Don's house. Seeing that it actually was an easy drive, she had looked at her 'to do' list. The following week she would visit the famous San Diego Zoo. Don had recommended setting aside at least two full days to really see the zoo since it was easy to miss whole sections of the huge complex. Trish had decided that the following Wednesday and Thursday would be perfect for the zoo. She would tour the entire zoo and take dozens of photos. Friday would be spent at Balboa Park with extra time devoted to the Museum of Man. She searched through her large assortment of things to do and see in the area and set several aside for further scrutiny. She had time for a nap.

CHAPTER TWELVE

The Awakening

<u>Friday, June 6, 1997</u>

Half the continent away, Thomas Stevens felt a sudden urgent need to tell Marilyn about the dreamcatchers. He was not certain where the thought had come from; perhaps his assistance was being requested once again. Things were quiet, but he was not in the best of health. Sitting at the dining room table, he asked Sarah how he should go about it since it was certain to be quite a shock and would probably cause Marilyn to question his sanity. He avoided mentioning his age and declining health as at least one reason for this sudden need to bring Marilyn or anyone else into the small group that was aware of the dreamcatcher phenomenon.

"Honey, just collect your notes and everything else that you've compiled over the years, place them here on the table and ask her to drop by. You know she'll rush right over. Visit with her for a few minutes and then tell your story; Marilyn will listen. Once she sees the information that you have collected, I think she will accept what you have to say." Sarah walked over to Thomas and gently placed her hand on his shoulder. "The real problem is: are those things still alive or active and can she take over where you left off? You and I both feel that you were somehow chosen to stop the dreamcatchers and you did, at least one of them. I don't know if you can just pass that responsibility along to someone that you choose. Perhaps that is beyond your ability or is not allowed; just like before, we don't know all of the rules."

Thomas thought for a few seconds before speaking.

"I don't think I'm up to chasing these things and that's assuming that they still exist. When I destroyed that dreamcatcher years ago, maybe it stopped the other two at the same time. If not, then perhaps the force behind their power somehow caused them to wait for an opportunity to return at a time when they would not be vulnerable."

"You mean that this force or the dreamcatchers are watching you and waiting until you cannot pursue them? Now you're starting to scare me."

Sarah pulled out the adjacent dining room chair and sat facing her troubled spouse. Looking deep into his eyes she spoke.

"Tom, if you are right about this then you *must* prepare her for the role that she must play. There might not be enough time for her to learn all the things that you learned over the years. Keep in mind, though, that she might not be able or *allowed* to continue what you have begun."

"I don't see any alternative; I'm just not sure where to begin."

"Just gather all of your information and invite her over. Tell your story and see what happens."

"I suppose you're right. Okay, I'll do it." His reluctance was readily apparent.

Fifteen minutes later he called her apartment. She was out, but one of her roommates said she would tell Marilyn to call her grandfather. Thomas thanked her and hung up. He breathed a sigh of relief and then went into the den to break out his notes and the old newspaper articles. Then he took a nap.

Thirty minutes later Sarah answered a knock at the door and ushered in a very nervous Marilyn.

"Where's Grandpa...is he okay?" Her face showed obvious concern.

As if on cue, Thomas walked into the living room, yawning and stretching. "Hi, Honey," he said to Marilyn while he walked over to kiss Sarah and then his granddaughter.

"I was worried...I had a bad feeling that something was wrong. Are you okay, Grandpa?"

"I am now...now that you're here."

Marilyn smiled and hugged her grandfather.

Sarah chose this moment to remind her husband of his purpose. "Tom, I'll make some coffee and you two can get started."

Marilyn looked at her grandmother and then back at her grandfather and her face showed extreme tension. She noticed how frail he had suddenly become; he seemed to have aged dramatically almost overnight. Something was dreadfully wrong.

"Grandpa, what's going on?"

"Nothing, Sweetheart. There is just something I need to tell you about. Come help me move some things out of the den." He turned and walked away slowly.

Marilyn looked at her grandmother with a quizzical expression and received a quick gesture to follow her grandfather. Marilyn complied and Sarah walked to the kitchen to clear off the dining room table and to start the inevitable pot of coffee.

In the den, Marilyn saw the two cardboard boxes on her grandfather's huge desk. Thomas picked up one and motioned for her to take the other. They walked to the dining room and placed both boxes on the table before sitting in adjacent chairs. Not a word had been spoken in the last minute and Marilyn was afraid to ask any questions...her grandfather's expression and demeanor were far too serious. She feared that some terrible news was forthcoming. She had noticed the word 'dreamcatchers' written on both boxes, but that meant nothing to her.

After what seemed to be an eternity, her grandfather spoke.

"Sweetheart, there is something that I must tell you and I think that you will have difficulty accepting it. I am getting a little too old to continue the things I did for several years and I think that I need to give this information to someone younger who can perhaps do what I did. Your grandmother can verify all of this information and it has been kept away from the public for reasons which will soon become clear to you. I don't know if I have the ability to transfer this task to you and I don't even know if you would even want to accept it. So I am going to tell you and show you things that you will find difficult to believe. I have newspaper articles, wire service tapes and original notes in these two boxes. I also have summaries of my notes since the originals were written on napkins, envelopes and whatever else was available at the time. I want to start by briefly telling you what I learned during the height of a host of coincidences that started years ago. After that, we will go through the clippings and the notes. First of all, do you know what a *dreamcatcher* is?"

From that point, Thomas spoke for twenty minutes and covered several years of his past that contained information relative to the dreamcatchers. He stopped only to take sips of coffee after it was delivered by a very relieved Sarah. Marilyn appeared to need to ask questions, but was discouraged by her grandfather. When he had finished, he pushed his chair back slightly and was surprised when Sarah joined them at the table.

"Any questions?" He smiled and waited for the barrage that would certainly come from his granddaughter.

"You are really serious, aren't you, Grandpa?"

She watched him nod his head and then she looked at her grandmother and received another nod. She was quiet for a few seconds as she considered the most implausible story she had ever heard. She was still waiting for them to tell her that it was a joke or the basis of a good story. She decided to reserve judgment until later. This revelation was overwhelming and she was not sure where to start.

"What's in the boxes?" She was clearly skeptical, but then she was a reporter and needed facts.

Thomas opened the first box which contained his original notes and two folders that each contained summaries of those notes. He handed her a folder and opened the other one.

"The dates are missing or approximated in some instances at the beginning simply because I didn't have any inkling that these things meant anything. As time passed and these unusual 'coincidences' seemed to be somehow related, I tried to establish a timeline. After that I updated my notes regularly with all the information I thought was relevant and sometimes I left out things that would later prove to be extremely important. The original papers have arrows and notes with references to numbered notes of similar things which are located elsewhere. Sometimes you will see your grandmother's handwriting as we tried to figure out answers or clues which came to me. The summaries have all of the information and they reference newspaper articles and wire tapes which are numbered accordingly. You can read these in detail at your leisure. Right now I want to briefly cover the summaries."

An hour later the grandfather and granddaughter closed their folders. Marilyn sat there thinking. She had questions and most of them would really focus on her grandfather's veracity. She would need to ask her questions very carefully.

"That's quite a story. Coming from anyone else, I would immediately dismiss it as pure fantasy. Grandpa, do you have any photos of these dreamcatchers? What about a photo of the Indian, Howling Wolf? I don't see any concrete proof, but the destruction of the three dreamcatchers by fire is fascinating with three separate accounts. So, Grandpa, where are the photos?"

Thomas smiled sheepishly. "There are no photos, not a single one. At the time I never even thought about my camera. I know it sounds a little lame, but I never even considered photos until it was too late. My old editor who died several years ago, your grandmother and now you are the only ones who know so much of this story; your parents don't even know about this. There are some people who know certain parts, but they have not spoken out over the years…at least not publicly. All of these things are considered coincidences and my strange dreams or visions have only been shared with those few people I just mentioned. I believe that there are still two dreamcatchers that can become alive or active at any time. I may be wrong, but I think that the one I destroyed somehow passed a warning to the other two and they remain inactive. The one that I eliminated seemed to become more mobile through the actions of people who fell under its influence. I am certain that it had grown in strength or power during the Second World War and if that is true, then the last two remaining dreamcatchers have been accumulating strength for a much longer period of time. It is possible that they are waiting for me to pass away and that is why I wanted to talk to you. I don't even know if there can be a transfer of my knowledge and what I think is a responsibility to combat these things."

"Grandpa, you're going to be with us for a long time, but I promise to start doing as much research as I can and go over these notes after I have had some time to digest what is definitely the most fascinating story I have ever heard. What is in the other box?"

"Mostly newspaper articles that relate to the deaths. The surprise is that no one else ever tied any of these incidents together. It is almost as if *something* prohibited anyone, and especially inquisitive reporters, from connecting these events even though newspapers always mentioned the irony of the nightmares and the causes of death. I know that it took me a while to learn, but now it seems so blatantly obvious that the facts were right there in plain sight for all to see."

"Well, Grandpa, you must admit that anyone who even remotely saw a pattern would avoid mentioning it. And I just realized why you were so reluctant to bring it up. So you're telling me that the newspaper articles actually state that the deceased person died from his nightmares or more accurately, was *killed* by his nightmares."

"More or less. Sometimes it is clearly stated and other times it is just implied."

Marilyn left after a few more minutes carrying her copy of the summary and a head full of curiosity, doubts and questions. She needed a quiet place to go over all that she had heard.

True to her word, Marilyn began her research immediately. She took great pains to ensure that her roommates did not discover her new project. That was an easy process since the other two women were more concerned with their social lives. After a 30 minute computer search, she located an old photo of a Native American named Howling Wolf. She made a copy of it and immediately took it to her grandfather.

"Is this the man you told me about...the one with the great powers who was in your dreams?"

Thomas stared at the photo in disbelief; it *was* the Indian who had appeared in his dreams! He appeared considerably younger in the photo, but it was clearly the same man.

"Yes, that is the man. I never thought to look for him, but I knew that he must have existed."

He walked slowly to the dining room table and sat. Marilyn followed and sat next to him. She looked at her grandfather who was now deep in thought and his facial expression gave her an immediate chill.

Sarah entered the room and smiled as she spotted her granddaughter. "Hi, Sweetheart. I thought I heard somebody come in." She turned her attention to her husband and noticed the strange look on his face.

"Oh my God! Tom, are you okay?" She rushed to his side.

Thomas replied with garbled words that Sarah was unable to decipher.

"I think he's having a stroke!' Sarah wrung her hands while she thought of what she must do.

Marilyn turned toward her grandmother, her face pale and she was trembling. "He said the dreamcatchers are on the move."

"He said *what*? That was just gibberish...something's wrong!" Confused, she moved rapidly toward the telephone.

"The dreamcatchers are on the move! Marilyn, we have work to do," Thomas said calmly.

His words stopped Sarah immediately. She turned, uncertain whether to rush to her husband or make the 911 call.

"Tom, are you okay?"

"I'm fine...what's wrong?" He was astonished that Sarah was in a near-panic state.

"Tom, you had this funny look on your face and mumbled some broken words that made no sense; you scared me."

Marilyn spoke immediately, "Grandma, he said that the dreamcatchers were on the move...it was clear as a bell! How could you have missed it? Are *you* okay?"

At that same moment the ancient Great Eagle re-appeared in the land of the Lakota and three lesser eagles soon converged on the same location. Suddenly one of the three departed to the southwest...toward southern California; the journey, by human standards, was instantaneous.

"Marilyn, it *was* gibberish; I know what I heard." She was somewhat indignant because her granddaughter had challenged her."

"Honey, I just had this vision...an eagle told me that the dreamcatchers were now moving and I simply repeated that to Marilyn. That's all it was. Marilyn seemed to hear me. Are *you* all right?" Thomas was clearly concerned.

"I know what I heard," Sarah's voice was rising.

Grandfather and granddaughter exchanged worried glances. There had been no conversation out of the ordinary except for the content as far as they were concerned. Perhaps Sarah had not been listening closely.

"If the dreamcatchers are on the move what do we do now, Grandpa? Where are they and how do we find them?" Marilyn was no longer wondering if she wanted to participate in this fascinating quest.

"I don't know...something will just guide me or us. It's a waiting game at least for a little while."

"Is there anything we need to do or get...I mean like maps or something?"

"Actually, we do need a road atlas; there is certain to be some chasing involved. Could you run over to Wal-Mart and pick one up?"

"Sure, I'll go right now." Marilyn picked up her purse, fumbled for her keys and left.

Sarah sat down next to her husband. "I'm sorry, but you frightened me. You were speaking in what I now think was another language but I thought at first that you were having a stroke. Since Marilyn clearly understood what you said then I must have been wrong. Do you think that she might have some of your abilities from the past?"

"I don't know...we'll be forced to wait and see."

Thirty-nine minutes later, a very pale Marilyn walked in through the front door carrying a road atlas; she was trembling. Her grandparents stared at her without speaking.

"I was in Wal-Mart and finally located the stand with the atlases. Just as I grabbed one this young boy ran past me and knocked it from my hand. It landed open, but upside down. When I picked it up and turned it over, there was the map of southern California, San Diego actually, staring me right in the face. I looked over at the boy who by then had returned to apologize after a scolding from his mom. I told him that I was okay and then I realized that he was wearing a baseball uniform. As he walked away I noticed that he played for a team called the *Eagles* and his mother was wearing a sweatshirt with a howling wolf on the front. After all you told me about how sometimes you just got hints out of the clear blue, I think I just got a hint or a message. I think that the dreamcatchers are somewhere in or near San Diego."

Thomas smiled and nodded his head. Marilyn sat next to her grandfather and waited for his comments; she was still trembling.

"You can't just rush out to San Diego and expect things to start happening. Your experience might have been a simple coincidence. If you are supposed to go to San Diego, I think that you will have more signs. If you look too hard for clues, you will start reacting to the wrong things. You will begin to know what you must do or where you must go...you will *feel* or *know* what is required. I'm sorry; I need to take a nap. Visit with your grandmother and she can tell you some of the things that we agonized over."

Thomas rose from his chair and walked stiffly to the bedroom. Marilyn noticed once again how frail he had become. She waited until she heard him close the door before speaking.

"He looks really bad. It's almost as if he has shrunk. I'm worried and I just assumed that he would travel with me. Now I don't see that as an option. What if I'm not ready; what if I'm not even supposed to be involved in this? I might do more harm than good."

"Your grandfather learned what to do. It was a slow, confusing process and then he learned to simply accept the clues or directions that were given to him. I watched him progress from complete confusion to confidence and acceptance that he was being led down the correct path. It was an agonizing process since there were no rules. When he first told me about the strange things that he was experiencing, I though he might be a little flaky in the head; I was ready to run for my life. You, on the other hand, have the benefit of his words and vast experience. You must also realize that you might not be the one to take his place."

"Well, I'm going back to the apartment and look over the notes and summaries again. Apparently I must wait for something to happen. This is more than just a little unsettling. Tell Grandpa I said goodbye."

Marilyn kissed her grandmother and left.

Back in her apartment Marilyn sat at the small desk in her bedroom and tried to relax while waiting for something else to happen. She dozed off several times and finally moved to her bed; she was sound asleep in less than a minute.

Shortly after the ancient Great Eagle had reappeared in the lands of the Lakota and dispatched one of the three lesser eagles to the southwest, the two golden eagles observing Bob Starnes' automobile wreckage and its deadly contents suddenly became extremely alert. After a few seconds they both launched themselves into the air and climbed to a point above Interstate 8. They searched the westbound lanes for something other than prey.

Fifteen minutes later two low flying eagles startled a westbound driver on the interstate. Sheldon Curry narrowly avoided plunging over an embankment in the southern California mountains. The shaken driver pulled over at a small turnout and walked around to settle his nerves. Once again he was startled by the two eagles; they were clearly not afraid of him.

"It must be mating season," he said half aloud.

Moments later the two huge birds flew toward him once again and at the last second, dropped rapidly into the valley below as if challenging him to see what they were doing. Fascinated, he walked to the edge of the guardrail and looked down trying to spot them. He was distracted by a bright reflection located several hundred feet down the slope near the base of a large dead tree. He strained to determine the source, but was unable to do so. Shortly thereafter the reflection disappeared as the sun slowly continued its relentless movement toward the west. The two birds did not return.

Sheldon's curiosity overcame his shattered nerves and it suddenly seemed so very important to find the source of the reflection. He was not normally an adventurous man, but he locked the car and began a slow, careful descent toward the general area of the source. It was now imperative that he locate the source of the reflected sunlight.

After thirty minutes and several slips and stumbles, he spotted the overturned wreckage of an old car that had most certainly been there for years or even decades. It was obvious to him that the car had come from the freeway above; he never considered that the Interstate highway was relatively new compared to the old car. Curiosity drove him to continue and he happened to spot what he assumed were the same two eagles now perched on the same branch of the dead tree watching him intently. At that instant both huge birds flew away. These eagles were a very dark brown with a few lighter feathers on the underside of their wings; he knew that they were definitely not bald eagles. He did not notice that they began to circle overhead, waiting.

Sheldon approached the wreckage wondering what had been left behind. Then he saw the human remains which would later be identified as Robert Starnes. He gasped and slowly realized that he was probably the first person to see the wreckage. After the initial shock, he was able to calm his nerves once again and methodically checked the wrecked car.

Virtually all of the glass had been shattered or knocked out. He was only able to see one occupant or, more accurately, the remains of one occupant. Strangely, the skeleton was intact and the clothing was in surprisingly good shape. Wild animals had not disturbed the remains even though there was easy access. He noted the presence of numerous articles that were certain to be of Indian origin. He knelt beside the old car and looked into the area of the back seat. Sheldon noticed two wooden boxes resting on what was probably an animal hide of some sort. They were both completely intact and looked as if they had been recently crafted. There was no dirt or dust on them. He retrieved one and noticed that there was no impression or discoloration on the hide where the box had rested.

With shaking hands he fumbled with the latch and opened the box. Sheldon stared in disbelief at something that he had no words to describe. He gently placed the box on the ground and reached inside the wreckage for the second box. To his surprise, it too was immaculate and left no trace that it had ever rested on what he was now convinced was a buffalo hide. He opened it and was once again overwhelmed by the contents. He placed it next to the first one and stared...they were identical. He suddenly felt the need to possess both objects. He thought about the owner or the descendants of the owner and realized that he could simply take the two boxes. The thought repulsed him briefly, but was quickly replaced by the *need* to have them. He realized that he must not disturb the site and decided to report his discovery, but only after he had his two prizes securely locked in the trunk of his car.

It took almost an hour to reach his car. He was exhausted due to the steep slope and holding the two boxes under one arm. After placing the two boxes in the trunk, he climbed in and started the engine. Just prior to moving back onto Interstate 8, he spotted the flashing lights on the California Highway Patrol car as it pulled in behind him. He briefly froze in fear, wondering how they had caught him so quickly. Then he realized that it was probably just a routine assistance check; he *hoped* it was a routine check. He shut off the engine and climbed out just as the Highway Patrolman did the same.

"Good afternoon, sir. Can I help you?"

"I, uh, need to report an accident, officer." Sheldon was sweating.

"Where did it occur?" The officer glanced around the immediate area.

Sheldon pointed over the guardrail. "Down there," he puffed. He saw the doubt in the patrolman's eyes as the officer looked at the undamaged guardrail.

"It looks like it happened a long time ago and there's a skeleton still inside."

Now he had the patrolman's full attention.

"A skeleton? You spotted it from up here? Show me where it is."

The two men walked to the guardrail and Sheldon pointed at the dead tree.

"It's right up against that big tree...the dead one." He paused to catch his breath before continuing. "I saw something reflecting the sunshine, probably the glass. Anyway, I got curious so I went down there. I just got back up here and was going to report it."

"Excuse me." The patrolman went back to his cruiser.

He returned a couple of minutes later.

"Okay, I need to get some information from you. Do you have a few minutes?" He broke out a pad and pen.

"Yes sir, just don't make me go back down there; I don't think I can climb back up again."

The next fifteen minutes was spent providing as much detail as Sheldon could recall. A second patrol car interrupted the process and the new arrival was given a quick update along with an introduction to Sheldon. The second patrolman suddenly decided that he would descend the steep slope to view the wreckage for the official report.

As the patrolman approached the guardrail, Sheldon spoke. "Be careful, there is a lot of loose rock; just head straight for the old dead tree."

"Thank you, but I've done this before." His tone was that of acute aggravation.

Sheldon looked at the original patrolman who smiled before speaking.

"One of us had to go down there and I'm senior. Don't worry, he'll get over it. Now, just a few more questions and we'll be finished. Let's sit in my cruiser...my portable radio seems to be dying. I would also like you to stay until George gets back up here if that is possible. He may have some questions after he's had a chance to examine the crash site."

Sheldon's pulse raced as he tried to think of anything he might have done that would indicate that he had disturbed the vehicle or its contents.

He was certain that he had not left any evidence that he had even been there except for possibly some tracks. He decided to remain.

"Sure, I'll stay. I'm a little rattled; that's the first dead person I've ever seen. Well, I mean except for funerals."

"We see accidents that we are not prepared for and I can tell you that it never gets easy."

"But this skeleton still had hair and skin. It was more like a mummy wearing clothes. I always thought that skeletons were just nice white bones. The worst part was that he was staring at me. I don't mean really *staring* at me; his face, his *head* was turned directly toward me. It seemed like he had been waiting for me. I looked for other skeletons, but I was not about to move anything around in the car. This may sound funny, but I didn't think that time mattered much any more to anyone who died in that car. I just wanted to get out of there and report it."

"You did the right thing. A recovery crew is enroute and they will determine how to proceed. The contents will probably be removed from the wreckage and the vehicle may remain. On the other hand, if there is any evidence of foul play then the wreckage will probably be removed, also."

The two men sat in silence for several more minutes.

"Unit 26, Unit 23." The cruiser's radio crackled, startling both men.

"Go ahead, 23."

"You can send the gentleman on his way. I'm coming back up."

"Ten-four. Okay, Mr. Curry, you can leave now if you feel up to driving. If not, we will provide you with transportation."

"I'm all right. I'm just glad you stopped when you did; I'm not so sure that I would have been very safe driving through the mountains trying to find a way to report this."

"In that case, thank you for your assistance. I don't think we'll need to contact you again. Be careful, Mr. Curry." He extended his hand.

Sheldon shook the patrolman's hand and glanced as his nametag. "I will, Officer Goodall."

He returned to his car and drove away. Neither man noticed the two eagles that suddenly stopped circling overhead and followed the Curry vehicle.

Twenty minutes later George struggled over the guardrail huffing and puffing. His uniform was soiled and the trousers were torn in several places. He crawled into Patrolman Goodall's cruiser.

"You look like hell." There was a smile on his face.

"Thanks, buddy. Looks like I'll be tossing these trousers."

"Hey, the guy tried to warn you."

"That's why I wanted him gone when I got back up here; I was not in the mood for some righteous sarcasm. Well, the crash site seems to be virtually untouched except for footprints. The car is an old Dodge from the mid-forties. Here is the plate information...notice that it's a 1947 California plate. One occupant, male, age could be anywhere from early twenties to forties with brown hair. I wasn't able to check for personal identification on the body. A few more hours won't make much difference."

George sighed before continuing. "There was nothing in the glove box except for maps of Nebraska, North and South Dakota, Texas and Kansas. It appears that the car left the road at moderate speed and first impact was on the front at a little more than ninety degrees from the horizontal on the only level area around. After impact, the car continued over onto the roof, finally coming to rest against that large tree. There was some damage to the right rear fender that may have occurred when the car went off the road. I would venture that the car skidded off the road either because of weather conditions or possibly because the driver fell asleep." He paused for a few seconds, still recuperating from the climb.

"There is one other thing: the body was not disturbed by wild animals and has remained there for probably fifty years. Most of the glass is broken and everything inside looks fresh except for the skeleton. There is no dirt, no leaves, no fading...everything is clean and well-preserved. I don't know how to put this in the report. I mean, except for the skeleton, the interior looks like the accident could have occurred in the last few hours. There's not even any rust on the damaged rear fender."

Patrolman Goodall thought for a few seconds before speaking. "That Mr. Curry also mentioned that the interior of the car was unusual. Then he said that he was surprised that the skeleton was more like a mummy than white bones."

"That's right...it *was* like a mummy. I don't know, but something about the wreckage is just not right. I don't want to put these thoughts into my report, though. Now if the medical folks want to introduce their ideas, then that's a different matter." George clearly wanted no part of what was certain to be a huge controversy.

Patrolman Goodall was silent for several seconds before speaking. "The only thing that bothers me is why this Curry guy stopped here and why he just *happened* to look over the guardrail and spot the wreckage. Is it possible that he knew something about the crash or was he just somehow drawn to the only place where you could spot it from up here? Think about it. They spent years building this interstate and yet nobody happened to see the old car down there. Curry said that he saw a reflection probably from some of the glass, but apparently nobody saw it during the highway construction. Somehow I don't think that it was Devine guidance that picked that man at that exact time to stop at that exact location and look toward that exact spot."

George shrugged. "Who cares? I just want to get the paperwork done and get back to work."

Twenty miles farther west, Sheldon Curry decided that he would try to sell one of the objects to that quirky store in El Cajon. After all, the store seemed to flourish as it sold all sorts of off-beat merchandise. It was worth a try and he would still have one of those feathered items for himself.

His thoughts were interrupted by brake lights ahead and Sheldon suddenly found himself sitting motionless in traffic. There was no movement at all for ten minutes and then two highway patrol cars worked their way past and disappeared. Forty minutes later the traffic started to move and eventually he made his way past the scene of an accident involving two vehicles. He waved at Patrolman Goodall just as he recognized him at the last instant; the patrolman did not see him as he concentrated on clearing the traffic jam.

By the time Sheldon reached the store in El Cajon it was closed. He sighed and continued north toward his home in Poway. He could stop there on his next trip to Yuma since he would drive by the store anyway. He drove to Santee and stopped at the Pinnacle Peak restaurant for dinner.

He parked his car and ambled into the restaurant, smiling as he looked at the thousands of cut-off ties adorning the walls. His own tie was up there somewhere; two of his friends had introduced him to the restaurant and the custom of cutting off the tie. His friends had removed their ties at the last instant and laughed as Sheldon watched his favorite tie become a wall decoration. He overcame his anger after biting into the best steak he had ever tasted. When one of the two friends picked up the tab, he was able to laugh about the experience. He became a regular customer.

Sheldon visited the men's room before sitting at his picnic-style table in the no frills restaurant and ordering his steak. Moments later a tall man wearing the khaki uniform of a naval officer stopped hesitantly.

"Mind if I join you? I've never been here before and this is not quite what I had expected."

"Sure. Name's Sheldon Curry and I would enjoy the company. You're a Major, right?"

"Lieutenant Commander, actually; I'm Navy. Name's Brad Chandler. You said Sheldon, right?"

"Yes. I sell solar water heating and storage systems, commercial and residential. I have the southern California district. I'm wrapping up a week-long trip and on my way home. I love the food here and stop in every chance I get. So how did you hear about this place; it's a little off the beaten path for you flyboys."

He grinned as watched the pilot unconsciously glance down briefly at the set of wings that rested just above three rows of military ribbons. He also broke out a business card and offered it to the pilot.

Brad took the card, glanced at it and placed it into his wallet.

"Three of us from my squadron were sent down here to San Diego to participate in the planning of a joint surface and air exercise. We were told that this place was a *must* and this was our last chance to check it out before leaving. The other two guys cancelled at the last minute and I've been waiting for this for the last two days. I'm staying for a few more days and trying to hook up with one of my friends who just reported to the USS Kitty Hawk, but he's still on leave and I can't seem to catch up with him. Anyway, I thought I would try and beat the crowd today and here I am."

At that moment a young waitress dressed more or less like a cowgirl arrived. She looked at Brad and then launched into her routine: "Hello, welcome to Pinnacle Peak. My name is Sherry and I'll be your waitress today. Have you been here before?" She checked his left hand for a wedding ring and smiled as she noted that there was none.

"No, ma'am, but I've heard a lot about this place. I want the biggest steak you have, medium, plus the beans and bread. Oh, and something diet to drink."

"I'll bring it out as soon as it's ready. You're welcome to watch it being cooked if you like. Just go right over there." She smiled and pointed at the area where the steaks were being cooked over an open fire. She then turned to Sheldon. "And I should be bringing out your order in just a few more minutes." With that she disappeared.

The two men talked about San Diego and all of the wonderful attributes of the entire area. Sheldon casually mentioned that he had recently acquired a pair of unusual Indian objects and had intended to sell one or both to a little establishment nearby. He chose not to mention how he had obtained them.

"What are they?" asked the curious but mostly polite pilot.

"I really don't know, but they're really cool. If you like, I'll show them to you after we eat."

Shortly thereafter their food arrived and the two men settled down to eat their meal. Brad was first to speak after tentatively taking the first bite of his steak.

"Now I understand why I've heard so much about this place. This is simply incredible."

Sheldon nodded and smiled as he tasted what he knew would be yet another perfect steak; he was not disappointed. Several minutes passed in silence as they enjoyed their meal.

"Did you notice how the pinto beans have a hint of chili flavor? I've never eaten at any place that features steak and beans. Perhaps this is what cowboys actually ate back in the old days and these people just decided to try it and see if it would catch on. I don't eat steak anywhere else. What do you think, Brad?"

"I must admit that I didn't expect much when I drove up...I was expecting something a little more elegant. I almost drove away, but curiosity brought me inside. I just can't get over how good this is and it seems like this is exactly the way it should be. The cut-off ties on the walls, picnic tables and the waitresses who look like cowgirls...it just fits."

"I don't know if you've noticed, but at least 50 people have arrived just since we sat down. This place must be a gold mine!"

Once the two men finished their meals, they paid their bills and wandered out to Sheldon's car. Sheldon unlocked the trunk and raised the lid. Brad gazed at the two wooden boxes and waited patiently as Sheldon selected a case and removed it. The salesman closed the trunk lid and rested the box on the lid. As Sheldon fumbled with the latch, Brad moved for a better view.

"Voila! Take a look at this!" Once again Sheldon was taken by the beauty of the feathered thing.

"Wow...I've never seen one quite like that before. It's huge and it's just...perfect. Can I pick it up?" Brad felt the urge to hold this magnificent creation.

"Sure, but be careful with it."

Brad gently lifted it and held it at arm length.

A passerby on his way to the restaurant entrance spotted the dreamcatcher and stopped. He stared for a few seconds before walking up to the two men.

"Is that for sale? I've never seen a dreamcatcher like that before. This has to be the best one I have ever seen. I'll give you fifty dollars for it right now. The workmanship is flawless."

The stranger immediately regretted his last comment; that would probably raise the price if it was for sale.

"I'm sorry, it's not for sale," an apologetic Sheldon responded.

"Okay one hundred cash, but I can't go any higher," he said as he removed his wallet from his hip pocket.

Brad quickly handed the dreamcatcher to Sheldon in a state of near shock.

"Well, I didn't want to split up the set, but at least I still would have one for myself. Okay, deal!"

The dreamcatcher was returned to its case and the exchange was made.

"My name's Dave Pearson and thanks for doing business." With that the passerby returned to his car and drove away. Apparently he was no longer hungry.

Overhead, one of two eagles followed David Pearson as he headed north. Two hours later he would have his new treasure mounted on the wall over the bed in his apartment.

"Brad, do you believe that? I was hoping for $25 or maybe $30! Do you want to buy the other one?"

"Nope, too rich for me, but can I take a look at it?"

Sheldon opened the trunk once again and brought out the second case. He opened it just as he had done with the other. Brad whistled softly as he gazed at the dreamcatcher.

"It must have really been a set; it looks just like the other one." Once again he felt a tremendous need to hold the dreamcatcher. Afraid that he might decide to spend the remainder of his cash, Brad sighed, "I need to head back to my room. I have a couple of calls to make. Sheldon, thank you for the excellent company and for showing me this dreamcatcher. I've only seen the cheap ones in the past and there is no comparison. I don't think you'll have any problem selling that one."

"It was my pleasure, Brad. Best of luck to you and perhaps some day we'll run into each other right here...I know you'll be back."

They shook hands and went their separate ways; the second eagle followed Sheldon's car.

Brad returned to his room at the North Island Naval Air Station Bachelor Officer Quarters. He decided to attempt another call to his old friend who was now assigned to the USS Kitty Hawk. He walked down to the pay phone and dialed the number that he had obtained from Information. His friend, Don, picked up the phone on the fourth ring.

"Lieutenant Commander Ahern."

"Don, it's Brad Chandler. Boy are you hard to track down! How are you doing, buddy?"

"Brad, good to hear from you. We moved back to San Diego two weeks ago and just found a house. Now I'm running around trying to get all of those little things done before officially reporting to the Kitty Hawk. Just a minute...."

Brad heard a brief muffled conversation.

"Sorry about that. Joan says 'hello' and hopes to see you soon. We have company right now."

The two men carried on a brief conversation before Don decided to invite his long-time friend to dinner at his house the following Wednesday evening...the invitation was quickly accepted. The two men spoke for another five minutes before hanging up.

Trish Favret had arrived at the Ahern residence promptly at six toting two bottles of wine, a red and a white. A pleasant looking woman had opened the door.

"Hi, I'm Joan. You must be Trish. Please come in."

"I'm really happy to meet you, Joan. I brought wine, but didn't know which to bring so now you have a choice."

"That wasn't necessary. As you can see, we are still unpacking some things and there are more boxes out in the garage. Don and the girls are out in the backyard. Let me take you out there."

The two women had walked toward the slider which opened onto the patio. Passing through the family room, Trish's eyes had been drawn to one wall which was covered with plaques and framed documents; in the middle was a photograph of Joan and Don exiting a church under arched swords held by twelve naval officers in dress whites.

"What is that?" Trish had asked as she gestured to the wall.

"Oh, that's Don's 'I love me' wall. He has a plaque from each place he's been stationed and then there are awards and special letters. There are more that aren't even unpacked...he ran out of room. He said that he would be forced to take over another wall and I told him that he is only allowed one. Now he is trying to think of a way to make the wall bigger. I actually had to remind him that we are only renting! I think he was serious about somehow making the wall bigger."

"I see the photo in the middle...good for you! That is a beautiful picture."

"That was the first thing he hung on the wall; he said it was the most important. Then he hung the other items around it. He put it up before the movers arrived. He had been carrying it around in his briefcase since we left his last duty station. Picture this room with nothing in it except that photo! C'mon, it's time to meet the girls."

The two women stepped out onto the patio. Don was busy at a huge grill and two young girls sat busily working at a picnic table.

"Girls, come meet your cousin, Trish!"

Adrianne, age 5, and Brianne, age 3 and a half, looked up and rushed to meet their cousin while Don turned and waved. The girls hugged Trish at the same time and then stepped back.

"I'm Brianne."

"I'm Adrianne and I'm 5."

"I'm Trish and I'm 7."

"No you're not! You're too big to be 7," Adrianne laughed. "Come see what we're doing."

"Okay, let's go."

The trio walked to the picnic table where the two girls showed her their coloring books. They resumed coloring immediately.

"Wow these are very pretty. Do you think I could have them when you finish them?"

There were two rapid affirmative responses and the two girls concentrated on finishing their artwork. Trish walked over to the grill where Joan had joined Don.

"What beautiful girls!"

"Thank you; they can be a handful. They have been so excited to meet you and I'm surprised that they let you leave them. I hope you like burgers. I haven't done any serious food shopping yet."

"Burgers are fine with me and I have to say that Don looks very comfortable next to that grill."

"Thank you and thank you for arriving on time. Any problems finding the place?"

"Nope, it was easy just like you said."

"Trish, you must excuse Don. He has this thing about being on time. I told him to wait to start the burgers just in case you were late. He smugly informed me that you knew how important it was to be on time."

Joan hugged her husband. Don winked at Trish.

"It's my military training...you never arrive late; people sometimes die if you arrive late."

"It's hamburgers, Don; it's just hamburgers!"

They all laughed and Don suddenly turned serious.

"By the way, we have a storm headed our way. It looks like rain for a few days. It's a little unusual for this time of the year and you might need to change some of your plans. You can borrow an umbrella if you like. There are dozens of things we are still looking for, but the umbrellas were in the first carton we opened; perhaps that was a sign. Joan, the burgers are now cooked to perfection; I've done my part. It's now up to you to maintain that level which I have established. I must rest now."

"See what I'm forced to put up with? And on top of that he drags me all over the country every few years and sometimes disappears on a ship for more than six months at a time."

Joan hugged her husband again. They made a great couple and Trish envied them.

"Trish, could you give me a hand? We need to bring out the other stuff. Girls, put your crayons and coloring books away, it's time to eat."

The two girls quickly gathered their coloring materials and took them into the house. Joan and Trish followed and returned minutes later with a tray of condiments, buns and silverware plus potato salad and chips. Don had already placed a checkered table cloth on the table and used a platter of burgers to hold it in place. Joan made one last trip to the kitchen and returned with a huge pitcher of lemonade and glasses. By that time the table was ready and the assemblage began a meal with good food and a lot of laughter. Both girls ate and showed excellent manners which was a bit of a surprise to Trish; she had witnessed terrible behavior by many young children whose parents never seemed to be the least bit concerned.

"This must be the perfect family," she thought to herself.

After the meal they all participated in the cleanup and soon everyone moved inside for the evening. Don fielded a phone call from an old friend and they spoke for several minutes. Don took Joan aside and mentioned that he had invited his friend Brad over for dinner Wednesday evening; she was genuinely pleased.

The girls were put to bed at eight and the adults visited for two hours while Trish learned more about her cousin and his family. It was clear that Joan loved this lifestyle although the six and sometimes seven-month deployments were difficult. Twice she had traveled overseas with several other wives who had followed the ship and met up with their husbands during the in-port visits. It had been fun, but after Adrianne arrived it was just too difficult. Don explained his career up to this day and his future aspirations. Trish discussed her role at the nuclear power plant.

As the conversation began to wane, Trish sensed that it would be a good time to leave. As she arose from the sofa, Joan suddenly asked her if she would like to come over Wednesday night for a real dinner...not hamburgers. Trish immediately accepted.

"What time?"

"Seven would be perfect."

"Then I will see you then. Thank you for a welcome meal and such good company. By the way, do you think the girls would like to spend Wednesday night with me at the hotel? That way you guys could have a little break."

"Trish you are a life saver! Adrianne has Thursday off due to some sort of teacher conference and I was debating if I should keep Brianne out of daycare that day. We could let them decide Wednesday night. Are you sure you don't mind?"

"I think it would be fun. Hey, I need to get moving! I'm going to revise my schedule due to the coming storm. Thank you again; this was a lot of fun. Joan, I'm so glad we finally met. Good night."

The couple responded simultaneously and watched Trish walk to her car; they waved as Trish drove away.

"Joan, did you forget that Brad is coming over for dinner Wednesday night?" He saw her smile. "Oh my God...you're fixing them up! That could be really interesting or possibly a complete disaster."

"Look, Brad needs to move on. The car crash was over six years ago. Besides, they're both coming over for dinner. You guys have a lot of catching up to do. Brad can choose to visit with you or visit with Trish. There is no pressure." She smiled smugly.

"Well, is there some reason that you failed to mention to Trish that Brad would also be here?"

"I didn't want her to have a ready-made excuse for not coming. She seemed to really enjoy this evening. I like Trish and I think that the two of them just might hit it off."

"Okay, but remember that she is just out here visiting."

"I know and now I am going to do whatever it takes to win you over to my side. Well, after I check on the girls."

Saturday, June 7, 1997

Marilyn slept soundly for several hours until awakened by a dream. There was the old Indian, Howling Wolf and an eagle. They both spoke to her and all she could remember was the phrase, "You must go." She was uncertain if the words came from Howling Wolf or the eagle, but it was clear and so very real. Her heart was pounding as she tried to remember everything from the dream, but only those three words and the two images remained. It was 4:00 A.M. and she toyed with the idea of phoning her grandfather, but decided that a phone call at that hour was not a good idea. Still, she had to do *something*. She paced back and forth wringing her hands and then realized that she was hungry. She quickly dressed and drove to a nearby restaurant for an early breakfast. She was both excited and a little frightened by the dream; she desperately wanted to talk with her grandfather.

She rang the doorbell at exactly 6:00 A.M. knowing that both grandparents always arose at that time. Seconds later her grandfather opened the door.

"What took you so long to get here, Sweetheart? Did you have a dream?" He was smiling. "I don't think you need another sign."

Marilyn followed him into the kitchen and noticed the pot of coffee.

"You had the dream, too?"

"Yes, and I saw you driving to San Diego; you must leave today. Go pack and fill your gas tank. Make sure to take a copy of my summary. Come back here for breakfast and we'll go over some things again."

"I ate breakfast before coming here...I've been up since 4 o'clock."

"You should have come over here immediately. I had the coffee ready at 4:15. I sent your grandmother back to bed when you didn't arrive right away. Now go pack!"

"Okay, Grandpa. I wish you were coming with me. I'm afraid that I don't know enough about my role in all of this. I'll be calling you...a lot."

Marilyn left to complete her preparations for the trip. For the first time in her life she was embarking on a huge journey without knowing what to expect. Her guidance would be coming from something that she did not understand and yet she would be expected to react to clues or directions that would just appear to her in dreams or visions. Her actions could then affect the lives of those who were under the influence of these dreamcatchers; she hoped that she was up to the challenges that would appear in her future. She also wondered if she might be a little crazy to be taking this whole thing seriously.

Thomas watched her drive away and returned to the kitchen table. He picked up his cup of coffee and cautiously sipped it...it seemed to have no taste at all. It dawned on him that his senses of taste and smell had faded. He decided not to mention that to anyone.

Marilyn's chosen route would be I-55 down to I-44 then onto I-40 to Barstow, California and then I-15 to San Diego. It was roughly 2200 miles and she wondered if flying would be a better choice. As she thought about it she suddenly remembered that her grandfather said that he had 'seen' her driving to San Diego; that was now resolved. She would take snacks and bottled water. She took comfortable clothes plus a nice suit and two dresses just to cover several scenarios. She also took an umbrella...it seemed important. After telling her roommates that she would be in San Diego for approximately one month, she called her parents in Ohio and then left the apartment.

Marilyn filled her gas tank and stopped by the bank for some cash. She considered what else she might possibly need to do before leaving and came up empty. She then drove to her grandparents' home. She knocked on the door and entered immediately.

"I'm packed and I just hope that I'm ready. Are there any other things I need to know?"

"Good morning, Marilyn." It was her grandmother's way of inserting some normalcy into Marilyn's now-turbulent and confusing world.

"I'm sorry, Grandma. I'm just worried about all of the little details right here, right now and then the longest driving trip of my life. Oh, and there's this little issue with dreamcatchers and people's lives. I'm frightened...I'm really frightened."

Marilyn's grandfather spoke from the kitchen.

"Ladies, would you care to join an old man who would like to be part of the conversation?"

Both women chuckled, walked to the kitchen and sat after Marilyn kissed her grandfather.

"Is your car all set? Everything packed? Is there anything that we need to keep an eye on for you?"

"No, Grandpa. I've loaded up the things I know I'll need and a few other essentials. I may need to buy some things and I'll do that as necessary. Right now I just have this sense of urgency to get on the road. Here's my route...all interstate."

She handed him the route which she had scribbled on a piece of paper.

"I don't know how long I will drive each day, so I didn't make advance reservations anywhere."

"Just don't drive when you're sleepy; you've got to rest. Also, call us collect and let us know how you're doing. Right now, though, you need to get on the road. Be careful. You will most likely encounter some bad weather along your route, especially afternoons and evenings...it's just that time of the year. Now it's time for you to get going. I am only rushing you because I sense a rising urgency in what must be done."

The threesome walked slowly out to Marilyn's car. Silently the two elders hugged and kissed their grandchild goodbye. Thomas noticed that the front seat contained a box with common necessities and the road atlas with small colorful paper tabs attached. He smiled knowing that there was undoubtedly nothing missing from her required items. He noticed the clothing on the hanger bar in the back seat area and knew that the trunk held suitcases.

Marilyn entered the car and started the engine. She wished desperately that her grandfather was going with her. Tears rolled down her cheeks as she backed out onto the street.

"Don't worry about me; I'll be okay. Bye!"

"Call us when you can; we know you'll be busy. I'll get you a contact name in San Diego. Remember, he or she will not know why you are there. Be careful! We love you!"

"I love you, too! Both of you!"

Marilyn sped away, wiping the tears from her cheeks.

Overhead, a very large yet mostly invisible eagle followed Marilyn's blue Honda sedan. Thomas suddenly looked up and spotted the eagle. He smiled, nodded his head and the eagle disappeared from his view.

"She'll be okay," he said confidently as the elderly couple walked hand in hand back to their house. They could do nothing more for now except wait and worry.

At that instant Marilyn was overcome by a feeling of complete serenity; there were no fears or uncertainty. She only needed to drive to San Diego. It was 10 A.M. and she reset the trip odometer to zero. She searched for a radio station for some weather information and twelve minutes later merged in with the southbound traffic on I-55. She accelerated to the speed limit and moved to the inside lane. Without warning, the car accelerated to 85 miles per hour. Initially she tried to slow down, but the speed remained at 85. She worried that something was terribly wrong, but once again that feeling of serenity returned and she simply accepted it.

Seventeen miles later she noticed flashing lights coming up behind her. She switched lanes while trying to slow down; her speed remained at 85.

"Great, just great. Nothing like a speeding ticket to start my journey," she said aloud.

A few seconds later, a state trooper passed her without paying any attention to her. Not knowing why, she smiled.

"That was lucky."

A few miles later she flew past a large sedan that had been stopped by a state trooper. She wondered if it was the same trooper that had passed her a few minutes earlier.

In San Diego, Trish Favret arrived at the Museum of Man in Balboa Park where she would spend the whole day.

After four hours Marilyn realized the need to stop for gas and took the next exit. For some reason she was not surprised when the car slowed; everything was back to normal. She visited the ladies room while the attendant filled the tank. Nine minutes later she again merged with the southbound traffic.

As soon as she moved into the left lane, the car accelerated to 85 miles per hour. She tried to take her foot off the accelerator pedal, but was unable; her speed remained at 85. Marilyn checked and noted that the cruise control was turned off. She accepted the situation and decided not to worry about it.

She refueled at Joplin, Missouri and the car had responded normally when she decided to exit for gas. Returning to the interstate, the car again accelerated to 85 in spite of her efforts to control it.

After almost an hour, Marilyn felt a strong urge to exit the interstate. She then thought she heard a voice say, "Leave the road now." She took the next exit and made a right turn onto the westbound road. She tried to relax and felt the urge to turn south at the next traffic light. One mile later she saw a sign indicating her route back to the interstate. After a left turn and traveling just over half a mile, she took the southbound on-ramp. Glancing to her left for the merge she was amazed to see the aftermath of a huge pileup of several cars and an eighteen wheeler; she had just avoided what would certainly have been a major delay. She was unaware that had she not exited, she would have been part of the multiple collisions. Thirty seconds later she was once again cruising along at 85 mph on the now deserted southbound side of the interstate. She never considered her detour to be anything other than a very lucky coincidence.

Marilyn reached the outskirts of Oklahoma City at 8:35 P.M. A few minutes later she was westbound on I-40. She stopped for gas at Clinton, Oklahoma and was amazed that she did not feel tired. Returning to the interstate, she was surprised when she moved to the left lane only this time her speed went to 90 miles per hour. Once again she simply accepted the situation. She was also amazed at the number of trucks on the road, but they were not an issue as she sped through the night. There were very few cars traveling westbound. She munched on her supply of crackers as she flew through the dark Texas panhandle.

Meanwhile northeast of San Diego, David Pearson, single at age 51, stared ahead into the heavy rain with the windshield wipers operating at maximum speed. He hated to drive at night in the rain and now some radio disc jockey was happily playing an old song about it never raining in California. Right now he also hated that disc jockey and wanted to change radio stations but was afraid to release his right hand from its death grip on the steering wheel. The winding two lane highway required all of his attention and he realized that he was sweating profusely. It was 10:30 P.M. on a Saturday night and he had not originally intended to remain long after dinner with friends; he had been unaware of the approaching storm. Now he was wishing that he had left before the rain began.

Suddenly he thought about the return of his nightmare from years ago. Three nights ago he had been flipping through the television channels and had stumbled upon a re-run of one of those irony-laced programs in black and white; it was the source of his childhood nightmares. He had switched channels immediately and found something else to watch. He had dozed off several times and decided to go to bed.

Hours later, Dave had awakened in a terrified state, drenched in sweat. The nightmare had returned. As he tried to calm himself, he wondered why he had chosen that particular time to surf the channels. Actually, he had not *chosen* to flip though the channels, he had been *compelled to do so*. There had been a sense of urgency to do that which seemed more than a little odd to a sleepy man suffering from acute boredom. He had watched perhaps five or possibly ten seconds of the old show before realizing what he was watching. He knew the story well even though it had been decades since that show had aired; he should remember it, it had haunted him for years before suddenly leaving him in peace.

Now he was struggling through this miserable rainstorm and his thoughts kept wandering back to the old nightmare. His concentration on driving gradually diminished and he chose to change the radio station which was now playing that song for the second time...something that the disc jockey *never* did. Dave glanced briefly at the tuning knob as he reached for it. In that brief instance he failed to see the caution sign which indicated a left curve and was startled moments later as he realized that he was in trouble.

In a panic state, he jammed his foot on the brake pedal and skidded onto the shoulder and then bounced and slid down the slope until a large boulder stopped the sideward motion of the vehicle. Without a seatbelt for restraint, Dave continued to move until first his head and then the rest of his body reached the intersection of the dashboard and the passenger's door. And then there was only blackness.

Another vehicle had been following Dave at a safe distance and cautiously pulled onto the shoulder and turned on his emergency flashers.

He quickly left his vehicle and stared into the darkness. Eventually he spotted the tail lights and returned to his car to grab a flashlight. Moments later another car arrived and the first Good Samaritan rushed over to the new arrival.

"Go get help! The car in front of me just went off the road. It's down the hill about a hundred yards. I'm going down there; I have a flashlight. Hurry...it might be serious!"

He left to start his descent as the second vehicle disappeared into the falling rain. One headlight and both taillights marked his destination and his flashlight gave him just enough light to prevent serious injury. It took almost three minutes and numerous slips and falls to reach the wrecked automobile.

He opened the driver's door and saw the driver slouched over against the passenger's side; he was not moving. He climbed into the front seat and switched off the ignition as a precaution.

"Mister, are you all right?"

There was no sound except ragged breathing and the rain beating on the roof. He was afraid to move the unconscious man and searched for a pulse since that is what was always done on television. He fumbled with the victim's left wrist before finally detecting a weak pulse. He was now out of ideas. He was afraid to leave the man and return to the highway although there was nothing he could think of to do. He looked into the backseat and spotted a jacket. He knew that he should keep the man warm for some reason, but could not remember why that was always so important. Then it came to him: prevent shock. He placed the jacket over the injured man as best he could and then closed the door to keep some of the warmth inside. He could think of nothing else to do.

Several minutes later he heard a siren, exited the wrecked car and started up the treacherous slope. He noticed that the falling rain was suddenly illuminated by the flashing lights and then the ambulance pulled to a stop. He waved his flashlight back and forth when he saw a member of the ambulance crew trying to locate the wreckage with a spotlight. He moved farther up the slope before stopping to shout.

"Hey! There's an injured man down here. He's alive but has a bad head injury!"

"Is he pinned in the wreckage?" In the background there was the sound of another siren.

"No, but you can only get to him through the driver's side and he's over on the passenger's side. The car is up against a big rock."

"Okay, we're coming down. That's a fire truck and they'll be sending down some more help."

Midway Clinic was the brainchild of three doctors who had pooled their resources and had acquired state and federal grants to construct a limited-care facility in a remote mountainous area northeast of San Diego. The idea stemmed from the all-too-often loss of life when severe injuries in this area took excessive time to reach a properly equipped facility in the San Diego area. Usually a combination of bad weather and hazardous road conditions resulted in delays that had cost the lives of several people each year; Midway Clinic was an attempt to reduce the number of fatalities and provide an additional source of medical care for local residents...an idea which was applauded by the local population. One individual (who preferred to remain anonymous) even donated a cashier's check in the amount of $100,000 to assist with the project. There had been numerous other donations, but they were generally small and much too sporadic.

A large portion of the available funding had gone toward construction of the facility. The construction costs, due to the location, had been far beyond what was anticipated which left certain trauma-related equipment unfunded. As an interim care facility, the idea was to stabilize serious injuries until it was safe to re-locate the individual to an appropriate facility. The clinic was staffed by several older doctors who had reduced or ended their own practices for various reasons and a few trauma surgeons who volunteered their services. It was hoped that the facility would eventually attract sufficient personnel to remain viable without outside assistance. Right now, though, volunteer assistance was the only thing keeping the project alive. Every conceivable action possible had already been utilized.

Older equipment had been obtained from various sources and was usually the result of replacement with newer equipment at the larger facilities; the purchase of new, state-of-the-art equipment had been out of the question for the clinic. Items were sometimes donated and sometimes offered at extremely low cost. Some items were in excellent condition while others required refurbishment which occasionally cost more than the acquisition cost. The clinic thus had a mixture of older items which were often completely foreign to the intended operators who would learn their quirks through experience, but it was always better than nothing.

Thus the clinic possessed an old Esten 1000. It was a machine designed to monitor and display a series of brain wave patterns that indicated the health of the brain. It was simple and reliable when new and the relatively low cost had made it available to numerous facilities that would otherwise have done without. Midway Clinic had acquired this one which was fully functional and had been used very little. It had a built-in test system which checked each individual function separately as a go-no go item and then displayed a continuous green or red indicator light for that function. The internal wiring was fixed... no modules that could easily be replaced if they malfunctioned. Repairs required the services of a specially trained technician or shipment of the unit to one of several repair locations scattered across the country; however, there was now only one facility that performed repairs on the Esten 1000 and it was unfortunately located on the opposite coast.

David Pearson arrived at the Midway Clinic in bad shape. It had been a difficult extraction from his automobile and the movement of the stretcher up the slippery hill had been even more difficult. The paramedics had stabilized him as much as possible, but it had become apparent that time would be a key factor in his survival. The only option had been the Midway Clinic due to the weather.

His pulse was still weak and he was on oxygen, but he was unresponsive to any stimulus. Upon arrival at Midway he was quickly moved to the emergency room and the paramedics passed their information while the trauma crew performed additional assessment. He was moved from the stretcher to the operating table and that is when he ceased to breathe on his own. Minutes later he was on a respirator and his evaluation continued.

Sunday, June 8, 1997

The ambulance crew was suddenly summoned to another automobile accident approximately five miles away; they were rolling in less than a minute. Things were suddenly becoming busy on this miserable night. But then, that was the reason for the existence of the Midway Clinic.

The trauma crew found only minor injuries to David except for the severe head injury. He had no broken bones, no apparent internal bleeding and they had already determined that he was comatose. There was definitely the probability of severe intracranial pressure, but there was no CAT scan or MRI capability available. After slightly more than an hour, he was relocated to Intensive Care with an Esten 1000, a respiratory unit and a separate vital signs monitor attached.

When the Esten 1000 was readied, it performed its internal self-test perfectly and each electrical sensor showed a constant green status light which remained as the electrical leads were plugged into the respective jack. The monitor indicated activity in all targeted areas of David's brain although certainly not to the levels that would be indicated for a fully conscious, responsive patient.

There was an unfortunate flaw in the design of the Esten 1000: once the circuitry for each individual monitor point was tested, the feedback loop for each parameter required a *false or out-of-range* condition to trigger the red alarm or failure status light. The feedback loops all received electrical power from a common source and the system would change the status of the suspect parameter to a red light and extinguish the green light. The monitor screen would then display a 'flat line' and an audible alarm would immediately sound. The flaw was that the failure mode in one part of the common electrical power source had no warning system of its own; without power, the system could not switch the indicator lights to red and extinguish the green lights. Under those circumstances, there would be no failure indications and all indicator lights would remain green. The remainder of the circuitry would then allow the 'flat line' displays on the monitor and the green lights would falsely indicate that the machine was performing properly. The patient would appear to be 'brain dead.' That failure would soon occur in the Esten 1000 attached to David Pearson; remarkably, it would be the first failure of this type.

Crossing into New Mexico, Marilyn set the clock back one hour and then refueled at Tucumcari. She took longer to get back on the road this time. She was beginning to feel the effects of fatigue and decided to take some extra time to walk around. She would probably need to start looking for a place to sleep.

Marilyn felt considerably refreshed as she crawled back into her car. As she increased speed on the on ramp, she just expected to go 85 or 90 miles per hour. After her speed steadied at 90, she began mentally going over everything she could recall about her new knowledge. Everything now seemed so clear and so simple. The only thing that bothered her was how she would be guided.

David Pearson slowly regained consciousness; he tried to open his eyes so that he could see his surroundings and determine where he was. He vaguely remembered going off the road and a wild ride down that slope. He recalled the huge bolder and maneuvering to try to miss it and then *nothing*. He decided that his head must be bandaged and his eyes covered and he automatically reached to feel the bandages. At that point he realized that he could not move his arm. He tried the other arm and it did not seem to work either.

"Hello, is anybody here?" He could not hear his own words, but he could hear other sounds. David knew that there was equipment operating in this place...it was a fan or something similar and at least one other rhythmic sound. He was not in any pain. And then he lapsed back into unconsciousness.

The Intensive Care nurse glanced at the equipment attached to her only patient and noticed only that his pulse was 80, now 79 and slowly dropping toward the 70 beats per minute that he had maintained for the last 23 minutes. Everything else showed no change.

She buzzed the doctor and informed him of what she had just seen and was told to keep an eye on the patient; perhaps he was trying to wake up. She hoped desperately that he would awaken and wondered why it was taking so long to ready the small space that would become the nurses' station. Remaining in this room was a waste of the clinic's meager personnel assets even though right now there was only one patient in Intensive Care. She heard the sound of an approaching siren; no, there were at least two sirens.

The same ambulance crew that had delivered David Pearson had returned with two patients from a head-on collision not far from the scene of David's crash. A second ambulance was right behind with two more and a San Diego County Sheriff's Deputy was bringing another patient along with a paramedic from the fire truck that had been summoned for David Pearson's accident.

There was complete chaos in the small facility as the medical staff performed triage on the five victims. This was suddenly a challenge that was not expected quite this soon. The paramedics were pressed into service and the systematic process began to move more efficiently. There was a wide assortment of injuries: head injuries, broken bones, lacerations and one of the drivers had been pinned in the wreckage; there would probably be an amputation of his left leg below the knee. Two victims were unconscious while the other three were now quiet and pain free due to morphine.

The clinic was now short one vital signs monitor and the decision was to temporarily utilize the one used by David Pearson. Everything appeared normal as the nurse disconnected the leads and noted that his pulse was steady at 70. She unplugged the power cord and quickly began rolling the unit toward the door. In her haste, she bumped the Esten 1000.

Inside, a small, slightly longer than necessary wire that carried the electrical current for the feedback loops flexed one final time before separating from its soldered connection. Three seconds later the monitor showed a flatline condition on all parameters while all status lights remained green. The audible alarm sounded just as the nurse wheeled the vital signs monitor through the door. She rushed back to David and noted the monitor screen and the green status lights. She quickly checked for a pulse which was fine and then checked for visual response to light and received none. She silenced the alarm and rushed the vital signs monitor to the emergency room. Another nurse grabbed the unit and rolled it over to a little girl who had been partially ejected through the windshield.

"Dr. Scheffer, the comatose patient in ICU just flatlined; his pulse was still 70; still no response to light stimulus!"

"Okay. There's not much we can do with him right now. Let's concentrate on the ones we have here. We'll get back to him when we get everyone stabilized!" Doctor Scheffer had made this type of decision many times; *concentrate on the ones you can save.*

Mary Croix was one of the volunteers who provided administrative services for the clinic. By a strange quirk of fate she had come in rather than sit at home in this miserable weather. She had finished the inventory of Mr. David Pearson's things and found that he was an organ donor and supposedly had a Do Not Resuscitate (DNR) directive on file at Sharp Memorial Hospital in San Diego. He had listed his apartment manager as his emergency contact but had indicated no next-of-kin which greatly saddened her. Mary verified the DNR with Sharp and requested a copy which was faxed to her twenty minutes later. She deposited the information in the plastic bin next to the entrance to the ICU and returned to her combination Information and Billing desk. She prayed that the newly-arrived victims would fare better than Mr. Pearson.

One hour and seventeen minutes later David Pearson slowly awakened for the second time. Once again he experienced the confusion of where he was along with the realization that he could not see but was able to hear. He tried to move, but found that to be impossible. He knew that he was wide awake and even tried to call out to anyone who might be able to come to him; once again he could not hear his own words. This time he started thinking in a logical manner.

'I was driving in the rain and skidded off the road. I bounced down the hill and saw the big rock and I remember that I was going to hit it. So I must have hit it hard enough to be knocked unconscious. So now I am in a hospital somewhere with severe injuries and may be paralyzed or on some kind of medicine to keep me from moving around. That must mean that I have a lot of internal injuries. So they are allowing my body to heal. But if my injuries are severe then someone must be keeping an eye on me and that means that he or she must be in the room with me.'

"Hello. Is anybody here?"

He was certain that he asked the question out loud, but was also certain that he did not *hear* his own words. There was no sound of movement and no reassuring words that would set his mind at ease. He could still hear the sound of something...a sound of something operating on a regular cycle that never varied. He realized that it must be some sort of breathing apparatus.

Dr. Scheffer was starting to feel the effects of bending over his third patient. He knew that he would be extremely sore later in the day but had finally reached the point where he could take a break. He had just worked on two of the most severely injured victims and they were both stable yet not completely out of danger.

"I'm going to check on the first patient, the head injury. My back is killing me and I need to walk around for a few minutes." With that, Dr. Scheffer left the operating room and headed for the ICU. The ICU nurse was preparing to enter the room having just been released by the emergency room.

"Dr. Scheffer, how did the surgery go?"

"It was slow, but both of my patients are stable and have good color; the other three are fine. If the weather improves then we can transport all of them to Sharp. Let's take a look at Mr. Pearson."

The nurse turned the door handle as Dr. Scheffer removed David Pearson's paperwork from the bin next to the door.

David Pearson heard the sound of the door handle. 'Someone is coming! Thank God! Now maybe they can tell me what's wrong.'

"Who's there?" David relaxed a little even though he still could not hear his own voice.

While the nurse took David's pulse, Dr. Scheffer looked at the Esten 1000 monitor and noticed the flat lines and the green indicator lights. He checked David's pupils for reaction to light stimulus and noted none.

"Pulse is a little over 70, slightly higher than previous, Doctor." She had used the six second count. She watched the steady rise and fall of his chest as the respirator did its job.

Dr. Scheffer moved to David's feet and checked for reaction to pain stimulus which was also absent.

"I noticed that Mary got a DNR on him and he's an organ donor. I'll be updating Sharp in a few minutes and we'll see how they want to proceed. He has no next-of-kin. I'm sure Sharp will want him after the others are transported. It's a shame, but at least others will benefit from his organs. Let's go check on the others."

The doctor added a few entries into David's chart and then doctor and nurse walked toward the door.

"Wait, don't go! I'm okay...I just can't move! I heard what you said and I tried to speak, but I can't! Please come back! Don't leave me...!"

Had the nurse checked his pulse at that instant, she would have noticed that his pulse was now racing.

David heard the door close. Then he realized that this was his old nightmare! He just needed some time to heal. On the old television program the victim was about to be taken off life support and a tear ran down his cheek. A family member had spotted it and told the doctor. At that point they realized that he was awake and hearing everything. The show ended with the viewer knowing that the patient would recover.

David had thought about how horrible the idea was and then the nightmares had begun! Now it was happening to him. He knew that he must find a way to communicate. Could he produce tears? What else could he do? His pulse would surely go up...they would see that! He had no idea that the vital signs monitor had been removed for another patient. A few minutes later David once again drifted into unconsciousness.

After checking first his two patients and then the other three, Dr. Scheffer consulted with the other two doctors. The first two patients would probably be transported first, before morning rush hour traffic while the other three would probably go later in the morning.

With notes in hand, the doctor called Sharp Memorial Hospital and advised them of the status of the five patients with his recommendation that the two most seriously injured be transported as soon as transport could be arranged. He also recommended that the other three be moved after morning rush hour due to the weather.

Then he informed his contact of David Pearson and was switched to another extension. There was a lengthy discussion on priorities and protocols; Sharp had an urgent need for a heart and both lungs and Mr. Pearson appeared to be a good match for each of the two recipients. After a quick computer check, they confirmed that a liver was needed in San Francisco and the corneas were needed in Seattle. Sharp would coordinate and have the Harvest Team assemble at Midway Clinic due to the urgency and the weather. They would have a plane available at the Gillespie Field airport for the San Francisco and Seattle run. Due to the bad weather, two separate ambulances would transport the heart and the lungs to Sharp...just in case. This was a complex process that was based on each member performing perfectly with time and weather being the wild cards.

At Sharp, coordinators commenced the phone calls that would start the process; the Harvest Team members received the first calls and were directed to report to Midway Clinic by 3:00 A.M. The last notifications would go to the families of the intended recipients when final approval was obtained. The legal requirements would be re-evaluated one last time and the final decision would be rendered after the Harvest Team assembled at Midway.

The last member of the Harvest Team arrived at Midway at 3:17 A.M. Weather conditions had failed to improve and thus it was decided that the two most seriously injured victims of the head-on collision would be transported along with the heart and lungs from David Pearson.

The team assembled and Dr. Scheffer immediately commenced the briefing with a summary of the status of David Pearson. All legal requirements had been met and the Harvest Team leader would specify the time that Mr. Pearson would be removed from life support. The organs for transport to San Francisco and Seattle must arrive at Gillespie Field by 5:45 A.M.

The two pilots for the Cessna Citation III reached Gillespie Field at 4:01 A.M. The pilot-in-command went directly to check the sleek jet while the co-pilot rushed to Operations and commenced flight planning; departure time was tentatively set for 6:00 A.M. Corporate pilots were accustomed to constant changes in itinerary, often just at the whim of the traveling executives. This was different; it was for very specific reasons and usually these things went very smoothly.

At 4:02 A.M. David Pearson awoke to the sound of his door opening. He hoped that the new arrival was bringing good news.

"Okay, let's get started." David recognized the voice that he assumed was that of his doctor.

David heard someone approaching his left side and noticed a bright light in first one eye and then the other. 'I can see light! I'm getting better! Thank God!' Then he heard the soft click of a switch and the cessation of the rhythmical sound. 'Good, they're taking me off the breathing machine. That's another good sign.'

"It's 4:03," it was the doctor again. "I'll make one last quick check of the Operating Room to make sure they're ready. You can get him ready to be moved."

"Yes, Dr. Scheffer."

It was the voice that he had heard before...probably the nurse. David could hear her moving and sensed that she was removing things so that he could be rolled to the Operating Room. He was relieved that they had finally noticed his improvement. He could hardly wait to thank them. And then he realized that he was becoming very tired.

"Hey, something's wrong! Help me! Put me back on that breathing machine!"

He tried to move; he had to get her attention. Nothing seemed to work. He could hear movement of something on wheels and things banging lightly against other things. He heard the door open and a different voice spoke.

"Dr. Scheffer will pronounce in the O.R. The team is ready to start removing his organs. I'll help you roll him down there."

Realization of the immediate future suddenly became crystal clear to David.

"No! I'm okay...just check my pulse! Don't do this; I'm awake! Listen to me...just put me back on the breathing machine." He knew that his heart was pounding. "You can't do this to me! Please, please help me! Don't let me die...please don't let me die...!" He felt himself slowly losing consciousness, but heard one final voice.

"His color is not good; it won't be long now," said the individual who was assisting the nurse.

As conscious thought began to disappear, David Pearson was confused as the vision of an outraged eagle appeared briefly and then faded into nothingness.

Once David was transferred to the operating table, Dr. Scheffer listened for a heartbeat. After several seconds he shook his head and spoke to those present.

"Time of death: 4:10 A.M. Okay, he's all yours." Then he left the O.R. to check on the living.

Marilyn stopped for gas at Gallup, New Mexico. She was fatigued, but very alert. She walked into the convenience store to let the clerk run her credit card. He wanted her to sign the receipt and then he would fill in the amount just to save her some time. He looked honest, but she said that she would gladly return just to put off getting back into her car any sooner than she had to. The clerk said that he understood.

While pumping gas, she noticed an unkempt man appear from around the corner of the convenience store. He glanced in her direction and then entered the store. Marilyn watched him wander around the aisles before coming outside and lighting a cigarette. When the pump shut off, she returned the nozzle to the stowed position, replaced the fuel cap and closed the access door. As a precaution she clicked the door lock button on the key fob...just in case. She noted the fuel quantity and the total cost and walked back to sign the credit slip.

Approaching the door, the unkempt man suddenly moved over and opened the door for her. Marilyn noticed a strong smell of alcohol. She warily thanked him and went inside. For some strange reason Marilyn decided not to use her credit card and dipped into her precious supply of cash. She took her cash receipt and the credit card paperwork. She then looked to see if the man was still standing by the door; he was gone.

"Do you need anything else? I need to re-stock some items and I always lock the door while I'm in the back room," the clerk sounded apologetic.

"No, I'm all set. Well, how far am I from Albuquerque?" She was surprised at her own question since it was not relevant.

"About a hundred and forty miles."

"Thank you...I'm behind schedule." She did not know why she had uttered her last statement.

Marilyn returned to her car and was startled when the unkempt man suddenly appeared from behind one of the pumps.

"Give me your purse and your keys...now!"

She saw the flash of a knife as the man moved toward her. She retreated and moved to the opposite side of the car, next to the driver's door.

"You locked it, remember? There's no place to go and no one to help you. Just toss me your purse and keys and I'll let you live. Give 'em to me, now!"

At that instant there was some sort of a commotion behind her yet she kept her eyes on the thug. She watched as his eyes widened and then he stepped back, tripping on the raised concrete of the pump island. His head slammed into the nearest gas pump and he disappeared from view.

Marilyn whirled around and briefly saw the largest bird she had ever seen; the bird, an eagle, simply disappeared. She felt unusually calm as she walked past the unconscious man and pounded on the locked door to the convenience store. The clerk returned and quickly unlocked the door.

"There's a guy out here next to my car. He pulled a knife on me and then tripped and hit his head. You need to call the police and an ambulance. I must leave now."

The clerk rushed to the phone while Marilyn returned to her car and drove away.

The police arrived five minutes later followed immediately by an ambulance. The two police officers recognized the man immediately, but were extremely interested in talking to the woman who had almost become a victim. The clerk informed the local police officer that he thought she was headed for Albuquerque since she had asked how far away it was. She was driving a blue car...he was fairly certain that it was a Honda. The ambulance crew was amazed at the injuries apparently delivered by the suspect's assailant. He had a shattered right ankle, a broken left arm and probably a concussion. He mumbled about a 'big bird' that had attacked him. Neither paramedic was surprised by the ramblings of a man clearly under the influence of alcohol. They did, however, find it hard to believe that an unarmed woman had been responsible for the severity of his injuries.

One of the police officers radioed the information to dispatch and after a quick consultation, the state police were contacted to watch for a blue Honda headed eastbound on I-40. Meanwhile, Marilyn was westbound on the interstate moving at 90 miles per hour. It was 5:06 A.M. and the first hints of dawn were beginning to appear.

At 5:33 A.M. an ambulance departed Midway Clinic for Sharp Memorial Hospital and a private vehicle departed for Gillespie Field to deliver its precious cargo to the waiting Cessna Citation jet. There would be no public disclosure of the irony to the media; even so, the event did not go unnoticed.

Marilyn thought about the eagle and then realized that she was undoubtedly being watched over by that eagle or *something*. At that instant, she was suddenly overcome with fatigue and fell asleep at the wheel with the speedometer indicating exactly 90. The car eased over into the right hand lane and maintained its position perfectly centered in the lane. Marilyn's eyes were closed and her chin rested on her chest.

Two hours later she was passed by another car, a red Porsche, whose passenger looked over at the driver of the blue Honda. She stared in disbelief before speaking to her husband.

"John! That driver is asleep! Honk the horn...wake her up!"

Her husband dutifully tapped the horn twice before speeding up.

"Aw, the driver is just playing with you. I think maybe you're the one who needs some sleep."

"Me? I'm not the one who just got a speeding ticket."

He briefly considered a response, but decided that it would be a losing battle. With that he dismissed the incident and went on with his plan to reach Las Vegas as soon as possible. There was money to be won and he was feeling lucky.

A few minutes later another car pulled up behind Marilyn's car and decided to stay behind the blue Honda which obviously contained a radar detector. That was always a good idea. The driver was soon surprised when he heard the short burst of a siren and noticed the flashing lights in his rearview mirror.

"Oh, crap...where did he come from?"

He slowed and pulled over while watching the Honda disappear ahead. He had his license and registration ready when the trooper approached.

"Why me and not the blue Honda in front of me, officer?"

"What are you talking about? You're only the second car I've seen in the last few minutes...just you and a red Porsche. Could I see your license and registration, please?"

In San Diego Trish awakened, looked at the clock, listened to the rain and decided to go back to sleep. She would take in a movie later on and look for a fancy restaurant and an elegant dinner. It was the first time that she had felt lonesome since her arrival.

Marilyn awakened feeling surprisingly refreshed; however, her neck was a little sore. She spotted a sign indicating that Kingman, Arizona was just ahead. She vaguely remembered leaving Gallup and knew that Kingman was on the western side of the state. The gas gauge and odometer confirmed that she had traveled more than 300 miles and she was surprised that she had no memory of virtually the entire portion of that leg of her trip. She did remember the knife-wielding man and the brief glimpse of the eagle and simply accepted that she had probably just 'zoned out' due to fatigue. She would check the atlas at the next gas stop which was now an immediate necessity unless she wanted to hitchhike.

She left the interstate and pulled in at a Union station. She let an attendant fill the tank while she consulted the atlas. Sure enough, she was at Kingman and it was 9:35 A.M. She paid with her credit card and moved her car to a parking space. She visited the ladies' room and went inside the small store for a bottle of cold water. Ten minutes later Marilyn was westbound once again and devouring some fig bars as she cruised along at 90 mph.

Crossing into California, she set the car clock back an hour and smiled as she realized that there were no more time changes for this trip. The trip odometer read 1883 miles as she passed through Needles. Next would be Barstow and switching to I-15 South and then on down to San Diego. The sky hinted that rain was probably in her near future as she continued westbound. Five minutes later the rain began. She felt fortunate to have missed the inevitable rainstorms for the past 1900-plus miles.

The transition to Interstate 15 went smoothly and two hours later Marilyn reached San Diego after a fuel stop in Ontario; the time was 11:29 A.M. Upon reaching the outskirts of the city she noticed that her speed was once again under her control or at least was under her *conscious* control. She thought of the eagle that she had glimpsed in Gallup and briefly wondered if perhaps the eagle had somehow been responsible for her ability to speed across so many states. She quickly dismissed the thought as just a little too farfetched.

Unknown to Marilyn, seventeen state troopers in six states pondered the mysterious temporary failure of their radar units that had occurred recently; the problem seemed to have resolved itself a few minutes after the occurrence. Four other troopers wondered why drivers they had pulled over had referred to a non-existent blue Honda sedan that they should have been chasing instead of pulling them over.

There was one other unusual item that would remain unknown to Marilyn: meteorologists along a large portion of her route were at a loss to explain how the weather had changed. Thunderstorms and rain showers had either disappeared or had occurred several hours later than forecast. These weather experts searched in vain for answers. Television and radio audiences just took it in stride; those weather people were good, but never perfect and they promptly forgot about it.

Marilyn continued toward downtown San Diego on Highway 163 in the rain and suddenly felt the need to exit onto Interstate 8. Headed eastbound, she exited once again and soon thereafter found herself at a fairly decent motel with a 'Vacancy' sign. Fifteen minutes later she was in her room and promptly made a collect phone call to her grandparents.

"Hi, Grandpa...I'm in San Diego!"

"That's impossible; it's at least a two and a half day drive. We were worried since you didn't call sooner. Are you really in San Diego?"

"Yes, I'm not really sure how I did it, but I'm here. I'm staying at the *Aguila Real* motel. The motel sign has an eagle on it and the clerk said that the translation of the name of the motel is *golden eagle*. I did not consciously pick this place...I just ended up here. I...I think I was *sent* here."

She considered telling him about the knife-wielding attacker and the eagle, but left that out to avoid worrying her grandfather. He already had enough on his mind.

"I don't have a contact name for you yet; I thought I had plenty of time. Give me your phone and room number and I'll get that to you tonight. Right now I think you might need to sleep."

They chatted for a few minutes and Marilyn was suddenly overcome by extreme exhaustion. She ended the conversation and immediately fell asleep for the next six hours. She was awakened by the ringing of the phone. Disoriented, she stumbled her way to the ringing phone.

"Hi Grandpa."

"How did you know it was me?" laughed the elder Stevens.

"Well, who else knows I'm here?"

"You sound like you just woke up. How do you feel?"

"The phone woke me up. I'm a little tired, but I'm also hungry. I think I'll get something to eat and move the rest of my things into the room."

"Good for you. Here is the name of a local contact that can probably help you. He is retired, but has some very good contacts all over the local area. Remember, he does not know why you are there and I do not think that letting him know would be a good idea. Tell him you are doing background research or something. His name is Albert Givens. Let me put on my glasses and I'll give you his number."

Fifteen minutes later Marilyn grabbed her umbrella and walked in the rain to a nearby restaurant. She ate a leisurely meal and marveled that she had arrived in San Diego so quickly. After that she stopped by the motel office and picked up a map of San Diego County before returning to her room. She then transferred her hanging clothes and suitcases to her room. She hung her clothes in the small closet, but decided not to unpack the suitcases...she could do that later. She showered and went to bed; sleep came instantly.

CHAPTER THIRTEEN

San Diego

<u>Monday, June 9, 1997</u>

Marilyn awakened after dreaming about the old Indian, Howling Wolf. "Look for the signs" was the message. Confused, she dressed and walked over to the restaurant for a substantial breakfast since a chance for a normal lunch did not seem probable. She looked for signs...at least she tried to look for signs, but nothing attracted her attention. On her way out she picked up a copy of the local paper.

Back in her room she began looking through the paper and spotted an article about a traffic accident that had occurred late Saturday night. A man named David Pearson had been seriously injured and died Sunday morning from his injuries. He had been taken to a place called Midway Clinic which suddenly seemed very important to her. She felt that it was *necessary* to go to this clinic; something was urging her to go there. Could this be one of the signs or was she just grasping at something that was not relevant? She toyed with the idea of dismissing the sense of urgency to investigate the clinic...but what if she were to be wrong?

One hour later Marilyn parked at the Midway Clinic. Inside she met Mary Croix, the volunteer administrative assistant who confirmed that David Pearson had been brought in late Saturday night. He had passed away early Sunday morning and was an organ donor. He had no next of kin, but his landlady, a Ms. Juanelle Thompson, had stopped by that afternoon to collect his few possessions. Perhaps she could provide some details. Then, to her own surprise, Mary provided Marilyn with the landlady's name, address and phone number.

Marilyn thanked her and left. She eventually located the landlady's apartment, but failed to meet up with the woman. Later, she tried the phone number and finally spoke to the landlady who invited her to stop by. Once she arrived, the two women discussed Mr. Pearson and Marilyn asked to see his apartment. There was nothing that even hinted that Marilyn was interested in renting the apartment and yet the landlady gladly opened it for her. Marilyn asked where the bedroom was and was quickly shown the room. There was no dreamcatcher, but there was a projecting nail on the wall above the bed.

"Was there a dreamcatcher hanging on that nail?"

"Well, yes there was, but I took it down when I started preparing the apartment for another renter. Is there something wrong?"

She seemed a little nervous. Marilyn decided to ease the landlady's fears.

"Not really, but there is something special about the dreamcatcher and I would like to take a picture of it. It has an interesting past and I have done research on others like it."

"Well since Dave had no next of kin and we have known each other for several years, I thought it would be okay if I gave it to my sister Carol. It seemed like the perfect gift for her."

"Could you contact her and let her know that I would like to see it? Here's where I can be reached," Marilyn said as she handed a piece of paper to the landlady.

"She has a doctor's appointment this afternoon, so don't expect anything until this evening."

"That's fine, but it really is important that I see the dreamcatcher. Thank you for your help."

"You're welcome and I will have her call you."

Marilyn left and returned to her motel room. She broke out her own notes and the summary provided by her grandfather and began reviewing the information while she waited for a phone call from Carol. She also called her San Diego contact, Albert Givens, just to say hello and let him know that she might need his help. He had numerous questions which were politely and skillfully deferred.

Trish Favret continued her exploration of Balboa Park. Determined to not allow the rain to spoil another day, she walked throughout the vast area of the park. She was tired and would sleep well that night.

It was Monday afternoon when Carol Kelso, age 34 and mother of two, left the doctor's office and confidently walked to the hotel one block away. It had taken five weeks, but Dr. Hemming had convinced her that she was ready. She had not been upset that it was still raining but had snugged her rain hood down tightly to keep her hair dry; she used a half-knot rather than a bow on the drawstring just to save time. She was very close to losing her nerve.

Carol entered the hotel and walked directly to the elevators. She hesitated for a few seconds, slid the hood from over her hair and then pushed the *up* button. A few seconds later the elevator arrived and she noticed that she was trembling. The petite woman took a deep breath when the door opened and then timidly stepped inside. She located the control panel and pushed the button for the second floor...it was better not to rush things...she would go all the way up soon. "Oh what the heck," she thought and pushed the button for the twelfth floor. She was staring at the panel debating if she should push the *close door* button when the door began to close automatically.

Startled, she whirled slightly and the longer of the two drawstrings for her hood swung through the rapidly closing door opening. For a brief instant she wondered what to do, but the gravity of the situation was not yet apparent to her. Then the elevator began the ascent to the second floor! Carol tried to grab the drawstring to pull it free, unaware that the large knot on the end was firmly clasped by the outer elevator door at the lobby level. At that instant the drawstring tightened and violently yanked her down to the floor of the elevator.

The pressure on her neck increased and the drawstring snapped at the knot which was caught at the lobby level. Carol clawed frantically at the noose that now had completely cut off her air supply, but was unable to loosen the drawstring. She knew that she was going to die in spite of the promises made by Dr. Hemming. The last image of her life was that of an angry eagle. She was vaguely aware of the door opening at the second floor, but she was not found until the elevator had been summoned down from the twelfth floor. By then it was too late...Carol was dead.

Dr. Hemming was astonished to hear of Carol's death. The police determined her death to be accidental, but was referred to the doctor by a close friend. The psychologist explained that he had been treating her for a fear of elevators...she was certain that she was destined to die in an elevator.

Carol had ridden in an elevator as a young teenager and the elevator had stopped suddenly between floors. Trapped inside, she had listened to the other occupants talk about all of the things that could go wrong and her fear had begun. A few weeks later, she and one of her friends saw a movie where the elevator had broken a cable and the safety brakes failed. Carol had rushed from the theater screaming along with the screaming celluloid elevator occupants as they plummeted to their celluloid deaths.

Until now, twenty years later, she had avoided elevators. She had come to this highly recommended psychologist for help in perhaps ending this fear. Carol had become tired of using the stairs and making excuses to her friends and co-workers. Her job had been moved from the first floor to the fourth floor of the building where she had worked. It had been time to resolve her 'irrational fears.'

One of Carol's sisters, a Ms. Juanell Thompson, had just *acquired* a special gift from one of her renters, a Mr. Dave Pearson who had just *moved out suddenly*. Juanelle had happily presented the dreamcatcher to Carol. Dr. Hemming had inwardly scoffed at the idea of this dreamcatcher helping his client, but reasoned that it could certainly do no harm.

He felt that it might have given her that last small amount of courage needed to try the elevator. He thought a lot about the irony of this particular case.

The local news media would also emphasize the irony in their reports.

Meanwhile, Marilyn Stevens waited for the phone call that would never come. She went to sleep at 10:30, planning to locate Carol Kelso first thing in the morning.

Tuesday, June 10, 1997

Marilyn slept soundly until just before dawn when she dreamed of the old Indian, Howling Wolf.

"Find it; burn it," was his simple message.

Marilyn bolted upright, wide awake. She switched on the television just as the news reporter began the coverage of a woman named Carol Kelso who had died in an elevator accident the previous afternoon. The woman's drawstring from her raincoat hood had somehow gotten caught in the elevator and she had died from strangulation. Ironically, she had just left her doctor's office where she was being treated for her fear of elevators. The television cut to a reporter who showed how the outer, stationary elevator door could pinch the drawstring when it closed. Then they showed the same sequence from inside the elevator...there was no problem until the elevator began its ascent or descent.

Marilyn suddenly realized that this Carol Kelso was the woman with the dreamcatcher! That landlady had mentioned Carol's doctor appointment and the woman had not called. This had to be the same woman. It was not a coincidence that her fear of elevators had ultimately resulted in her death. Marilyn's dream and her timely decision to turn on the television were clearly the signs that she was waiting for; now it was time to act. There was no longer any doubt that she was being assisted by something that was both mysterious and powerful.

She picked up the phone and placed a collect call to her grandfather.

Thomas Stevens answered the phone on the third ring.

"Stevens' residence...yes, speaking...yes I will...thank you operator."

"Grandpa, it's Marilyn! Something just happened!"

"Slow down, Honey. Tell me what happened."

The sound of his voice had an immediate calming effect. She told him about the dream and the newscast before realizing that she needed to go back further. Marilyn mentioned the newspaper article about David Pearson and his death. She had felt the need to go to the clinic where he had died. From there she had followed her reporter's instincts and located the landlady. She told him how she had planned to talk to and hopefully to visit with this Carol person yesterday, but the woman had failed to call...because she had died in the elevator accident.

"Maybe I could have saved her if I had been more aggressive."

"First of all, she did not die in an accident; she was killed. It sounds like she was killed before you had a chance to intervene. Your first clue came from the dream and then came the newscast so don't blame yourself. You said that in your dream the Indian said 'Find it; burn it,' instead of 'them.' That seems to mean that only one is active. Now you must concentrate on locating that dreamcatcher. That would be the fourth one; there should be one more. Make certain that you have a foolproof method of starting a fire when the time comes. And if you can, get a photo. Be careful. I think that your starting point would be the landlady and right now she is probably mourning the death of her sister. You have work to do."

"Thank you, Grandpa. I'll try to keep you updated. Oh, and I bought one of those propane lighters, the kind for lighting charcoal grills and it stays in my purse. I also bought a can of lighter fluid. I guess I'd better get started. I love you and tell Grandma that I love her too. Bye."

"I love you and am very proud of you. Call us when you can."

Marilyn returned the handset to its cradle and sat there. What should she do next? She would call the landlady. It was still early and the woman had most certainly not slept well. She would wait until after 8 A.M. before trying to call her. She was not yet certain how to convince the landlady that she needed access to the dreamcatcher at this terribly inconvenient time; it was doubtful that the truth would be very effective.

Marilyn left the motel and walked over to the nearby restaurant. On the way in she purchased a copy of the *Union-Tribune* and after being ushered to a booth, ordered breakfast and began reading the article about Carol Kelso. She read how investigators had discovered the half-knot on the drawstring which probably explained Carol's inability to remove it from her neck. The real puzzle was how one end of the drawstring could have protruded through both the inner and outer elevator doors while they were closing. The reporter who wrote the article had purchased a similar coat and tried numerous times to duplicate that feat; he had succeeded once. The timing had to be precise and he had been forced to cheat in order to accomplish it, but it *was* possible. He subtly implied that it could not have been an accident. Marilyn decided to give the reporter a call after breakfast. She wrote down the phone number for the newsroom.

Leaving the restaurant she passed the pay phone and tried calling the landlady; there was no answer. She then dialed the newsroom number and asked to speak to the reporter, a Jack Arrington. She was informed that he was not in yet, but would probably show up around nine o'clock or so. Marilyn thanked the receptionist and returned to her motel room. She located her stenographer's notebook and made a series of entries regarding her trip to California. After that she added all of the information that she had accumulated since her arrival.

At the same time, Trish Favret left her hotel and commenced a day of leisurely exploring the Mission Bay area. She was disappointed in the weather, but she had no desire to remain in her room all day. This was her vacation and she was in San Diego; a little rain would not stop her!

Marilyn became restless and returned to the pay phone. Once again she was unable to reach the landlady and decided to drive to her apartment. Once there she rang the doorbell and pounded on the door, but nobody was home. She returned to her car and scribbled a note imploring the woman to contact her. She also wrote that she would phone her precisely at noon. Marilyn returned to the door and wedged the note into the door frame. She then left and headed for the newspaper building to hopefully meet with the reporter.

Before she had even left the parking area of the apartment complex, a sudden gust of wind dislodged her note and deposited it in a large puddle. Had she been there when this occurred, she would have wondered how the wind could gust so strongly within the confines of the apartment complex.

Marilyn drove to the downtown area of San Diego and managed to find the *Union-Tribune* building without asking for directions. Parking was at a premium due to the rain, but on her second trip around the block she happily parked in a recently-vacated spot right in front of the building. Once inside she obtained directions to the newsroom and went in search of the reporter.

Jack Arrington was seated at his desk when Marilyn approached. He glanced up at her.

"Can I help you?" He was in his mid-thirties and appeared to be quite interested in his visitor.

"My name is Marilyn Stevens and I would like to discuss one of your articles."

He gestured for her to take a seat.

"And which article would that be?" he smiled hoping that it appeared that there were so many articles to choose from. He was trying to impress her but was not certain why. "Your name sounds vaguely familiar."

"It's a fairly common name. I want to learn more about Carol Kelso. You hinted that something was suspicious about her death."

"My editor cut part of my article that mentioned foul play. You certainly read that I had to work hard to make that knot get caught in the outer elevator door. I tried, oh I would say probably thirty times to make it happen accidentally the way I think she might have moved and it was impossible. The only way I got it to work was to flip the cord directly through both sets of doors at exactly the right instant. Believe me, when that happened all hell broke loose! That coat was immediately yanked out of my hands and I'm glad that I was not wearing it. I found the knot when I returned to the floor where I got the cord to go through. Here is a photo of the coat with the drawstring pulled tight...the loop is less than an inch in diameter and the half-knot could not be loosened by hand. Now back to the part where I finally made it happen. Either she did it intentionally or someone else either inside the elevator or outside on the first floor did it. There is no suicide note and there is nothing to indicate that she just did this on a sudden impulse. That leaves one other possibility: someone else did it."

Marilyn was now sitting on the edge of her chair. The photo made it clear that a tremendous amount of force had been applied to Carol's drawstring and Jack's description of the knot had made it readily apparent that she could not have loosened it.

"What if something else caused it?" she asked quietly.

"What do you mean?" He stared at her with a blank expression.

Marilyn realized that she had vocalized her thought and quickly recovered.

"Couldn't it just be a bizarre set of circumstances? Sometimes things just happen."

"Look, Marilyn, I deal in facts. I am a reporter and sometimes things are not what they appear to be. My editor told me to leave it alone. I checked and could find no reason for someone to kill her; she had no enemies. Her ex-husband pays alimony and child support and is the logical suspect. He lives in Phoenix and I spoke to him in Phoenix late yesterday afternoon. It is possible that he hired someone to do this, but from all indications, they got along very well. That leaves someone else who simply seized the opportunity when it presented itself. It might have been intended as just a simple prank that got out of hand."

"What about the police; aren't they even a little suspicious? I can't believe that I'm the only other person who thinks that something is wrong."

"The police consider it a freak accident; case closed. They have no intention of investigating further. You are the only other person who has questioned the circumstances under which Carol Kelso died. You're a reporter, aren't you?"

"I'm a freelancer just visiting the area and your article got my attention."

"I knew it; I must have read some of your articles and that's why your name is familiar."

Marilyn decided that it was time to leave. She did not want Jack to arrive at her identity and her relationship to a certain famous reporter.

"Well I'm trying to relax and enjoy my visit, but I got carried away by reading between the lines. I just had to ask you about the article. Thank you for sharing your thoughts. I have so much to do and see and the rain is not helping."

"Take my card...maybe we could discuss this further or perhaps something will happen regarding a real investigation into the cause of her death. Thanks for stopping by."

He rose to his feet as she stood. He was still trying to figure out the real reason for her interest in this case; there was much more to this woman than just a freelancer on vacation. It was time for some research on her. He watched her walk away and then turned to his computer and began typing.

Marilyn walked quickly to her car and drove back to her motel. She tried calling the landlady even though it was not yet noon. There was still no answer. She left a message on Juanelle Thompson's answering machine and returned to her room. She went over all of the information she had developed and updated her notebook. Everything hinged on the landlady. There was a growing sense of urgency.

Several hours later, Juanelle Thompson returned to her apartment for the third time. The grieving woman had taken the responsibility of making all arrangements for her sister's funeral. She had tried to delegate some of the tasks to her other two sisters, but one had taken Carol's two children and the other was still hysterical. This time she spotted the flashing light on the answering machine and checked the messages. She froze when she listened to the message from Marilyn. She had completely forgotten about the dreamcatcher and just realized that Carol had never gotten an opportunity to show it to that Stevens lady. She vaguely remembered that she had given the dreamcatcher to her neighbor after watching the news at noon. She regretted her lapse in memory and was sorry that she had not contacted that nice lady, but her priorities had changed with the death of her sister. She had felt an urgent need to put the dreamcatcher to good use and perhaps that had clouded her judgment. She would call the Stevens lady tomorrow; there was too much going through her head right now.

Juanelle left the apartment and drove to her sister's house; perhaps she could console her.

The Wayside House was intended for and named for those unfortunate souls who had fallen by society's wayside. The occupants included those who had committed all sorts of crimes against mankind and some who had simply lost their jobs due to their own physical or mental weaknesses. They were all welcome except for those who were so violent that they created a danger to the other occupants or the staff. The Wayside House was supported by several church groups, local activists and volunteers who saw the plight of the residents and hoped to someday re-establish them as productive citizens.

The city of San Diego applauded these types of efforts and assisted with brokering assistance deals with those who owned property and operated local businesses. A growing homeless population was not a good thing for the tourist industry.

Thirteen new residents had just arrived at Wayside resulting in a full house of thirty-two. These new arrivals had been the only survivors of a truck crash that had destroyed a similar house two days earlier; the other nineteen occupants had been fatally injured in the 2:07 A.M. crash. Ironically, the survivors had received only minor injuries some of which occurred as they tried to escape from their pitch black prison. It had taken forty-five agonizing minutes to rescue the thirteen terrified women from the building that had collapsed on them. Even two days later they were still shaken by their ordeal. They were kept together as a group and were moved into an open living bay on the second floor that had just been refurbished. The staff thought that sharing their ordeal with each other more or less constantly would give them a strong bond and allow them to gain strength from each other as they put that terrible experience behind them. They were often referred to as the 'Lucky Thirteen.'

One of the caregivers brought in and hung a beautiful wall decoration, a dreamcatcher, and explained that it would take away their bad dreams. Her neighbor had given it to her after the neighbor's sister had passed away in an elevator accident. The neighbor was going to show it to some woman who wanted to take a photo of it but had seen a news broadcast about the thirteen women at Wayside; the grieving woman felt that someone should benefit from this beautiful dreamcatcher even though it had not helped her sister. She had felt compelled to donate the dreamcatcher after seeing that the walls of their sleeping bay were mostly barren. She never watched the mid-day news, but had tuned in for some strange reason and heard the mention of the Wayside House. After the broadcast she had immediately delivered her sister's dreamcatcher to the caretaker who agreed to take it when she went in for her 2-10 P.M. shift. Later, the caregiver had delivered the dreamcatcher and shortly thereafter it was hanging on the wall of the sleeping bay occupied by the Lucky Thirteen.

The presence of the dreamcatcher immediately made the new residents smile; for the first time in many months they all experienced feelings of serenity and hope. Their fears and bad dreams began to diminish, for some at a faster rate than for others. The dreamcatcher was clearly the focal point of their sleeping bay; it made the new residents happy.

C.E. "Stan" Standley

Wednesday, June 11, 1997

It was the fifth straight day of rain in the San Diego area. That was certainly unusual for that time of year and it was depressing to those accustomed to spending time outdoors. Trish suddenly decided to visit Old Town and the Mission Valley area, thankful that she had dinner plans. She found herself eastbound on Interstate 8 in moderate rush hour traffic. She simply drove and looked for something that appeared to be interesting; the rain was still wreaking havoc with her plans.

At some point Trish did something that she seldom ever did: she cleared her mind of those things which she wanted to do and just let *fate* take over. It was then that she felt the need to exit the interstate; it was just after 9:00 A.M. and she made a brief stop before resuming her journey. The sun would finally return a couple of hours later and Trish would spend the next few hours driving around aimlessly.

Marilyn Stevens had attempted a phone call to Juanelle Thompson but had to leave a message instead. She left word that she would call back at 10:00 A.M. and desperately needed to talk to her.

At the Wayside House the thirteen new arrivals were undergoing a group session which was facilitated by an experienced staff member. They were sitting on the floor in the middle of their bay, arranged in three rows with the facilitator out in front. It was clear to the facilitator that the group was rapidly moving forward and becoming more at ease. She gave some of the credit to the new dreamcatcher, but smugly felt that she had been primarily responsible; regardless, the progress of the entire group had been astounding and that was what really mattered. She sadly remembered that the dreamcatcher had been removed as 'being inappropriate.'

One of the problems with buildings that have flat roofs is drainage. The Wayside House was one of those older two-story buildings that had suffered neglect over the years and the flat roof had gradually begun to sag in the middle area. A slow, steady buildup of leaves and other debris had accumulated and finally blocked the four drains. There were four main vertical support beams for the center portion of the roof and all had experienced water seepage for many years; the subsequent rotting was hidden from view. There was now seven inches of rainwater on the roof.

At exactly 10:00 Marilyn phoned Juanelle Thompson. Ms. Thompson answered immediately.

"Thompson Apartments."

"Good morning, this is Marilyn Stevens. I spoke to you a couple of days ago about that dreamcatcher that you gave to your sister. I am so sorry to hear of the loss of your sister and I hate to bother you now, but I simply must find that dreamcatcher. Can you tell me where it is?"

"I'm sorry, it's just that my sister's death has been quite a shock to our family and our world has suddenly been turned upside down. I forgot about your request to see it and gave it to one of my neighbors who took it to her workplace. She works at the Wayside House, but I don't have the address."

"That's okay...I can find it. I'm so sorry to have bothered you at this time, but it is urgent that I locate that item. Again, I'm truly sorry for your loss."

"Thank you and I hope you find it."

Marilyn hung up the pay phone and frantically searched the yellow pages of the phone book under "Shelters." After locating the Wayside House, she scribbled the address in her notebook and after consulting her map, headed for the shelter. She felt an unmistakable need to hurry.

At 10:16 A.M. the fourteen women in the open bay all experienced the vision of an angry eagle followed by a loud groan which caused them all to look upward. At that instant the entire roof section above the open bay, along with tons of water, came crashing down. Only the facilitator survived.

Marilyn saw the police cars and then the fire trucks and ambulances while she was still three blocks away. She parked as close as possible, grabbed her umbrella and hurried to the small crowd that was being prevented from approaching closer. She asked the nearest bystander what had happened and was informed that the roof of the shelter had collapsed and there were some fatalities.

Marilyn asked the posted police officer if she could speak to someone from the Wayside House administration.

"You a reporter?" he asked.

"Yes, but that's not why I'm here...I'm trying to locate someone."

"A spokesman from the shelter will address the media in a few minutes. You can probably get some answers then."

"Thank you, Officer."

Marilyn stepped back and watched the frenzied actions of the fire and medical personnel as they disappeared inside and apparently searched for survivors. Periodically some would exit carrying a stretcher with a body completely covered by blankets. She counted six since she had arrived.

Suddenly there was a commotion from inside the building and two more EMTs rushed inside. Five minutes later a small group exited with an obvious survivor; one held an IV aloft while another was apparently maintaining pressure on an injury. They hurried to an ambulance which departed minutes later with siren wailing and lights flashing.

Marilyn debated remaining for the press conference or searching for a phone. If she could reach someone inside by phone, then perhaps she could get some information about the dreamcatcher. At that instant she wondered if the roof collapse could be related to the presence of the dreamcatcher.

She suddenly felt sick to her stomach as the possibility that she might have prevented the tragedy with an earlier arrival struck home.

While Marilyn agonized over this alarming possibility, three members of what appeared to be the staff from the shelter walked toward the small assortment of bystanders and reporters. A pleasant looking man under obvious duress moved closer to the outstretched microphones and began to speak.

"I am Daniel Overton from Wayside House. This very sad morning at approximately 10:17 A.M. there was a collapse of the roof and ceiling apparently due to the extensive rain which has fallen over the last several days. There have been some fatalities, but at least one survivor has just been transported to Sharp Hospital. We are attempting to identify all of those who were in the area of the collapse, but right now we are trying to avoid hindering those who are searching for victims. That is all of the information that I have at this time."

Reporters jockeyed for a better position from which to ask questions. Marilyn quickly moved to the far side of the group of reporters and made eye contact with one of the two women accompanying Mr. Overton. Marilyn motioned for her to approach.

Seeing no microphone and no notepad, the woman warily moved toward Marilyn.

"I'm trying to locate someone who might know something about a dreamcatcher that was delivered here perhaps yesterday; it is very important."

"That would be Brenda. She works at the registration desk and was told to get rid of the thing. You're talking about that round thing with the feathers on it, right? Mr. Overton said that it was not the type of thing for decorating places that rely on state funding."

"How can I reach Brenda...it is extremely important."

"She left for the hospital a few minutes ago. Her best friend was found alive in the rubble; she is the survivor that Mr. Overton just mentioned."

"Thank you! I must leave now."

"They took her to Sharp Hospital. Do you know how to get there?"

"No, can you help me?"

"Sure, just get back on I-8 West and go north on 163. There are plenty of signs."

"Thank you, again," Marilyn said as she turned and walked to her car.

Minutes later she merged into the westbound traffic on Interstate 8 and soon spotted the sign for Highway 163; she was relieved to see the hospital indicator on the same sign. She walked into the emergency room 10 minutes later and went straight to the Admissions/Information desk. The lady at the desk confirmed that a patient from Wayside House had been brought in but did not have any other information on her status. Marilyn asked if anyone from Wayside House had shown up...someone named Brenda. The answer was a simple "No."

Marilyn walked over to the seating area. "Is there a Brenda here from Wayside House?"

Blank stares and head shakes were the only responses. Marilyn sat where she could see new arrivals. She knew she was getting very close. There was a television in the waiting area and the Wayside House story was the *Breaking News*. The group known as the "Lucky Thirteen" had perished in the roof collapse; one survivor, a staff member, was now hospitalized with serious injuries. Marilyn watched the brief interview that she had witnessed earlier. The reporter emphasized the irony of the "Lucky Thirteen" surviving one tragedy only to lose their lives in another almost identical situation a few days later. Those words started a building anger and public indignation that would reverberate throughout the city.

The rain stopped a few minutes later and bright sunshine returned within the hour. The media soon created a flurry of righteous indignity that survivors of one terrible tragedy would be placed in such an unsafe building. Local politicians called for a complete investigation into the facts surrounding the collapse of the roof. Where were the building inspectors? How many more buildings of this type existed?

The search for the blame would continue until the public tired of hearing the story and after the last funeral, media coverage would all but cease. The politicians would stop their posturing and resume their daily routines having extracted as much attention as was possible. Most would be pleased with their performances; the public would surely see how concerned and how sincere they were.

Marilyn waited for Brenda for two hours. She tried calling Wayside House but the line was constantly busy. In desperation, she drove back to Wayside House. The area was cordoned off and a large crowd of curious onlookers had gathered. There were several news vans there, but no serious activity. She approached one of the three police officers who prevented access to the damaged building.

"Is there anyone from the staff that I can talk to? I am trying to locate a staff member who has some information that I need."

"Yes ma'am, you and 20 or 30 other reporters. You are welcome to wait right here and perhaps someone will come out and talk to you, but good luck with that. I'm sorry...there appear to be some serious liability issues here and everyone has been instructed not to talk to the news people."

"Officer, I'm not here as a reporter. I'm trying to find a staff member named Brenda who has some information about an object that was recently delivered here. Obviously the timing is bad, but it is imperative that I speak to her. Her best friend was the survivor that was taken to Sharp Hospital and she was supposedly going there. I waited for her at the hospital for over two hours, but she never showed. I just want to leave her my phone number or speak to her briefly."

"Okay, write down your name and number and I will see to it that this information gets inside to whatever staff is still here. It will be up to them to pass it along to this Brenda person." He handed a note pad to her.

Marilyn quickly wrote her name and the number for the motel. She also wrote that she would be at the Sharp emergency room until at least 5:00.

"Thank you, Officer," she said as she returned the note pad. "I'm going back to the emergency room."

"I'll take it inside. Good luck, Ms. Stevens."

A look of surprise came over his face as he looked down at the note...she had not included her last name. He wondered briefly if she had spoken it and then dismissed the thought entirely.

"Thank you," Marilyn said as she turned to leave. She took one step before realizing that she had not given the police officer her last name nor had she written it on the note. She turned back toward the police officer who was walking toward the entrance to the building. It was yet another sign.

Marilyn returned to the hospital and was in the process of locating a decent parking space. She and another driver, a woman, simultaneously reached a parking space quite close to the emergency room. Marilyn deferred to the other driver who quickly parked in the space. Marilyn continued and spotted the back-up lights of another vehicle nearby and parked her car a few seconds later.

Walking briskly toward the emergency room, she spotted a woman standing near the crosswalk; she was apparently waiting for someone. Marilyn smiled and nodded her head as she approached.

"Thank you for giving up that parking spot. I was glad that you were able to park close by."

"It just seemed that you might need the parking space more than I did...and you're welcome."

"Are you here to check on someone?"

"Actually, I'm searching for someone who might be here, but not as a patient. What about you?"

"A good friend was injured in an accident and I was told that it would be awhile before they could tell me anything."

The two women walked to the entrance door and Marilyn allowed the stranger to enter first. They both went to the Admissions/Information Desk.

"Can I help you?" asked the woman with a 'Volunteer' tag on her blouse.

"I'm here to find out the status on a Dianne Waverly; she was brought in from the Wayside House."

Marilyn's purse dropped from her hand. She tapped the woman on the shoulder and then retrieved her purse.

"Is your name Brenda?"

"Just a second," said the Volunteer somewhat aggravated.

"Yes, it is, Brenda Wiggins," replied the stranger as she turned toward Marilyn with a look of surprise that was quickly replaced with a smile. "Do I know you?" Her smile slowly changed to a quizzical expression.

"No, but perhaps you can help me with some information."

"Pardon me, ladies," it was the Volunteer again. "First things first. Dianne Waverly is out of surgery and in the recovery room. I should have more information in a few more minutes. Any questions?"

"No, I'll check back in a few minutes," the relief was evident on Brenda's face. She turned toward Marilyn. "So how can I help you?"

"Uh, ma'am, you're next," stated the Volunteer.

"I'm okay," she replied to the Volunteer. "Please come with me for just a couple of minutes. My name is Marilyn Stevens."

The two walked over to a deserted area. Brenda was becoming suspicious.

"Are you a reporter? We are not allowed to talk anyone about what happened today." Her eyes were beginning to water.

"Yes, I'm a reporter, but that's not why I'm here. I need to ask you about an object that you might know something about. Do you know what a *dreamcatcher* is?"

"Sure I do. Why do you ask?" Brenda stepped back slightly; she was suddenly very suspicious.

"I am trying to locate a certain dreamcatcher that has a very strange reputation. I believe that it is at the Wayside House."

"Actually, it was taken away early this morning. Upper management decided that it was not a proper thing to have in the house so it was given to me to dispose of. It was a gift and when I saw it, I really wanted it. This probably sounds strange, but it seemed to be telling me to keep it. Anyway, out of the clear blue, in walks this really nice tourist who said she was looking for something. I don't know why but I showed her the dreamcatcher. She offered me thirty dollars for it and I gave it to her, wooden case and all. Then she just left. Am I in some kind of trouble? I'll give back the money."

"No, I just need to know where the dreamcatcher went. Do you have any idea where I can find that woman? Did you get a name or anything? You said she was a tourist."

"No, I don't...wait a minute. She had an eastern accent and I asked her where she was from. She's from Massachusetts and we talked about the area since I've always wanted to visit that part of the country. She wrote a local phone number on her business card so we could talk about some of the sights to see if I do go up there."

"Do you have her card with you?" Marilyn held her breath.

"No, it's on my desk at the Wayside House."

"Brenda, I cannot express how important it is that I talk to this person. Did she say where she was staying?"

"No, she just wrote down the phone number and I think she put her room number on the card. It was a San Diego number...I do remember that."

"Is there any possibility that we could go to Wayside House and you could get the business card; I just need the name and phone number."

"I called the Wayside House private number before I came here and spoke to my boss. He said that all occupants were being re-located and that the building was undergoing some very intense scrutiny due to what happened. No one is allowed back inside due to the investigation. Supposedly we will be able to retrieve personal items later. My area is near the front door and is not anywhere near the damaged spaces. I could try calling and maybe get permission, but my boss made it sound like *nobody* from the staff would be allowed in after the personnel and their records were removed."

"Could we call right now? This is extremely important."

"Sure, there's a pay phone right over there."

The two women walked to the pay phone and Marilyn held out a handful of change. Brenda took the necessary coins and dialed the number. She listened to it ring for several seconds, shook her head and hung up the phone. She retrieved the coins and handed them to Marilyn.

"I'm sorry."

"Brenda, give me your phone number. I might have a way to get you into the building...under police escort, of course. Could you help me out if I can make that happen? Let me give you my number."

"Please be careful...I could lose my job over this, you being a reporter and all."

"Don't worry. I won't do anything to jeopardize your job."

Marilyn turned toward the pay phone; she would call Albert Givens, the contact provided by her grandfather. She quickly located his phone number and dialed.

"Mr. Givens, this is Marilyn Stevens."

"Hello, my dear; what can I do for you?"

"I'm afraid that I must ask you for a really big favor."

"If I can lend assistance to the granddaughter of my most favorite colleague, then it would be an honor. Now, how can I help?"

"Have you been following the story of the roof collapse at that shelter...the one with the Lucky Thirteen?"

"Sure, it was quite the tragedy."

Well, there's a lady who works there who needs to get me a phone number, but the police have the building locked down due to an investigation into the cause of the collapse. Her desk is near the entrance, well away from the damaged area. I was wondering if she could go in under police escort just to her desk to get the phone number. That's where I need your help. Do you have a police contact that could approve that?"

"I believe I do. What is the lady's name?"

"Brenda Wiggins; she is the daytime receptionist for the Wayside House."

"Okay. I'll get right on it. Give me a number where I can reach you."

I'm at the *Aguila Real* motel. I don't have the number with me. If you reach me, fine; if not, please leave me a message. And Al thank you...this is very important."

"Okay, young lady, but you must tell me what this was all about. I mean, when it's over."

"I will, I promise."

She hung up the phone and spoke to Brenda.

"I think we'll be getting some help soon."

Unfortunately, Albert Givens would spend several hours tracking down a certain detective who would ultimately provide Brenda Wiggins with a police escort into the Wayside House to retrieve the phone number. Albert finally located the detective at a favorite hangout that catered to the police. Feeling no real sense of urgency and due to the late hour, the two men decided that the escort into the Wayside House would not occur until the following morning. And it was time for another drink.

Marilyn stopped for gas and then ate dinner before returning to her room. She immediately looked for a flashing red light on her phone and was disappointed when there was none. She waited impatiently in her room wondering when the phone would ring. She was very close to locating the dreamcatcher. She knew she was close. Perhaps another sign would soon appear.

That evening Trish showed up at Don's house promptly at seven o'clock. She was met at the door by Joan sporting an impish smile that would not disappear.

"C'mon in, everyone is in the family room. I can hardly believe that the sun finally came out."

Two men stood as the ladies entered the room. Trish immediately locked eyes with a tall and quite handsome man who smiled before speaking.

"I'm Brad."

"I'm Trish."

"Well now that everybody knows everybody, Trish would you like something to drink?" Joan asked after a quick grin aimed at her husband.

"Uh, a glass of wine would be fine. I'll come with you."

The two women walked to the kitchen.

"I suppose that Brad being here is a coincidence," Trish whispered to Joan. "He's gorgeous."

"Actually Don invited him and since I was planning on cooking a nice meal anyway, what's one more at the table. I hope you're not offended."

"Are you kidding? Is he single?"

"Brad lost his wife and son about six and a half years ago in an automobile accident. He never re-married. After meeting you I thought that the two of you should be introduced. I hope I haven't embarrassed you."

"Far from it; pour my wine and I'll return. I'm sorry; do you need any help with dinner?"

"Not right now, but when I do I'll get Don."

A similar conversation had taken place between the two men. Trish returned to the family room and once again both men rose as she entered the room.

"Thank you, gentlemen; I am not accustomed to men rising when I enter a room. I like it, but it's okay with me if you remain seated."

The three adults sat. Brad was first to speak.

"Don says you work at a nuclear power plant. You don't glow, do you?"

"Not at the plant," said Trish as she playfully lowered her gaze.

They all laughed.

"And what do you do, Brad?"

"I do the same thing Don does, but I'm so much better at it," he said with a grin.

"Let me get this straight. You're a guest in our house and you're going to eat our food and you have the audacity to insult me in front of our special guest?"

"I thought *I* was the special guest." Brad feigned great disappointment.

There was laughter once again.

"Where are the girls?" Trish finally asked.

"Oh, they're next door. I'll go get them after we three *adults* eat. I probably should take Brad over there now. You can decide, Trish."

"I vote to let him stay."

Brad thanked her with a smile and a nod of his head.

Moments later, Joan summoned her husband for assistance which allowed Trish and Brad to learn more about each other. There was none of the awkward conversation that sometimes kills a potential new relationship; they both were completely honest. Politics and music were the first topics which were followed by movies and recreation. The two were in agreement in most areas, but there was some lively discussion about areas where they disagreed. It was during one of those discussions that they were summoned to the dining room table. They promised to resume later.

The dinner was quite elegant; Joan and Don had set a table which could have adorned any of several magazine covers. Trish was especially impressed at the appearance alone; the food was even more impressive. The two couples thoroughly enjoyed the meal and the visitation.

After coffee, they cleared the table and moved to the family room. Don excused himself and went next door to collect Adrianne and Brianne. He returned shortly with two very excited daughters.

"Girls, Trish has something to ask you," Don said as the girls rushed to greet their cousin.

"What is it?" asked Adrianne as she hugged Trish.

"Yeah, what?" chimed Brianne as she competed for Trish's attention.

"Well, how would you like to spend the night with me in my hotel?"

Both small heads with hopeful expressions snapped toward their parents; neither spoke for a few seconds until Adrianne finally could not wait any longer.

"Can we?"

"Go pack your suitcases. Take some clothes for tomorrow and your pajamas. Adrianne, help your sister," Joan said with a grin.

The two girls quickly disappeared.

"You realize that you just sent Trish back to her hotel," Don laughed.

"I sure did...just as soon as I said it was okay. I don't suppose that the girls would sit here patiently while we chat for a while."

"It's all right with me; the look on their faces made me happy. We can chat some other time. Don't get me wrong...I would rather visit with the adults," Trish said as she smiled at Brad.

Brad smiled back as he formulated a plan of his own. He was not ready to say good night to Trish.

Joan picked this time to go the kitchen and returned with the coffee pot.

"Time for final refills. The girls will be ready to go soon and Don and I always make a point of not letting them dictate what we do. They, hopefully, will return and wait patiently for your departure. This will be tough on them tonight since it just reeks with exciting adventure for them. So, Trish, you are now in charge of the restraint...you decide when to leave. They will probably not try to convince you to leave, but Brianne is just getting the idea of how this works. I guess you could say that she is the *wildcard*. Don or I will intervene if it comes up."

Right on cue, Adrianne and Brianne walked into the family room with their suitcases. Both girls were wearing sweaters and were obviously ready to leave. Adrianne, standing next to Trish, spoke.

"We're packed."

Hearing no acknowledgment, Adrianne gently nudged her sister and they moved to a large chair located in the departure path. They placed their suitcases on the carpet and eased onto the chair without saying a word. Don took the opportunity to resume conversation.

"Brad, you drove down from Lemoore in your own car, right?"

"Sure. It's not a long drive and I really didn't want the hassle of a rental car or flying down and then picking up a rental. There's always something wrong with a rental car."

"Well thank you very much for that comment...I had no choice," responded Trish with a slight smile. "Now I'll start worrying about my rental car."

Trish glanced at the two girls who were fidgeting while they waited. It was more than she could bear.

"I need to leave pretty soon...I have a lot to do."

Both girls immediately stood and picked up their small suitcases. All four adults smiled.

"I should leave, too. I hate to eat and run, but I must admit that tonight I had the best dinner I've had in years. I'm driving back tomorrow and plan to get an early start. The food and the company could not have been better," Brad said as he looked at Trish.

Joan glanced at Don and gave him her best triumphant smile. He returned the smile and threw in a wink for good measure. The four adults then stood simultaneously. With the two girls out in front, they moved toward the front door. Adrianne quickly gave her parents a hug and kiss and Brianne eventually gave up her position next to the door to follow suit. Brad shook Don's hand and gave Joan a kiss on the cheek.

"I think I'll escort Trish and the little people to the hotel just to make sure they get there okay. Thanks again for a nice evening and I will be in touch now that you guys have settled in."

"Thanks, Joan, for everything," said Trish as she squeezed her hand. "Good night, Don."

"Good night! Drive carefully."

Brad followed Trish and the girls back to her hotel. He escorted them to Trish's room on the third floor and she invited him inside for a few minutes.

"Okay, everybody in," Trish said as she opened the door.

The Shaman's Legacy

The girls rushed in followed by Trish and Brad.

"Trish, did you buy some things from here to take back with you?" asked Adrianne. "We always get to buy something from each new place we go."

"Gee, not that much so far, but I've visited a lot of great places. Wait a minute...I did buy something really neat today."

Moving to the small closet, she brought out a wooden case and placed it on the small desk.

"What's inside?" asked Brianne.

Trish opened the case and stepped back. Brad was the first to speak.

"When did you get that?"

"I bought it this morning. Why?"

"I've seen it before. Well, maybe not the same one. Where did you find it?"

Brad's intense interest in the dreamcatcher was surprising to Trish.

"You know, it was the strangest thing. I was driving along Interstate 8 and suddenly had this powerful urge to change my route and ended up at some kind of homeless shelter. Don't ask me why. Anyway, I felt this need to go inside and a nice lady named Brenda showed me this box. When she opened it, I was immediately struck by the beauty of this dreamcatcher. I mean, I felt like I *must* have it. I paid 30 dollars for it and was happy to do so. She said that it had been hung on the wall but had later been removed because it was inappropriate. She thought it was unfair because it had been displayed in a room housing some women called the "Lucky Thirteen." We chatted for a few minutes and she asked about my accent. She wanted to know a little about the Massachusetts area where I live and I gave her my hotel phone number so we could talk about that later...I just wanted to leave with my prize before she changed her mind. That's it, nothing spectacular."

"I was at this steak place and a guy had two of them; they were identical to this one. After we ate, he was showing me one of them when some other guy saw it and bought it right on the spot for 100 dollars! You got quite a bargain. He even asked me if I wanted to buy the second one but I declined."

Adrianne and Brianne had stared at the dreamcatcher long enough.

"What is it? It's very pretty," said Adrianne as she looked at the object in the wooden box.

"It's called a *dreamcatcher*," said Brad as he carefully lifted it for them to see.

He once again felt the strong need to possess it.

"It catches your good dreams and makes the bad dreams go away."

That was when Brad noticed that apparently the one who had constructed this dreamcatcher had not made a hole for the bad dreams to escape. He was disappointed since it was supposedly what the dreamcatcher was all about. He suddenly felt that he must drop that thought. He also experienced a chill and his instincts warned him that something was not right; he handed the dreamcatcher to Trish and the ominous feeling immediately disappeared.

"Can we hang it up?" asked Adrianne.

"Yeah, can we, please?" questioned Brianne with her most charming smile.

Trish glanced at Brad and his blank stare was immediately replaced with a smile.

"Do you have one of those wire clothes hangers like you get from the cleaners?"

"Sure. Let me grab one."

Trish handed the dreamcatcher to Adrianne and removed a blouse from one of her hangers and handed the hanger to Brad. She then folded the blouse and placed it on the dresser.

Brad quickly fashioned a makeshift hook and retrieved the dreamcatcher from Adrianne. After very carefully bringing the lower end of the improvised hook through the top of the dreamcatcher, he centered the dreamcatcher atop the large painting which adorned the wall above the king-size bed. He stepped back to admire his handiwork. He noticed that the strange feeling had not returned. In fact, he felt wonderful.

"Wow! It looks great. It makes me want to take down the painting." Trish was obviously impressed. "Okay girls now it's time for a surprise. We are going to have a pajama party tonight, but first we need to do some shopping. Brad would you like to come with us to a couple of shops in the lobby?"

"I'll pass. I could watch a little television though; I would hate to spoil the fun. You ladies go do what women do best," he chuckled. He was certain that this special treat was really for the two girls.

Adrianne and Brianne were already at the door and grinning from ear to ear. Neither had said a word. Perhaps it was because they were not sure what a pajama party was or maybe they were just too excited. Trish grabbed her purse and headed for the door.

"We won't be long."

Trish wanted to give him a goodbye kiss, but decided that it might be a little awkward.

"Have fun, ladies."

Brad located the remote and brought the television to life. He found a show that seemed interesting and sprawled on the bed. He wondered if he should even be here in this room, but then he really did not want to leave. Trish had not left any subtle hints that he should go...at least he did not think she had. He was sound asleep within two minutes.

Forty-five minutes later Trish and the two girls returned with their new items. Trish had hurried the girls through their small shopping spree just so she could get back to Brad. They entered the room without waking Brad and the room was quiet until Brianne opened her shopping bag.

"Uncle Brad, look what I got!" she said as she pulled a plush white bathrobe from the bag.

Brad went immediately from fitful sleep to a wide awake state. He was sweating and his heart was pounding.

"Are you okay, Brad?"

"Sure...I, uh, was just dreaming that's all." He looked at his watch. "Now that must be a new record for three women shopping."

"We got robes!" said Adrianne. "Look!"

"Girls, it's time to get your pajamas and go change in the bathroom. Don't forget your robes!"

The two girls carried their small suitcases and their new robes to the bathroom.

"Brad, are you okay? You were sweating and this room is a little on the cool side."

"It was just a bad dream, that's all. I'm fine. Actually, I need to be going. I'm driving back to Lemoore in the morning. I'm scheduled for a flight Friday morning. Oh, and 'Uncle Brad;' where did *that* come from?"

"Adrianne just wanted to know what to call you. And just in case you're not aware of it, Friday is the thirteenth...you're not superstitious, are you?"

"Well, the Navy doesn't just shut down because of superstition; that wouldn't look right to the rest of the world, now would it? Actually, I'm taking flying lessons...I'm working on my private pilot's license."

"You're a Navy pilot and you are learning how to fly? That seems a little strange."

"Military aviation and civilian aviation have different rules and the aircraft are different. Since I want to fly recreationally, I must learn the rules that will apply to me. And the aircraft are at opposite ends of the performance spectrum. Maybe someday I can take you flying."

"I would like that; I've never ridden in a small plane before."

He stood and decided to kiss Trish without the presence of the two short witnesses.

"I'm not going to shake your hand in farewell," he said while watching her reaction.

"Well, what do you have in mind?"

She turned her head slightly and glanced at him out of the corners of her eyes as if daring him. The effect was devastating and Brad kissed her very gently. At that moment Trish wished that her two young cousins were not there. She initiated a kiss of her own which was interrupted by the return of her two cousins. Brad said farewell to the threesome and reluctantly left for his own room at the Naval Air Station.

Trish allowed the two girls to stay up past their normal bedtimes. There was the inevitable pillow fight and both girls soon showed obvious signs of fatigue. The two girls initially were going to sleep in the second bed, but asked if they could crawl into bed with Trish if they got scared. Adrianne reminded Trish that she was afraid of monsters, especially at night. Then she mentioned that Brianne had nightmares about big dogs, having been bitten by a neighbor's dog a few weeks earlier. Trish solved that problem by telling them to jump into bed with her if they wanted to; there was no need for a second invitation.

And they all slept beneath the beautiful dreamcatcher that hung from the painting on the wall above the headboard.

Thursday, June 12, 1997

Thursday dawned as beautiful a day as was possible; it was cool, but not cold. Marilyn was up at 5:30. She showered, dressed and ate breakfast and was back in her room at 7:00. She was watching television and waiting. It was a few minutes after 8:00 when the phone finally rang.

"Hello, Al?"

"Yes, my dear. I have good news: you can tell the lady from the Wayside House to go see Officer Daly. He will escort her into the building, but only to her desk. She can retrieve what she needs and then leave."

"You don't sound so good, Al. Tough night?"

"Let's just say that it took longer than I expected. It seems that the public is furious with the accident and the police are trying to help keep a lid on this. They don't want those sneaky reporters snooping around while the investigation is underway...you know what I mean. Let's just say that it took awhile to get my contact to loosen up."

"Yes, I was just watching the news and it's already beginning to get ugly. I need to get started. Thank you so much for your help, Al."

"You're welcome. Remember, you still owe me an explanation."

"And you will get it...hopefully very soon. Gotta run!"

Marilyn hung up the phone abruptly.

She dialed Brenda's number and let it ring several times.

"Come on, pick up the phone!"

When the answering machine activated, she left a message for Brenda to go to Wayside House and ask for Officer Daly. Once she had retrieved the information, she must call back with the information and, if necessary, leave it as a message.

Marilyn sat in front of the television set deep in thought. During a commercial, the words 'Hurry to the place!' appeared on the screen and she jumped in surprise. Two minutes later she was on her way to Wayside House.

She was able to park much closer due to the absence of news vehicles and spectators. She spotted the ambulance as soon as she stepped from her car and a bad feeling came over her as she hurried to the police officer posted next to his cruiser.

"What happened?"

"Some lady was being escorted inside to retrieve something important and fell when she started down the steps...she hit her head on the railing. Here comes Officer Daly; he was escorting her." He hesitated briefly before speaking again.

"Hey Daly, can you talk to this lady?"

"Ma'am, can I help you?" He asked the question while still several steps away.

"The woman, is her name Brenda?"

"Yes it is. And you are...?"

"Marilyn Stevens. Brenda was retrieving an important phone number for me. You were supposed to escort her inside to her desk and then bring her out as soon as she had the information. I think she said it was on some woman's business card. Is she okay?"

The siren on the ambulance suddenly 'chirped' and the two police officers scrambled to move the yellow and black tape as the ambulance began to roll. The ambulance sped away and shortly thereafter the siren began warning drivers to clear a path.

Officer Daly returned to Marilyn.

"The paramedics said she has a concussion and some minor injuries from the fall. She was unconscious for several minutes. She fell right in front of me just as I finished locking the door for her. I think she was putting the business card in her purse when she stumbled."

"I don't mean to sound uncaring, but where is her purse?"

"It's in the ambulance. I tossed her keys into the purse and zipped it closed. It will be kept at the hospital until she's released."

"Is she going to Sharp Hospital?"

"Yes...it's closest."

"Thank you, Officer Daly," she said as she turned and ran to her car.

The police officer waved to her back and shook his head.

"It must be important," he said to the other police officer.

He watched her make a u-turn and speed away. He shook his head once more.

"It must be really important."

Twenty minutes later Marilyn sat in the waiting area of the Emergency Room. She had confirmed that a Brenda Wiggins had been admitted with head trauma. The Volunteer at the desk promised to keep her updated even though she was not a relative.

Shortly after 11:00 a woman approached her.

"Are you Marilyn?"

"Yes"

"My name is Michele Andrews, Brenda's sister. The lady at the desk said that you were interested in my sister."

"Without going into a lot of detail, your sister had gone into her workplace to get a name and phone number for me. It is urgent that I talk to this person. Anyway, she fell and hit her head. The police officer who was escorting her in and out of the building said that she had found the card with the name and phone number and was putting it into her purse when she fell. I simply must have that name and phone number. It might be in her purse."

"I suppose I could ask for her purse...I was listed as her closest relative. I'll be right back."

Marilyn watched her walk to the desk and begin a conversation with the Volunteer. Moments later she returned.

"They will bring the purse out to me shortly and we can look for the card. They still don't have an update on Brenda's condition."

"I hope she's okay. Excuse me, I need to make a phone call."

Marilyn walked over to the pay phone and placed a collect call to her grandfather. After a few seconds she heard her grandfather's voice.

"Marilyn?"

"Hi Grandpa! I'm sort of stuck right now. Let me fill you in on everything that has happened since we last spoke."

Marilyn spoke almost nonstop for ten minutes with only a few pauses to answer questions. Then she reached the present and the fact that she was waiting at the hospital for Brenda's purse.

"You know, Grandpa, people are so slow to respond; it's really difficult. How did you ever track down the dreamcatcher that you destroyed?"

"That was a long time ago and life was much simpler. I did a lot of driving and it really did take a long time. You are dealing with people who have busy and complex schedules."

"I know, but each time that I get a new clue it comes with a big delay. For once I would like to be able to move forward immediately after receiving a sign. I'm close to finding the dreamcatcher; I know it"

"Well, if it isn't just because of busy lifestyles, then there is one more possibility. What if the dreamcatchers or the power behind them can somehow erect obstacles in your path? You know...like some sort of self-preservation ability."

"Don't you think that to be a little far-fetched? These are dreamcatchers."

"Go back and examine each clue or sign. See if there was some sort of delay or dead end. Perhaps the dreamcatchers now know what you are doing and can delay you."

"But Grandpa, why wouldn't they just eliminate me as a threat?"

"Maybe they can't. Maybe they must follow some sort of rules that do not allow you to be harmed. I will tell you one thing, though. When I destroyed that dreamcatcher years ago, that object that arose from the flames shrieked at me and the way it looked at me was one of the most terrifying things I have ever seen. I think that these dreamcatchers have become stronger and wiser, but if they could stop you, they would have already accomplished that. I don't mean to frighten you, but that's just what pops into my mind. I'm sorry, Sweetheart, it's time for my nap."

"Thank you, Grandpa. I love you. Tell Grandma I miss her."

"I will, Sweetheart. Call us anytime."

The line went dead. She hung up the phone and thought briefly how weak he sounded and returned to her seat next to Michele.

"I had to talk to my grandfather. He's my advisor on things like this."

"I don't know what you mean...things like this."

"Oh, well...tracking down artifacts and things like that. It's very difficult sometimes. He has a lot of experience and I'm a novice."

"Artifacts? What sort of artifacts?"

"I'm trying to locate a special dreamcatcher with a cloudy history. I am supposed to locate it and photograph it."

Marilyn hoped that her vague explanation would be sufficient.

"Would this be the dreamcatcher from Wayside House?"

"Yes. How did you know?"

"Brenda offered it to me, but I have too much stuff in my house as is."

"She sold it to a tourist lady who just walked in and was curious about the wooden case that it was in. As soon as she saw it she had to have it. They struck up a brief conversation and Brenda wanted to talk to her about visiting the New England area someday. She wrote the lady's name and phone number on her business card so she could talk more about going up there. That card will get me in touch with the tourist."

"So, finding that card is not a life and death matter."

Michele's voice indicated aggravation.

"Actually it is. I wish I could tell you more, but right now I must locate the dreamcatcher."

The two women sat in silence for a few minutes until Michele was summoned to the desk by the Volunteer.

"Your sister's purse will be brought out in a few minutes. Also, a doctor will speak to you in a minute or so."

"Thank you...I'll be over there," she said as she gestured to her previous seat.

She returned and sat next to Marilyn.

"The doctor's coming out and someone's bringing Brenda's purse. I'm sorry if I was a little cross with you earlier. I just have a lot on my mind right now."

"It's okay...I'm a little pushy sometimes. Well, most of the time."

A doctor wearing scrubs entered the waiting room and most of those in the room followed his path to the desk. He conferred briefly with the lady at the desk and then looked toward Michele and Marilyn. They stood simultaneously and held their breath as he walked toward them.

"Ms. Andrews...I'm Dr. Seguin. Your sister is in the recovery room. She's doing fine. She struck her head on a steel railing for the steps where she works. She has a concussion and was unconscious for awhile, but she has no permanent damage. She'll be moved to her own room a little later and you'll be able to visit with her for a little while then. We'll be keeping her overnight and she will probably go home later tomorrow. I don't expect any complications, but she will need to take it easy for a few days. Do you have any questions?"

"You said no permanent damage...what does that mean?"

"She is a little disoriented which is to be expected and after striking the railing she landed face down suffering several facial lacerations and contusions. She will be sore for several days. Right now she needs rest. So visit with her and I'm certain she will have you check on a few things for her. This would be a good time for you to let other family members know her status. She'll be fine. I'm sorry, I must check on two other patients."

"Thank you, Dr. Seguin."

He smiled and gave her a small wave as he left the area.

"Michele, that's good news!"

"Yes it is. Of course now it will be a long wait before she reaches her room."

"You're probably right," sighed Marilyn.

At that moment, a young lady entered the waiting room carrying a purse. She walked straight to the desk and conferred briefly with the Volunteer who suddenly looked toward Michele and motioned for her to approach. Michele hurried to the desk, briefly examined the purse and signed a form provided by the Volunteer. She then returned to her seat next to Marilyn.

"Well, I passed the test...I knew her name and address so they let me take her purse...after I signed for it. Okay, what are we looking for?"

"Supposedly it is a business card with a name and local phone number on it. I would assume that it has a New England company on it."

Michele systematically went through the purse, but failed to find the card. She made a second search as Marilyn looked over her shoulder.

"I don't think it's in here."

The Shaman's Legacy

"Wait...the police officer that was with her said he thought that she was putting the card in her purse when she fell. Maybe it's still there. I'm going back to see if they will let me look for it. I hope everything works out. Thank you for your help."

Marilyn squeezed the other woman's hand and left. Twenty minutes later she was parked near the Wayside House. She walked over to the nearest police officer and asked for Officer Daly.

"You're the lady who was here earlier. Officer Daly got pulled off this detail. Can I help you?"

"He was helping the lady who was injured locate a business card for me. He thought she was putting it in her purse when she fell. It wasn't in the purse, so perhaps it is on the steps or close by. Is it possible for me to look for it...I don't need to go inside."

"Okay, just the area of the steps, nowhere else. Understood?"

"Yes, officer."

He lifted the police tape and Marilyn quickly ducked under it. She went straight to the concrete steps and quickly spotted what must have been blood on the bottom two steps. The card was not on the steps so she commenced her search in the shrubs next to the steps. She carefully and methodically checked the area, but found nothing.

"Gravity and wind are the two forces that were in play," she stated aloud. Marilyn tried to envision the probable sequence of events. Brenda was trying to put the card into her purse when she fell. She reasoned that when Brenda fell she probably dropped both her purse and the card as she tried to avoid the fall. There were only a few variations of what Brenda's arm motions could have been. Thus the wind was the key. She tried to remember if the wind had been blowing the previous day. It could not have been significant or she knew she would have remembered it. And then she remembered the gentle movement of the end of the police tape.

She grabbed her purse and located several of her own business cards. She released them from different heights and locations and was astonished that they fluttered down within a relatively small area. She then returned to the area she had previously searched only this time she worked her way toward the steps while carefully maneuvering through the landscaping.

"It's got to be here," she whispered.

"I beg your pardon," said the police officer who had wandered over to keep an eye on her. "Looks like you could use some help. I've done a little searching myself. Tell me exactly what you are looking for."

"A business card...I assume it's probably white or beige. It should really stand out; it has to be right here." Her aggravation was obvious.

Then, in a moment of extreme clarity, she remembered her grandfather's comment that possibly the dreamcatchers could somehow erect obstacles to thwart her efforts to locate and destroy them. What if that was happening right now? And almost immediately she either heard or felt something directing her to the downspout.

"Wait; the downspout!"

The police officer turned abruptly, first toward Marilyn and then toward the downspout.

"What?"

"The downspout...I need to check the downspout!"

Marilyn struggled through the soggy mulch and varied array of plants toward the downspout. In her haste, she snagged her right foot on some of the vines that constituted part of the ground cover. She positioned her arms to cushion her fall and tore the downspout from its mounting.

"Great...just great!" It was embarrassment more than anything else.

"Ma'am, are you okay?"

The police officer gently assisted her to her feet.

"I'm fine. I picked a great day to wear yellow!" She was now angry with herself.

She stepped away from the police officer and brushed the leaves and mulch from her arms and blouse as best she could. She looked down, but the card was nowhere in sight.

The police officer picked up the downspout and tossed it out of the way. It struck the ground and bounced. A collection of small twigs and other nesting materials flew from the lower end of the downspout. Amid the substantial variety of construction materials were numerous pieces of white paper. All of the nesting material was dry. Obviously the downspout had not been performing its designed function.

"The business card...I think I just found the business card!" Marilyn exclaimed.

She rushed to the nest.

"Don't touch it! It probably belongs to a mouse judging by the size of the nest."

"But I need that card, even if it is in pieces."

"You don't want to touch that nest. Ever hear of Hanta virus? Let me get a plastic bag. I'll be right back."

Marilyn knelt in front of the nest; she was no longer concerned about her appearance. She had the answers right in front of her...it was just a matter of assembling the pieces. She fumbled in her purse and retrieved a pair of tweezers. She heard the police officer approaching.

"This should work."

She turned and saw the plastic bag and some latex gloves.

"I have some tweezers."

"Put the gloves on. Don't disturb the nest any more than necessary. Would you like me to help?"

"No, I can manage. Thank you...you've been extremely helpful."

The Shaman's Legacy

A slightly embarrassed Marilyn took the gloves and put them on.

"What is so important about that business card?"

"It has some very important information written on it. With that information I might be able to prevent something terrible from happening."

"Such as...?"

"It is extremely complicated and I just don't have time to explain it," she said as she extracted the first piece of the card and carefully placed it into the bag.

"Okay, I'll be over at my post. The mayor is coming in a few minutes. I don't think you should be here when he arrives. There will be a hoard of news people arriving shortly."

"Thanks for the warning, Officer...."

"Hughes, Don Hughes. And you are?"

"Marilyn Stevens."

"I am very pleased to meet you, Marilyn Stevens. Maybe we could have dinner sometime."

"Perhaps. Thank you again for your help."

She continued retrieving the pieces of the card. She would love to have dinner with the police officer, but right now she needed to focus on solving the current problem. There was something about the police officer that she found refreshing. Perhaps another time and another place....

"You're welcome and good luck." He turned and walked back to his cruiser.

It took five minutes for her to pick the remaining pieces from the nesting materials. Convinced that she had all of the pieces, she closed the bag and stood. She looked down at her tan slacks and saw the soaked area of both knees. At that moment the Channel 39 news van arrived.

"Wonderful, just wonderful," she muttered.

Marilyn held her head high as she struggled from the landscaped area. She nodded at Officer Hughes who had a huge smile on his face that slowly turned to sympathetic concern. He walked over to her and took her arm.

"I'll escort you to your car."

"Maybe you should put me in your cruiser...that would bring less attention to me, don't you think?"

They both laughed. Upon reaching her car he opened her door and turned toward the news van. The camera was on the two of them and the news reporter was walking rapidly toward them.

"Get in and go. Make a u-turn and get out of here. I know that something important is going on and you don't need any more attention. Now go!"

"Thank you, Don."

He turned and faced the reporter.

"Step back, please," he said as Marilyn wheeled around and left.

"Who was that, Officer? What was in that bag?"

"I'm sorry, I am not an official spokesman and this is part of an ongoing investigation. The mayor should be arriving any minute now."

The reporter turned to the videographer, "Did you get a shot of her license plate when she drove away?"

"Of course, I zoomed right in on it. Illinois plate."

"Good. We want to check on that, later."

Marilyn returned to her motel and began the process of re-assembling the card. She quickly discovered that the task would not be easy. She moved all of the edge pieces into one area of the desk after checking for printing. There was no printed name on the front of the card...it was generic. She laid the pieces out based on the front; the name and phone number were written on the back. She had tried assembling the back so she could quickly get the information, but it just did not work.

Now she had enough information that she could turn the pieces over. As long as she kept them in the same relative position, she should have the answers. She had assumed that the task would be the same as reconstructing a document that had been torn into several pieces. Apparently, mice that are building nests only care about making lots of small pieces that are very similar.

After what seemed like an eternity, she had the majority of the card re-assembled. There were numerous gaps and she scoured the remaining pieces for traces of the written information. She found several, but none contributed significantly to the solution. It was clear that key parts of the card were missing. She knew that she had picked up every piece that she had seen so, obviously she had missed some. Marilyn wondered if it was her own error or if perhaps the dreamcatcher had somehow intervened.

She had the area code and the first number of the prefix. She had partial numbers for the remaining six digits. For the first name she had 'Tr' and a large gap followed by what appeared to be an 'F' for the last name. There was also a '3' that was larger than the other numbers and two other partial digits that seemed to be larger than the others; the second digit could be a '6' or '0' while the third could be a '1,' '4' or '5.' Her notebook was covered with possible numbers and letters that could complete this small puzzle.

"Damn that mouse," she said just before she fell asleep at the desk.

Trish considered herself fortunate to be in San Diego on such a remarkable day. She had taken the two girls home after a leisurely breakfast at the hotel and had visited with Joan for more than an hour. She mentioned that Brad had called her the night before after the girls had fallen asleep and they had talked for over an hour. Joan beamed.

Trish suddenly remembered her impending zoo visit and thanked Joan once again for such a nice evening and her choice of guests. She hugged Joan goodbye and left.

Trish reached the zoo just before noon and purchased a two-day ticket. Once inside, Trish methodically worked her way around the zoo grounds until arriving at the Reptile House. She had hated snakes ever since that day when a small garter snake invaded her house. Her brother had captured it and then proceeded to chase Trish who ran screaming until she collapsed from exhaustion. Over the years she had come to believe that the snake really had been harmless, but the thought of touching even a harmless snake was still terrifying to her. She had occasional nightmares involving rooms full of snakes that were not afraid of her and most of them had fangs!

She suddenly glanced at her watch and decided to leave for the day; tomorrow she would start her visit right here at the Reptile House. Why should she get caught in rush hour traffic...tomorrow would be better. Somewhat disappointed in herself, she left the zoo, picked up some fast food and returned to her hotel. She wondered if Brad had made it home.

Brad reached his home in Grangeville at almost exactly the same time having run a few errands. He entered the house and went straight to the phone then dialed a number in San Diego; he asked for room 304.

Friday, June 13, 1997

Marilyn awakened at 5:30 A.M. The dream was still fresh in her mind. 'Hurry, find it! Burn it!' was the terse message. The urgency was clear. She stared at the partially assembled card which had been rearranged when she had dozed off the night before. She checked her notes. There had to be a way to track this down.

"I'll call Al Givens...he has contacts everywhere," she thought.

She located his number and dialed it without even bothering to check the clock. The phone rang eight times before he answered.

"It's 5:45! What the hell do you want?"

"Al, it's Marilyn Stevens and I need your help again. I'm sorry to call so early."

"It's okay...I thought it was my ex-wife. How can I be of assistance?"

"I'm closing in on the thing I need to fix, but I must track down a person. I have only a partial name and a partial phone number. I need a way to try and locate a San Diego hotel and a tourist that is staying there...I just don't have a way to do it."

"Where are you staying? I'm sorry...I forgot where you told me."

"A motel called *Aguila Real*, just off Interstate 8 in Mission Valley."

"It's right next to a restaurant, right?"

"Yes it is."

"I'll meet you at the restaurant at 6:30. Bring all of your notes and information. And will I finally get some idea of what this is all about?"

"Well, some information to be sure, but there is a lot that even I don't know. What I'm looking for is critical and I need this information as soon as possible."

"Okay, I'll see you at 6:30."

Brad Chandler shut off his alarm clock. He sat on the edge of his bed for several minutes, struggling with a feeling of acute dread and a rising sense of urgency to get on with his day. He finally rose and started his morning routine. In the kitchen he pushed the 'brew' button on the coffee maker and then quickly showered and shaved. He dressed casually and returned to the kitchen for some coffee and, after several sips, quickly made a ham and cheese sandwich. He ate the sandwich and polished off a second cup of coffee with this unusual compelling force urging him to hurry. Twenty minutes later he was northbound on Highway 41 headed for the Adams Flight School at the Fresno Airport.

John Hefner had finished the wiring installation and had just connected the two wires for the ventilation fan and switch to an old 6-volt lantern battery. He carefully installed the intake tube where it was not noticeable; the exhaust tube was hidden just as well. He marveled that the solution had come to him so clearly. It was a very professional installation and had been quite inexpensive with just a cooling fan for one of those home computers, some sheet metal, wires, a switch, a few screws and some duct tape. None of the purchases would have drawn any attention to him. He moved to the front of the van and started the engine. He climbed into the rear of the van and after flipping the fan switch, reached for the end of the exhaust tube and smiled as he felt the air flowing out of the freezer. He meant to return the fan switch to the 'Off' position but forgot to do so.

The magnetic signs for his appliance repair van had been obtained in Oregon and contained phone numbers obtained from Directory Services in San Diego and Los Angeles. He had several different sets of signs...just in case. The same flexibility was evident in his jumpsuits which had a place on the back and one above the left front pocket where the company information could be placed, held there by Velcro. His name was there for all to see; he was Bob from *Bob's Appliance Repair*. The golden signs with black lettering proudly proclaimed that Bob's did "Repairs, Replacements and Removals."

John had transferred all of his tools into the windowless black work van and then placed the six-foot stepladder on top and strapped it down. His spare parts were properly secured and the extension cords were neatly coiled and attached to the expanded metal that separated the back of the van from the front seat area. It was now time to do some reconnaissance. He drove away whistling.

Marilyn showered and made herself presentable...she was not interested in impressing anyone. She felt the unrelenting urgency of something of immense proportions and felt queasiness in her stomach; something was clearly about to happen. She checked her purse for the propane grill lighter and the can of lighter fluid and then walked to the diner. An unshaven and slightly disheveled Albert Givens sat in a booth facing the entrance. He motioned for Marilyn to join him.

"You made good time, Al."

"My dear, the intrigue is suffocating. Your coffee will be here momentarily and you should order your breakfast. You already have a menu."

"I don't need a menu, but I do need the coffee."

The waitress appeared with her coffee and Albert's breakfast. Marilyn quickly ordered and began sipping the coffee. After several quick sips she opened her notebook and pushed it over to Albert. He began looking at her notes as she spoke.

"Here's what I do know: I am looking for a female tourist from Massachusetts. She is or was staying at a local hotel. Her first name begins with the letters 'Tr' and her last name begins with an 'F.' You can see the area code and the first number in the prefix. There is also what appears to be a 3-digit number beginning with a '3' followed by either a '0' or '6.' The final digit is a '5,' '4' or '1.' These numbers are larger than the phone numbers and appear after the 'F.' The last name would either be very short or just an initial. If we could find the right hotel then we could go from there."

"That's true, but there are privacy policies at hotels; they typically do not confirm the presence of their guests."

"I know...that's why I need your help. If we can locate the person, then we go to the hotel and I can ask her to hand over something that she recently purchased. If she is not there, then I need someone to open the door. If what I am looking for is there, then I must remove it and destroy it."

Albert's jaw dropped. He stared at her for several seconds before speaking.

"Let me get this straight. You intend to ask this lady to turn over something she bought so that you can destroy it. If she is not there then you want to break down the door, steal it and then destroy it, right?"

"That sums it up pretty well, but I was hoping that if she is not there, then perhaps we could get the hotel people to open the door for us. You have contacts; I cannot do this alone. Will you help me?"

The waitress arrived with Marilyn's breakfast. In spite of Marilyn's excitement, she tried to appear calm and nonchalantly began to eat. Albert stared at her for a few more seconds and began devouring his own breakfast. He abruptly stopped.

"Does your grandfather know anything about this?"

"Actually, Al, he sent me here to do this with some urging from another source. Right now I can tell you that if we can obtain this object and destroy it, you will see something that you will find difficult to believe. Grandpa destroyed one years ago and I had trouble believing it. I still have trouble believing it, but I have seen things that defy rational explanations. I must keep you in the dark about much of this, but if it happens the way it is supposed to happen then you can get more of the story and what a story it is."

"Okay, let's finish eating then you and I are going to take a quick trip. Getting the hotel listing will be easy and we either find the hotel outright or at least narrow the search."

They each took several more bites and Albert signaled for the bill. He left a twenty on the table and they left. Twenty minutes later they entered the same newspaper building that Marilyn had visited previously. Albert was greeted by a large number of employees who were in obvious awe of this well-known newsman.

He stopped to visit with one of the more seasoned reporters. He introduced Marilyn and asked if he could get a listing of all San Diego hotels with the area code from Marilyn's notebook. When the listing appeared on the computer screen, he asked if the list could then be sorted by the first digit of the local prefix and everything except that series be deleted. The resulting list was still too long. He asked to eliminate anything with 'motel' in the title and the list became manageable.

"Can you print me two copies? I'll owe you."

Several minutes later Marilyn and Albert went over the list.

"Do you have any more information that we could use to narrow the search?"

"Well, there are pieces of the rest of the hotel phone number, but I couldn't discern the actual digits."

"Okay, we're going back to your place!"

At the flight school Brad parked his car, walked in and quickly glanced at the status board for the airplanes and instructors. He noted that his instructor, Frank, was out with a student and that the Cessna 182 was still assigned to him and a green tag indicated that the aircraft was ready to go.

"Good morning, Mr. Chandler. It looks like a great day for a solo cross country flight," said Cheryl, one of the flight instructors.

She smiled, wishing that he had been her student. He was single and very eligible.

"Hi, Cheryl. Yeah, I don't think that weather will be a factor today. Did you guys get me permission to land at that private field north of Pahrump?"

"Yep. They know you're coming. Make sure you have your logbook so they can sign it off. By the way, why such a long flight and through the mountains? Everyone else stays down here in the San Joaquin Valley."

"Two reasons. It's scenic and it's more of a challenge. Besides, I need to know more about how the airplane reacts at higher altitudes and want to build up more flight time before I carry any passengers."

Brad thought briefly of Trish and smiled. He thoroughly examined the maintenance records on his chosen airplane and noted that there were no outstanding maintenance actions. Satisfied, he filed a visual flight plan after receiving a weather briefing by phone and headed for the green and white Cessna. Brad's preflight inspection was thorough and no new discrepancies were discovered. Fifteen minutes later he was airborne and enroute to his first visual checkpoint, the dam at Pine Flat Lake. The second leg of the flight would take him to the dam at the Courtright Reservoir and from there he would continue to Big Pine. That third leg was the high altitude portion of the flight through the Sierra Nevada Mountains. From there he would fly the valley route down to Lone Pine and then over to Stovepipe Wells. The last leg would take him straight to the private airport.

Brad reached the first checkpoint right on schedule and enroute to the second checkpoint he commenced a gentle climb in preparation for the third leg. He had no intention of climbing any higher than necessary as he crossed the rugged mountains.

Brad smiled as he crossed the second checkpoint right on schedule. He then made a gentle right turn for the leg to Big Pine. The terrain was rising rapidly and he was glad that he had started his climb early. Looking into the early morning sun was difficult, but the absence of a realistic horizon made it a necessary requirement. In a few more minutes he would reach the highest point on this leg and judging his clearance above the steep slopes was difficult. Brad was prepared to make a quick turn, if necessary.

Approaching the highest elevation for his current leg, Brad realized that he needed a few hundred feet more. He increased power and readjusted the nose of the airplane. He considered making a 360 degree turn while climbing, but it appeared that he would safely clear the terrain on his present heading...an abrupt turn was always an option. He relaxed somewhat as he passed over the highest ridgeline on this leg and prepared to reset engine power for cruise flight.

Without warning, the engine abruptly quit! Brad quickly lowered the nose to establish a safe gliding speed and began checking for possible causes of the engine failure. He switched the fuel selector from 'both' to first the left tank and then to the right tank; the engine continued windmilling, but failed to catch. He surmised that lack of fuel was not the problem. He tried switching the magnetos from 'Both' to 'Right' and then 'Left' to no avail; he thus eliminated ignition problems. Each check was conducted while maintaining a safe flying speed and searching for a suitable landing area.

Brad cycled the mixture control, the prop control and the throttle and received no indication that any of these had any affect. It slowly dawned on him that he should have made an immediate turn to the west when the engine failed; it was now too late...he was going down in the mountains. He switched the radio over to the emergency frequency and broadcast a 'Mayday.' He received no acknowledgement.

He searched for any place that would give him a chance of surviving the inevitable crash; there were no level or open spaces, just rugged slopes on his left and right. He had no choice but to continue his descent and hope for an opening.

Brad suddenly realized that he was living his nightmare. Although he was not in his 'Hornet,' he was unable to land or eject from this stricken aircraft. The nightmare had returned at the hotel while Trish and the girls were shopping. He thought briefly of Trish...he should have cancelled this flight and stayed in San Diego.

Up ahead he saw where the two slopes converged leaving only a very small opening...that would be his only chance. His only hope was to glide through the middle of the opening as low and as slow as possible and pray that both wings hit their respective slope simultaneously. If he were to be injured, there would be little hope of getting out of there alive: that is, if he even managed to survive the crash. He tightened his harness and quickly re-tried all of his earlier attempts to bring the engine back to life; nothing worked. Time was running out!

Marilyn unlocked the door to her motel room and went straight to the desk. She moved the pieces of the business card back to their previous locations. Albert peered over her shoulder.

"Where are the missing pieces?"

"I don't know...these were in a mouse nest and I thought I had all of them. Maybe the mouse ate them. You can see partial numbers. Maybe we can get or eliminate enough to be able to identify the hotel."

"You're right. I'll make six columns with 10 digits in each and we can mark them as 'no' or 'maybe.' With luck we can catch a break."

He noticed that she was staring straight ahead.

"Al, turn on the television!"

"What?"

"Turn on the television!"

He hesitated briefly before grabbing the remote and pushing the power button.

"What channel?"

"It doesn't matter."

Confused, he watched a furniture commercial materialize and Marilyn turned toward the set just as a phone number flashed on the screen. She quickly wrote a phone number on her note pad. Albert peeked to see what she had written.

"What's that you just wrote down?"

"The phone number from that commercial."

"That's not the same number that was on the screen, Marilyn."

"It's the number for the hotel," she calmly replied.

"Okay, I give up. What are you talking about?"

"I was just given the phone number for the hotel we're looking for."

"Given? Given by whom?"

"Al, if I told you, you would not believe me. Trust me."

A number of questions flooded Albert's brain, but he resisted his impulse to begin asking them. He decided to humor her.

"So what do we do now?"

"We can call that number and get the name of the hotel or just find the number on the list."

"And you really think it will be there? Okay, I'll look for that prefix."

He started his search, placing a dash next to the phone numbers with the same prefix.

"There are 27 possibilities and the tenth one matches the number! It's the Imperial Hotel, Al."

At that point she picked up her list and circled the number near the bottom of the first page. Albert watched her warily; she had not even consulted her list but knew exactly where to go.

"Where did you come up with that?"

"Al, there are things that exist that we as intelligent, sophisticated people don't even know about. There are some who know and can't even begin to explain. Grandpa was one of those people and somehow I am being brought into whatever this is. I am asking you to just go along with me...I am learning to accept things that are not possible or have no explanation. Call the number...you must dial '9' first."

Albert stared at her. "She is not some flake," he thought. He picked up her note pad and dialed the number that she had written on the note pad. The call was answered after one ring.

"Imperial Hotel," said a pleasant female voice. "How can I help you?"

"Uh...sorry, wrong number," he said as he abruptly hung up the phone.

"Are you starting to believe me now?" Marilyn's expression showed no trace of surprise.

"I need to sit down for just a minute. I'm going to ask a few questions before I do anything else. Remember, I deal in *facts*. What is this that you or *we* are dealing with? Why are you and your grandfather involved in this big secret?"

"Al, I'm asking you to trust me and help me finish what I must do. There are lives at stake and time is running out for those people. I must locate a thing called a dreamcatcher, one of several that have some ability to cause the deaths of certain people. A woman from Massachusetts bought the one that killed those women at the Wayside House. It will kill her and move on to kill others."

Marilyn glanced at the television set. The word 'hurry' appeared on the screen.

"We must go to the hotel now!"

"Wait a minute, I still have questions."

"Al, take me to the Imperial Hotel right now!"

The urgency in her voice made it clear that she was serious. They left the room and piled into Al's car. He remained silent as he headed for the hotel until he could stand the silence no longer.

"Do I run traffic lights or wait for them to turn green?"

It was his way of gauging the urgency. Breaking the law for bona fide reasons was one thing and *bending* the rules was acceptable in many situations, but this was a situation that was dubious at best. He decided to play along until encountering some serious consequences. He now wished that it *had* been his ex-wife who had awakened him with a phone call.

"Just get me to the hotel. And what female names begin with the letters 'Tr?' Trudy is all I can think of at the moment."

Trish sat on a bench next to the Reptile House trying to summon up enough courage to go inside and view the many snakes in their special enclosures with the glass viewing windows. She would be safe...the glass would protect her. She was enjoying the warmth of the sun and beginning to win her mental battle with her snake demons. She had been disappointed with herself for avoiding the chance to face her fear of snakes yesterday.

Trish moved her purse to make room for two elderly ladies who obviously felt the need for a brief rest. She placed the purse on the ground next to her feet and read through the literature that discussed the venomous snakes on display. Her attention was drawn to the *Malayan krait* (Bungarus candidus) which was a featured specimen. Just looking at its photo gave her chills and the power of its venom made her wonder why such a snake would be on display. She was forced to admit that the snake was actually quite beautiful despite its deadly potential. Still, in spite of her fear, she would at least enter the building. It was 9:17 A.M.

At that moment, far below the surface of the earth, two tectonic plates moved in response to the enormous pressure that had been building up between them. The resulting earthquake caused the startling and frightening shaking that is characteristic of moderate quakes. The three women quickly stood and tried to maintain their balance. Seeing the terrified look on Trish's face, the woman closest to Trish spoke.

"It's okay, dear; it's just a small earthquake. It'll stop in a few seconds."

The words were not particularly soothing to Trish, but she noticed that most other zoo visitors were paying only scant attention to the shaking of the earth. They were smiling as they moved to maintain their balance.

"They're not really concerned," she said in a soft voice.

About twelve seconds after the quake began, the corner foundation of the reptile house broke apart from the main building. This was due to a structural fault that had occurred during the construction of the building many years earlier when Carlos Montoya failed to ensure that the air pockets were removed from the fresh concrete. There was now a three-quarter inch gap that continued up the wall before becoming a mere crack. Visitors and staff had fled the building at the first tremor and no one was there to see the Malayan krait as it escaped. The nature of the deadly serpent was to seek freedom and its nocturnal nature caused it to search for a darkened location. After traveling a mere five feet, the snake sought sanctuary in the perfect location which, unfortunately, was Trish's special tourist purse; it had fallen over as the earth trembled. By this time the tremors had ceased and the zoo visitors were excitedly expressing their thoughts.

Adrianne Ahern was thrilled. The five year old had been selected Student of the Month after only one week in her new kindergarten. One of the perks was delivering the class mail to the mail box near the front of the school. There had been two letters being mailed to adults who had made presentations to the students. After happily skipping down to the mailbox, she had deposited the two letters and turned to retrace her route. It was then that the earthquake had struck. Adrianne had sat down next to the mailbox after experiencing difficulty standing; she had not been frightened.

Meanwhile, Adrianne's teacher had watched her as the young girl deposited the letters. She had also been watching as she saw Adrianne sit and then had heard the announcement for all students to move into the hallway. The teacher had immediately and very calmly directed the children to move quickly and quietly into the hall which was the designated location for the best protection during earthquakes. She had known that Adrianne would be safe outside.

Albert noticed a shaking that was both fascinating and a little unnerving. The frenzied movement of the street lights and traffic signals convinced him that it was just another earthquake.

"I think it's an earthquake...first one I ever experienced while driving," he said calmly.

"Should we pull over or something? Maybe we should just stop," Marilyn ventured.

"No, we're headed for the hotel; we'll keep going."

The first aftershock would occur just prior to reaching the hotel.

John Hefner had been in the back of his van which was parked near a school. He had left the engine running and was checking everything one last time when the quake hit. The tires reduced the effects of the shaking, but the right rear door swung open. John saw a little girl sitting next to a nearby mailbox. He looked through the front of the van and saw no one coming. He then grabbed the jar with the saturated cloth inside and loosened the lid. He quickly moved his toolbox just as the shaking ceased.

"Hey, little girl, come here; I need help!"

Adrianne looked at the man in the van.

"I'm here to fix a stove in your cafeteria and my toolbox fell on my foot. Can you help me?"

Adrianne looked around for help, but there was no one else in sight. She began walking slowly toward the van. She stopped at the back of the van and looked at the man carefully.

"The earthquake made the toolbox fall on my foot and I just need a little help to move it. Please help me. What's your name? My name is Bob."

He smiled and then winced as if he were in great pain.

"I'm Adrianne," she responded as she slowly climbed into the van.

John waited until she was within reach and then grabbed her and covered her mouth so she could not scream. With his free hand he removed the lid from the jar and removed the cloth. He held it over her nose and waited until she went limp and quickly wrapped duct tape around her wrists. Then he reached over to the chest freezer and lifted the lid. He carefully placed the unconscious girl into the freezer and closed the lid. Then he locked the lid and put the key in his pocket. Finally, he made certain that air was coming out through the exhaust tube. He quickly returned the cloth to its jar and tightened the lid. He placed the jar back into its storage place, calmly exited the van and closed the rear door; there was no time to lock it.

John walked around to the driver's door carefully scanning the area for any witnesses. Seeing none, he climbed in and moved the shift lever to 'Drive.' Moments later he was headed for the safety of Interstate 5.

This one had been incredibly easy and his ventilating system would keep her alive until he reached his home; that had not been the case in several other abductions. And when he was through with her, he could simply plug the freezer into an extension cord and not worry about those awful plastic bags. Right now, though, he needed to reach the safety of the interstate. The news media referred to him as "the monster," but they just did not understand.

The school janitor peeked through the window at the corner of the building and watched the van drive away. He noted the signs on the black van and the stepladder on top. He then raced to the chaotic office as fast as the crowded hallway would allow.

The shaking stopped and all 12 of the largest children at the day care center stood still, wondering what to do next. They were outdoors so they could burn off some of their excess energy and had gotten more than they had expected. Even so, they thought it was fun just trying to remain standing. Sally, one of the teachers, was told to let them stay outside unless they were frightened. The adults would clean up the inside and make preparations "just in case." The children soon resumed their outdoor routines.

Sally expected that there would be aftershocks...this was not her first 'quake. Sure enough, several minutes later a large aftershock occurred. None of the children panicked and were still surprisingly calm. They began to wander back toward the sliding patio door and re-enter the center. Brianne Ahern, though, noticed that the side gate to the front yard area was now standing open. That was something that she had never seen before and she was unaware that the movement of the earth had allowed the latch bar to be released and the aftershock caused the gate to swing open. She walked toward the gate to close it and suddenly stopped. She stood there for a few seconds and spotted a pit bull as it investigated the open gate. She thought of the last dog that she had encountered and unconsciously rubbed the scars on her left arm.

Brianne turned and ran. The pit bull instinctively gave chase and began to rapidly overtake the small girl. Meanwhile, Sally closed the slider as what she assumed to be the last of the 12 children stepped inside. Brianne was still 10 feet away from the door when the pit bull knocked her legs out from under her and then wheeled to face his prey.

Brianne lay on her back, frozen with fear. She did not cry or move as the pit bull moved toward her throat. He stood there ready to attack. The dog only needed a sound or movement of any sort to trigger an instantaneous and deadly attack. He stood over the defenseless child, saliva dripping onto her face.

It was then that Sally realized that Brianne had not returned with the other children. She looked out and saw the most frightening sight she had ever encountered. She, too, froze somehow knowing not to do anything that might cause a deadly response from the pit bull.

"Please, please, Brianne...don't move," she whispered softly, but knew that it was just a matter of time. Something had to give...something horrible. Sally could not look away; spellbound, she awaited the inevitable.

John drove two blocks and turned right onto the street that would take him to the northbound on-ramp for Interstate 5. Just a little over a mile to go before he joined the safety of thousands of other vehicles. This had been so easy; it was almost as if it were destined to happen. He smiled and began humming. Then he remembered the signs and the stepladder. He pulled over and pulled both magnetic signs from the driver's side and then the two from the other side. He tossed them into the back of the van and quickly untied the cords that secured the stepladder. He then carefully placed the ladder into the van next to the freezer and closed the door; this time he locked it. Had he taken time to check the freezer's exhaust vent he would have discovered that the battery was almost dead and very little fresh air was being drawn into the freezer.

Once back inside, he waited for an opening in the traffic and that was when a large aftershock occurred. It was not especially noticeable for those in their vehicles, but underground utilities had already been affected by the original earthquake and this aftershock added to what had already transpired. Electrical power failed in several areas and that included the area where John sat, ready to merge into traffic.

An opening appeared suddenly and John took advantage of the break in traffic. The traffic quickly slowed as the two sets of traffic lights ahead failed and bedlam ensued in the intersections as drivers fought to reach destinations that were suddenly very important due to the earthquake. The on-ramp was less than half a mile away.

The first set of traffic lights was for a rather unimportant cross street and traffic moved slowly but steadily through the intersection. The second set of lights was more difficult to navigate due to the intersection of two major streets. The rules of courtesy were ignored as drivers fought their way through with varying degrees of success. Timid drivers or those in small vehicles gave way to bolder drivers or those with larger vehicles. Approaching the intersection, John became more aggressive when he spotted the sign for the northbound on-ramp to Interstate 5. Just another minute or so and he would be safely on his way out of town.

San Diego police officer Scott Winters turned on his flashing lights and hit the siren. His new destination was the busy intersection half a block north; he had just been assigned traffic detail. He carefully navigated his way to the intersection and parked in the middle. He exited and brought all traffic to a complete stop. After clearing the intersection he then resumed the north-south flow and then cleared the left turn lanes. At this point he decided to clear the left turn lanes first for the east-west traffic.

His radio crackled with the news that a small girl had just been kidnapped from a nearby school and was possibly headed for Interstate 5; the vehicle was a black van with gold signage and a ladder on the roof. This intersection was on the most probable escape route. The police officer made a mental note of the description of the van and started moving the traffic in the left turn lanes. After the last turning vehicle cleared the intersection, he started the through-traffic moving.

A nervous John Hefner was dreading the trip through the intersection after spotting the traffic cop. Regardless, once clear of the intersection he should be okay. Luckily he had removed the signs and the ladder...his police scanner was well worth what he had paid for it; smiling, he turned it off so he could concentrate.

Meanwhile in an uncharacteristic glance away from the traffic he was controlling, police officer Winters looked skyward and spotted a huge eagle. His gaze immediately returned to the traffic he was directing just as a black work van approached the intersection. His attention focused on two separate areas: the driver's door and the area in the middle of the van. He could clearly see two rectangular areas that were slightly cleaner than the surrounding areas; the average person would have seen no difference. Scott would never be able to explain how he had spotted the difference.

He blew his whistle and stopped all traffic before racing to his cruiser and speeding after the van; he knew it was the right one even though he did not know how he knew this. He alerted Dispatch of his pursuit and caught up with the van just as it entered the on-ramp. He bumped the siren and, using the PA system, told the driver of the van to "Move out of the way!" He was prepared to force the vehicle off the ramp if the driver tried to make a run for it; the van moved to the right.

As he accelerated past the black van, he eased to the center of the ramp and suddenly slowed. Simultaneously, he thrust his left arm out of the window and motioned for the van and other vehicles to stop. After stopping his cruiser, he exited and calmly started walking back toward the following traffic. Passing the van, he spoke to the driver whose van was now blocked.

"Just hold on for a couple of minutes, sir...we need to open up a section of the interstate for some emergency vehicles."

John Hefner acknowledged the police officer's words with a nod of his head and began to relax.

Once past the driver's window, police officer Winters whirled while simultaneously drawing his automatic. In a split second, the driver of the van was fixated on the business end of the officer's service weapon.

"Freeze! Hands where I can see 'em!"

John Hefner complied. He could bluff his way out of this; he had done it before.

"You just scared the crap out of me! What's going on, officer?"

"What do you have in the back of the van?"

A northbound California Highway Patrol cruiser with lights flashing pulled over and blocked the on-ramp as a second San Diego Police cruiser worked its way down the on-ramp. Both officers quickly converged on the van with weapons drawn.

"Just my tools and an old freezer that I exchanged a few days ago. I'm an appliance repairman."

John's explanation faded away as he watched the Highway Patrolman walking directly toward the front of the van. A second later he saw the second policeman with his weapon pointed at his head. It was now time to be quiet.

Officer Winters spoke loudly and slowly.

"Now, very slowly turn off the engine and set the parking brake. Keep one hand in sight."

John did as instructed; the fan inside the freezer had stopped rotating.

"Now, slowly open the door and step out of the vehicle."

Once again John did as instructed. Once outside the vehicle he automatically placed his hands up and out with legs spread and then leaned against the van. The Highway Patrolman took a position on John's left while the second police officer took a position on his right.

Officer Winters holstered his weapon and patted John down and cuffed him. Then he calmly walked around to the back doors: they were locked.

"Where are the keys?"

"Left front trouser pocket. There's also one on the keychain in the ignition."

Officer Winters retrieved the ignition keys and selected the other similar key; the door unlocked easily. For some strange reason he only opened the right door. He noticed that a stepladder was blocking his entrance and started to unlatch the left door. As he looked around the inside of the van he spotted something that caused his heart to skip a beat: mounted low on the expanded metal divider behind the driver's seat were two hand grenades with wires running from the safety pins toward the back of the van! He looked down at the left door and saw two similar wires emerging from a pulley system and attached to the door. He withdrew his hand from the latch.

"I've got two hand grenades back here, part of a booby trap. Whatever you do, don't open the left door." And then under his breath, "Appliance repairman, my ass."

He returned to his cuffed suspect.

"What's in the freezer?"

"Power tools, mostly. You know...the expensive ones. People keep stealing stuff from my van."

"Any more booby traps?"

"No sir. I, uh, figured that any thieves would get the hint when the grenades went off."

"Sure," the police officer's voice was laced with sarcasm. "Is there a key to the freezer?"

"Left front pants pocket," he replied somberly.

Trish retrieved her purse but failed to notice the slight increase in weight caused by her new and deadly passenger. She was still quite nervous and slowly continued her exploration of the huge zoo. Unfortunately, the first aftershock occurred a few minutes later and convinced her that it was now time to leave. It was at that moment that she considered that dangerous animals like lions and tigers could possibly escape and thus it was definitely time for her to leave. She walked rapidly to the exit gates and then went straight to her rental car.

As she approached her car, she automatically slipped her right hand into her purse to locate the keys to the Toyota Corolla; as usual, the keys had settled to the bottom of the purse. She began fishing around in the purse for the elusive keys and suddenly touched something that clearly did not belong there! And then she felt it move! She instinctively froze.

Inside her purse, the deadly serpent was prepared to strike Trish's hand. There was hesitation as the reptile instinctively waited for the situation to resolve itself without expenditure of its precious venom. Trish's knees shook violently. Not knowing what was inside her purse was terrifying enough, but she lacked the courage to look. She knew that her hand was shaking and that she might be able to yank her hand clear. She would not have made it...the beautiful yellow and black snake was still fully alert and poised to strike with lightning speed.

Alfred parked his car in the loading/unloading zone at the Imperial Hotel. Marilyn exited the car and rushed to the lobby as a skeptical and reluctant Alfred followed. She went straight to the registration desk. She looked at the clerk's nametag.

"Deb, I need your help...I must find a tourist here from Massachusetts. Her first name starts with a 'T' and her last name starts with an 'F.' It is truly a matter of life and death."

"I'm sorry, ma'am, we do not give out guest names."

"Then could you check to see if you have any guests from Massachusetts?"

"I suppose I could do that. Just a minute, please."

Marilyn could hear the clicking of the keyboard.

"Okay, we have three families from Massachusetts...well, actually one is a single."

"I understand the hotel policy, but does the last name of that single begin with an 'F?' Surely you could tell me that."

"Yes it does."

"And the first name...is a 'T' the first letter?"

"No...I mean no, I can't tell you."

Marilyn stared deep into the eyes of the clerk who suddenly showed signs of distress. Without warning, her expression softened and a smile appeared.

"Deb...I need the name and room number."

"Her name is Patricia Favret and she is in room 304. Thank you for choosing the Imperial Hotel. I hope you enjoy your stay."

"Patricia...Trish, of course!"

Marilyn turned and headed toward the elevators. Albert suddenly realized what she had accomplished and hurried after her, leaving a confused clerk wondering what had just happened. Neither spoke until the elevator left the lobby.

"What was that...hypnotism?"

"I don't know for certain. I just knew that I had to do that."

"How are you going to open the door, or do I dare ask?"

"Hopefully Patricia will open it."

The elevator stopped at the third floor. Marilyn stepped out as soon as the doors opened. She briefly glanced at the arrows on the sign in front of her.

"It's to the left," she said as she strode away. "It's the third door from the end of the hall."

A cleaning cart partially blocked the hall ahead of her as the housekeeping crew attempted to get an early start. Upon reaching the door to room 304, she knocked loudly; after a few seconds she knocked again. She then headed for the cleaning cart. She reached the cart just as the housekeeper exited a room with an arm full of linens and towels.

"My name is Patricia Favret and I'm in room 304...I can't find my key. Can you open my door?"

The housekeeper dropped her burden into the hamper, sighed and walked toward room 304 without speaking. At the door she paused and looked at Marilyn.

"This is it?"

"Yes, 304."

"Okay," said the housekeeper as she unlocked the door and pushed it open.

"Thank you," Marilyn said as she stepped inside.

"Yes, thank you very much," said Albert as he handed the housekeeper a five dollar bill and followed Marilyn into the room.

She stopped suddenly as she spotted the dreamcatcher hanging from the large painting on the wall above the nearest bed.

"It's so beautiful. It's just hard to imagine how dangerous it is."

"And you think it's dangerous. You sure you want to destroy that?"

"We have no choice. Could you get it down, please?"

While Albert awkwardly moved onto the bed and lifted the dreamcatcher from the improvised hook, Marilyn located the wooden case which rested on the coffee table. She opened the case, knowing in advance that its purpose was to protect the dreamcatcher. Albert brought the dreamcatcher over to Marilyn and carefully placed it in its cushioned resting place. He treated it as if it were a great treasure. He continued to stare at it and felt it calling to him to hold it, to caress it and to *protect it.*

"Are you sure we need to destroy it"

"Yes, Al," she replied as she closed the case and latched it.

He felt a slight relaxation in his sudden need to protect this incredible work of art.

Marilyn picked up the case and headed for the door.

"Let's go, Al...we're not finished yet."

He followed reluctantly, wondering if perhaps he could take it and that would eliminate her misguided need to destroy it. He could convince her to surrender it to him. He could manipulate people...he had been doing that for years.

In the elevator Marilyn noticed a slight change in his demeanor; it was not hostility, but he was clearly unhappy with the idea of disposing of something with such incredible beauty. She had to admit that the dreamcatcher was far more beautiful than her grandfather had indicated.

Suddenly an overpowering sense of urgency struck Marilyn; she realized that her heart was pounding and breathing was difficult. The elevator stopped and the doors opened. She stepped into the lobby and raced toward the hotel entrance. Albert followed, still nursing the thought of preventing her from destroying the dreamcatcher.

Passing the relaxing/waiting area of the lobby, Marilyn glanced at the television; the word 'Hurry!' was flashing on the screen.

"Hurry, Al!"

Deb, the desk clerk, looked up and wondered who the two people were that were rushing out of the hotel. She could not recall having seen them before.

Marilyn reached the car and yanked the door open. She climbed in and held the wooden case on her lap as if trying to prevent its escape. Albert crawled in moments later.

"Let's go! Find a quiet place...an alley or something...hurry!"

"You know, I could keep it in a safe place," he said as he started the engine.

"Drive, Albert, now!"

He sped away. One minute later he braked hard and made a right turn into an alley. He immediately spotted a dumpster and stopped next to it. Marilyn stepped out with her special burden and suddenly remembered her purse and camera. She grabbed both of them and rushed toward the dumpster.

She placed the wooden case on the asphalt and pulled the can of lighter fluid and the propane lighter from her purse. Kneeling in front of the wooden case she raised the pouring spout on the can of lighter fluid and set it next to the wooden case. Then she reached for the latch on the case. She noticed a child's crushed plastic toy next to the case.

Albert stood next to the dumpster wondering if she needed any material from the dumpster. There was cardboard, wood and even some pipe inside...clearly this dumpster was used by many people.

Marilyn opened the case. Once again she was overwhelmed by the beauty of the dreamcatcher. She noted the incredible craftsmanship and remembered her camera. She grabbed it and stood over the dreamcatcher and snapped a photo. The word 'Hurry' flashed inside the viewfinder. She was unaware of the change in Albert as he stared at the glorious dreamcatcher. Suddenly he smiled.

Marilyn knelt and set the camera to one side. She picked up the can of lighter fluid and the miniature torch.

Albert reached into the dumpster and pulled out a piece of pipe. With tears running down his face he took a step toward Marilyn.

At that instant, Marilyn looked up into the bright morning sun and spotted an eagle as it landed in a nearby tree. She took a deep breath and returned to her task.

Albert raised the pipe over his head and took a small, measured step toward Marilyn.

Neither heard the squeal of braking tires.

Marilyn doused the wooden case and the dreamcatcher with lighter fluid.

Albert raised the pipe higher and paused briefly while gauging his intended point of impact.

Marilyn pushed the safety catch and started to squeeze the trigger on the torch.

Neither Marilyn nor Albert heard the sound of the shots!

Albert crumpled and crashed into the dumpster; the pipe clanged against the dumpster, struck the asphalt and rolled a short distance. Simultaneously, Marilyn lit the torch and placed it next to the drenched wooden case.

Whoosh!

She struggled to her feet with camera in hand as she watched the flames build. Only then did she become aware of Albert's lifeless body. Marilyn suddenly had difficulty breathing.

"Ma'am, are you okay?"

Marilyn heard a voice that came from behind her, but did not reply nor did she turn. She stepped back slightly as the wooden case began burning fiercely. Then the dreamcatcher suddenly began to burn brightly. She quickly positioned her camera; she would have proof.

There was movement in the raging fire and then an eagle suddenly arose, staring straight at her. A high-pitched scream that came from the eagle was deafening and terrifying. She could see intense hatred in its expression. She automatically snapped a photo just before the eagle spread its wings and flew away toward the east. Then Marilyn's knees buckled. She did not see the sentinel eagle as it launched itself into the air and sped away.

Her collapse was softened by the police officer who had fired the two shots. He eased her to the ground.

"Ma'am, are you okay?"

Her eyelids fluttered briefly and then she opened her eyes. She was disoriented, but otherwise uninjured. She stared at the police officer before looking around.

"I know you...you helped me at the Wayside House. You're Don."

"Yes ma'am, Don Hughes. I need to call this in. Unfortunately, I need to know what just happened. I know that this has something to do with that business card from the other day."

"Oh, my God! What happened to Al?"

She stared in horror at the pool of blood that slowly moved from beneath him.

"He was going to kill you; I shot him. Look, I just witnessed something else that I know I saw, but really can't describe. I need some answers real quick! I need to call this in immediately!"

The police officer looked at his watch; the time was 9:51.

Officer Winters carefully extracted the small ring of keys from the suspect's pocket and returned to the back of the van accompanied by the Highway Patrolman. After carefully looking for additional signs of booby traps, he very slowly and very carefully removed the step ladder. He then eased himself into the van and moved a large toolbox. He cautiously opened the toolbox and located a set of diagonal cutters. Then he carefully stepped over to the grenades and cut the wires attached to the safety pins. Back at the freezer he selected the odd looking key utilized by many freezer manufacturers and, with shaking hands, inserted it into the lock. He noted the time on his watch...it was 9:51.

He turned the key and took a deep breath before slowly lifting the lid and looking inside.

"Get an ambulance...now!" his voice was choked with emotion.

Officer Winters leaned over into the freezer and picked up the motionless little girl. She was breathing! He stepped from the van very carefully with his precious bundle. Tears rolled down his cheeks as he thought of his own daughter who was about the same age. He looked around for the suspect who was now sitting in the back of the second police cruiser. He briefly considered removing any possibility that the monster sitting in the back of the cruiser would be freed on some small technicality.

The second police officer said simply, "Don't do it Scott. We got him; we caught him in the act."

Sally was terrified at what was about to happen, but was unable to look away. At that moment she noticed a smile slowly spreading across Brianne's face. Her heart ached as she waited for the dog to react. Tears flowed freely as she prayed that the dog would simply turn and leave.

At that second all hell broke loose! A huge bird, an eagle, slammed its massive talons into the neck and upper jaw of the pit bull. The startled animal immediately attempted to shake loose from its captor but to no avail.

Amid the frantic beating of wings and the uncharacteristic cries of the crazed dog, Brianne eased away from the melee and crawled toward the slider. A hysterical Sally opened the slider, stepped out, grabbed the still smiling girl and pulled her inside to safety.

In a brief instant that she would never forget, Sally watched as the eagle turned toward her, meeting her gaze. Then without warning the eagle released its grip on the dog and climbed skyward. She turned toward Brianne who stood next to her calmly waving at the eagle. When she looked back, the eagle was gone, having returned to its normal life as a skilled hunter. Shaking violently, Sally sat on one of the tiny chairs trying to catch her breath and was approached by Brianne.

"That was a bad dog like the one that bit me. The big bird was my friend."

With that, the little girl joined her playmates who simply dismissed the incident as if it had never happened. Sally then noticed that the dog had disappeared. The entire incident had lasted a mere 20 seconds. She looked at the clock on the wall; it read 9:51.

She slowly rose to join her fellow workers who were calming the very small children and picking up the objects that had been displaced during the earthquake and aftershock. Sally suddenly glanced out through the slider and noticed something unusual; there was a large feather on the ground where the altercation between dog and eagle had occurred. She hesitated momentarily before opening the sliding door and retrieving the feather. She examined the feather briefly and a feeling of deep serenity replaced her anxiety. Sally decided not to mention what she had just witnessed, but kept the feather.

Brad was bracing himself physically and mentally for the crash. At that instant, the engine suddenly roared to life! He instinctively raised the nose of the airplane while holding his breath. And then he could see that the airplane was climbing. He still had to contend with the narrow opening since turning left or right was out of the question. As the plane climbed, the opening increased in size and suddenly he was clear! He glanced briefly at the clock; it read 9:51.

"Just hang in there, girl...I'm not touching anything!" he said aloud.

He was puzzled about the engine failure, but he would think about that later. Right now he was just happy to listen to the wonderful sound of that engine. He remained in that valley until he had enough altitude to cross the eastern ridge. Somewhere in his joy he had reset engine power for a normal climb and now he was easing the power back as he began his descent to match the terrain. He would skip Big Pine and just pick up U.S. 395 southbound and follow the remainder of his planned route. His pulse had already returned to its normal rate.

Trish held her breath. She still wanted to yank her hand free to avoid whatever was inside her purse. She had no idea how long she had been standing there motionless, but was aware that her left arm was beginning to ache. She noticed what appeared to be an eagle overhead...probably an escapee from confinement thanks to the earthquake. The waiting game continued for a few more seconds before she had a thought materialize: *just gently place the purse on the ground*. She slowly lowered the purse and when all of the weight was gone from her left arm, slowly removed her right hand. Once her hand was free she let go of the purse and it fell over on one side. She quickly stepped back.

A sleek, dark head appeared as *Bungarus Candidus* looked for an opportunity to escape. Moments later it returned to the safety of its hiding place.

Trish very calmly walked back to the zoo entrance and told the woman at the ticket booth that there was a very poisonous snake in her purse and she wanted to go home. She noticed that it was 9:52. She also asked if it would be possible for someone to come remove it real soon because she really needed to go to the bathroom.

In the brief moments immediately following the shooting, a confused and distraught Marilyn tried to explain what she had been doing. Officer Hughes finally told her to stop. He called in his report and very carefully placed the lighter fluid and propane lighter into Marilyn's purse. He then placed the purse and camera into Albert's car. That was when they both realized simultaneously that there was no evidence that there had been a fire near the dumpster. Marilyn noticed that the child's plastic toy had not been melted by the intense heat; she pointed that out to Officer Hughes who was concerned with numerous other things.

San Diego police assets were at a premium with the sudden demands brought about by the earthquake; off-duty police officers were called in to assist with the increased workload. There were numerous security alarms to investigate and countless accidents caused by the failure of traffic lights in several areas. There was also the abduction of a 5-year old girl and the police shooting in an attempted murder.

Marilyn was examined by the ambulance crew and declined treatment. She wondered how she would break the news to her grandfather, but knew that she needed to do it soon before names went public. She was allowed to take her purse and camera when she was taken to the police station to make her statement.

For some strange reason, she was only required to give a statement and was only asked a few questions to clarify what had occurred. She was beyond suspicion of any wrong doing. She thought of numerous questions that should be asked, but were not. She was then provided with a ride to her motel.

Police Officer Hughes was subjected to what was normally an ordeal. He provided his statement which was basically that he had observed a vehicle headed the opposite direction at a high rate of speed suddenly brake hard and make a right turn into an alley. He had turned on his flashing lights, made a u-turn and drove into the alley. He had then observed an older man remove a metal pipe from a dumpster and move toward a woman who was examining an object on the ground. He had stopped his cruiser and stepped out just as the man raised the pipe over his head. At that point he had drawn his weapon and fired two quick shots. He had then rushed to assist the woman who collapsed as he approached.

His report was corroborated by the woman he had protected and the shooting was later ruled a "good shoot." There were numerous questions that he felt *should* have been asked, but for some strange reason, were not. The entire incident had been bizarre and he needed to talk to this

The Shaman's Legacy

Marilyn Stevens...she could probably give him some answers. Besides, he was told to take a few days off. Maybe they could finally have dinner together.

Reporter Jack Arrington was saddened and shocked when he learned of the death of Albert Givens. His source had mentioned that he had been shot while trying to kill a woman named Marilyn Stevens. Jack immediately remembered the woman who had visited him there at the newspaper...there was something so familiar about her. He began a search which culminated with the revelation that she was none other than the granddaughter of the famous Thomas Stevens! He became so excited that he stopped his present assignment. What did she know that would cause Albert to try and kill her? This was going to be the biggest story of his career. He needed to find her before someone else did!

The Channel 39 reporter was able to trace the license plate of the lady in the blue Honda to a Marilyn Stevens, but failed to find any other information. She promptly gave up.

Back at her motel Marilyn tried to relax. She was not certain if her grandfather and Albert Givens had been close friends; she hoped that they were simply professional acquaintances. She tried to think of a way to mention the shooting in a way that would allow her grandfather to gradually learn what had happened. Finally, she decided to just tell him what had happened.

Marilyn walked to the pay phone and once again called *collect*. Once the connection was made, she said her greetings and blurted out that she had destroyed one of the dreamcatchers.

"Did you get photos?" was the immediate question from the other end of the line.

"I snapped one of the dreamcatcher lying in the open case and then another when the eagle arose from the flames...Grandpa, that was terrifying! That was just before the police officer shot Albert Givens who was trying to kill me with a pipe!"

There, it was out in the open.

"Al was trying to kill you...that's ridiculous! What happened?"

"Grandpa, he was helping me locate the dreamcatcher and when we finally found it, we were both overwhelmed by its beauty. Then Al started saying that he could keep it rather than destroy it. He was very serious about that and his attitude became sort of hostile. If that police officer had not arrived when he did, we would not be talking right now."

"I just can't believe it, unless...."

"Unless what, Grandpa?"

"Unless he was under the influence of the dreamcatcher. Could it be that they now can affect people directly rather than just through their nightmares?"

"If that were true, why not just make me not set them on fire?"

"Well, maybe it's because of who you are or perhaps you are under the protection of an eagle. It could be that your will was too strong to be broken. Al has always been a borderline alcoholic and he might have been easy to manipulate. I guess we'll never know. What's next on your agenda?"

"I think I want to relax for a couple of days. The police officer who saved my life had helped me earlier. It is so ironic that he would appear out of nowhere and at exactly the right minute to protect me. He saw what happened when the dreamcatcher burned and I need to talk to him about some of this. He asked me to dinner and I think that if he's really serious, I just might accept."

"Have you considered that he might have been sent to protect you? It's just a question. By now you have most certainly come to believe that there are some powerful forces at work here. Do not forget that there is another dreamcatcher that is still unaccounted for."

"I know and that's another reason why I think it might be wise to stay here for a few days just in case."

"Well, okay. I'm sorry...it's time for my nap. Give us a call tomorrow if you can, but call earlier. I love you."

"I love you, too. Goodbye."

Joan Ahern picked up Brianne from the daycare center and drove to Sharp Hospital. Don was already there and met them as they entered the lobby. A San Diego Police detective approached them and introduced himself. He explained that Adrianne was fine and they would be allowed to see her in a few minutes. He ushered them to a quiet area and began the explanation of what had transpired during the past hour and a half.

When he had finished, he answered their questions and escorted them to Adrianne's room. A tall police officer named Scott Winters sat next to her bed making her laugh. He stood as they entered the room and quietly left so as not to disturb their reunion; tears ran down his cheeks as he left.

Scott Winters was haunted by the thought of what would have happened had he not spotted that van. He would never associate that eagle with his ability to see where the signs had been located on John Hefner's van.

Brianne never spoke of the encounter with the pit bull and although she mentioned her friend, the big bird, her parents assumed that she was talking about a television character.

Trish went back to her room and somehow failed to notice that the dreamcatcher was missing. She quickly dialed Brad's phone number. He was not home so she left a message about her exciting trip to the zoo. Brad, meanwhile, was debating the merits of telling Trish about the mysterious engine failure...it might scare her from flying with him. He decided to drive back to San Diego for the weekend; he would call her as soon as he reached his house.

CHAPTER FOURTEEN

The Last Dreamcatcher

Sheldon Curry left the Pinnacle Peak restaurant for his home in Poway, California. He had been genuinely impressed with Lieutenant Commander Chandler; he felt like he had known him for years. Sheldon would have preferred to sell the remaining dreamcatcher to his new friend, but sometimes things just do not work out right and that was okay with him.

Overhead the second golden eagle followed the salesman's car as it traveled northward. The huge bird was experiencing difficulty sensing where the object it was sent to watch was located; it was forced to maintain visual contact with the thing that carried the object unless it flew in close proximity. The dreamcatcher was learning to hide.

Sheldon reached his home just before dark. His wife, Margaret, was visiting her sister in Sacramento and would be returning the following day...he had the house to himself. He pushed the button on the garage door opener just as he pulled into the driveway. Like many Californians, he used his garage as an additional storage room with no room for cars.

He unloaded his luggage and placed it in the garage. The last item he removed from his car was the case containing the dreamcatcher. He carried it inside and placed it on his workbench. After locking the car, he closed the garage door and opened the door leading into the house. He turned on a few more lights inside before returning to the garage.

The dreamcatcher suddenly became semi-dormant and began slowly growing in strength.

Sheldon walked over to the workbench and opened the wooden case. He stared at the dreamcatcher but this time did not feel the overpowering need to touch it. He was just looking at an object that was certainly beautiful, but was just another of his acquisitions. He would set it aside for another time. He closed the case and thought about protecting the case from damage. He looked around for a box that would hold it and spied a special gift that he had purchased for himself. He had bought a deluxe set of outdoor cooking utensils that came inside a plastic carrying case. He had purchased the set because they were stainless steel and the outer box had billed them as "The last set of grill tools you'll ever buy."

He removed the box from the shelf and carried it to the workbench. He placed the wooden case on top of the box and was delighted to see that it appeared to be a perfect fit. Placing the case beside the box he was surprised that the third dimension was also very close. He broke the tape seal, opened the box and removed the plastic case. He mentally crossed his fingers and eased the wooden case into the cardboard container. It actually was a perfect fit! Well, he needed to add some wooden strips to make an allowance for the latch on the wooden case. What were the odds that he could be this fortunate...it was clearly fate.

Sheldon checked his scrap barrel and selected a flat piece of quarter-inch balsa trim; it was perfect. He measured and cut two pieces to fit on either side of the latch and shortly thereafter resealed the box which was now protecting the wooden case. It also disguised the actual contents of the box. There was one final detail to be completed: the label. He removed a plastic container from another shelf and removed a stick-on label. He placed it perfectly centered on the end of the box. After that he removed a marker from the label container and printed 'D. C.' on the label so that he would know the contents. After putting the label container away, he cleaned up the small amount of sawdust he had created and moved the box with its new inhabitant to its new resting place. He briefly marveled about his good luck in finding a perfect container; it was almost as if he had been destined to do all of this.

Sheldon moved his luggage and other travel items into the house and then brought in the plastic case with the last set of grill tools he would ever buy. He relocated the plastic case to his outdoor grilling area and returned to move his luggage into the bedroom. He chose not to unpack until later and headed for the kitchen. He spotted the flashing light on the answering machine but decided to ignore it until he had quenched his sudden thirst. He washed his hands and quickly dried them before opening the refrigerator. He grabbed a bottle of water and removed the cap. He finished the entire bottle before remembering the blinking light on the answering machine.

He sat on one of the counter stools and pushed the 'play' button. He listened to and discarded six nuisance messages before reaching the last one for that day. It was from his boss.

"Sheldon, it's Jerry. It's late Friday afternoon and I have some bad news. The company is shutting down next week due to low volume. We have a meeting first thing Monday morning. We are all in shock. Sorry to tell you this way, but I didn't know when you'd get home. You can call me...I'll probably be up late tonight. See you Monday morning."

There was a beep and then the announcement that there were no more messages.

Sheldon sat there in a near panic state. This could not be happening to him! He had bills and still owed more than $250,000 on his home.

Margaret was not working and they had maybe $25,000 in savings. Jerry must have been kidding; the company was financially stable or at least it *appeared* to be. Besides, he had just secured two more large accounts. Maybe Jerry meant that the company was temporarily shutting down for a few weeks until business picked up. Jerry's monotone had not reflected anger or surprise and that was a little troubling to him.

He toyed with the idea of calling Jerry for clarification, but something told him that it might be bad news. He mulled that thought over for several minutes. He would need to tell Margaret something when she returned and she would demand an explanation or he could just pretend that everything was fine until after the Monday meeting. At least then he could tell her facts rather than supposition.

Sheldon slept fitfully that night. He awakened several times and had difficulty returning to sleep on each occasion. He thought about the chances he had been given to leave the sales arena and move into another area; he regretted that he had lacked the confidence to do so. He felt betrayed that his company had withheld the information about the fragile nature of the business; perhaps bringing that information to the sales staff would have changed the outcome that was now lingering over the heads of Sheldon and his co-workers.

Margaret had married him in spite of what she had considered to be a waste of his true potential. He was a salesman and very good at his chosen profession. He had convinced her that he would move into the coveted Director of Sales position and that would essentially curtail his constant travel. A few years later, rumors began that the new Director would soon be announced and it was expected that Sheldon would fill that slot; he was, after all, a superstar.

Neither Sheldon nor Margaret had considered that a stranger would be hired to fill that spot. The owner of the company had brought in his new son-in-law, Jerry, and proudly introduced him as his new Director and favorite golf partner. The bi-weekly sales meetings had been replaced with weekly reports which were not shared and thus the competition between the salesmen was not as lively as it had been in the past. True, there were no 'butt-chewings' for poor performance, but there was also no recognition for good performance. Sheldon had approached his boss with some strong recommendations for improvements which would be "taken into consideration." That had been eighteen months ago and nothing had changed.

He tried to think of ideas for the Monday meeting. Surely reorganization was an option. Perhaps some of his earlier recommendations could now be acted upon. He knew that he could turn the company around...he just needed the chance to prove it. Of course, the current Director would have to go and the odds of that happening seemed pretty slim.

Margaret arrived home the following afternoon and immediately sensed that something was wrong. Sheldon shrugged off her questions as just being tired after a sleepless night. She knew there was more to the issue, but chose to let him decide when to bring her into his confidence.

Monday morning finally arrived and Sheldon nervously dressed as if he were meeting his biggest client. He would fight to keep the company alive...he had a lot of ideas and could be very convincing. He assumed that all employees had been informed of the company's plan and were suffering from high anxiety levels. There were approximately 60 employees who could band together; some would simply leave and go elsewhere while others would rather fight to keep the company going. Sheldon could feel the confidence and energy growing inside!

He bounded out the door, much to Margaret's surprise. There was no doubt that the day would go well. Sheldon was smiling as he entered the door to the company's administrative area. He was early, but was surprised to see at least 30 fellow employees who stood in small groups talking quietly. The majority of them stared at him as if he were from another planet. They assumed that he had not heard what was coming. A few thought that he must be bringing good news.

Sheldon walked over to the two members of the small Research and Development group. He did not know them by name, but they knew who he was...everyone in the company knew him. He pulled them aside.

"I'm Sheldon Curry from Sales. I need to ask you some questions."

"Jim Peterson, R&D."

"Terry Carter, R&D."

They shook hands.

"I have a feeling that today's meeting is going to be bad news. I may have a plan. I need to ask one question: do you have or have you made recommendations of any sort for changes to our product lines?"

"Sure we did, but they were rejected and we were told that the company would remain with its present line rather than venture off into uncharted waters," said a startled Jim.

"Well, I got the distinct impression that we are closing the doors forever and it's a done deal," ventured Terry.

"Do you think that the majority of employees sincerely want to keep the company alive?"

"There are a few who have started looking elsewhere and one or two that I know of who are content with just retiring," answered Terry. "What are you thinking?"

"I think that we could take over the company, buy it."

"You do realize that the company is going out of business...there was no mention that someone was buying it. Besides, the debt is apparently large," was the quick response from Jim.

"No one wants to see the company go under because everyone loses. If we could put together a plan to buy the company and turn it around, I think we might be able to pull this off. It would take a commitment from everyone and certainly some sacrifice, but I think we can do it. Let's wait until after the meeting just to see what the current plan is. How could we get everyone together on short notice?"

"Are you kidding? We just need to mention the time and the place," said Terry as he rubbed his hands together in anticipation.

"Okay, just keep it quiet for now...we're drawing a lot of attention."

Promptly at 8:00 A.M. the doors to the largest meeting room opened and the crowd of workers which now included all but two entered. Almost half were able to sit...the remainder lined the walls of the room. There was total silence. There were no managers present.

Theodore Pruett, the owner, cleared his throat in preparation.

"Good morning. I'm sorry to announce that the company is going out of business. We have been losing money for months and we've reached the point that we can no longer operate. We have been unsuccessful in finding a buyer and I must inform you that we will be locking the doors forever, today. Thank you for your contributions over the past twelve years. Joe Hunt from Human Resources will explain your options. Again, thank you for your support," he said as he left for the golf course.

Mr. Pruett left the room amid the whispers as realization of the imminent closure set in.

"Okay, folks, I wish I had lots of good news, but due to the severity of the company debt, we will not be receiving great severance packages."

Joe Hunt covered the information he had accumulated and dutifully reported it to the stunned assemblage. When he finished, he asked for questions and was surprised that there were so few. It was as if life itself had been drained from his audience. He asked for questions one last time and there were none.

"In that case, I will begin dispensing the severance packages and pay checks."

He called the names in alphabetical order and watched as each individual quietly came forward and accepted their last compensation. The recipients slowly left the building and assembled in the parking lot. Most had opened their package and decided to look through it later. Each individual examined the final check and wondered how far they could stretch it. They milled around murmuring to each other. They waited and hoped for a miracle.

The last of the recipients to arrive outdoors was Sheldon Curry. The crowd fell silent as he walked into their midst. There was an air of anticipation, of hope and he realized that he was expected to say something.

"Go ahead, tell them about your plan," said Terry Carter.

Sheldon thought for a few seconds before speaking.

"We can buy out the company. It will take a serious commitment from each of us, but I know we can turn this company around. We need ideas and a plan. If you want to give it a try, meet back here in the parking on Wednesday at 1:00 P.M. and bring your items for consideration. The company has never adapted to a changing market and now that's exactly what we must do. We need to look at developing new products and new markets. I want to present a plan to the bank on Friday morning. Wednesday we will decide what we intend to do. I, for one, do not intend to let the company just roll over and die!"

The crowd burst into applause while nodding in agreement.

"One last thing: R&D and Sales please remain for a few minutes. We have some potential fires to put out. Thank you everyone...see you on Wednesday!"

The workers dispersed except for R&D and Sales.

"Okay, there are two things we must do immediately. First, any recent sales where the equipment has not been delivered and installed will need to be reinforced with a phone call to the buyer and pass along assurances that we are going to honor their purchase agreements. Let them know that we intend to re-organize and grow. Also, contact your past clients and let them know the same thing. We all know how fast rumors can spread."

"Second, R&D: think smaller items with large markets. I think of motor homes and boats when I think of California. Most boats with engines need battery chargers. These could be small units powered by wind or solar energy. Make them small and dependable at a reasonable price. Motor home owners need to keep the batteries charged when not in use...same as with boats. The motor home could also benefit from a solar heating system that would extend their precious supply of propane. These are just a couple of items that I have been asked about in the past, but never seriously considered bringing up. Think about it. Then come back here Wednesday with some ideas. Don't let past rejections or radical ideas stop you. There is tremendous potential here. I would like to bring Marketing in on this on Wednesday as part of a brainstorming party. Friday I want to float a rough plan past the bank. It may be the toughest sale of my life. Now let's go get to work."

One hour later Sheldon broke the news to Margaret. He began with the news from the company and then provided his bold plan. Surprisingly, she immediately saw this as a huge opportunity.

"We need to sell the house and move into an apartment," she said. "I have some friends in the real estate business and they could get the ball rolling quickly. We will need to get rid of a lot of stuff or store it somewhere. With the proceeds from the sale, we should be able to show enough good faith money to the bank for enough time to let the new company start to grow. Actually, we need everyone in the company to chip in and show commitment."

Sheldon sat in stunned silence...Margaret was already ahead of him.

"Next," she continued, "are you buying the corporation or just the company assets?"

"The corporation...name, assets, debt and everything that goes along with it. The family apparently intends to walk away from the whole thing. I'm certain that the bank will jump at our offer if we show a good plan and I think they'll even help us when they see the growth potential. We will be meeting Wednesday to see how the remainder of the newly-unemployed feel about my proposal. Right now they seem to be very enthusiastic. Friday I plan to meet with the bank; the Operations Officer is one of my customers and he has been extremely pleased with our product."

"How do you plan to re-structure the corporation?"

"I haven't thought that far ahead, but if the family is walking away from their corporation, I think they will walk away from their stock, too. I haven't spoken to an attorney, but everyone who remains and assists in the re-building process will own stock according to their contribution. With success will come payback of any money paid in to offset our initial efforts to re-start the company. There is much to be done and I'm not the most knowledgeable person to be discussing these aspects."

"Who is going to run the company...I think it should be you."

I think that will be up to the other employees. I think I'm up to that challenge, but it might be better if I ran the Sales Department. We have a huge selling problem just to get everything started and we cannot afford to let any part of the company lag behind."

Wednesday afternoon at 1:00 P.M. revealed every single employee there in the parking lot except for the former management. Sheldon welcomed the crowd and had them meet in their respective groups. Each group elected a leader/spokesman and began collecting the written and oral ideas. Each employee was also handed a Pledge Sheet which would indicate a dollar amount that the individual would voluntarily contribute to assist in operating expenses as the company moved forward. The pledge could be a cash contribution or a wage reduction...anything to show a commitment.

One hour later all of the inputs had been collected and the employees agreed to meet at 10:00 the next morning. Sheldon and the group leaders then adjourned to the nearby home of the head of the old Legal Department. The inputs were brought forth by each group leader and analyzed; some were accepted outright and others held as future possibilities. Surprisingly, none were rejected due to elements that sparked other possibilities.

Next came proposals to bring before the bank as part of the plan for a new, efficient and profitable organization. It was agreed that Sheldon with support from R&D and Marketing would bring the plan before the bank. A rough outline of the proposal was constructed and refined during the following three hours. Sheldon took the outline home for Margaret to help with formalizing and entering it into their computer. Margaret informed him that their house was essentially sold without even going on the market and she was already searching for an apartment; they would realize a profit of approximately $200,000.

The following morning the Pledge Sheets were collected and the eager employees were briefed on the plan which would go before the bank. Word would be passed by phone as soon as the bank reached a decision. The mood was one of cautious optimism. The group leaders went over their copies of the outline and made recommendations. Sheldon then took the Pledge Sheets and change recommendations home to prepare his plan for presentation to the bank. He was amazed at the contents of the Pledge Sheets...each employee had signed one and the rough total far exceeded his hopes.

Sheldon's plan was approved and accepted by the bank in record time; the Pledge Sheets were instrumental in extending the time for the company to demonstrate the ability to get back on track. The bank was pleased with the support shown by the employees and was willing to make several unexpected concessions. Sheldon began calling the group leaders at 11:15 A.M. and employees were then phoned and told to report to work on Wednesday morning. There were numerous administrative actions to be accomplished.

Sheldon worked through the weekend with the group leaders and an attorney specializing in corporate law. Margaret had acquired their new apartment and was left with the task of relocating their possessions to their new residence or to local storage. While clearing the garage she came upon a box that obviously contained some exotic outdoor cooking utensils with the letters "D.C." on a label. Rather than bother her busy husband, she picked up a birthday card and took the box down to the nearest UPS office. She sent it to David Curry, Sheldon's brother; the box would arrive in Seattle several days before his birthday. She would not mention it to Sheldon until he realized that he had failed to send the gift. As far as she knew, this was the first time that her husband had purchased a gift for his brother. The subject would never come up.

The fifth dreamcatcher was now on the move and it was no longer dormant. The eagle that acted as a sentinel would follow the dreamcatcher to Seattle and then establish its new residence near the home of David Curry.

The UPS package was delivered to the Curry residence two days later and David was there when it arrived. After removing the outer wrapping, he saw what he assumed to be outdoor cooking utensils; unfortunately, he had just replaced his previous set and promptly moved his gift to the attic without bothering to open it. The dreamcatcher became semi-dormant once again, waiting and slowly increasing in power.

Six weeks later, Sheldon Curry, Director of Sales, would proudly announce to his sales personnel that the first two items of the new product line were going on the market with five more coming in the next few months. Even sales of their existing line would increase substantially thanks to nation-wide media coverage of the employee buy-out. There was already a search underway for an additional facility and employment applications were being taken. Sheldon no longer spent most of his time on the road.

Marilyn Stevens had felt a sense of uneasiness and experienced a vision: Howling Wolf told her that the dreamcatcher was on the move. She waited for more precise information, but it never came...at least not right away. She was distracted; Don Hughes, San Diego's newest police detective was becoming a major part of her life.

They had gone to dinner one week after the shooting. Don had spoken of his incredible luck in being there when she needed him. Marilyn then felt the need to reveal more of her role yet was apprehensive due to possible effects from the revelation of her mission in San Diego. She had two photos that were impressive: one showed a beautiful dreamcatcher in a wooden case and the other was a photo of the alley with a completely blank area in the shape of a large bird. The explanation might be more than Don could handle. Of course, she had her grandfather's summary and her own notes, but those were not really proof. She would see how their budding relationship progressed.

Her grandfather had received copies of the two photos and smiled as he held what he considered to be validation of everything he had endured in this fascinating yet bizarre experience. The massive stroke occurred three days later.

Marilyn experienced a dream in which Howling Wolf told her that her grandfather was nearing the end. Her grandmother called just as the morning news revealed that one of America's best loved reporters had suffered a massive stroke. Marilyn called Don and told him the news and explained that she was flying back to Chicago. She was surprised when he told her that he wanted to go with her. Five hours later their airplane lifted off the runway at the San Diego International Airport and headed eastward for O'Hare International.

In Chicago they rented a car and headed straight for the hospital. Marilyn's grandmother met them at the hospital entrance; the remainder of the immediate family was either in his room or in the nearby waiting area. Visiting hours had been extended by the hospital as a special courtesy and reporters were restricted to the lobby.

After hugs, kisses and Don's introduction, Sarah ushered them to the elevator. Free of the probing eyes and ears of the reporters, they were able to speak.

"Grandma, how is he doing?"

"He has a lot of paralysis on his right side and is unable to speak. He can hear and can nod or shake his head. He's not in pain, but he dozes off a lot. He is very weak. He is waiting for you. I'm just so glad that you could get here."

"Nothing could have prevented me from coming, nothing."

Sarah hugged her granddaughter. An uncomfortable Don remained silent, unable to say or do anything for either of these two strong women. The elevator chimed as it reached its destination.

The doors opened to reveal 10 adults and their nine children staring into the elevator. Sarah and Marilyn stepped out followed by Don. Marilyn immediately spotted her mother and brother and rushed to them.

"Where's Dad?" she asked as she hugged her mom and then her brother, Michael.

"He and your Aunt Kathy are in your granddad's room. Come with me."

Marilyn grabbed Don's arm and followed her grandmother and mother to the room adjacent to the Nurses' Station. Her dad and aunt met them just outside the door.

"He's asleep," her dad stated before welcoming his daughter.

Sarah entered the room while Marilyn hugged her aunt.

"This is Don, Don Hughes. This is my Aunt Kathy and my dad."

They both awkwardly shook Don's hand, not knowing why he was there. Their confusion was obvious to the detective.

"Marilyn has been helping me with a case and I felt that I should come with her," he said lamely.

"Marilyn, would you come here; I want to try and wake up your grandfather."

She entered the room and stared at the most influential man in her life. He looked so frail. Her eyes filled with tears as she approached his bed.

"Honey, wake up. Marilyn's here."

Thomas Stevens' eyes opened immediately!

"Hello, sweetheart; what took you so long to get here...did you walk? And where is your young man? I need to meet him."

There was complete silence for several seconds and then complete bedlam. Marilyn moved closer to the bed and leaned over to hug her grandfather. Sarah moved to the door.

"Don, come on in," she said and then ushered him to the opposite side of the bed.

The room began filling immediately and a nurse quickly arrived when she saw the commotion; her initial thought was to clear the room until she saw the patient with both arms wrapped around his latest visitor. She quickly returned to her station and paged the doctor.

Thomas broke the hug with Marilyn and held her hand. He looked up at the detective.

"You must be Don."

"Yes sir...Don Hughes," he said as he automatically extended his right hand.

He then remembered that Mr. Stevens was paralyzed on that side and was surprised when he felt the strong handclasp.

Thomas squeezed Marilyn's hand.

"He has a good heart," Thomas said as he looked first at Marilyn and then at Don. "Don, this is a very special woman who has inherited a special role in life; she will need your help and wisdom at times. Take good care of her."

Thomas then looked at each of the adults in the room as he spoke.

"I am a happy man. I have had a long and wonderful life with an incredible wife and family and they are all here right now. I have no regrets. I would like to have more time to spend with all of you, but that is not to be. Don't mourn my passing; instead, celebrate each day and the chance to do good in the world. Above all, cherish your families."

With those words Thomas Stevens returned to his previous state. All eyes turned to the monitor which showed a steady pulse. The room slowly emptied except for Sarah, Marilyn and Don. At that moment the doctor arrived. He eased past Marilyn and quickly examined Thomas.

"The nurse said that he had returned to normal all of a sudden, but I don't see any change."

"For perhaps a minute he was completely normal and spoke to all of us. I think he was telling us goodbye," said Sarah very softly.

"I really don't know what to tell you...I've heard all kinds of similar stories, but I think that it's just our way of dealing with reality. Our brains can sometimes provide us with what we *want* instead of what actually *is*."

The doctor turned and moved toward the door. Sarah looked at Marilyn and then Don; she smiled. The couple also smiled although Don was just trying to be polite.

Suddenly, there was the soft sound of wings fluttering and their eyes were drawn to the monitor where the image of an eagle had appeared.

The eagle lowered its head slightly and the image faded only to be replaced by an old man with an injured right ear and a bald spot nearby.

"He was a good man," the old man said just before his image faded away.

The monitor then alarmed and showed a flatline condition. The doctor immediately returned to the room and examined Thomas.

"I'm sorry," he said as he removed his stethoscope from his ears and glanced at the clock. He left the room and spoke to the remainder of the family before he walked away.

Sarah hugged Marilyn but there were no tears. Don stood there saddened yet grappling with the images that he had just seen and the words that had come from that image. He was visibly shaken.

The remainder of the family began entering the room in various degrees of distress and grief. One glance at Sarah and they each drew strength from her and remembered the words that Thomas had spoken. An unexplained calmness came over each of them as they remembered his influence in their lives. This was a process that would continue for days and even weeks.

Marilyn kissed her grandfather for the last time, took Don's trembling hand and led him from the room. In the waiting area he spoke.

"Did you see that monitor?"

Marilyn took a deep breath and thought for several seconds before speaking.

"Don, you have just been given a brief glimpse of things from my grandfather's life; recently I have been brought into something that I cannot completely explain. I promise that I will tell you everything, most of which will be difficult to grasp. I have been debating whether I should tell you certain things and I think that I was just given permission to do so."

"You're not an alien, are you?" he asked nervously, trying to mask his growing concern with an attempt at humor.

"No, Don. And this is not the place for the explanation. It has been a long, stressful day and tomorrow I will tell you things that you may not believe. Tonight you were granted a look at something that I now share with only my grandmother. The remainder of my family has no knowledge of the things you will learn tomorrow...that is, if you choose to stay."

"Stay? You think that I would leave simply because a hospital monitor suddenly became a television set and an old man spoke to us? Lady, if nothing else, I need to hear what's coming next! And right now I'm thinking padded cell. I'm just kidding; I'm a little rattled right now, that's all. I've been in love with you since the first moment I saw you and I'm just so happy that I was able to find you again even though it was under really bad circumstances. I don't normally have such good luck."

"Well, Don, starting tomorrow you are in for the biggest surprise of your life. We will find a quiet place away from the family and I will tell you all that I know."

"Marilyn," it was Sarah's voice. "Do you and Don have a place to stay? I have a full house, but I can make room."

"We're okay...I reserved rooms for us before we left. What about funeral arrangements?"

"You know your grandfather; he had taken care of everything except the dates. Your father and I will take care of the details tomorrow. I think that you might need to borrow some of your grandfather's things that he has always kept in the den, you know, to talk about with Don. We also need to consider what to do with those things. Actually, I guess that is your decision. Now go visit with your other family members; your dad, Aunt Kathy and I will need to address those awful news people in the lobby...you know how they are," she said with a smile.

The two women hugged.

"Tom, Kathy...let's go meet the reporters," Sarah sighed.

The trio walked to the elevator and was joined by the doctor after he hung up the phone. The remaining family members migrated to the waiting area just as the television flashed the words 'Breaking News' on the screen. Don walked over to the set and adjusted the volume. They watched the reporter as he announced that the hospital and the Stevens family had just called a brief press conference; the elevator doors were in the background.

The room was completely silent and the sound of the elevator chime seemed to reverberate throughout the lobby area. The doors opened and the doctor followed by Sarah, Kathy and Tom moved to a small lectern. The doctor tapped the microphone to ensure it was working.

"I regret to inform you that Thomas Stevens passed away a few minutes ago after suffering a massive stroke late last night. His widow, Sarah Stevens has a brief statement."

He stepped back and allowed Sarah to move forward. She moved to the microphone blinking back tears as the word 'widow' sunk in. She paused, took a deep breath and looked around the room. She noted the two policemen assigned to crowd control with their hats held over their hearts; she nodded to them and then in a strong voice she spoke.

"My husband had a long and wonderful life. He passed away with his entire family present and was somehow able to speak to all of us. I know that we all share special memories of him and some of you here and at home may recall portions of his life's work which he loved so much. Those of you fortunate enough to have met him know that he was a truly remarkable reporter who preferred to report the human side of the news and the good that is often untouched in favor of the more spectacular and often depressing events. He did not suffer in his final hours and we thank you for your thoughts and prayers. I now ask that you allow us to have some privacy until we can give you more information. Thank you for your patience."

They turned and re-entered the elevator amid complete silence. As soon as the elevator closed, the doctor answered questions from an unusually polite group of reporters.

Marilyn took Don around to the individual family members and performed the introductions. There was much speculation about this man who seemed to be more than a friend to Marilyn and yet no one had even heard about him. This was Marilyn…the girl who did not date and never had a boyfriend. They searched for an engagement ring but there was none. They also noticed that there was none of the touching or hand holding that was to be expected. And there was the obvious question: why was a police officer traveling with her?

After what seemed to be an eternity to Marilyn, she left the hospital with Don and they drove to the hotel. After check-in the two took the elevator to their floor and Don properly escorted Marilyn to her room. There they paused awkwardly at the door.

"Don, I've had a long trying day and I need some rest. I recommend that you get some rest too; you just might be overwhelmed tomorrow. See you about 7?"

"I don't suppose you'd like to start right now with the big mystery explanation. After what I witnessed tonight, I'm probably not going to sleep very well."

"No, Don," she sniffed, "I need some time to myself. I thought I was prepared for the loss of my grandfather. I knew that he was showing signs that his health was rapidly deteriorating, but this was the first time that I have experienced something like this. Ever since I first told him that I wanted to be a reporter, he has patiently taught me how to do the job that I love so much. Then just a short time ago he introduced me to a part of his life that is both fascinating and frightening. He was somehow able to pass this knowledge along to me and to see that I actually could pick up where he left off. Then he passed away. It was as if he held on long enough to be satisfied that I could complete what he started and then he, well, you know. Right now I just want to be alone with my thoughts."

Don hugged her and in that instant knew without a doubt that this was the woman with whom he wanted to share the remainder of his life.

"Okay, I understand. Just remember, I'm right next door if you need me."

They kissed tenderly and Marilyn unlocked her door.

"I love you," Don said for the first time.

She turned and kissed him again and softly whispered to him.

"I love you, too."

She entered the room with her luggage and went straight to the bed. She flopped onto the bed and cried softly for almost an hour. When the tears subsided, she showered and went to bed. Her thoughts then turned to her grandmother and how her life had suddenly changed. Marilyn wondered what to do; she could remain in San Diego only if she knew that her grandmother would be okay. It also seemed to hinge on Don and his reaction to what he would learn tomorrow. She toyed with the idea of calling Don and starting the explanation before deciding to put it off until morning. Then, abruptly, she fell asleep.

Meanwhile Don was wide awake. He thought about what he had seen earlier; he knew that Marilyn and her grandmother had also seen it and were not surprised at all. While he was trying to process this, he remembered thinking how lucky he had been to prevent her from being killed by that lunatic reporter. Even the shooting investigation had seemed ridiculously abbreviated and, at the time, he had been extremely relieved that the process had been completed so quickly. Now these seemingly unrelated events were beginning to merge into a mystery that seemed to engulf this wonderful, but mysterious woman. He was reluctant and yet eager to hear her explanation. The best thing was her final statement just before she disappeared into her room.

He partially unpacked his suitcase and then requested a wakeup call for 6:15. He fell asleep fully clothed after another half hour.

Don was awakened by a ringing telephone.

"Detective Hughes," he stated automatically.

"This is civilian Marilyn Stevens in the room next door...are you awake?"

"Well, I am now. How can I be of assistance, ma'am?"

"I just wanted to remind you that you're taking me to breakfast and that I am starving. It's a couple of minutes after six and I can be ready in ten minutes."

"Last night you said 7 A.M. and I still have not received my 6:15 wakeup call. That's probably because it is not yet 6:15. So if you'll hang up, I'll go back to sleep."

"I'm leaving for breakfast at 6:30. In case you forgot, we did not have dinner yesterday. What part of 'starving' do you not understand? If you are late then you will be forced to use your detective skills to find me. Or, at the risk of bruising your ego, you could ask the Chicago police for some 'professional courtesy' in helping locate me. I would recommend that you hang up and get serious."

Marilyn hung up and smiled.

Fifteen minutes later she was sitting in the lobby skimming through a courtesy copy of the newspaper. She wondered how her grandmother had fared. Hopefully the extra family members would be keeping her busy or listening to her if she just needed to talk. Marilyn knew that her parents were staying there at the house but was not certain how many others were also there. She assumed that everyone would end up there at some point today.

At 6:29, Don tapped her on the shoulder.

"There's a rumor going around that you're a little hungry...care for some breakfast?"

Marilyn stood and kissed him without even thinking about it.

"We can either eat here or at a good place about a block away. I'm not usually impressed with hotel food and I think it would be better to make the short trip. It's your choice."

Don took her hand and the couple left the hotel. Six minutes later they were seated in a booth and looking at the menu while the waitress poured their coffee. They both ordered simple breakfasts and the waitress scurried away.

Marilyn was first to speak.

"How did you sleep?"

"I think I now know what *jet lag* means. I had some trouble going to sleep probably due to the two-hour time difference or perhaps it had something to do with something I witnessed last night. And, of course, there is a little bit of anticipation about what I am going to learn today. Other than that, I slept like a baby until I was rudely awakened by the phone. How did you sleep?"

"I cried for awhile; Grandpa was a major player in my life. I mean my mom and dad were always there, but Grandpa did all of these things to make me self-reliant and taught me everything about being a reporter. I doubt that very many people had such a teacher that genuinely cared about their success. I learned very little in school except grammar. In college there was a lot of theory, but not much that I had not already learned. I never mentioned Grandpa, but my teachers and professors all knew who he was. Occasionally I would challenge them and offer another perspective, but I listened dutifully and searched for those things which might serve me well. Grandpa and I often argued over this other point of view and I think I learned something about humanity that is not taught in school. I always hoped that he would help me get started in my career, but he made certain that I did everything on my own. And he was right. Now I am sitting on top of something that I cannot report on because it goes beyond the laws of nature and science that we have all been taught. We will get to that later."

"Would you care to start now?" Don asked tentatively.

"No, you will need to read some things while I explain...no, *try* to explain them. We need to be at the house for that. I also need to find out what Grandma plans to do. That house is huge and I think it is too much for her. I'm not sure how to approach that issue. Maybe Mom and Dad or my aunt and uncle will help her sort that out."

The waitress returned with their orders and the couple began eating in silence. Both were wondering why their own future was being so carefully avoided. They had each hoped that the other would give a hint or perhaps an outright statement about hope for a future together, but inside they each feared what they might hear.

They continued their meal with no further references to the future and returned to the hotel. From there they drove to her grandmother's house and judging by the number of cars parked outside they were probably the last to arrive.

They entered the house and were greeted first by Marilyn's grandmother and then by her parents.

"Have you two had breakfast?" her grandmother asked and was obviously prepared to cook for two more.

"We've already eaten, but I know there's a pot of coffee somewhere around here. Don, would you care for a cup?"

"Please," he responded while smiling at Marilyn. "I will probably need it before the inquisition begins."

"Oh come on...everyone is just curious since they know very little about you and especially about us. By the way, my dad knows that you saved my life although he doesn't have any details. I have no idea whom he might have shared that information with. So as far as I'm concerned, it's just a good thing that you came along when that crazy man tried to kill me. That's my story."

"I think I understand what you're saying, but I am actually here to protect you in case there are others who might also wish to prevent you from any further investigation. That should be sufficient for your family."

At that point Sarah decided to speak.

"Why don't you two just announce your plans...I've seen the way you look at each other. You remind me of a young couple that I knew years ago. Stop wasting valuable time. Marilyn, take Don into the den and have that special talk. The box and summary are sitting right where you and your grandpa left them several weeks ago. Now take your coffee and go!"

Blushing profusely, Marilyn picked up her cup and headed for the den; Don smiled sheepishly at Sarah and followed. They almost made it to the den but were intercepted by Marilyn's parents. Her father looked first at Don and then spoke to Marilyn.

"Marilyn, your mom and I would like talk to you and Don for a minute. This might be our only chance to find out a little more about what happened in San Diego. The fact that you're being escorted by a policeman is a little troubling to all of us. We just want to know some facts."

"Grandpa needed me to check on something in San Diego. I spent time chasing down some leads and apparently I stumbled onto something that was very sensitive. I was working with a former reporter that Grandpa had told me to check with and at some point he began to act strange. We were looking at some proof that Grandpa wanted me to locate and the next thing I knew Don appeared out of nowhere and shot him. I vaguely remember hearing the shots and the sound of a metal object, a pipe, striking a nearby dumpster before hitting the ground and then I saw the reporter on the ground."

Don chose that moment to add his perspective.

"I was in my cruiser on a routine patrol and spotted a suspicious vehicle headed the opposite direction. I saw it turn down an alleyway. We had just experienced a minor earthquake and drivers were not cooperating very well, but I eventually was able to turn around and drive to the alley. I stopped my cruiser just as the man raised a steel pipe to strike your daughter who was kneeling next to a small object in the alley. I drew my weapon and fired two shots. If I had arrived a couple of seconds later, we would not be discussing this. We have been unable to determine if this was a single individual acting alone and must assume that there could be others involved. I don't mean to frighten you, but that is the reality. Your daughter has additional information right here that we are going to sift through and maybe gain some valuable clues. The timing is bad and I'm sorry that we must meet under the present circumstances. That is really all that I can tell you."

"Well, the newspaper has a photo of the two of you arriving at the hospital and you are identified as a San Diego police detective and mentions that you shot her assailant and hints that she might be in protective custody. That is enough to make us worry."

"I'm sorry Dad, but we need to start going through the stuff in the den. Grandma might be needed to help, but we will try to avoid that. If you'll excuse us, we want to get started and get this over with. Try not to mention any of this to the reporters who were surprisingly absent when we arrived."

Thomas Jr. nodded agreement just as Sarah approached with a cup of coffee.

"Don, I thought you might need more coffee."

"Thank you, ma'am. Okay, if you will excuse us, Marilyn and I have some work to do."

The couple entered the den and closed the door. There on the desk was the summary folder and the box labeled "Dreamcatcher."

"Don could you bring that box and the folder over to this coffee table and we will get started."

The Shaman's Legacy

Marilyn was nervous; she would tell how she was given this knowledge and what she had experienced up until today. Then they would go through the summary folder. After that she would show Don the two photos in her purse. She would watch Don very carefully throughout what she now considered to be an ordeal. There was a lot for him to absorb and much of it could not be explained.

"Several weeks ago, Grandpa called me and told me to come over and that there was something he needed to tell me. He told me that I might have difficulty believing parts of it. That turned out to be a gross understatement! I actually had trouble believing *most of it*. Grandma was right there and verified some of what he said. There was no proof, only the word of a man who has always reported the facts. Now sit back and listen to a story that begins a long time ago."

It took half an hour for her explanation which Don interrupted on two occasions to clarify what she had said. Next they went through the summary which required another half hour and Don simply read it while Marilyn looked over his shoulder; this time he asked no questions. Marilyn then retrieved her journal which documented her movement from Chicago to San Diego and contained several references to the police detective seated beside her. His first question was: how was she able to drive that far in a day and a half, virtually non-stop?

"Welcome to my new world," she simply said. "You tell me."

Then she removed the lid from the box. There on top of the clippings and rough notes were two photos. Don picked them up and studied them.

"These were taken in the alley!"

Yes. That one is the dreamcatcher. The other photo is a picture of what came out of the fire."

"But it's only a shape or outline."

"And what would you say it resembles?"

"It's obviously a large bird. Remember, I saw it and heard it, too"

"Apparently it could not be photographed. It is or was not just my imagination...I actually saw an eagle. That photo is my proof and it *is* proof."

"You would have difficulty convincing anyone that the photo is proof of anything."

"Last night, looking Grandpa's monitor, what did you see?"

"I saw an eagle and then an old man, possibly an Indian who spoke to us."

"Let me show you something else."

She fumbled through the box and showed him an old photo.

"Recognize anyone?"

"My God! It's the man whose image was on the monitor! But how...?"

"Once again, welcome to my world. Any more questions?"

"So now you have some sort of special powers?"

"I'm not aware of having any type of powers; I think I am just a receptor for thoughts and knowledge that allow me to locate and destroy the dreamcatchers. In other words I can provide the physical means to accomplish what needs to be done. I have been guided by these images and thoughts just as my grandfather was. I don't know why he was chosen but I think that I was chosen to replace him...this thing or these things knew that he was nearing the end of his life and had him teach me to do what he had done in the past. I don't really know this to be true; it just sort of seems to make sense. I was skeptical at first, but strange things began to happen that kept directing me to go somewhere or locate someone and I slowly began to listen to these thoughts and follow them. Sometimes the directions are precise and other times they are vague. There is one other thing: one dreamcatcher remains and they seem to become more powerful as time goes by. The one I destroyed had learned to hide somewhat and I imagine that the remaining one can do the same. I have not received any hints about where the last one is and that bothers me tremendously."

There was a soft knock at the door.

"Marilyn?"

Recognizing her grandmother's voice, Marilyn quickly moved to the door and opened it.

"Yes, Grandma?"

"Can I come in for a minute? I think you might need some reinforcements."

"Sure, come in."

"Don, by now you have probably heard the most outrageous story of your life. I need to say some things that might add to the credibility of what Marilyn has told you. Think back to the first time you saw her. Why were you there and why was Marilyn there? What single item brought the two of you together? Think about it. Was there a reason that you were there...something that was out of the ordinary?"

"Actually, yes; I was re-assigned there on short notice when the officer assigned to the detail suddenly became ill. That's nothing unusual, it happens on a regular basis."

"Did you feel an immediate attraction toward Marilyn?"

"Yes, I even asked her to dinner."

"And do you always ask members of the public that you assist to have dinner with you?"

Sarah smiled as she watched him.

"No."

"Doesn't it seem at least a little odd that you were available to respond to prevent Marilyn's death?"

"I was fortunate to be in the area, that's all."

"Think back to that day, before the incident. Can you recall anything unusual?"

"No...well, there was the earthquake and then my patrol was shifted. Wait a minute! Just before spotting the car with Marilyn and the reporter in it, I was distracted by a brief shadow and instinctively glanced in that direction. Oh my gosh...I remember now! There was a huge bird flying unusually low and it was an eagle!"

"Do you still consider this to be one big coincidence?"

"I, uh...."

"Don," Marilyn interjected, "this is just one small revelation. My questioning after the incident was very superficial, but at the time I was relieved after what I had just been through. I know that your statement and actions were also completed very quickly which seems odd to me. Do you have any reason why you were cleared so quickly?"

"No, but it was an open and shut case. I thought about that last night."

"Let me put it another way. Do you know of any other case that was closed so quickly?"

"No."

"Why did you place the lighter fluid and my camera back into Albert's car?"

"I don't recall doing that."

"Could it have been that you were ensuring that there would be no questions asked that would force you to mention some things that were beyond explanation?"

"I don't know."

"Well, Don, do you routinely disturb a crime scene?"

"Of course not."

Sarah spoke once again.

"Don, your involvement was carefully orchestrated by forces that we do not understand. You and Marilyn were destined to meet and meet again to ensure the destruction of the dreamcatcher. This is how it happened to me and my husband. I never received any proof, just a whole bunch of impossible coincidences that finally proved to me that Tom and I were brought together for a purpose. Last night I received that proof just as you did. Did we actually see those images on the monitor or were they just images imprinted in our minds? I don't know and I don't think it matters. You have been included in Marilyn's future for a reason. You may never know how or why, but apparently you will also play a role in locating and destroying the remaining dreamcatcher. I have said enough. Now please excuse me."

Sarah left the den smiling. She wondered what Don had to be thinking.

"Well, I'm sure you now have some questions," Marilyn said softly.

"Look, this is an awful lot to absorb. Neither you nor your grandmother seem to be bothered by any of this; how can you just accept it?"

"It hasn't been easy. I'm not delusional...at least I don't think so. I don't talk to these things, these images, but they speak to me. The television sometimes has words on the screen that no one else can see. The word 'hurry' appeared in the viewfinder of my camera while I was taking the photo of the dreamcatcher in the alley; that word is not in the camera."

"I've never asked you...where did you get the dreamcatcher?"

"I stole it from a lady's hotel room...Albert helped me."

"You *what*?"

"We had to get the dreamcatcher and destroy it. I kept getting messages that helped me locate it and I was told to hurry and destroy it. Remember, these things *kill people*. It has something to do with their nightmares."

"So do you honestly think that this dreamcatcher killed people in San Diego?"

"There was a guy that was critically injured in a car wreck who had it. Then it was given to a woman who died in a mysterious elevator accident. From there it went to the Wayside House where those thirteen women died and from there it went to the lady that I stole it from. This information was in my notes, but I didn't present it to you in this manner because you already had enough to digest. Everyone who died had slept under the dreamcatcher and this was the pattern that my grandfather had discovered years ago; he also learned that they all had died in a manner that mimicked their worst nightmare."

"I remember the lady who died in the elevator accident and obviously the women who died at Wayside House; what about the lady that you stole it from...what did she die from?"

"That's just it, she didn't die. I think it was because I was able to destroy the dreamcatcher before she died from whatever was going to kill her."

"Well did she sleep under it?"

"It was hanging from a clothes hanger hooked over her bed so I would assume that she did. You know, thinking back I received numerous directions to *hurry* that morning. There was a sense of extreme urgency to find and destroy the dreamcatcher. In retrospect I think that the lady, a Patricia Favret, was in extreme danger."

"She was staying in a hotel...was she a tourist? Maybe we could talk to her."

"Yes, she's visiting from Massachusetts; she was still registered there two days ago. I wanted to pay for the dreamcatcher. I was going to push some money under her door but decided to talk to her."

"Then you would be forced to explain why you stole it and that might be a little sticky."

The Shaman's Legacy

"Well, when we get back to San Diego perhaps you could intervene and offer restitution on my behalf...assuming that she is still there. Something like the good cop who tries to rescue an extremely nice lady from a budding life of crime."

"That might work. Let's take a break from this; I need some time to think about all that I've heard and seen in the last few hours."

"Okay, time to visit with the family; I'm sorry...I meant start the *inquisition* as you call it."

"Well, in that case, you should at least be dressed properly," Don said as he dropped to one knee and produced a small jewelry box. "Will you marry me?"

Marilyn watched him open the box and stared at the most beautiful solitaire ring she had ever seen. She looked at Don with her mouth open and then, dumbfounded, simply nodded.

The embrace and kiss that followed were both long and passionate. And suddenly, Marilyn took Don's hand and led him to the kitchen where her grandmother was arranging various foods on the table. She glanced up as the couple entered the kitchen.

"Well it's about time," she said as she saw the expression on Marilyn's face.

"Don just proposed," Marilyn said while lifting her left hand with its new adornment.

The older woman hugged first her granddaughter then her future grandson-in-law.

"I wish Grandpa could have been here to see this."

"He knew, Marilyn, he knew. Remember, he told Don to take good care of you. He knew it when you first told him that the same police officer who had helped you earlier showed up just in time to save your life. That was one of the first things he said to me after you called him. Remember, he and I went through a similar thing years ago. Believe me, he knew. I think you should now go make your announcement to the rest of the family...I'm tired of playing dumb!"

With that, the couple left the kitchen and moved to the living room and faced the silent stares of the remainder of the family.

"Everyone, I need to re-introduce Don Hughes, my fiancé."

There was a collective gasp of surprise followed by chaos as family members rushed to congratulate the couple. No one considered this announcement to be ill-timed considering the loss of the family patriarch...it just fit in with so many other quirky things that seemed to surface on a regular basis.

At that moment the morning news segment on the television began a brief story on the life of Thomas Stevens, one of the most noteworthy news reporters of all times. There were numerous old photos and film clips including one of him shaking hands with an older man with an injured right ear and a bald spot right next to it.

"Who is that man?" asked Thomas, Jr.

"An Indian named *Howling Wolf*," replied Don without even thinking.

Marilyn smiled at her grandmother just as Don realized what he had said.

"How did you know that, Don? You're a cop from San Diego," again from Thomas, Jr.

"Uh...Marilyn told me that they had worked together a few times."

The family resumed viewing the special report and Marilyn squeezed Don's hand.

"Grandpa and Howling Wolf never met," she whispered.

"But they were shaking hands in the film clip...how could...?" Don turned to Marilyn, "I have the feeling that I should no longer be surprised no matter what happens. Obviously the rest of the family saw the same thing; heck, the whole country saw it."

"Maybe, maybe not. Perhaps only our family was allowed a glimpse of something that happened which was beyond our realm of understanding."

On that day and for many days thereafter, condolences arrived from around the world. Presidents, past and present, heads of state, lesser officials, former co-workers, old friends and thousands of others sent brief messages of sympathy. Some provided photos and news clippings of this man who had touched their lives. Others wrote of their personal interactions with him...many were written in a shaky, almost illegible manner; the events mentioned indicated that these were elderly men whose memories were sharp although their bodies were injured or deteriorating as they aged.

The news media camped out on the lawn but chose not to ring the door bell. Periodically, a family member would go outdoors to speak to them. There were others who came and some had signs of remembrance. The biggest surprise was a group of Native American elders who appeared and requested to address the family. They were admitted to the residence and told their story of this white man who was special to them and was admired throughout the land of the Lakota and beyond. They were all dressed in ceremonial clothing which created quite a stir among the news media; the Stevens family was both surprised and pleased by their presence.

As they prepared to leave, the leader went straight to Sarah and took both of her hands in his. He spoke words which she did not understand, but knew what he meant. The elder then turned to Marilyn and Don and held a hand from each in his own. Again he spoke softly in his native tongue and both clearly understood his message. Then he turned to leave and was followed by the remainder of the group, each of whom nodded first to Sarah and then to Marilyn and Don. Those acts were witnessed by the rest of the family and yet no one questioned why Marilyn and Don were singled out for special attention. The elder spoke briefly to the members of the news media and then they all left.

The same group returned three days later for the funeral which was restricted to family and special friends. Thousands of onlookers of all ages lined the route from the funeral home to the cemetery. The Navy's Blue Angels performed the "Missing Man" formation as a prelude to the brief graveside ceremony and a Marine Captain from the Honor Guard presented the flag that had draped Thomas' coffin minutes earlier to Sarah. The Lakota elder then placed an ornate peace pipe on the coffin after uttering a special incantation. A brief, but mostly upbeat service followed.

Marilyn and Don were married in a civil ceremony on the day following the funeral. This was done for the convenience of the family members since they had already assembled. To some it would have been considered odd or in poor taste to have a wedding immediately following a funeral, but it was exactly what the late Thomas Stevens would have expected.

Tom Jr. and his wife, Mary, would move in with Sarah at her request. Marilyn made arrangements to have her personal things shipped to San Diego. Her roommates were surprised to learn of the wedding, but were really impressed with her new husband. The newlyweds flew back to San Diego the next day; there was additional work to be done concerning the recent destruction of the fourth dreamcatcher.

Marilyn phoned Patricia Favret's hotel from the San Diego airport and was relieved to find that she was still registered there; she was not in her room and Marilyn left a message that she would call back later. The couple left the airport in their own cars and drove to Marilyn's motel where she collected her belongings and checked out. Don mentioned that the name of the motel meant "golden eagle" in Spanish and asked if that was why she chose to stay there; she replied that she was "sent there." Don did not even question her reply. "Why bother?" he thought as he shook his head.

Don led the way to his apartment and on the first trip with their luggage he unlocked the door, picked her up and carried her across the threshold as she giggled.

"I had heard about this custom and never thought it was actually done except in the movies," she purred.

"Apparently I saw the same movies, but I never thought I would do it."

After several trips to and from the cars, Marilyn considered herself a new resident.

"You know that I must tone down the masculinity factor of this place, Don," she said with a smile.

"I didn't know I was bringing home a bride; otherwise, I would have dressed the place up with a plastic flower in a vase or a doily or something."

"Careful, we both have some serious adjustments to make...let's not rush anything."

"Rush anything? A couple of weeks ago we didn't even *know* each other! But I understand what you're saying. Right now I'll just concentrate on remembering to call you 'Marilyn' or 'Honey' instead of 'Alice, Beth, Carol, Diane, Ester, Flo...ouch! You hit pretty good for a girl. In my line of work we call it 'battery' in case you forgot."

"So, call a cop. Go ahead, dial 911. I'll even write the story...*Little Girl Beats Up Big City Cop*."

"Okay, that did it! Call that lady that you stole the dreamcatcher from and let's go make things right with her. I'll just listen and learn how to handle these things since I'm new at the business."

"Isn't there another tradition that you should be concerned with...I mean, we are still considered newlyweds, aren't we? This is our first home and we have an obligation to it and to each other."

An hour later Marilyn picked up the phone and called Patricia Favret's room; this time she answered.

"Hello?"

"Hello, my name is Marilyn Stevens and I need to discuss something with you. Normally I would say let's meet somewhere, but this is a very unusual matter and I am bringing a San Diego Police detective with me. Would it be okay if we stopped by for a few minutes in about an hour?"

"Have I done something wrong?"

"Oh, no! You may have some information that the detective needs to help clear a case and since I am involved, I really do need your help."

"I guess that would be okay. You said in an hour so I guess I'll see you then."

"Thank you...goodbye."

Marilyn hung up the phone and faced her frowning husband.

"Honey, your last name is now *Hughes* in case you forgot," said Don with a tentative grin.

"This way you can be the detective who is ensuring that I do the right thing and you are trying to keep me out of jail. I don't think it would be wise to greet Patricia as husband and wife."

"That makes good sense. So then I will take the lead and explain the situation and then turn everything over to you for your admission of guilt and offer of restitution. That should work. One other thing: you didn't verify who she was when you called her."

"It wasn't necessary, I *knew* it was her."

"Silly me...I should have known. I'm still learning."

An hour later they stood outside room 304 and Don, detective shield in hand, knocked on the door. After a few seconds the couple heard the bolt retract and the door opened slightly. Don held the shield so that it could be seen and the door closed slightly as the chain was removed. The door opened to reveal a woman and a man staring intently at the two visitors.

"I'm detective Hughes and this is Marilyn Stevens. May we come in?"

The door opened further and the woman stepped closer to the man.

"I'm Patricia Favret and this is Brad Chandler. Please come in. I'm sorry...there are only two chairs."

"That's okay, this shouldn't take long. Several days ago there was a shooting in a nearby alley and I am trying to clear up a few items. Marilyn was the woman who was almost killed by that old reporter. During the course of the investigation she revealed that she had removed an object from your room. Can you confirm that something was missing?"

"Yes, there was a thing called a dreamcatcher that was hanging over the bed and it was missing; I didn't notice it until Brad pointed it out. There was no damage to the door and the hotel couldn't find anyone who knew anything about it. I didn't file a police report since nothing else was missing and I didn't pay that much for it."

Marilyn chose that moment to enter the conversation.

"I want to apologize for taking the dreamcatcher, but it was necessary. I have been tracking it but it was always being presented to someone else and I finally traced it to your room. I had hoped to buy it and provide you with a profit. So now I would like to offer you double what you paid for it."

"Couldn't you just return it to me?"

"Well, it had to be destroyed," Marilyn stated matter-of-factly.

"Why would you want to destroy something so beautiful? That doesn't make any sense."

"Let me ask you a few questions. On the day that you discovered that the dreamcatcher was missing, do you recall anything unusual or dangerous that had occurred recently?"

"Yes, actually...I was at the zoo and a deadly snake somehow got into my purse right after the earthquake. I was reaching for my car keys and felt it move. I didn't know at the time that it was a snake; I just knew that whatever it was, it was alive!"

Don chose this moment to speak.

"Ms. Stevens, perhaps this is not the best time to discuss this."

"Detective Hughes...I know exactly what I'm doing."

Brad and Trish exchanged glances wondering what was going on.

"You slept under the dreamcatcher the night before, right?"

"Yes, but why does that matter?"

"Because that dreamcatcher was going to kill you."

"Okay, that does it...what's going on here?" Trish asked shakily.

"Wait a minute," interjected Brad, "I slept under it, too."

"And did you have a near brush with death right after that?"

"Well, I didn't mention this to Trish, but I almost crashed that Friday morning after my plane's engine quit. Just before impact the engine began running again. Oh my gosh! Trish...Adrianne and Brianne also slept under the dreamcatcher and you said that Adrianne had been abducted by that pervert but was rescued that morning. Ms. Stevens would you please try to explain what you think was happening?"

"The short version is that I managed to destroy the dreamcatcher before it killed all of you."

"Are they all like that...I saw two of them and they were identical."

"The one I destroyed had killed at least fifteen people and we know that there is one more somewhere. I need to find that one, also."

"There was a guy that had two of them and sold one for one hundred bucks to another guy who was walking by while I was being shown the first dreamcatcher. The guy's name was Sheldon something and I had his card but it sort of just disappeared."

"So this Sheldon guy has the other dreamcatcher. Was it in a wooden box?"

"Yes."

"Can you remember anything else about this man?"

"He was on the road a lot. Everything was on his business card. If I could just find it...."

"Trish, Brad, move over here next to me," commanded Marilyn.

The couple complied. Marilyn looked at each of them and set her jaw. She then closed her eyes and her brow wrinkled as she concentrated. A few seconds later, she relaxed and handed a one hundred dollar bill to Trish.

"Thank you for selling me that nice dreamcatcher. Don, it's time that we were leaving."

"Thank you! I know I can put the money to good use."

Marilyn and Don left the room leaving a slightly confused couple behind. Neither said a word until they reached the elevator.

"Marilyn, didn't you say that you had no special powers?"

"Now I don't need to explain it other than admitting that I can erase some memories. I don't really know how far I can go with this. I can also force people into action...doing something that is against their will. I don't know if it is always available to me or if it just pertains to the dreamcatcher thing."

"So you could use it on me, make me do things that are against my will. I suppose you could erase portions of my memories of things that happened before I met you. Actually, there are some things that I would love to forget...do I have a say in this?"

He smiled weakly.

"Honey, I have already changed your life. I would never touch upon your previous life...that is what makes you who you are. As long as you provide me with everything I ask for and treat me like a princess, I'll leave your brain alone." She laughed and hugged him. "Right now, though, I need to settle in and try to figure out how to locate the other dreamcatcher. I know that I will need your help since you may have access to information that I can't get. I need to talk to a certain reporter who helped me a few days ago. If he is smart, he has already been trying to find out why I am here...I am sure he already knows who I am."

"Are you going to fry his brain?"

"No, silly, not even if I could. Well, if he were to start digging up information and figuring out what was going on with dreamcatchers and strange deaths, then I might be forced to intervene. Now take me home and let's forget about everything except us."

One week later Marilyn happily announced her new position as a Special Correspondent to the *Union-Tribune*. She was welcomed to the newspaper's readers in a special piece that dwelt mostly on her famous grandfather and her narrow escape from death thanks to her new husband. Marilyn was given tremendous latitude in assignments; she was on a small retainer and could produce as much or as little as she chose. She and Don spent considerable time trying to backtrack and locate the fifth dreamcatcher but could not find the man named Sheldon who was apparently the key. Neither was able to associate the name of Sheldon Curry with the last two dreamcatchers even though he was mentioned numerous times by various news media as the man responsible for breathing life back into a failed company. They both were familiar with the story, but it was as if they were being prohibited from even questioning whether this particular Sheldon could put them on the trail of the missing dreamcatcher.

As weeks turned into months with no clues to direct their search, the couple continued a routine which slowly drew their attention away from the final dreamcatcher. By this time Marilyn had entered all of the old data into her own computer database; it would be available when the need arose.

Donilyn Hughes was born on March 14, 1999. Marilyn's focus on the dreamcatcher was diluted even further.

CHAPTER FIFTEEN

Twenty-Eight Years Later

Diane Begley was in her junior year at the University of Washington, Seattle campus. The end of the Autumn Quarter was approaching and the weather had been unusually mild thus far. She chose this Thursday morning after her last exam to drive around the local area with two friends. She spotted the dark sedan as soon as she left her parking spot and glanced back periodically as the driver maintained a discreet distance. Diane noted that there were two and possibly three occupants in the sedan. She was not worried...she had two others with her.

Driving down one of the nearby residential streets, she spotted a yard sale and, on a whim, decided to stop and examine the goods. The sedan stopped half a block away and Diane knew that the occupants would leave her alone. The three girls left Diane's car and wandered over to the various tables. Only Diane checked the sedan periodically. There was no one else at the yard sale except for a lady sitting near the front porch.

There were the usual small appliances, clothing, games and toys. Diane was looking for something unique, something special or a little off-beat. It would be a special gift for her dad. She had been unable to locate something suitable in the Seattle area and time was running out. As she approached the last of the offerings, the lady seated in a lawn chair stood.

"Come take a look at this," she said as she moved toward the porch steps.

There was a box that proclaimed that inside was 'The last set of grill tools you'll ever buy.'

"I don't even own a grill," said Diane as she turned to leave.

"You *really do need to see what it is* and it's not grill tools; oh, and my name is Amanda, Amanda Curry."

With that, the woman opened the end of the box, tilted it and let a wooden case slide out. She allowed the cardboard box to fall away and held the beautiful case so that Diane could open it.

"Go ahead, open it up," Amanda said with a pleasant smile.

The Shaman's Legacy

Diane opened the case and gasped as she spotted the dreamcatcher; she had found the perfect gift for her father! It was almost as if fate had brought her to this place.

"It's a dreamcatcher...how much do you want for it?"

She held her breath hoping that she could afford it. It was the largest one she had ever seen and it was so beautiful. It actually seemed to be calling out to her.

"I was planning on selling it for $50, but I see how much you like it and...."

"It's not for me, it's for my dad!"

"Well, in that case...$25. I was hoping that it would go to someone nice. If you can't afford it, just give me what you can. It belonged to my dad and it's been up in the attic for years. His brother gave it to him for his birthday right after my dad had eye surgery almost thirty years ago. They replaced his corneas and restored his failing vision."

"I have $25! I'll take it. Leah, Caitlyn...come look at this!"

Diane glanced down the street and noticed that the driver of the sedan was trying to see what the commotion was all about. Amid the 'oohs' and 'ahs' Diane handed Amanda a twenty and a five. After putting the wooden case back into the cardboard box, the three young ladies and one dreamcatcher piled into Diane's car and returned to their dormitory. That is how Diane Begley came to possess the fifth dreamcatcher.

She had not seen the sentinel Golden Eagle that had suspiciously watched her as she carried the dreamcatcher to her car. Inside the wooden case, the dreamcatcher had suddenly awakened and seconds later the eagle had plummeted to the ground, dead; the dreamcatcher had then returned to its dormant status. It was far more powerful than it had been when it first arrived in Seattle years ago.

Diane had never even looked back for the sedan as the trio discussed first the new item and then getting together for dinner. She was flying home the next day while Caitlyn and Leah were taking their last quarter finals. There would be no partying since all three of them took their education very seriously and good grades were essential. She had already placed Caitlyn on her insurance policy so that she could leave the car with her.

She proudly showed her new treasure to her roommate, Gwen, who examined it very carefully and asked how much she paid for it. She seemed shocked that Diane was able to acquire such an incredible work of art for such a price. She asked if there were any more like it and then helped Diane wrap the box in bubble-wrap for the flight home. Diane was uncertain if she would return for the Winter Quarter which would commence in early January. The Autumn Quarter had been difficult for her due to repeated absences; she needed a break.

Gwen was a few years older than Diane and was truly a *straight arrow*. Like Diane, she was a lot of fun but not a party animal. They shared two classes and were friends, but not best buddies. They were roommates since they were from the same part of the country and the University always tried to match students for compatibility reasons. Their interests were incredibly similar.

The next day they were to fly home to spend the holidays with their families; Gwen chose the same flight since she lived approximately twenty miles from Diane's home and was a little nervous about flying. Gwen took care of the flight arrangements except for Diane's air fare. She had booked the flight early to get decent seats due to the Christmas holidays.

Upon arrival at the airport and checking their luggage curbside, they learned that their 8:05 A.M. flight to Boston had already been cancelled or possibly seriously delayed due to an engine problem; the earlier passengers had scrambled to find other flights. Many were successful and were able to leave earlier than originally planned; the remainder proceeded to the departure gate and hoped for the best. There were apparently no other seats available. As the two women discussed their plight, Gwen was paged and was asked to stop by the ticket counter.

Diane watched hopefully as Gwen spoke to the ticket agent and then showed her ID before finally turning and pointing at Diane. She then smiled and thanked the ticket agent. She informed Diane that the problem had been corrected and that the flight would be departing approximately forty minutes late. There was also a potential weather issue as an *Alberta Clipper* raced toward New England.

The happy women proceeded to their gate and awaited the boarding announcement. They listened as their fellow travelers were summoned to the counter to make various adjustments. They had minimized their carry-on luggage just to avoid the frantic battle to grab their possessions from the overhead bins when disembarking in Boston; they complimented themselves on their wise decision.

Several minutes later they heard the boarding call for their flight and moved quickly toward the jetway, amazed at the amount of items being carried aboard by their fellow passengers. They were motioned to the front of the line since they were carrying very little.

"Please go ahead since you don't appear to have anything for the overhead bins," the agent said as she checked the boarding passes, "and you are, actually *both* of you, are seated in the rear of the cabin. That's even better. Have a nice flight."

The two women ended up in the third row from the back of the plane; they had an aisle seat and a middle seat on the right hand side of the cabin.

"Well, at least we're close to the restrooms," said Gwen, "That is probably a good thing for me since I get nervous. That's why I grabbed an aisle seat."

They watched with a perverse sense of humor as their fellow passengers tried to stow their luggage and gifts. Everyone wanted their overhead items as close to the front of the plane as possible and seemed not to care how much they inconvenienced the passengers behind them.

"So much for holiday cheer," sighed Gwen as she observed several passengers becoming increasingly vocal in their displeasure.

"Yeah, I'm glad we boarded before the mob."

Eventually the flight attendants began expediting the movement of passengers, baggage and gifts. Several minutes later the passengers were seated and the cabin door was closed. At this time both women noticed that the last five rows of the cabin were vacant except for them.

"I can't believe that we're leaving with empty seats...there's more than twenty vacant ones," Diane whispered.

"Well, we are leaving late and I think that any more delays during this time of the year would create even more delays. You can bet that the pilots will be trying to make up for our late start."

They were interrupted by a flight attendant.

"You are welcome to move around if you like. We originally had a full cabin, but obviously several passengers jumped ship when they heard of the delay or possible cancellation."

"Thank you," Diane said and then to Gwen: "No offense, but I'm moving over to the window seat. I want to sleep and try to ward off jet lag."

"No problem; I plan on napping for the same reason."

Sixteen minutes later their Boeing 797 lifted off the SEA runway and turned eastward while climbing to cruising altitude. The passengers settled in for the four hour flight, thankful that they were finally on their way. Their only concern was the cold front headed for the Boston area; the Captain had advised them of the possibility of a delay upon arrival.

An hour prior to their expected arrival time, the Captain announced that the cold front had slowed significantly. They were assured that they would be placed into a holding pattern for up to one hour; another option was to divert to the Manchester, NH airport. A chorus of groans filled the cabin. The airline would, of course, provide bus transportation from Manchester to Boston.

"Hey, Diane," Gwen whispered, "did you hear that? We might be going into Manchester. My dad could pick us up and we could drop you off. It's not that much out of our way."

"But how would he know that we are going there instead of Boston?"

"Trust me...he's been watching the weather. I'll bet that right now he is somewhere in between the two airports waiting to know which one. He would probably let your family know the plan since the roads are most likely in bad shape. When we land we can let everyone know where we are just in case they go to the wrong location. Meanwhile we can wait inside a nice warm terminal."

"As long as your dad doesn't mind dropping me off. Oh, and that's only if we can know for certain that both families know where we are. There is no sense in two families driving in bad weather," Diane added with a touch of uncertainty in her voice.

Five minutes later the Captain announced that due to the large number of aircraft awaiting clearance into Boston, they would be proceeding direct to Manchester.

"Now we need to make sure our luggage doesn't go to Boston when we get off in Manchester," Diane stated as she thought of the dreamcatcher.

"I don't think we have to worry...I'm sure that there will be quite a few of us who will be happy to be arriving in Manchester. We will probably be required to claim our stuff and either leave with it or take it to the bus."

Once again the Captain addressed the passengers.

"Ladies and gentlemen, this is the Captain speaking. We are commencing our descent into Manchester, New Hampshire. There are five aircraft ahead of us, but we shouldn't be delayed. Bus service to Boston will be provided as a courtesy. It is still snowing heavily in Boston, but it has almost stopped in Manchester. We are sorry for any inconvenience, but this time of the year everything hinges on the weather. We should be on the ground in approximately forty minutes. The flight attendants will be coming through the cabin soon in preparation for landing. We can expect a little turbulence as we approach the airport so I will be turning on the seatbelt sign in about five minutes. Again, sorry for any inconvenience and on behalf of the entire crew, thank you for choosing us as your airline. Happy holidays."

Forty-five minutes later the airplane touched down and after another ten minutes it reached the terminal. The aisle filled with anxious passengers even before the *Fasten Seatbelt* sign was turned off. Neither Diane nor Gwen even bothered to move other than to release their seatbelts; they looked at each other and shook their heads. A flight attendant smiled as she approached and spoke.

"It will take a little time for the aisle to clear. I plan to stay back here out of the way. Are you taking one of the buses to Boston?"

"We don't know at this stage. My dad is probably waiting on us right now at baggage claim," ventured Gwen.

"Yes, but here or in Boston?" asked an apprehensive Diane.

All three women chuckled.

"You need to check at the gate for messages. Also, listen for any pages that might direct you to one of the courtesy phones. I would guess that you're home from college."

"University of Washington at Seattle; we're both juniors. Diane is planning to take the next quarter off while I go back to the grind. I guess I'll be breaking in a new roommate," Gwen announced.

"I just need a break...this last quarter was really tough on me. I must study real hard unlike Gwen who just needs to show up for class to get good grades. I guess you could say that I'm burnt out and jealous."

"Who knows, maybe after some holiday relaxation you might be ready to go back. I left school after two years and never made it back, but some day I plan to finish. This lifestyle is not quite as glamorous as you might believe. If I could do it all over again I would finish college. Look, I think I see some movement in the aisle."

Gwen stood and eased into the aisle as Diane slid over until she could stand. They both stretched and collected those few items that they had carried with them.

Gwen faced the flight attendant.

"Thank you, Karen, for taking care of us. I hope you have a Merry Christmas and Happy New Year."

"The same from me," added Diane.

"You're both welcome. I hope to see you onboard again."

With Gwen leading the way, the two women began moving toward the front of the cabin. Gwen was paged just as soon as she left the jetway. They both hurried to the nearby courtesy phone.

"Gwen Adams," and after a few seconds, "Hi, Daddy! We just got off the plane."

Diane moved away to give her a little privacy. She noted that the gate area had very few people waiting for their departures. She strolled over to the nearby flight status screens and noted the delays and cancellations next to most flights. She watched as several cancellations changed to delays leading her to believe that the weather was beginning to improve significantly. She glanced toward Gwen just as she hung up the phone and walked over to her.

"My dad and Mom are at the baggage claim...well Dad is and we are taking you home." Your dad got delayed by the weather, but he called the airline and they informed him that my dad would meet the plane up here and take you home. So everything worked out okay."

"Then let's go get our stuff and get out of here. Was your dad excited?"

"Well, he's not one to let his emotions show in public, but he sounded really pleased. My mom is not quite so reserved and she will probably hug you. Dad said that she's a brunette this month...she's a little vain since she's prematurely gray. Poor Mom."

"I've never seen a photo of your dad, just your mom."

"He's tall and looks like a Marine...you'll know what I mean as soon as you see him."

They worked their way toward baggage claim and Gwen suddenly spoke.

"Okay, see if you can pick out my dad."

"Gwen, he's the guy in the dark suit looking around for us."

Gwen grabbed Diane's arm.

"Come on!"

Diane reluctantly allowed herself to be dragged to what should probably be a private greeting.

"Hi, Daddy!" Gwen shouted as she rushed ahead with arms outstretched.

Diane watched them hug and kiss each other's cheek. Abruptly, Gwen's dad broke the embrace and looked at Diane.

"You must be Diane."

"Yes, sir," was all that she could say.

He looked like a Marine...a no-nonsense Marine.

"Dad...where's Mom?"

"She's out there arguing with the policeman who said I couldn't park there. She'll keep him busy until we get the luggage. I feel sorry for the poor cop! How was the flight?"

"Not too bad, just long. We were lucky to get out of Seattle. Wait, there's one of Diane's bags!"

The threesome turned their attention to the baggage carousel and soon had the four bags and the bubble wrapped package containing the dreamcatcher. They moved the baggage out through the sliding doors and into the cold. Parked next to the pedestrian crosswalk was a dark SUV; a policeman and a petite woman stood nearby.

"See, here they come now! I told you they'd be right out. Give us just a minute and we'll be gone. Hi Honey!"

The woman rushed to Gwen who hugged her with one arm while trying to maintain her balance.

Diane followed Gwen's dad and watched him open the rear door of the SUV even though he had a large suitcase in each hand. He placed both bags inside and then relieved Diane of first the suitcase and then the dreamcatcher. He then took Gwen's bag and placed it with the others.

"Let's go," he said as he slammed the rear doors and walked to the driver's door.

"Hello, Diane. It's nice to finally meet you."

She seemed shorter than in the family photos and the change from blond to brunette made a striking difference. She smiled warmly as she extended her hand to Diane and then reconsidered.

"It's just like having another daughter," she said as she hugged Diane.

"Let's go ladies! It will be slow going for several miles and I'd like to get home before dark. The snowplows will be out in full force as it is."

Gwen and Diane piled into the back seat and moments later the SUV departed to the obvious relief of the police officer. Gwen and her mom played catch up on all of the recent news and periodically brought Diane into the conversation.

Once they were established southbound on I-93, the road conditions improved dramatically. Crossing into Massachusetts they began catching up with the cold front and the flurries began to change to steady snow. An hour later they left I-93 and finally reached the Begley residence amid a heavy snowfall. Mr. Adams waved politely to a neighbor who sat in his car apparently waiting to pull away from the curb.

They said their farewells in the SUV and the young women promised to stay in touch during the holidays. Then Gwen's dad helped her with her luggage and they trudged through the snow to the front door. He waited patiently until Mrs. Begley answered the doorbell and politely declined her invitation for them to come in for a visit, citing the weather and his desire to get home before dark. Diane and her mom waved farewell to the other ladies while Diane's mom thanked Gwen's dad for bringing Diane home safely. The two women waved again as the snow-covered SUV backed out of the driveway and disappeared into the falling snow.

The mother and daughter hugged once again.

"Where's Dad...I thought he would be home by now."

"Come look at the television. Boston is getting clobbered. All the main roads are passable, but the rest are in bad shape. You probably noticed that our street had a single snowplow pass and we've gotten at least three more inches since then. Your dad will be here as soon as he safely can. Now, what's this nonsense about you not returning to school for the next quarter?"

"I'm just tired. This last quarter was too demanding with all of my absences and I need a break."

"You mean that the school didn't take into account that the absences weren't your fault?"

"Mom, if you miss classes then you must make them up if you want to pass the course. I borrowed notes from Gwen and other classmates but there was just too much added on to the regular class work and reading assignments. I'm just burnt out. I want some time to relax and I especially want to see my nephew. Are they coming over soon?"

"Probably tomorrow if this storm moves out, but it has stalled and right now the weather experts aren't sure what's going to happen in the next few days. Care for some hot chocolate?"

"Sure. Let me put my stuff in my room and then I will show you what I got for Dad."

Diane moved her two suitcases to her room and then returned for the dreamcatcher. She was in the process of removing the bubble-wrap when her mother walked into her room.

"I don't think he needs any barbeque tools."

"Just wait...this will blow your socks off."

Diane removed the last traces of bubble-wrap and opened the cardboard box. Then she eased the wooden case from the box and placed it on the bed.

"Open it," she said as she stepped aside.

Her mom fumbled with the latch and then lifted the lid. When she saw the dreamcatcher she released the lid and brought both hands to her face.

"My gosh...it's beautiful! Where did you get this?"

"At a yard sale. I don't even know why I stopped there. I, well there were actually three of us, was starting to leave when the lady said I needed to see something and here it is!"

"Can I pick it up?"

"Of course...it won't bite."

Mrs. Begley gently lifted the dreamcatcher and was rewarded with a feeling of warmth and serenity unlike anything she had ever experienced. She looked at the impeccable workmanship and then eased the beautiful object back into its case. Diane watched the expression on her mom's face and knew that this gift would be a welcome addition; she smiled and mentally patted herself on the back for her choice of presents. She did not realize that it had *not* been her choice at all.

"I think you hit a homerun with this. Your dad will be thrilled."

"I want Linda to see it and if she agrees then it will be from both of us."

"I don't think that will be a problem. Now let's go get some hot chocolate," she said as she turned to leave the room.

"Okay, just let me put this away and don't tell Dad what I or *we* got him."

"I promise, but it won't be easy."

Twenty-three minutes later Robert Alan Begley entered the house.

"Anybody home? I see tracks in the snow!"

Diane ran from the kitchen and fiercely hugged her dad.

"It's so good to see you! It's so good to be home!"

"I'm glad that you made it home okay. The roads are a nightmare."

"You can thank Mr. Sam Adams for picking me up at the Manchester airport and transporting me safely home."

"Sam Adams? You must be kidding."

"Gwen said that everyone calls him that and, of course, his name is not Sam or Samuel. Come on, have some hot chocolate...Mom just made it."

"There's always room for hot chocolate on a snowy day. Hi Hon," he said just before he kissed his wife hello.

The snow continued to fall as darkness approached. Christmas lighting displays cast an eerie glow from beneath their snowy blanket. The street lights accentuated the windblown snow as it silently fell. Inside, the Begley family enjoyed a leisurely early dinner and visited, happy to be completely free of the demands which normally plagued them. The older daughter, Linda, called a little after 6 P.M. and said that they would come down the following day after the roads were cleared. She chatted with Diane for a few minutes and then had to hang up and answer the very vocal demands of Robert Patrick Allen.

Linda, her husband Jack and six month old Robert arrived at the Begley house just before noon. Diane rushed to greet her sister and husband before taking Robert and rescuing him from his snowsuit and cap. She was surprised at how much he had changed since she last saw him. They visited for a few minutes before Robert decided to take a nap. The two young women moved him into Diane's room which had a small crib next to the wall. Linda gently placed the infant in the crib and carefully covered him. They both stood there for a few moments and marveled at the little boy.

That was when Diane suddenly remembered the dreamcatcher. She quietly closed the door and removed the wooden case from its hiding place in the closet. She then placed it on the bed and opened it.

"Wow! That is beautiful. What is it?"

"It's called a *dreamcatcher* and its purpose is to capture your good dreams and let the bad ones escape. I got it for us to give to Dad. Mom has already seen it and loves it...she knows Dad will love it, too. When they move into their new house we can give it to them as a housewarming gift. What do you think?"

"I like it, but where in the world did you find it?"

"At a yard sale, of all places."

"It's really cool. Could we hang it over Robert's crib while he naps? That would make it even more special for Dad."

"Sure, just take the sound monitor off the wall and set it on the dresser and I'll hang the dreamcatcher on the screw."

Diane carefully placed the dreamcatcher over the head of the screw. The lower feathers reached down to the level of the sleeping infant. She thought about moving it higher and suddenly felt the onset of a headache. She decided to forego the relocation of the dreamcatcher and the headache faded away.

"Let's go find out what the plan for lunch is," whispered Diane as she turned on the power switch for the monitor.

They quietly closed the door as they left the room and headed for the kitchen.

Two things happened immediately in the bedroom: the dreamcatcher rustled slightly and a feather moved toward the crib; simultaneously, Robert's eyes snapped open and he reached for the feather. As soon as he gripped it, the dreamcatcher seemed to shrink slightly and lost a miniscule amount of its mass; little Robert gained the same amount of mass as the frontal lobe of his cerebellum changed in the areas affecting behavior. Abruptly, Robert released the feather, smiled and fell asleep once again.

At that same instant, the ancient Great Eagle appeared once again in the land of the Lakota and was soon joined by the three lesser eagles. Moments later, one of the lesser eagles left for a location in Massachusetts near Boston.

The Begleys and the Allens dined on pizza that afternoon and talked about all of those things that affected their lives. After their late lunch, Jack shoveled the sidewalk and driveway while Mr. Begley enjoyed the rare opportunity to watch some football. The women doted on little Robert and Diane held him at every opportunity.

It was during this time that Linda noticed that her son seemed to be uncharacteristically interested in everything around him. He turned his head toward the source of any sound or movement just as if he were considerably older. He seemed to be taking notice of everything and she had the distinct impression that he was *understanding those things that he heard and saw*. She was convinced that he had suddenly changed dramatically...something that she kept to herself. She began to experience severe headaches each time she thought about it; the headaches disappeared when she stopped thinking about the changes. She also noticed that little Robert frowned when she had those thoughts.

The Allen family left late in the afternoon and Diane took the opportunity to look at the undisturbed snow in the back yard. The yard was always her favorite place after a snowfall and it made her happy just to be there. It was then that she spotted the sentinel eagle perched on a branch of a large oak tree. She was amazed at the size of the bird and her amazement grew as she walked toward it. She was pleased to see how it watched her yet chose not to fly away. She wondered if she could feed it something and then decided that it probably would prefer to catch its own meals. She stared at it for several minutes until the approaching darkness convinced her to return to the house.

For the next three weeks there were parties and visits to be made. The weather was typical for New England: sudden, unpredictable changes which resulted in constantly changing plans. Her mom and dad spent considerable time meeting with all sorts of people and Diane caught up on her sleep and visited with many of the friends with whom she had grown up. Invariably they would choose to come to the Begley residence rather than plan a gathering at some public location...that was just too difficult considering the season and the unpredictable weather.

New Year's Day had brought the hope for better times and a new start for the entire family. Diane's parents moved to their interim home in northern Virginia while the Allens put their house on the market and moved into the Begley house. Diane chose to remain at her childhood home and help her sister with the move; her priority was actually to spend as much time as possible with her nephew.

It was at this point that Gwen called. Her parents were smothering her and she was wondering if she could stay with Diane for a few days. Diane explained that her sister and her family were buying the Begley house and she needed to check with them. Diane called her back a few minutes later and told her to come on over. The house was large enough to easily accommodate a huge family and Linda considered herself fortunate to now have two free babysitters although she wisely chose not to make that statement.

The arrangement worked well; it seemed that everyone benefited from the changes and life was far more relaxed. There was time to watch movies and even the news although it was depressing, especially on the international scene. Threats against nations continued and minor skirmishes seemed to erupt almost daily. That's when the television channel was invariably switched.

Finally, after what seemed to be an eternity, it was time for the Begleys to move into their new home. Diane and the Allens drove down to Virginia; the dreamcatcher's wooden case was now suitably wrapped and a card announced the presence of a housewarming gift. The entire family had a quiet dinner together. Afterward, Diane and Linda presented the gift to their dad who was pleasantly surprised. He stated that his first task in their new home would be to mount the beautiful work of art over their bed.

The Allens left for their hotel while Diane remained with her parents. Tomorrow was moving day among other things and everyone was fatigued and excited. Still, sleep did not come easily.

The day dawned clear and cold. The Allens arrived just after 8 A.M. and breakfast was delivered to the apartment shortly thereafter. While they enjoyed their first meal of the day, Robert Begley revealed that his nightmare had returned not once, but twice during the night. He abruptly finished his breakfast and walked over to the portable crib.

He lifted his grandson and held him at arms length. Little Robert smiled broadly and winked at his grandfather.

"He just winked at me," the amazed elder Begley stated softly. "He really did."

"Relax, Robert, he's a baby...it's just a coordination thing," Shirley Begley stated with a grin.

Linda started to speak, but a splitting pain in her head stopped her.

"Wow! Now he's frowning," said Robert as he pulled the tot closer and hugged him.

Linda's pain immediately subsided just as the doorbell rang. Diane went to the door and opened it. To her surprise there stood Gwen and Diane could see her parents sitting in their SUV.

"Got a minute? There's something I need to tell you."

"Sure, let me get my coat. Is something wrong?"

"No, not at all."

Diane grabbed her coat and stepped outside.

"So what's going on, Gwen?"

"Your dad asked that you be allowed to lead as normal a life as possible under the circumstances. I am Secret Service and was assigned to protect you while you were at school. The two people out there in the SUV are also Secret Service and certainly not my parents. I wanted to tell you my status when we first met, but your dad wanted you to have as much freedom as possible. You had mentioned the strange car that followed you sometimes...if you think back, it never happened when you and I went places together. I came to enjoy your friendship and I am especially glad that this ruse is over. We will be transporting you, your sister and her family to your Dad's inaugural ceremony; your parents will be traveling with others and on a different route and time schedule. You probably have a lot of questions; I will answer them later. Please do not be upset with me. I think you'll enjoy living in the White House."

Diane stood there in shock. She was not angry.

"But you don't *look* like you're Secret Service."

"Precisely. That's why I was chosen. A lot of strings were pulled to make sure that we ended up as roommates. Go back to your family...this will be a day you'll never forget."

Diane hugged her awkwardly.

"Is your name really Gwen?"

"Yes, but my last name is not the same as you know me. That will not be revealed just in case we work together again. I'm sorry, I must leave now."

Gwen turned and walked to the SUV. The front seat occupants waved as the SUV departed. Diane watched it leave and then went back into the apartment.

"Gwen just told me who she really is. Did all of you know?"

The adults nodded and little Robert smiled.

"I just wanted you to be safe and to be spared the headaches caused by the security restrictions placed on you. Perhaps I should have told you."

"It's okay, Dad, I just need to adjust that's all. You look really tired."

The President-elect slowly turned toward his daughter and sighed loudly before speaking.

"It was that same nightmare, the one with the map of the country and the mushrooms. There was also an evil looking eagle...I don't know why that is so terrifying."

In San Diego, Marilyn Stevens Hughes suddenly awakened her husband.

"Don...I just had a terrible dream. After all these years Howling Wolf just re-appeared and I think we have some urgent work to do."

"I know. We need to go to Washington, DC and quickly. I have a *really* bad feeling."

The End